RETURN TO HUCKLEBERRY HILL

Had she fainted? Her head spun in several different directions like a yard full of pinwheels. Was she still standing or had she fallen over?

"Stay still, *heartzly*." Reuben's low voice sounded like a caress against her skin.

Yep. She had fainted, and she was still unconscious. Reuben would only have called her *heartzly* in her dreams.

Groaning softly, she lifted her hand to her forehead and opened her eyes. Reuben's face was mere inches from hers, and he didn't seem inclined to pull away. His expression was saturated with concern as he tightened his arms around her. She sat on the ground while Reuben knelt beside her, keeping her upright with his firm embrace.

"Did I faint?"

"About fifteen seconds ago. Hush. Don't try to talk."

The last thing she needed in her already frazzled state was to be this close to Reuben Helmuth, who smelled so *gute*, it should probably be against the *Ordnung*. She tried to push away from him so she could stand up, but he only pulled her closer. If she didn't give up the struggle, he'd persist in drawing her dangerously close to his heart. . . .

Books by Jennifer Beckstrand

The Matchmakers of Huckleberry Hill
HUCKLEBERRY HILL
HUCKLEBERRY SUMMER
HUCKLEBERRY CHRISTMAS
HUCKLEBERRY SPRING
HUCKLEBERRY HARVEST
HUCKLEBERRY HEARTS
RETURN TO HUCKLEBERRY HILL

The Honeybee Sisters
SWEET AS HONEY
A BEE IN HER BONNET
LIKE A BEE TO HONEY

Anthologies
AN AMISH CHRISTMAS QUILT
THE AMISH CHRISTMAS KITCHEN
AMISH BRIDES

Published by Kensington Publishing Corporation

Return To Huckleberry Hill

JENNIFER BECKSTRAND

ZEBRA BOOKS
KENSINGTON PUBLISHING CORP.
http://www.kensingtonbooks.com

ZEBRA BOOKS are published by

Kensington Publishing Corp.
119 West 40th Street
New York, NY 10018

All Kensington titles, imprints and distributed lines are available at special quantity discounts for bulk purchases for sales promotion, premiums, fund-raising, educational or institutional use.

Special book excerpts or customized printings can also be created to fit specific needs. For details, write or phone the office of the Kensington Sales Manager. Attn.: Sales Department. Kensington Publishing Corp., 119 West 40th Street, New York, NY 10018. Phone: 1-800-221-2647.

First Printing: June 2017
ISBN-13: 978-1-4201-4411-6
ISBN-10: 1-4201-4411-1

eISBN-13: 978-1-4201-4412-3
eISBN-10: 1-4201-4412-X

10 9 8 7 6 5 4 3 2 1

Printed in the United States of America

Chapter One

Reuben Helmuth had a sinking feeling in his gut the minute Delores Johnson answered her door, and it wasn't because Delores was glaring at him from behind her screen.

The Christmas Eve night was bitter cold, and Reuben's breath hung in the air as he tried to keep the tune while Benji Troyer sang loudly off key right next to Reuben's ear. Poor Benji couldn't have carried a tune if it had a handle.

Delores Johnson, one of the *Englischers* who lived in their mostly Amish community, had never possessed a pleasant disposition, but tonight she looked downright hostile. She narrowed her eyes and scowled directly at Reuben as if she blamed him for her being alone on Christmas Eve. Or maybe she didn't like the way he sang or the fact that she had to strain her neck to look up at him. Maybe she was annoyed that she had to stand there and listen while the warm air seeped through the screen door and out of her house. Reuben never could tell with Delores.

Delores's bad mood wasn't the reason Reuben felt

unsettled all of a sudden. His throat tightened and "O Come All Ye Faithful" died on his lips. Irrational as it was, he felt vulnerable and exposed, as if everyone behind him was laughing at a joke he wasn't in on. He casually turned around and glanced at *die youngie* behind him. Most of them were bundled up like snowmen with coats and scarves and winter hats, but they were smiling and singing as if they weren't paying Reuben much attention at all.

But where was Linda Sue? He could have sworn she had been right beside him not five minutes ago.

He scanned the group of young people, looking for Linda Sue's lavender scarf among the sea of black coats. She wasn't there, and yet right before they'd made the trek up Mrs. Johnson's driveway, Linda Sue had been by his side. Hadn't she? Their youth group was traveling door to door on foot, singing carols and delivering goodies to the shut-ins. It would have been impossible for Linda Sue to get lost.

He smiled, even though Mrs. Johnson's frown could have given him a rash or something equally as itchy. Tomorrow was Christmas, and he was going to propose to Linda Sue. His heart skipped about in his chest like a moth around a flame. They'd be married in September, and he couldn't be happier. He and Linda Sue were perfect for each other. She was the bishop's daughter. His *dat* was a minister. Both of their families were respected and loved in the community. Linda Sue was the prettiest girl in Sugarcreek, and Reuben's *mamm* had always said he wasn't too bad to look at.

It was a match made in heaven with *Gotte*'s approval, for sure and certain.

They finished the song, and Mrs. Johnson opened

her screen door just wide enough for one of the girls to hand her a basket of Christmas goodies. "Thank you for stopping by," Delores said. "I love having you Amish folks come see me. Come anytime."

After seeing her lemon-sour expression, Reuben wasn't entirely convinced of her affection. Maybe she was offended by Reuben in particular.

Reuben took another look around as the group started moving down Mrs. Johnson's driveway and on to their next destination. No Linda Sue. His best friend, John King, was nowhere to be seen either.

"Ruth," he said, tapping the girl next to him. "Have you seen Linda Sue yet? I've lost her all of a sudden."

Ruth, a mousy girl of barely sixteen, turned bright red. She looked almost guilty, which made no sense. She was probably flustered at having an older boy like Reuben Helmuth talk to her. He had that effect on girls. John teased him about it all the time, but he couldn't help that girls found him good-looking.

Ruth shuffled her feet and clasped her gloved hands together. "I . . . well . . . I . . ."

Ruth's sister, Jolene, hooked her elbow around Ruth's arm, and the two of them simultaneously burst into a fit of the giggles. "She and John fell behind," Jolene said. "At the bridge that crosses the creek."

Benji Troyer, with his brother Andy and cousin Enos, ambled past Reuben. Benji's lips twitched in amusement. "They've been falling behind a lot lately."

Andy and Enos glanced at Reuben and down at their feet and snickered softly while Reuben stared at them and tried to figure out why they were acting as if their suspenders were cinched too tight.

Reuben didn't especially like how Benji was smirking.

He planted his feet and folded his arms across his chest. "What do you mean?"

"John and Linda Sue," Benji said, not even trying to hide a self-satisfied grin. "If they're not with you, they're with each other."

Reuben casually shrugged his shoulders and pretended that he already knew it and couldn't care less what Benji and everyone else thought. He wouldn't give Benji the satisfaction of knowing something Reuben didn't know, even though it felt as if someone had just thrown a snowball at his head.

A hard, cold snowball. With a rock in the middle.

That was what had been nagging at his gut all afternoon. Something had been different between Linda Sue and John for weeks. Whenever the three of them were together, it was as if Linda Sue tried to pretend John didn't exist and John would turn so painfully cheerful as to be annoying—as if he was trying too hard to be someone he wasn't.

What did Benji know that Reuben didn't?

He refused to lower himself to ask.

Clenching his teeth, he glanced in the direction of the bridge. "You go on to the next house. I'll find Linda Sue and catch up."

"Maybe she doesn't want to be found," Benji said. "Girls are like that, you know."

Reuben turned and strolled away as if he hadn't a care in the world, even though his neck and shoulders were so tight he thought they might snap.

Jolene and Ruth were still giggling, and he heard two or three other girls join in. Then Benji murmured something under his breath, and Andy and Enos laughed softly.

Reuben's face flamed with embarrassment and

anger, and he felt the heat all the way to his ears. They were laughing at him! Him. Reuben Helmuth, the boy no one laughed at. The boy everyone loved and would never dream of making fun of. The boy with his own hefty bank account and too many friends to number. He was practically engaged to the bishop's daughter. Everybody respected him. And nobody would ever dream of laughing.

Until now.

What had Linda Sue done?

The narrow bridge across the creek was only a few hundred yards through the trees. John and Linda Sue stood on the bridge with their heads together, whispering as if they were engaged in some secret and intimate conversation.

Reuben furrowed his brow and cleared his throat, even though he wasn't the one doing something inappropriate. His frown deepened when Linda Sue and John flinched and practically jumped away from each other as if they'd been caught with their hands in the cookie jar.

"Is everything okay?" Reuben said, trying to keep his voice light and carefree. After all, John might have been helping Linda Sue get something out of her eye. John was Reuben's best friend. He would never do anything to jeopardize that friendship. Linda Sue was the bishop's daughter, and she had been in love with Reuben for years. Reuben had finally taken notice of her, and she had felt herself doubly blessed. She'd never trade her prosperous and happy future for a pig farmer.

John looked as if there'd been a death in his family. He gazed at Reuben, every line of his face etched with pain as his eyes flashed with pity.

Pity? Surely he didn't feel sorry for Reuben. Reuben was everything that John wanted to be. John was the one Reuben and his other friends had pitied. Nobody pitied Reuben Helmuth. He wouldn't allow it.

Reuben's lungs seized up when John grabbed hold of Linda Sue's hand. Linda Sue didn't even try to pull away. "We've got to tell him, Linda Sue."

Linda Sue finally turned her eyes to Reuben. They were moist and pleading. "I didn't want to do this at Christmastime," she said. With her hand still in John's, she took a step toward Reuben and reached out her free hand. He stepped back, quite sure he didn't want whatever she was trying to give him. "I'm sorry, Reuben. We didn't mean for this to go on so long without telling you. It just . . . it just happened, and I haven't been able to confide in you for a long time."

Reuben couldn't believe, *wouldn't* believe what he was hearing. "What do you mean?"

"You won't listen."

"I sit at your kitchen table every week late into the night. We talk about everything. What do you mean I won't listen?"

A tear meandered down Linda Sue's cheek, as if she cared. As if she felt real and sincere remorse. "You don't know how many times I tried to tell you about my growing feelings for John."

"Tried to tell me?" Reuben said, unable to keep the bitterness off the tip of his tongue.

John pulled Linda Sue to him. How could she let him when John smelled like the pigs, and he wasn't near good enough for the bishop's daughter? "She tried to tell you, Reuben, but you're too wrapped up in yourself."

Every word that came out of John's mouth pulled

Reuben's nerves a little tighter. "So whatever is going on here is my fault?"

"Of course it's not your fault," Linda Sue said, her eyes glowing with compassion.

She must have been trying to win an award for being sensitive. He found it offensive. Reuben Helmuth didn't need anyone's compassion or pity or sympathy. It was humiliating that she thought he did.

"No one is to blame. These things just happen," she said, as if that would make everything all better.

"What things?" Reuben said, knowing he didn't want the answer. He was shaking with rage and cold and pure and utter shock. What would people say?

John dropped all pretense and put both arms around Linda Sue. "We love each other, Reuben, and we have for several weeks. We're going to be married, Lord willing."

Linda Sue had the gall to give him that kindly smile she saved for old ladies and small children. He thought he might be sick. "We would be so happy if you would come to the wedding."

Come to a wedding that was supposed to be his? His humiliation was complete.

Die youngie would never stop laughing at him.

Chapter Two

Three days after Christmas, and the snow kept falling. The drifts were already piled up past the porch, and Huckleberry Hill looked like a marshmallow-and-mashed-potato wonderland—which also sounded like a brilliant idea for a new recipe. Maybe Anna could try it out for New Year's Eve. On a night like this, it felt wonderful *gute* to hibernate in a cozy house and let the bears and the bunny rabbits enjoy the weather outside.

Anna Helmuth adjusted her glasses to get a better look at her letter, and her shoulder creaked like a rusty hinge. It seemed that her body made a new groan or whimper every time she got up in the morning. Walking around the house was getting to be noisier than a buggy rolling over cobblestones. Anna supposed it was only to be expected that an eighty-four-year-old should have a few squeaky joints. She didn't consider herself aged by any means, but the body the *gute* Lord had given her had seen quite a bit of use. She had given birth to thirteen children, after all.

But it wasn't her own children who occupied Anna's

thoughts these days—she'd done all she could to rear them, and if they had turned out poorly, she didn't have time to feel guilty about it.

Nae. Anna fretted over her poor, unmarried grandchildren. Too many of them were hopelessly in need of spouses, and if Anna and her husband Felty didn't help them, their posterity would very likely wither and die on the vine.

The thought of unwed grandchildren put Anna in quite a dither. Something had to be done.

"Felty dear, how do you spell 'parsimonious'?" she said, holding her pen at the ready.

Felty, Anna's husband of sixty-five years, sat in his recliner reading *The Budget* as he did every Wednesday evening. He lowered his paper and squinted at the ceiling as if the answer were written in the bumpy plaster above. "Annie-banannie, I don't even know what 'pars-pneumonia' means. You're so much smarter than me. In school, I was always the first one to sit down during a spelling bee."

"Now, Felty. I'm not that smart, but I know what 'parsimonious' means because it sounds like 'persimmon,' and I just remember that persimmons are cheap at the store, and 'parsimonious' means cheap or miserly."

"Very clever, Banannie, but who are you writing a letter to, and will they know what 'parsimonious' means even if you spell it right?"

Anna raised her eyebrows and peered over her glasses. "Elsie will know. She's smart as a tack and very avuncular."

"For sure and certain our granddaughter is smart, but why are you writing her a letter with big words like 'parsimonious' and 'have-an-uncle-yooler'?"

Anna leaned closer to Felty and took him into her confidence. "I'm hoping my big vocabulary will convince her to come to Huckleberry Hill yet. The school will be needing a new teacher in August, and Elsie needs a husband. We can kill two birds with one stone."

"That is a very *gute* plan, Annie."

Anna crossed out an entire sentence, dotted her last *i* with a heart, and picked up her letter. "How does this sound? *Dear Elsie, I hope this correspondence finds you in good health and very comfortable at home. Your* dawdi *and I have very avuncular feelings toward you and want you to abide with us and teach the scholars at the school next year. The school board is not parsimonious. You will be compensated well. What do you say? Would you like to come to Huckleberry Hill?*" Anna eyed Felty expectantly. "What do you think of that?"

"There are so many big words in that letter, she's sure to say yes."

"I hope so. I got a headache just trying to spell everything correctly."

Three loud taps at the door nearly peeled Anna out of her skin. "Do you think that's Elsie already?"

"She's smart, Banannie, but I don't think there's any possibility she got your letter before you sent it."

Anna folded her letter carefully, slipped it into her apron pocket, and ambled to the door, trying to ignore all the creaking her knees did. Her shoulders were doing quite enough creaking for everybody.

She opened the door and peered into the darkness. A snowman stood on the porch with his hat pulled low over his eyes. Well, it wasn't truly a snowman, but his trousers and coat were covered with snow, his hat caked with ice, and the small duffel bag he carried in one hand could have been a giant snowball. Anna drew her brows together. It most surely wasn't Elsie. She was too smart to be out on such a bitter night. "Can I help you?" Anna said, hoping that whoever was standing on her porch would feel welcome in her home, even if he wasn't very bright.

He took off his hat and lifted his head. The dull-witted boy turned out to be Anna's very icy grandson Reuben, who Anna knew wasn't dull-witted at all. His eyes caught the light from inside the house, and Anna caught her breath. No wonder she hadn't recognized him. She'd never seen Reuben slouch his shoulders so low or have such a gloomy cast to his expression. "Hello, Mammi," he mumbled. Something was very wrong. Reuben never mumbled.

Anna threw open her arms. "*Ach, du lieva*, Reuben. *Cum reu, cum reu.* You look as if you've just come from Alaska." When Reuben didn't seem inclined to move, she grabbed the front of his coat, pulled him into the house, and wrapped her arms tightly around him, being careful not to crush the precious letter in her pocket. It had taken far too long to write to have to compose another one.

Reuben tried to pull away. "Mammi, I'll get you wet."

Anna refused to let him go. "*Ach*, I'd rather have my hug."

Felty rocked his recliner back and forth until he built enough momentum to toss himself out of the chair and onto his feet. He joined Anna and Reuben in a three-way hug.

Reuben grimaced. "Now everybody is wet."

"My dear boy," Anna said, hurrying to the drawer for a dish towel, "why in the world are you out on a night like this? You could have been swept away by a blizzard or frozen solid to a light pole. What will your *mamm* say?"

Felty took Reuben's bag. "Did you ski all the way from Sugarcreek?"

Reuben drooped even lower. "I'm sorry I didn't write. I got on the bus in Ohio yesterday, arrived in Shawano station this morning, and walked from there."

"You walked from Shawano? That's ten miles!" It was fortunate Reuben didn't have creaky knees.

"I needed the time to think," Reuben said. From the look on his face, he'd been thinking about very serious things. Too serious for a young man who was usually so perky.

Reuben used Anna's towel to wipe the melting snowflakes from his face, then he lowered his eyes and studied his snow-covered boots. The caked snow was sliding slowly to the floor and melting into an impressive puddlc. "Can I stay for a few days?" He expelled a quick breath from between his lips. "*Ach.* I hate to ask a favor of anyone. I don't want to impose."

Ignoring her squeaky shoulder, Anna reached up and patted Reuben on the cheek. "Grandsons are never an imposition." She took the towel from his hand and caught a bead of water that was about to drip from his earlobe. "Go dry yourself off in the bathroom, change into some warm clothes so you don't catch your death of cold, and we'll have a talk."

"It's all right, Mammi," Reuben said. "I used some cinnamon bark and lavender." Despite his fine collection of essential oils, he must have seen the wisdom in dry clothes. He trudged down the hall, leaving a trail of melting snow in his wake. Anna would definitely be getting out the mop.

But there were more pressing matters at hand. She turned to Felty and fingered the letter in her pocket. "If Reuben is going to stay, we can't hurt his feelings by inviting Elsie."

"For sure and certain," Felty said.

She pulled Elsie's letter from her pocket and gave it one regretful glance. She would never want Reuben to think he was unwelcome. What had to be done, had to be done. She quickly ripped the letter into strips, then ripped those strips into small squares, then ripped those small squares into even smaller bits. Not even Elsie would be able to put the pieces back together. Reuben would never know that Anna had been about to invite someone else to live with them. His fragile feelings were safe.

Anna frowned. Reuben's feelings had never been fragile before, but something had definitely changed. She didn't like seeing her grandchildren unhappy. Something would have to be done. She would need to find him a wife without delay.

Reuben ambled down the hall in dry, wrinkly trousers, an equally wrinkly blue shirt, and bare feet. "There's a wonderful-pretty doily on the back of the toilet."

Anna bloomed into a smile. "How nice of you to notice. I've taken up crochet recently. *Die youngie* were growing tired of my pot holders."

Still looking as dejected as ever, Reuben leaned over and planted a kiss on Anna's forehead. "How could anyone not love your pot holders?"

Felty smoothed his long, gray beard. "Is your *fater* going to be worried about you?" Felty was so smart. It was a *gute* way to ask Reuben about his troubles without really prying.

"I left a note," Reuben said, this time studying his feet. He had nice long toes, like Felty. Anna loved long toes. "I told them I didn't know when I'll be coming back. Do you . . . do you care if I stay? Maybe for a week, until I can find another place?"

Anna blew air through her lips. "Another place? You don't need another place. You stay here as long as you like." Elsie would just have to be patient. That was all there was to it.

Reuben didn't smile, but his expression seemed to grow a few degrees warmer. "*Denki*, Mammi. I will stay."

Anna still had a handful of paper scraps—nothing that Reuben would ever mistake for a letter, but she didn't want to give him any reason to suspect. She tossed the scraps into the air. "Hooray!"

Reuben lifted his eyebrows as the bits of paper descended to the floor like snowflakes. One side of his mouth curled reluctantly. "Mammi, you are my favorite person in the whole world."

Anna smiled. "And you are definitely one of my favorite grandsons." She studied his haggard expression. It belonged to a much older man. Poor thing. What had he been through? "If you spent the whole day walking, you must be hungry. I made cheesy banana bread this morning."

A spark flickered to life in his eyes. "A new recipe?"

"I made it up by myself. I just throw this and that into the bowl, and it usually turns out well." Anna made a beeline for the fridge. "I have a whole loaf."

Without a word, Reuben pulled the broom and the mop out of the closet. While Anna sliced bread, Reuben mopped up the watery trail he'd made down the hall as well as the puddle by the front door. Then he swept up Anna's confetti and deposited it into the trash. He'd always been a *gute* helper like that. Surely it wouldn't be too hard to find him a wife.

"*Cum*, Reuben," she said, setting the entire loaf of cheesy banana bread on the table with a plate of creamy butter she'd churned this morning. It was probably why her shoulder was creaking tonight.

Reuben put the mop and broom away and sat at the table. Without waiting for an invitation, he picked up a piece of the brown bread with orange cheese bits and slathered it with butter. He took a huge bite, dispatching of almost a third of the slice, and leaned back in his chair. "This tastes like it was baked in the ovens of heaven," he said. "No one cooks like my *mammi*."

Anna stood at the counter, folding and unfolding a dish towel. "There's lots more where that came from. I've invented a recipe for peach venison stew and one for Chinese dumplings. If you substitute tongue for the pork, it makes them nice and chewy."

Reuben took another hearty bite of cheesy banana bread. "I can't wait to see what recipes you have in store."

Anna's smile only widened. Her dear grandson would never suspect that she had more in store for him than gourmet food.

She was going to get him a wife.

Chapter Three

Reuben took a rake to Mammi's flower beds as if he were trying to get revenge on the dead leaves that had been there since autumn. Backbreaking work and aching muscles distracted him from his dark thoughts. They'd weighed heavily on him for three months. He'd rake the whole hill if it would help.

He'd only intended to stay for a week, but Mammi's cooking had been too *gute* and his heart had been too heavy to even consider leaving. Mamm and Dat had written ten letters, urging him to come home, but he couldn't bear the thought of such humiliation. He'd been cooped up in Mammi and Dawdi's house all of January, February, and March, shoveling coal, driving Mammi and Dawdi to *gmay* in the sleigh, waiting for spring. At last he could take his frustrations out on the clods of dirt in the yard.

A chilly morning in early April was a perfect time to try to work himself to death. His shirt was already drenched with sweat, and he swiped away a trickle of moisture from his temple. If it had been any warmer, he would have been dizzy with the heat.

Reuben kept his head bent over his rake as he made his way around Mammi and Dawdi's house, dragging the dead leaves from the foundation, pulling weeds from under the rosebushes, and being careful not to disturb the tulips and daffodils making their way out of the soil.

It felt like an anvil was tied around his neck, as if he wouldn't be able to lift his face to *Gotte*, even if he had wanted to. *Gotte* had seen to it that Reuben was completely miserable. He didn't much feel like having a conversation with Him.

John and Linda Sue had humiliated Reuben but good, and he didn't wonder but the whole community was laughing and gossiping about him behind his back. John had made a fool of him, and even with three months of brooding behind him, Reuben's pride still smarted something wonderful. Better to stay in Bonduel where people didn't know of his disgrace and wouldn't think less of him. Maybe they'd come to admire and like him. Maybe here he could be as popular as he had once been in Sugarcreek. It would never be the same back home.

Mammi and Dawdi hadn't asked any questions, and he hadn't volunteered any answers. Though they'd given him a roof over his head and food fit for a king, he simply couldn't bring himself to tell them anything. Linda Sue had rejected him—Reuben Helmuth, the minister's son—for a pig farmer. The humiliation smarted like a carpet burn to his cheek.

It galled him that even though John had been the one who betrayed their friendship, it had been Reuben who'd left Sugarcreek in disgrace. For sure and certain, John had set out to purposefully embarrass him.

Linda Sue and John had been so smug, standing

hand in hand on the bridge, pretending to feel so bad about hurting Reuben's feelings like that. Whoever heard of breaking up with your boyfriend on Christmas Eve? Wasn't that a sin or something? Linda Sue had even managed a few tears, as if she truly felt bad about leading him on and making him believe that she loved him when she had been seeing John behind his back. The crying, the deep distress, had been an act, and he couldn't have been more humiliated if one of his brothers had joined the army.

John had been Reuben's best friend, but he was also a poor, redheaded pig farmer who had no business even hoping for the bishop's daughter. Reuben had been replaced by a nobody.

Dawdi ambled around the side of the house singing to himself. If he ever forgot the words to a song, he just made up his own. Dawdi was clever that way. "*Denki,* Mammi, for praying for me," he sang. "If you had not prayed I don't know where I'd be. I thought you were old-fashioned, but you loved the Lord, and your prayers flew to heaven as your tears fell to the floor."

Reuben raked another pile of leaves onto the tarp he'd laid out on the lawn. Dawdi reached down and picked up two corners of the tarp.

"I can move it, Dawdi." Dawdi was well into his eighties. He shouldn't be lifting anything.

"Not all that heavy with two of us," Dawdi said, motioning for Reuben to grab the other two sides of the tarp. "Besides, I've got titanium knees. I can lift just about anything."

They dragged the tarp to the edge of the woods, Reuben trying to take most of the weight in his arms.

"I've never seen this place so cleaned up," Dawdi

said, tilting the tarp and shaking the leaves among the trees. "Like as not, some of those leaves have been sitting around the foundation for a generation."

"Mammi wants it to look nice for *gmay* tomorrow."

"It will look better than nice. I didn't even know there were daffodils hiding under there." Each holding a corner, Reuben and Dawdi dragged the empty tarp over the grass and spread it next to the yet-to-be-raked leaves. "We got a letter from your *dat* this morning," Dawdi said.

Reuben felt the heat travel up his neck. Another letter from Dat. How long before Mammi and Dawdi started asking questions? How long before they figured out why their grandson had shown up at their house a few days after Christmas and didn't show any signs of leaving?

Not long, apparently. "Do you want to talk about it?" Dawdi said.

"*Nae.*"

Dawdi stroked his beard. "You've been as silent as a skunk on the prowl since you got here."

Reuben picked up his rake and attacked the thick and rotting clump of leaves that congregated against the house. "I don't want to relive my humiliation," he said, nearly spitting the words out of his mouth. He paused raking and bowed his head. "I'm sorry, Dawdi. I didn't mean to speak to you that way."

"A broken heart is nothing to be ashamed of."

"My best friend betrayed me."

"You bear no shame for that," Dawdi said.

"I'm angry I trusted him."

Dawdi nodded, and the lines in his face deepened. "You were hurt by someone who was supposed to be your friend. It's what you do with your anger that matters now. You've got all the time in the world to figure it out here on Huckleberry Hill. Elsie would be happy to let you stay as long as you like."

Cousin Elsie who lived in Charm, Ohio? "*Denki,* Dawdi." People at home would be laughing about him for years. The girl he loved had rejected him. A broken heart and a large helping of humble pie waited for him in Sugarcreek. He never wanted to go back. But he couldn't stay on Huckleberry Hill forever.

"There's no rush to make plans," Dawdi said. "But your *dat* and I both agree that it's time for you to go back to church. Staying away never did nobody no good."

Reuben hadn't been to *gmay* since he'd come to Huckleberry Hill. At first it was because he didn't think he'd be in Bonduel that long. He'd been too low to want to meet anybody new, let alone try to make friends or forge new relationships that would be so temporary. Then it was easier to be the hermit everyone thought he was. Hermits never got their hearts broken. Hermits never got betrayed by their best friends. Hermits didn't have friends.

But Dawdi was right. Reuben had been baptized, and *Gotte* expected him to be in church, no matter how mad Reuben was at *Gotte* at the moment. No matter how painful, he needed to quit being a baby about it. "*Jah.* I know I need to go back to church."

Dawdi folded his arms. "Tomorrow will be a wonderful-*gute* day for it since it's at our house."

"Okay. I'll come. I just don't like being laughed at."

"I can't imagine anyone will laugh at you. They've been curious as cats to know who the boy is hiding on Huckleberry Hill. The girls caught wind that you are handsome, and they've been holding their breath in hopes you'll show up."

"I'd rather they left me alone. I don't have the heart for it."

Dawdi rested a firm hand on Reuben's shoulder. "No one's asking you to pick a new girlfriend. It's *gmay*. You don't have to flirt. You only have to show up and listen to the sermons. That will be plenty of excitement for everybody for one day."

"It's a sad day when I'm the most exciting thing to happen at *gmay*."

"Exciting things happen at *gmay* all the time. Two weeks ago little Jake Zimmerman and Yost Kiem were fighting over a copy of the *Ausbund*, and Jake yanked it out of Yost's hands so fast, it hit him in the face and gave him a bloody nose." Dawdi motioned toward the house. "I can't prepare for all the excitement on an empty stomach. Your *mammi*'s made Spam sandwiches and orange Jell-O with pickles."

Reuben propped his rake against the side of the house. "Lead the way."

At least he didn't have to pretend to be enthusiastic about lunch. The best thing about being on Huckleberry Hill, besides his grandparents, was the food. Mammi wasn't a timid cook. She experimented with new combinations and flavors, and Reuben loved her sense of adventure—and her lentil, raisin, and green bean soup.

If only everybody could cook like Mammi.

Chapter Four

Reuben hadn't felt like singing for three months, but he felt obligated to sing in church. The elders wouldn't like it if he sat there during the singing like a mute songbird. They were halfway through "*Das Loblied*," which took nearly half an hour to sing, but his mind wasn't on the words. Instead, he was thinking of Linda Sue and her hazel eyes, which were so deep he had often imagined he could swim in them. He used to sneak glances at her during the minister's sermons. Church would always remind him of Linda Sue.

No wonder he'd stayed away for so long.

Linda Sue had a quiet, humble way about her that Reuben liked very much. She wasn't loud and never drew attention to herself, even though she was pretty and the bishop's daughter to boot. Reuben had loved sitting with her in the evenings on her *dat*'s porch swing, maybe gazing at the sunset or laughing at a joke.

That was all behind him now. John King had seen to that. Would Reuben ever be able to smile again?

He shifted his weight on the bench to get comfortable, if that was possible tightly sandwiched between two young men he didn't know. Should he try to make friends with them, or would they prove as disappointing as John had?

More than anything else, Reuben wanted to be liked again. He wanted people to admire him, respect him. And he didn't want to be laughed at. Was there any hope of that in Bonduel?

Although Mammi and Dawdi's house had a nice big room—as did many Amish homes—specifically for the purpose of holding church services, the space was still filled to overflowing. Each home in the district took a turn hosting the *gmayna*, and Mammi and Dawdi held church here every six months or so. Reuben had helped them clear the sofa and Dawdi's recliner from the room and had helped the men set up benches last night. The table had been pushed to the side and the kitchen chairs had been lined up along the wall to make room for benches. The front door was open, and some of the men sat on Mammi's porch, craning their necks to see into the house. It wasn't even sixty degrees, but no one seemed to mind the cold. Wisconsin springs were no match for hardy Amish folks.

After Reuben had raked the yard clean yesterday, he had helped Mammi sweep and mop her formidable wood floor and cleaned the toilets until they sparkled. Mammi had been impressed with Reuben's toilets. If there was one thing his *mamm* had taught him, it was how to use a toilet scrubber.

The *Vorsinger* started them on the fourth verse of "*Das Loblied*," and Reuben glanced up from the *Ausbund*. The girls and women were sitting on the neatly lined up benches directly across from him.

A girl on the end of one of the benches leaned sideways so Reuben could see her face from behind the girl sitting in front of her. He caught his breath. She smiled as if her being there was the most natural thing in the world. His heart galloped so fast, his lungs couldn't keep up.

He stared at her breathlessly until she winked at him, and then he thought he might burst into flames.

What was she doing here?

Fern King, John's pesky little sister, was sitting in Anna and Felty's great room as if she had a right to be there. As if her brother hadn't betrayed Reuben a mere three months ago. As if she lived just down the road instead of hundreds of miles away.

If Reuben had been at anyone else's house, he would have stood up, stormed out of church, and marched home. Instead, he was forced to sit there—his throat on fire, his jaw clenched so tightly his teeth were likely to crack—while Fern eyed him with that smug smile she always wore, as if Reuben were someone she barely put up with. *Ach!* She was fully aware that Reuben had been putting up with John's baby sister ever since she had been old enough to tag after him.

"Rube! Wait for me. I want to come."

"John, Mamm says you have to let me play with you."

"I want to shoot the BB gun too. Dat says to give me a turn."

He scowled at her, which only made her smile wider. If she had come to gloat, she'd be sorely disappointed. Reuben didn't plan on giving her the time of day, let alone a chance to exult over him in his grandparents' own home. He still had some pride left.

He refused to glance in her direction for the rest of the service, but she might as well have been the only person in the room. Until *gmay* ended, he could think on nothing else but Fern and her aggravating smile.

He barely registered the sermon about the Golden Rule. He couldn't even remember singing the last hymn. His anger was so thick, he could have chewed on it.

Finally the service ended, and the women congregated around the counter and the kitchen table, readying food for the fellowship supper. The men carried the benches outside and assembled some of them into tables. Throwing on his jacket, Reuben didn't waste time lollygagging inside. He had no intention of being cornered by Fern King. If she'd come all the way to Wisconsin to scold him, he wasn't going to give her a chance to say anything.

An older man with a graying beard took the other side of Reuben's bench, and they lifted it together on top of another bench to form a table. "Reuben Helmuth, isn't it?"

"*Jah.*"

"I'm Menno Glick. I knew your *dat* before he married and moved to Ohio. How is he?"

"He's in very *gute* health. Hasn't spent a day of his life in the hospital," Reuben said. Out of the corner of his eye, he saw Fern amble onto the porch and lean on the railing. She was waiting to pounce. He could see it in her eyes. Reuben turned his face from her, wanting to growl like a bear and scare her away.

Unfortunately, Fern wasn't the type to spook easily.

"Your *dat* is like Felty, hardly sick a day in his life, except when he wore out his knees."

Keeping an eye on Fern, Reuben made himself extremely busy with the benches. She didn't spook easily, and she was persistent. She'd once camped out all night at the entrance to Reuben and John's secret hideout just so they'd let her in.

He picked up a bench and carried it around to the side of the house, out of Fern's line of sight. After setting the bench down, he jogged into the trees and made a run for the barn. He could hole up there until the fellowship supper was over.

Once he reached the barn, he realized it was a *deerich*, foolish plan. The barn was the first place Fern would look for him. He circled around the barn and took the back way to the trail that led to Mammi and Dawdi's huckleberry patch, almost a two-mile walk from the house. Fern wouldn't be able to find him.

He picked his way over the muddy trail. There were still patches of dirty snow surviving in the shade of the tall maples. In the shade, the air was as crisp as a Granny Smith apple. He was glad he'd brought a jacket.

Reuben had fond memories of picking huckleberries on Huckleberry Hill. On picking days, they would hike to the huckleberry patch, each carrying a bucket and a thermos of water. Dawdi would fill his pocket with raisins, and Reuben would stuff his mouth alternately with raisins and huckleberries. Mamm had frequently scolded him for eating a good portion of the huckleberry harvest, but Mammi had never minded. The berries were for eating, she always said. After picking, they'd have a picnic under the canopy of trees, then head for home, where Aendi Diana would make enough huckleberry pies for the whole family.

The huckleberry bushes were beginning to bud with their creamy white, bulbous flowers that looked to Reuben like tiny, upside-down butterkin squash.

This was a place where Reuben could forget about his humiliation for a little while. Maybe this was a place where he could heal.

Or maybe not.

He heard muffled footsteps and knew immediately who was coming down the trail. With a stifled groan, he turned and watched as Fern strolled toward him with that irritating smile on her face, heedless of the mud puddles or the obstacles on the path. And the foolish girl hadn't even worn a shawl. Sure as rain, she was going to catch cold.

Unlike John's carrot top, Fern's hair was a deep auburn, like maple leaves in late autumn. Her hair brought out the reddish flecks in her brown eyes and the abundance of freckles sprinkled across her nose and cheeks. He had once considered her pretty—even though she was John's kid sister—but now that Reuben disliked her brother so much, he couldn't be objective about Fern's looks. She was too much like her brother, and her brother was a horrible friend.

He gave up trying to escape and folded his arms across his chest, waiting silently for her approach as he glared in her direction.

At the end of the trail, she stopped to catch her breath, letting her gaze travel over the huckleberry patch. "Beautiful," she said, her eyes dancing with amusement. "I've always been a faster runner than you. It's useless to run away."

"You might as well turn around and go back the way you came. I won't talk to you."

She held a slice of bread in each hand. One was topped with cheese spread, the other with peanut butter. "Which one do you want?"

Wasn't it just like her to pretend nothing was wrong, to pretend that her brother hadn't stolen his girlfriend. "I don't want either."

She held out the slice with peanut butter spread on it. "I snuck a taste of the peanut butter. It's very *gute.*

Extra sweet." When he didn't reply, she took a step toward him and raised the bread closer to his face. "*Cum*, Reuben. If you're going to yell at me, you should at least eat something to give you the energy for it." Her chin trembled, and he could see a flock of goose bumps on her arms.

Reuben shrugged the jacket off his shoulders and draped it over Fern's arm. "Put this on and go back to the house. Give it to my *mammi* when you leave."

She tilted her head and lifted both hands. "I can't put it on. My hands are full."

Oh, *sis yuscht*, that girl knew how to get on his nerves. He took both slices of bread from her, and she flashed a self-satisfied grin before sliding her arms into his jacket, which was way too big. She pressed the fabric close to her nose and breathed in. "You smell like cedarwood."

He and Fern had spent too much time together over the years. She could probably identify forty essential oils by their smell. He would have been impressed if he weren't so irritated. He tried to give back her slices of bread, but she slipped her hands behind her back. "They're all yours."

While he didn't want her to think she'd won any sort of victory, he really was hungry after three hours of sermons and songs and prayers. He took a bite of the peanut butter slice and then the cheesy one. Her smile only got wider. Leave it to Fern King to think she'd beaten him.

It was hard to frown and chew at the same time, but that didn't stop him from trying. "You're not welcome here, Fern. You can gloat just as easily from Sugarcreek as you can from Bonduel yet."

"Why would I gloat?"

"Because your brother got the girl I love."

Her smile disappeared as she took another step forward. He took a step back. "For sure and certain, Reuben, I feel terrible about what happened. I came to see if there was anything I could do to make it up to you."

He took another step away from her. "How did you know I was here? I only told my *mamm* and *dat* where I was going."

"I pried it out of your *mamm* three days ago. She's worried about you. As soon as she told me where you'd gone, I hitched a ride with a funeral van headed to Appleton. I had to see if I could help."

Reuben very nearly snorted. "I'm fine, and it's none of your business."

She reached out to . . . he didn't know what she reached out to do. Touch him? He wouldn't allow that. He'd stepped away from her so many times, he was practically strolling backward. She dropped her hand to her side, and the sleeve of his jacket immediately swallowed it. "I know how bad it must have hurt, and I'm sorry, that's all."

"*You're* feeling sorry for *me*? Don't make me laugh."

She looked him up and down as if he were a tree she was planning to chop down. Then she grinned. "Still as stuck-up as ever, I see."

Fern loved to insult him by telling him how stuck-up she thought he was. As if he cared about her opinion. "Just because I won't trip all over myself to lick the dust—or the pig manure—off John's boots doesn't mean I'm a snob. It wonders me why I ever let him be my friend."

Fern seemed to be laughing at him with her eyes.

"You wanted some admirers from among the poor of Sugarcreek."

Reuben narrowed his eyes. "I don't care how much money your *dat* makes."

"*Ach*, but you do, Reuben Helmuth. John is a wonderful-convenient friend. You can always feel superior to him because your family is wealthy, and ours is poor."

Reuben couldn't even begin to defend himself against that accusation. His family was rich. So what? It wasn't his fault Fern was ashamed to be poor. "Maybe John made friends with me so he could steal my girlfriend."

Fern arched an eyebrow. "You two have been friends almost since the moment you could talk. I doubt there was a secret plan to steal Linda Sue at the age of two."

"At least you admit he stole her."

"Now you're being ridiculous," she said.

"Go ahead and mock me. Better yet, go back to Sugarcreek and join the whole community in mocking me. That should make you happy."

Fern smiled and huffed out a breath. "I don't rejoice in your pain, Reuben. I am very sorry about the way things turned out, but you don't know the whole story. Linda Sue was very unhappy. Go back to Sugarcreek and talk to them."

"I never want to lay eyes on John again. Don't you think I've been humiliated enough for a lifetime?"

Fern shook her head as if he were a lost cause. "Can't you find it in your hard heart to forgive them?"

He ground his teeth together. "If you hate me so much, why are you here?"

She surged forward, and before he could react, she wrapped her fingers around one of his suspenders. "Because I don't hate you, you silly goose. You may be arrogant and selfish and prone to hold a grudge, but you're like a big brother to me."

He backed away again, and his suspender slapped him in the chest when she let go. "You don't make me sound like a very nice big brother."

Fern giggled. He pulled his frown deeper into his face. She truly enjoyed poking fun at him. "You are the nicest, Reuben. You have many faults, but I care about you, and I know you care about me."

"I don't care one whit about you."

"Aren't you the boy who pulled my buggy out of the mud and helped me wash it before Dat could find out? Aren't you the boy who put more than one Band-Aid on my knees over the years?" She snatched one of his slices of bread and took a bite. "I tagged after you and John like a hungry mosquito, but you were still willing to teach me how to ice-skate. You held my hand on the ice, Reuben. I had a wonderful-serious six-year-old crush on you." Her brown eyes got sort of soft, like chocolate tapioca pudding. "I don't want you to be sad. You tell me how I can make it better, and I'll do it. You just have to ask."

Reuben looked away and stared at a very interesting tree branch to his right. "You're John King's sister. There's nothing you can do but make it worse."

"Jesus said to forgive seventy times seven. You need to forgive my brother."

"Like that," Reuben said, snapping his attention back to Fern. "You make it worse like that. You have no right to preach to me when your own brother betrayed his best friend. Go home and remind him of his own sins, and leave mine out of it."

"Believe me, John feels very bad about how he handled things between you, but you left him no choice."

"Go ahead and make it out to be my fault. That's what John and Linda Sue did."

Fern growled in exasperation. "I didn't mean it that way. You, Reuben Helmuth, need to quit lying to yourself and try to see things clearly."

"For someone who says she cares about me, you seem to have kept a very long list of my faults. I don't need your sermon." Reuben turned his back on Fern and marched down the trail toward Mammi and Dawdi's house, completely disgusted with himself. He'd promised himself he wasn't going to say a word, and he'd done at least half the talking. He should have given Fern nothing but his silence. She was John's sister. He didn't owe her anything.

He could hear her following him along the path and picked up his pace. Fern might be a fast walker but his legs were longer, and he'd rather get his fingers caught in the wringer washer than let her catch up to him.

He strode out of the woods, across the lawn, and up the porch steps. Inside the house, he waited at the window, gazing at the trail that led into the forest to make sure Fern made it back safely. With his jacket. Maybe he just wanted to make sure his jacket made it home okay.

It only took a minute of waiting until he saw her emerge from among the trees. She glanced around her, took the front flaps of his jacket in both her fists, and buried her nose in the soft fleece lining at the neck. She must have really liked the smell of cedarwood.

Either that, or she was blowing her nose on his jacket.

She could be irritating like that.

Chapter Five

Fern King knelt beside her rickety bicycle, gasping in pain and chastising herself for being so impatient. A long, crooked gash zigzagged along her ankle, and blood trickled cheerfully down her foot and into the dirt. Oh, *sis yuscht*. It was going to smart for days. If she had been wearing shoes, her foot wouldn't have slipped and she wouldn't have scraped her ankle against the pedal, but shoes cost money and she never wore them if she could possibly help it. She had her pair for church and another sensible black pair that she wore during the winter. They lasted longer if she went barefoot all summer long.

Of course, no one could claim that it was summer yet, but it seemed wasteful to wear her shoes on a fine April day like this. Unfortunately, she hadn't anticipated having to wrestle her bicycle up Huckleberry Hill.

Gingerly putting weight on her foot, Fern stood and retrieved the bottle of water Wally Schmucker had given her this morning. Fern had only been in Bonduel two days, but it was plain that Wally had to tiptoe around his wife something wonderful. But he also had a kind heart and didn't want Fern to go thirsty, not when she hadn't had a chance to get to the store for her own groceries. Fern had been grateful for anything Wally was willing to lend her, including his old bike.

She opened the bottle that Wally had sneaked out of the house and poured a generous amount of water over her bleeding ankle. It rinsed away the old blood, but new blood immediately rushed in to take its place. *Ach, vell.* It would stop bleeding eventually.

Fern tossed the half-empty bottle into the wire basket on the front of her bike. Grabbing the handlebars, she pushed her bike up the hill, limping all the way. The pain was bearable. She'd be fine.

Even when she had been riding, the trip had been slow going. Wally Schmucker had been very kind to let her borrow the bike, but the poor thing was obviously close to death. It squeaked like a closet full of bats and glowed orange with rust—*gute* thing she was up to date with her tetanus shot. The back tire wobbled precariously, even though Fern had taken a wrench to it this morning.

But she couldn't be ungrateful. The Schmuckers were relatives, very distant cousins on her *dat*'s side, and Barbara Schmucker hadn't wanted to let her stay at all. Wally had been very kind to find a place for her to sleep, even though she had shown up uninvited at their house on Saturday evening. Barbara had insisted that Fern could only stay for a few days, but after seeing Reuben yesterday at *gmay*, it was obvious that a few days would not be enough. She didn't hold out much hope that Barbara would understand, but perhaps Fern could convince Wally that she wouldn't be any sort of bother.

She didn't intend to give up on Reuben Helmuth, no matter how hard he tried to push her away. He was like a brother to her. She'd do anything to help. If worse came to worst, she would find a place to camp. It was nearly warm enough to sleep outside if she had to.

Fern was nothing if not persistent. Reuben Helmuth should have already figured that out by now. And she wasn't going to stop pestering him until he snapped out of his whiny, woe-is-me mood. He was wearing his self-pity like a badge, and Fern couldn't allow that.

The bike squealed its way up the hill. If Fern had been at home, Mamm would have stuck her head out the front door for fear the pigs had gotten into the yard.

She reached the crest of the hill, and Reuben's grandparents' house came into view. Delicate purple crocuses peeked up from the grass, and with a few more warm days, the daffodils would be blooming in the flower beds.

The barn door opened, and Reuben emerged carrying a bulging burlap bag over his shoulder. With bowed head, he trudged toward the house and didn't see Fern until she cleared her throat and spoke. "*Gute maiya*, Reuben."

He stopped short, as if he'd run headlong into a brick wall, and stared at Fern like an unwelcome surprise. Fern grinned and shrugged. She *was* an unwelcome surprise. Reuben was a big boy. A little discomfort would do him some good.

"What are you doing here?" Could he possibly have sounded more hostile?

It really irritated him when she smiled, but she couldn't help it. Reuben looked as forlorn as a lost puppy dog—cute and adorable and in need of a hug—and she was so glad to see him and so eager to help him be happy again. "I came to scold you into a *gute* mood."

"My mood is none of your business."

"But you're so fun," Fern said in her best little sister whine. "You're the one everybody wants to be around because something exciting happens whenever you're there. You are always laughing and joking, making even the worst days better."

"Until three months ago," Reuben said. "Then your brother humiliated me, and everybody is laughing at me. You don't know anything about how I'm feeling."

Fern gave him a patient smile. "Okay. You're right. I don't know. But I do know that if you could forgive John and Linda Sue, you'd be happier, and you'd be able to come home."

"If I forgive John, it would be like admitting he was right when he wasn't."

The bike screamed in protest as Fern pushed it to the sidewalk and lowered the kickstand. The blood dripping from her ankle must have caught his eye. He glanced down at her foot and quickly looked away. Scooting the burlap bag more securely onto his shoulder, he started back toward the barn. "Please leave me alone."

She would have chased him all over Huckleberry Hill, but her ankle needed to be tended or she'd leave a blood trail that would probably attract a wild and ferocious animal. Were snakes attracted to blood? She didn't really want to find out.

The bleeding had mostly stopped, but the cut

looked quite ghastly. Would Anna Helmuth object to blood on her floor? Fern didn't know much about Reuben's grandparents except what she'd heard from Reuben. He had told her that his *mammi* was the best cook in the world and that his *dawdi* could make up songs like a writer. They seemed like people who wouldn't mind giving a Band-Aid to a passing stranger.

Besides, Reuben was going to need plenty of persuasion. It wouldn't hurt to enlist the grandparents' help. Reuben was living with them. He couldn't shut them out the way he did Fern.

She limped up the porch steps, tilting her foot so she wouldn't get blood on the stairs, and knocked on the door. She heard a bright, chipper voice inside. "*Cum reu.*"

Fern opened the door and poked her head into the room. The kitchen and family room were one big space, with a nicely lumpy sofa sitting in the great room, a massive recliner to its left, and a rocking chair across from it. An ample wooden table stood immediately to her right, and a counter with a sink jutted out from the wall. A ball of white fur slept on the rag rug next to the sofa. A dog. *Gute.* Fern loved dogs. Anyone who owned a dog couldn't be half bad.

"I'm sorry to bother you," Fern said, keeping her feet securely planted on the porch. She didn't want to track blood into the house.

Reuben's *mammi* stood behind the counter at the stove with her hands clasped around the handle of an enormous pot. From the door, Fern could see the big rolling bubbles of water threatening to escape the pot. Something in there must have been boiling wonderful hot. Fern felt hollow inside just imagining what must be in that pot. She hadn't had dinner last night. Or breakfast this morning.

Anna Helmuth looked up and smiled as if Fern were her favorite person in the whole world. "Well, hello, dear. Do you think you could help me?" She had her oven mitts around the handles of the pot, attempting to lift it from the stove, but it looked like it weighed almost as much as Anna did.

Fern nearly barreled into the house before stopping herself. "My ankle got cut. I'm dripping a little blood."

"Plenty of people have bled on this floor," Anna said, grunting and straining to lift the pot. "I'm not persnickety about a little blood. I've got to get this off the stove before the oysters overcook."

Not sure if she should be alarmed that plenty of people had bled on Anna's floor, Fern rushed into the kitchen, snatched a towel from the cupboard, and wrapped it around the lip of the pot. Anna gripped the handles, and Fern held tight to the pot, and together they lifted it to the sink where Anna directed Fern to pour the boiling water. Steam rose clear to the ceiling, and both Fern and Anna leaned back to keep from getting burned.

Once half the water was gone, Anna pressed the lid to the top of the pot and used it to stop the oysters from escaping as Fern poured out the rest of the water. Once the water was drained, Fern set the pot on a cooling rack next to the stove.

"*Denki*, dear. I have never cooked oysters before, and I want to make a special meal for Reuben tonight. He is so very sad, and I thought oyster and water chestnut salad might cheer him up."

"Sounds like a very unusual recipe."

"*Ach, vell,* I made it up. The best ones are usually the ones I come up with when I'm being creative." Anna winked and tapped her temple with her index finger. "It keeps me sharp."

Reuben had said that his *mammi* was a *gute* cook, but Fern wasn't too sure about the sound of oyster and water chestnut salad, even with a stomach so empty it echoed.

Anna caught her breath. "*Ach, du lieva.* Your foot is bleeding."

Fern looked down at her ankle. The oozing blood had left a trail from her ankle to her heel that looked quite spectacular. "I'm sorry for getting your floor dirty."

Anna swatted her apology away like a mosquito. "It will wipe right off, but *cum,* sit down. What a very thoughtful girl you are. You cared more about my pot than you did your ankle. I hope your foot doesn't fall off because of your unselfishness."

Fern giggled. "It's just a scratch. My foot slipped off my bicycle pedal." She went around the counter and sat down at the kitchen table while Anna gathered some supplies from her drawers in the kitchen.

She came to the table and sat in the chair next to Fern. "Can you lift your foot and rest it on my leg? I'm afraid I don't bend so well anymore. Every bone in my body clanks if I try."

Fern raised her eyebrows. "Of course, but you don't need to do that. I can clean it myself."

Anna tapped her leg where she wanted Fern to prop her foot. "Stuff and nonsense. You saved my oysters. The least I can do is tend to your foot. After caring for thirteen children, I'm practically a nurse."

Smiling at this charming *fraa* who had no doubt

seen her share of skinned knees and fat lips, Fern set her foot on Anna's leg and let her tend to her ankle.

Anna dabbed carefully at Fern's cut with a soapy towel. Her hands were gentle but thorough, as if she'd done such a thing hundreds of times before. "What is your name, dear?"

"*Ach*, I'm sorry. My name is Fern King. I'm visiting from Ohio."

"Who are you visiting?"

"Barbara and Wally Schmucker. Barbara is my *dat*'s second cousin."

Something awkward and uncertain flitted across Anna's face. "You're staying with Barbara?"

Fern was staying on their property. Anna didn't need the details. "*Jah.*"

"Wally is a dear man," Anna said, wiping the dried blood from Fern's foot. "Patient and long-suffering. He does what he can, you know." She leaned closer to Fern. "Barbara has an extra toe on her left foot, but none of us has ever loved her less because of her little deformity."

Fern grinned. "I'm glad to hear it."

"I saw you at *gmay* yesterday and thought, *What a pretty girl.* You left before we could get acquainted."

"Barbara wasn't feeling well. Wally was eager to get home to her."

Anna nodded, and Fern could tell she was forcing a reassuring smile onto her lips. "Barbara takes lots of naps. She was the best quilter in Wisconsin once." She dried Fern's foot with the edge of her towel. It looked as good as new except for the three-inch gash at her ankle. Anna picked up a tube of antibacterial ointment and studied Fern, her eyes twinkling like sparklers on the Fourth of July. "You seem like such a delightful girl, Fern. Do you have a boyfriend?"

Fern couldn't hold back a wide smile. *Mammis* never failed to ask about boyfriends. "*Nae.* I haven't found one who can keep up with me. I can't abide the sluggish ones."

"I don't blame you, dear. I fell in love with Felty because he was so lively. I knew I would have many exciting adventures if I married him." Anna spread the ointment on Fern's cut. "I ask because I am looking for a wife for my grandson Reuben, and you might be just the girl. He's very handsome and very thoughtful and any girl would consider herself blessed to marry him."

Fern bit her tongue to keep from laughing. Reuben would be quite irritated if he knew his *mammi* was trying to marry him off. Fern itched to tell him. She loved it when he got irritated.

"He's going through a bit of a rough patch right now. He may seem a little grumpy at first, but he's always been one of my most cheerful grandsons. He's from Ohio too." She examined Fern's cut and pulled out four Band-Aids from the box. "Of course, I would have to interview you to make sure you and Reuben would suit, so don't get your hopes up just yet."

"I would never get my hopes up with Reuben," Fern said, smiling in resignation. "He refuses to talk to me."

Anna eyed Fern as if she wore a feather on her head. "You already know Reuben?"

"I came from Ohio just so I could talk to him."

"Really? About what? Did you try to propose?"

"*Nae.* My brother and Reuben's old girlfriend are engaged. I feel terrible about what happened and was hoping I could talk Reuben into coming home. If he would just listen to John, I know my brother could make things right between them."

Anna leaned in again and lowered her voice to a whisper. "We know all about his disgrace. Our son wrote to us."

"It wasn't exactly a disgrace, though I'm sure Reuben thinks it is. My brother and Linda Sue didn't plan to fall in love. John was Reuben's best friend, and Linda Sue was Reuben's girlfriend. He's the one who brought them together." Fern smiled and shook her head. "I'm sure Reuben would be very irritated if I pointed that out to him."

"So Linda Sue broke his heart?" Anna said.

"*Jah*, I suppose she did. You would like Linda Sue. She's very quiet, hardly says a word unless you ask her a question."

Anna pressed her lips together. "I have a hard time being fond of a girl who hurt my grandson's feelings. Although, maybe they weren't a *gute* match. It takes skill to find just the right match for someone. Not everyone is good at it."

"Reuben thought they were perfectly suited. Linda Sue is the prettiest girl in Sugarcreek, and her *dat* is the bishop. Reuben always hoped to marry a bishop's *maedle*. He thought it would make him more important."

Anna's lips twitched. "You think my grandson is proud."

Fern was sure her eyes were dancing like Anna's were. "*Jah*, and I've told him so many times. He doesn't pay me any heed."

Anna looked as if she was trying to hold in her laughter. "I think he would appreciate a girl who is honest with him."

"But who among us isn't tempted by pride? Poor

Reuben simply has more reason to be proud than most of us. He's handsome, smart, rich, and the minister's son. His blessings are almost unbearable for him."

"It was probably a *gute* thing that your brother knocked Reuben's pride down a peg or two."

"I hate to see him so unhappy, even if it was for his own *gute* yet."

"When people praise me for my cooking, I am tempted to be proud," Anna said. "My son, Reuben's *fater*, and my daughter-in-law have gotten very wealthy selling that smelly oil stuff, though why anyone would pay good money for it, I'll never know."

Fern laughed. "Essential oils. They've done very well, but they give much of their money to the church."

"Of course they do. We taught Reuben's *dat* David whom to thank for his blessings. He's no slouch."

"And neither is Reuben."

Anna squeezed Fern's hand. "I know that for sure and certain. He may be proud and a little big for his britches, but he also has a heart of gold."

"He does," said Fern, suddenly feeling very sad for Reuben. "I'm very sorry about what happened. I just don't know how to make it better. Linda Sue isn't suddenly going to change her mind."

Anna finished laying the Band-Aids over Fern's cut. "You're here, and Linda Sue isn't. Even though you don't particularly like him, I'm still willing to match you up, if you think that would help."

Fern took her foot from Anna's lap. "*Ach*, I like him very much. He's like a big brother to me, a misguided brother, but still. . . ." She bent over and smoothed the Band-Aids with her finger. "He was always watching out for me, like a brother should, even though I often ruined his fun by tagging along or tattling. He saved my life once."

"I've always known he was a very nice sort of boy. Did he donate blood?"

Fern curled her lips. "John and Reuben and some of their other friends went swimming, and I insisted on going, like I often did. John was always annoyed with me so he usually ignored me. If Reuben hadn't been looking out for me, I would have drowned."

"Thank the *gute* Lord he was there," Anna said. "Since he saved your life, we might be able to talk him into marrying you."

Fern couldn't suppress her laughter. Reuben would choke on his own tongue if he knew what they were talking about. "I truly love Reuben, but I couldn't marry him. He's too stuck-up. And he would never dream of marrying me. I'm from a poor family, not to mention the sister of the boy who stole his girlfriend. It would be humiliating to marry the daughter of a pig farmer."

"But Reuben's best friend was the son of a pig farmer."

Fern wrinkled her forehead. "I suppose he thought John looked up to him."

Anna stood, went around the counter, and peered into her pot. She took a slotted spoon, fished an oyster shell from the pot, and carried it to the table like she might carry a compass ahead of her. "Would you like to try an oyster, Fern? They're very nutritious."

Fern attempted a smile. Inside the half-open shell was a grayish-black, shiny blob that looked about as appetizing as shoe rubber. Swallowing hard, she stifled a shudder. She wasn't quite that hungry yet. "You should save them for Reuben. He has a big appetite."

"He surely does." To Fern's relief, Anna didn't try to persuade her. She took the pot back to the stove and covered it with the lid, probably to make sure those things wouldn't escape. "Reuben eats when he's upset. That's why he needs a girl."

"I'm not sure having a girlfriend would cheer him up," Fern said.

"There's nothing like a wife to cure what ails my Reuben. The trouble is, ever since he showed up at our house, I've been wracking my brain, but I just can't think of a girl who's right for him."

Fern leaned her chin on her hand. "And you've got to get her to Huckleberry Hill. Reuben's not likely to go into town to see a girl, even if she's perfect for him. He'd move to Montana if he thought you were trying to get him married off."

"It wonders me if knitting some pot holders for him might help. Or I wouldn't mind crocheting some dishrags."

Fern clapped her hands. "Anna, what about starting a knitting group and matching him with one of the knitters?"

Anna's smile froze in place, as if she were trying to be encouraging even though she thought Fern's suggestion was slightly odd. "Well, dear, I'm already in a knitting group, and the youngest member is seventy-three. I don't think Reuben is that desperate."

Fern laughed. "What I meant was, what if we started a knitting group with some of the unmarried girls in the district? That would give them an excuse to come to Huckleberry Hill without making Reuben suspicious. Each girl would have a chance to get to know Reuben while we knitted."

Anna tapped her fingers to her mouth. "That just

might work. So few of *die youngie* know how to knit these days. It would do them *gute* to learn."

"But you would have to pick the girls. I don't know anybody in Bonduel but you, Reuben, and the Schmuckers."

Anna's eyes seemed even more lively than usual. "It's what I do best. We'll find a girl for Reuben yet." She grabbed a notebook and pencil from the kitchen drawer and sat down at the table next to Fern. "No knitting group of this kind would be complete without Dorothy Miller. She knits almost as well as I do, and she can help me help the beginners."

"*Gute.* Is she someone who might catch Reuben's eye?"

Anna scrunched her cheeks until her eyes nearly disappeared. "*Ach, vell,* she's well into her thirties, but Reuben won't believe it's a real knitting group unless he sees that at least one of the members knows how to knit."

Fern wasn't sure about that, but Anna knew a lot more about knitting groups than she did. "Who else should we invite?"

"Lorene Zook might suit," Anna said, jotting down the name in her notebook. "She's on the downhill side of twenty-three."

"Not too old."

"*Nae.* And she has very nice teeth. They're on the large side, but Reuben isn't so shallow that he would reject a girl because of her teeth. Or her mole."

Fern pressed her lips together. She wasn't so sure about that either.

Anna nibbled on the pencil eraser. "You say Linda Sue is quiet. Maybe Reuben would like someone like

Eva Raber. She's as quiet as a bowl of potatoes. And of course we should invite Clara and Carolyn Yutzy. They're twins, and I have never been able to tell them apart. But don't tell them I said that. I don't want to hurt their feelings."

"How old are they?"

"*Ach*, twenty or so. Young enough, but not too young."

Fern wanted to ask if they were pretty, but since Anna didn't want to believe that Reuben was shallow, she decided she better not burst his *mammi*'s bubble. "That's five girls. Anyone else you think we should invite?" Someone really pretty. Preferably a minister's daughter with lots of money.

"Sadie Yoder is the bishop's daughter. She's got beautiful golden hair and a very nice dimple, and she knitted a scarf for the auction last September."

"Sounds perfect."

Anna's pen was working furiously now. "But we can't invite Sadie without inviting Esther Shirk. They're always together, those two, even though I don't think Esther has ever picked up a pair of knitting needles."

"What better place to learn than the knitting group?" Fern glanced over Anna's list. "Do you think they'll come?"

Anna's eyes sparkled. "They all got a *gute* look at Reuben yesterday. They'll come."

Fern raised a teasing eyebrow. "Are you saying they're shallow enough to notice how handsome he is?"

Anna nodded. "That's exactly what I'm saying. I'm not beneath using Reuben's good looks to our advantage, especially if it will help him find a wife."

"I only want him to be happy."

"Me too, dear. Even someone as proud and self-centered as my Reuben deserves to be happy." Anna wrote down directions to the new knitting group members' houses and tore the page out of her notebook. Fern took the paper and stuffed it into her pocket. Hopefully her bike would live long enough to get her around town to recruit members for the knitting group.

She bit her bottom lip. She'd have to tell them at least part of why they were being invited to join the knitting group, or they might wonder why a girl from Sugarcreek, Ohio, was asking them to come to Huckleberry Hill and knit. But Anna was right. If they knew it was Reuben, they'd come. Cheerfully. Reuben was handsome enough to attract lightning.

But he wasn't just handsome. The girls would soon find out that there was no more exciting person to be around, plus he was the best volleyball player in Ohio. If he had his way, they would also find out that he was rich, devout, and very likable. And quite proud of himself.

Fern felt sort of heavy as she said good-bye to Anna and ambled down the porch steps. It was unlikely the girls in the knitting group would ever truly see the real Reuben. He was arrogant, to be sure, but he would also wrestle a porcupine for the people he loved. He'd secretly give his best friend money so he could fix the roof and feed the horse. He'd make an annoying kid sister feel special, even when she didn't deserve it— even when he had a thousand better things to do. His smile was like sunshine reflecting off the lake on a summer day.

Once outside, Fern paused and looked toward the

barn for any sign of Reuben. Not that he'd want to see her, but it might cheer him up if she smiled at him one more time. Nope. He was probably locked in the barn nursing his wounds and pouting about how unfairly he'd been treated. It was just as well she left him alone today.

Fern dragged her feet to her bike and glanced down at her four Band-Aids. Lord willing, she'd be able to ride all over town without any more mishaps.

Strange. She thought she'd parked her bike pointing the other way.

Gingerly, she nudged the kickstand with her foot. Instead of giving her the usual screaming protest, it folded up noiselessly as if it didn't mind being shoved. She decided to walk the thing down the hill. The tire was likely to fall off, and she'd rather not break her leg today. Or her neck.

She grabbed the handlebars and pushed the bike forward, only to stop in her tracks. Her bike no longer squeaked, rattled, or wobbled. She could have sneaked up on an unsuspecting boy with this bike. The chain links had been brushed and oiled, the shaft of her handlebars lubricated, and her basket wiped clean. Leaning over, she took a better look at the back tire. She tried to wiggle it back and forth, but it stayed solidly in the hub. She got even closer. This wasn't the same bolt she'd fiddled with this morning.

With her heart beating inexplicably fast, Fern glanced up, half expecting to see Reuben standing over her with a self-satisfied smile on his lips and that attractive tease in his blue eyes. There was no doubt in her mind that he had fixed her bike. He'd heard her clattering up the hill earlier and seen the blood dripping from her cut. He had decided to take matters into his own hands.

Fern smiled to herself. Reuben might have hated her brother, but this probably meant he didn't hate her. Either that or he couldn't in good conscience let his best friend's sister ride a bike in such poor condition.

Reuben came around the side of the barn, glanced in her direction, and then made as if he hadn't seen her.

She wasn't going to let him get away with that. She waved her arm as if she were flagging down a car. "*Denki* for fixing my bike."

He frowned before turning away and swinging the barn door open. "I don't want you to kill yourself on your way out of town," he called back.

"Don't worry," Fern said, unable to keep the mischief out of her voice. "I'm not leaving anytime soon."

Reuben pretended not to hear.

Chapter Six

Fern considered herself a poor knitter, but when she saw Esther holding her knitting needles like a pair of hammers, she decided that maybe she had underestimated her abilities.

Nine of them, plus Anna, congregated in Anna's great room, crammed onto the sofa and sitting on the hard kitchen chairs they'd dragged from under the table. Anna sat in her rocker, and Fern had made herself comfortable on the floor on Anna's rag rug.

"Dangle the tail over your thumb," Dorothy said, looking slightly exasperated that Esther couldn't even cast on.

"I don't especially like knitting," Esther said, although she was making a valiant attempt. Some people just weren't cut out to be knitters.

"You're doing a wonderful-*gute* job, dear," Anna said. "The baby who gets your blanket will jump for joy."

Anna was trying to be encouraging, but not even Esther could possibly believe that babies could jump.

They were each knitting a baby blanket for the

hospital in Shawano. Some new mothers didn't even have blankets to take their babies home in after delivery. Anna was making her blanket with bright yellow yarn, already miles ahead of the rest of the knitters. Dorothy hadn't even started a blanket because Esther's difficulties took all her attention. Esther's attempted blanket was a soft pink, as was her best friend Sadie's. Lorene Zook and Carolyn and Clara Yutzy were working in various shades of light blue, and Eva Raber's blanket was black. Fern wasn't sure why Eva chose to make a black baby blanket, but at least she had agreed to join their knitting group. Fern had never met anyone who had so little to say for herself.

Fern's blanket was green, suitable for either a boy or a girl. She had found some yarn that was as soft as a bunny rabbit. It had been a little expensive, but every baby deserved something soft to be cuddled in, even if Fern was almost out of money.

"Esther," Sadie said, holding up her needles and showing off three whole inches of knitted stitches, "you're too slow. Have you got ten thumbs?"

Lorene laughed hysterically. And loudly. When they had made up their list of knitting group members, Anna had failed to mention that Lorene's laugh could have frightened the hide off an old horse. She laughed like a duck in fear of its life, her hornlike blasts giving everybody a shock when they first heard her. Fern was pretty sure Reuben wouldn't take much interest in Lorene. Big teeth and a mole in the middle of her chin were minor compared to that horn of a laugh. Lorene was a *gute* girl, loud and friendly, but unless she learned to tone it down, no boy would volunteer to marry her. Perhaps she'd find someone hard of hearing to share her love.

Esther gave Sadie the stink eye. Fern wasn't sure why Sadie and Esther were friends. They seemed not to like each other very much. "I'm trying," Esther said, sniffing in Sadie's direction. "Don't distract me. Every time I try to release my thumb from the loop, I get tangled in the yarn. This is a waste of time. When do we get to see Reuben?"

Fern slumped her shoulders. The knitting group had already met twice this week, and Reuben might as well have been in Ohio. When the knitters came over, he disappeared as if he knew exactly what they were doing there and exactly who had asked them to come. She had expected more effort from him. It was very important to Reuben to be liked. Fern would have thought he'd jump at the chance to meet the girls in the knitting group.

A frown tugged at Fern's mouth. Reuben was just being stubborn—wearing his imaginary shame like a badge of honor. He would not be coaxed into being friendly if he didn't want to be friendly. Fern would have to use force.

Lorene's smile was so wide, Fern could see all her fillings. "I'd like a chance to flirt with Reuben. Isn't that our reason for being here?"

Carolyn shushed Lorene almost before the words were out of her mouth. "Don't you remember, Lorene? It's a secret. What do you think Reuben would do if he knew Fern had asked us to come and try to cheer him up?"

Fern hadn't told anyone in the knitting group that Anna wanted Reuben to marry one of them. That information might have kept some of them away—Eva Raber specifically—or might have made some of them too eager. They thought they were here to cheer

Reuben up, which was completely true. If one of them caught Reuben's fancy, it would definitely make him happy.

Fern frowned to herself. It was a *gute* idea, even if she was having doubts.

"If Reuben knew Fern asked us to cheer him up, it might put him in a worse mood yet," Carolyn's sister Clara said.

Fern had liked Clara and Carolyn the minute she'd met them. They were sturdy brunettes, on the tall side, with sensible faces and intelligent eyes. Fern couldn't tell them apart, but when they came into the house today, they had announced that Clara was wearing blue, and Carolyn was in burgundy. They were thoughtful that way, not expecting Fern to be able to tell them apart and not putting her in the awkward position of having to ask who was who. Clara was older than Carolyn by ten minutes—they'd informed Fern of that first thing—but Carolyn was definitely the bossy one—bossy in a nice way. She simply saw how things were supposed to be done and gladly let everyone know what was required of them.

"I'd like to get another look at Reuben," Esther said, yanking her finger from a knot she'd tied herself into.

Clara grinned. "When I saw him at *gmay*, I remember thinking he had a very *gute* face, even if it looked like he'd never smiled in his life."

"I pretended to trip when I walked by him after services," Sadie said, before bursting into a fit of giggles.

"Were you hoping he'd catch you?" Esther said, as if she thought it was the dumbest idea in the world.

"*Jah.*" The giggling got louder. Sadie laid her knitting on the end table, stood up, and spread her arms out from her sides. "I sort of hopped like this and flew through the air like a bird." She clapped her hand over her mouth to stifle her laughter. "I stole a glance at him, just to see if he was looking my way. He was studying his fingernails. Didn't even notice. I huffed and walked away. He didn't notice that either."

"I'm glad you didn't actually fall," Clara said. "But maybe he would have noticed that."

"I could have done a cartwheel, and Reuben Helmuth would have pulled out his clippers and trimmed his toenails." Sadie looked at Anna. "No offense to your grandson, Anna. Like as not, he had other things on his mind."

Anna smiled that serene smile she got whenever she talked about Reuben. "He's such a dear boy. Always very careful with his toenails."

"But we can't cheer him up if he won't come in the house," Lorene said.

Fern dropped a stitch in her blanket. It was worthless to bring potential wives to Huckleberry Hill if Reuben refused to show his face when they came.

Anna's fingers seemed to fly off her hands, she was knitting so fast. "Lorene is right." She paused to glance at Fern. "It was a very *gute* plan, Fern, but we need to make some improvements to it. I hope you're not offended."

"I want Reuben to be happy." She'd like to see his smile again.

Carolyn set her needles in her lap. "We'll have to take the knitting group out to him."

"That would be a *gute* idea in June," Anna said. "But I can't knit in the cold. My fingers stiffen up."

Carolyn nudged Clara with her elbow. "What I mean

is, one of us will have to put down our knitting, go outside, and trick Reuben into talking to us."

"Okay," said Clara. "We could take turns every time we have knitting group. One of us goes out to be with Reuben instead of knitting, and then we swap. That way we could each get a shot at cheering him up."

Anna's eyebrows rose so high, they almost disappeared under her *kapp*. "What a *wunderbarr* idea, Clara. It would be like rotating the milk so it doesn't go sour."

"I . . . I'd rather not," Eva Raber said.

Everyone paused to look at her. She hadn't uttered a word since she had come into the house.

Dorothy glanced up from the knot she was trying to untangle. "I'd rather not either."

"Don't worry, Dorothy," Anna said. "We invited you for the knitting."

"I'd rather not," Eva said again.

Anna patted Eva on the leg. "No one has to do anything she doesn't want to do. We are content to enjoy your company inside the house. We'll let the other girls have the adventure."

Fern hid a smile. Trying to crack Reuben's crusty shell would indeed be an adventure. He was determined to stay in a bad mood. "Who wants the first turn?"

"We've only got ten minutes left," Esther said. "It wouldn't be fair."

Carolyn let out some slack in her ball of yarn. "You go, Sadie."

Sadie scrunched her lips together. "You heard Esther. It's not fair if I only get ten minutes."

"You could go out next time too," Carolyn said. "Introduce yourself now and spend the whole time with him on Friday."

"That's not fair either," Lorene said.

"We could set a timer," Clara offered.

"Now, girls," Anna said. "You'll all get your chance with Reuben. Let Sadie go out and talk to him. Maybe she'll catch him off guard and get him to smile."

Sadie giggled behind her hand. "I'm sure I can do it."

Esther put down her sorry attempt at knitting and folded her arms. "Well, I hope you don't think I'm petty, but if Sadie gets an extra ten minutes, then I think I deserve an extra ten minutes too."

Sadie pursed her lips and blinked rapidly. "We all think you're petty, Esther."

Fern did not laugh, even though she wanted to. Reuben was too good-looking for his own good. "Esther," she said, "I'll see to it that you get your extra ten minutes in the rotation. Is that fair?"

Esther didn't look convinced. "How are you going to do that?"

"We could set a timer," Clara said.

Fern reached over and patted Esther's foot. "I'll keep careful track of the time. Once we've been through a complete rotation, you'll get your extra ten minutes."

"I suppose that will work."

Sadie practically jumped to her feet and deposited her knitting on the sofa where she'd been sitting. "I'd better make hay while the sun shines."

"He's in the garden digging a hole," Anna said.

Grinning from ear to ear, Sadie donned her black sweater and strutted out the door. Fern felt a twinge of something unpleasant in the area of her liver. Sadie was very pretty. Did Reuben like dimples? What about golden yellow hair? Linda Sue's hair was plain brown, but maybe Reuben would have liked her that much better if she had been a blonde.

Sadie only had ten minutes. She couldn't solidify a relationship in ten minutes. She certainly couldn't ever be a friend like Fern was to Reuben. Fern and Reuben were like brother and sister. Not even a girlfriend could get closer than that, could she?

Ten minutes felt like a month of Sundays. What were they talking about? Would Sadie be taken in by Reuben's handsome face and not even care that he was proud and self-centered? Reuben didn't need an admirer. He needed someone to scold him and keep him humble and teach him not to take himself so seriously. Would Sadie be able to do that?

Probably not in ten minutes.

Even if Sadie puffed him up, Fern would be able to cut him down to size. It was what she did best. Reuben didn't realize how blessed he was to have a friend like Fern King around.

At eleven o'clock, the knitters packed up their yarn and needles. Everybody but Eva, Dorothy, and Anna seemed to have an ear to the door, even though they stood several feet away from it. Fern jumped, actually jumped, when Sadie came strolling back into the room. She wasn't smiling, but she wasn't frowning either.

They all stared at Sadie with unconcealed curiosity.

"Well?" Lorene said. "What happened?"

"He's digging a trench," Sadie said. A smile crept slowly up her cheeks. "And he has muscles." She glanced at Anna in a moment of contrition. "I hope you don't mind that I talk about your grandson that way."

Anna waved her hand in the air. "Felty has muscles

too. It's one of his best qualities. I'd have to be dead not to appreciate them."

"Go on, Sadie."

"I introduced myself, and he smiled and told me he was very happy to meet me." Sadie cooed. "I think I'm cheering him up already."

Fern bit the inside of her cheek. Reuben hadn't smiled at her once since she'd been to Bonduel. What an aggravating boy! He was punishing her, of course, for being related to John, but more than that, he couldn't stand that she was poor and redheaded and persistent.

Well, let him be as unfriendly or as charming as he wanted. Fern could see right through him. Reuben Helmuth's pride was smarting, and even deeper than that, he was hurting. He thought Linda Sue and John had made a fool of him. His own embarrassment made him believe that he wasn't the most important and well-liked boy in Sugarcreek anymore. It had to hurt.

"I can't wait to come again on Friday," Sadie said.

"It's my turn on Friday," Esther said.

Sadie turned up her nose at her best friend, grabbed her knitting from the sofa, and stuffed it into her bag. She and Esther hooked elbows and sashayed out the door as if they'd never been arguing over who got to lay eyes on Reuben Helmuth next.

"Can I be next in the rotation?" Lorene said.

Dorothy stayed long enough to unravel everything Esther had done on her blanket and roll the yarn up into a tight ball. She sighed and smiled at Anna in resignation. "I hope Esther is better at cheering people up than she is at knitting. Some people were just not meant for handicrafts."

When everyone had gone, Fern replaced the kitchen chairs under the table and sat down on one.

Anna sank into the chair next to her. "The knitting group takes more out of me than I thought it would," she said. "Oh, the worry of making sure everyone does their stitches right."

Fern patted Anna's hand. "Don't worry about that. You're the head of the knitting group. It's your job to knit. Dorothy, Eva, and I can supervise."

Anna placed her other hand on top of Fern's. "I'll do my part. We've all got to make sacrifices for the good of my grandson. I just hope Esther's blanket will do her proud. What if the hospital refuses to take it? It would be a definite stain on our knitting group's reputation."

"I don't think we have a reputation."

"Only because they haven't seen Esther's blanket yet."

One of the advantages of being in charge of the knitting group was that Fern got to stay at the Helmuths' as long as she wanted after the rest of the girls had gone home. She didn't have to put herself into the rotation, and she didn't have to justify herself to Esther. She didn't intend to squander the time.

Reuben was digging trenches, and Fern didn't see any reason why she couldn't help him. She was plenty strong for a girl. It came with working a pig farm. Fern carefully took off her *kapp* and laid it on the table. She pulled a plain blue scarf from her pocket and tied it quickly around her head. The work outside was too dirty to wear a *kapp*.

Even though she would rather have gone without shoes, it was hard to thrust a shovel into the dirt without them. Fern had learned that the hard way when she was five. "Anna, do you think I could borrow your boots to help Reuben dig trenches?"

"What a nice girl you are. Of course you can wear my boots, but I don't know that they'll fit."

Fern was seven or eight inches taller than Anna and no doubt had much bigger feet. Anna was just a tiny thing, not more than five feet tall, but maybe Fern could squeeze into her boots. They stood on the mat next to the door. Fern tried to slip her feet into them, but they pinched something wonderful, and that was before she'd even shoved her feet in all the way.

"Do they fit?" Anna said.

Fern shook her head. "You have tiny feet." She'd have to settle for no shoes at all. Even though Reuben would most likely scold her for going barefoot on such a brisk day, it wouldn't do to ruin her good pair of shoes. With no source of income in sight, Fern was living off the kindness of the Schmuckers and the Helmuths. She had only enough money to buy a bus ticket home and couldn't spare it for anything so expensive as a new pair of shoes.

"Felty's boots are on his feet at the market," Anna said, "but you could wear his galoshes. There are plenty of puddles out there to splash in."

Galoshes would be better than nothing. Fern found Felty's black galoshes in the closet and slipped her feet into them. Felty was tall and lanky, like his grandson, and Fern felt like she was wearing canoes on her feet. "Where can I find a shovel?"

"Out in the toolshed to the left, behind the barn. The door sticks, so be careful. Our grandson Titus pulled it too hard once, and the door smacked him in the forehead. It was a truly lovely goose egg." Anna retrieved four cookies from the cookie jar. She had served a plate of them to the knitting group earlier, and Fern had to concentrate hard not to shrink away in fear. Anna's ginger snaps were strong enough to clear out your sinuses. "Here," she said. "Take Reuben a cookie. Two for you and two for him."

In her oversized galoshes, Fern shuffled to Anna and took the nice, round balls from Anna's hand. They wouldn't crack if she pitched them against the pavement. Those cookies could clear out your sinuses *and* break all your teeth. "*Denki*, Anna. I'm sure Reuben has worked up an appetite." She put on her sweater and slipped the cookies into her apron pocket.

Anna threw up her hands. "*Ach*, one more thing." She went to the long closet where Felty kept his galoshes and pulled out a furry navy-blue scarf. "I crocheted this," she said, "but don't tell the knitting group. They'll think I betrayed them." She slid it around Fern's neck. "It will keep you from getting a cold. Nothing brings on the chills faster than a cold neck."

"*Denki*, Anna. It's very soft." Fern wasn't used to something as extravagant as a scarf. "I'll bring it back when I'm done."

"You keep it. That scarf will either save your life or get you a husband one day. Mark my words."

Fern smiled. She didn't see how a scarf could do either, but it was definitely worth a trial. She tromped down the porch stairs and out to the toolshed. It was slow going. She was in danger of tripping over her feet with every step.

After finding a shovel, she surveyed the farm in an effort to locate Reuben. He could have been digging trenches just about anywhere. Dragging her shovel behind her, she doddered behind the barn and to the other side, where she spotted Reuben digging at the edge of a small orchard of peach trees.

She shouted and waved to get his attention, as if she were in a big crowd and he couldn't possibly see her unless she jumped up and down and flailed her arms like a windmill. Unfortunately, she nearly lost her galoshes every time she jumped, so she couldn't be as enthusiastic as she wanted to be. Still, Reuben got the idea.

He glanced up, then looked again, and amusement traveled across his face before he replaced it with a barely contained scowl. "Playing in the rain?"

She tromped toward him, being careful not to lose her galoshes. She'd have to butter him up, since he was determined to push her away. She reached into her pocket and took out all four of Anna's cookies. Only after she pulled them out did she realize that maybe the golf ball–sized pebbles might make him grumpier. They were nearly inedible.

Well, it was too late now.

"A gift from Anna," she said, holding them out to him. She half expected him to snatch them from her hand and throw them at her. They would definitely hurt.

"That's very nice of Mammi. She knows how much I love her cookies."

Fern studied his face for a hint of annoyance or even teasing, but she didn't see either emotion. It was impossible that he actually liked Anna's cookies.

"Don't you want one?" he said.

"*Nae. Denki.*"

He must have seen the involuntary wince that accompanied her answer. "You don't like ginger snaps?"

"Well . . ." She shifted her feet and nearly pulled one of them out of Felty's boot.

"Well, what?"

"Anna's cookies are too hard to chew or swallow. And . . . nobody likes them." She said the last sentence quickly, just in case it offended him.

Reuben frowned in puzzlement. "I like them. Mammi isn't afraid to use her spices."

Fern bit her bottom lip. "Everybody loves your *mammi*, but I'm afraid she has a reputation as not a very *gute* cook." It was one of the first things Fern had heard when she came to Bonduel.

"Just don't tell my *mammi* that. It would break her heart."

"*Ach*, of course not. I would never in a million years hurt her feelings, but you asked. I thought I should be honest."

"You always are." She got the feeling that he didn't think her honesty was such a good quality. "I don't mind if you don't like Mammi's cookies. That just leaves more for me." He took all four from her— leaving her very happy that she would not have to eat them—and stuffed three in his pocket and one in his mouth. She could hear his teeth scrape against the hard cookie and the loud crack when he finally chewed the thing in half. Lord willing, the sound was the cookie and not one of his teeth.

She waited until he swallowed. She almost wished she could take a drink of milk on his behalf. "Sadie said you're digging trenches."

His face lost any hint of good humor. "What did you tell her about me?"

"Who?"

"Sadie. Did you tell her that your brother made a fool of me?"

"My brother didn't make a fool of you. Linda Sue broke your heart. It happens to everybody."

Reuben seemed to catch her words and chew on them painfully and with more effort than he chewed on Anna's cookies. "Everybody knew but me, and they were laughing at me behind my back. You can't begin to understand my embarrassment."

Poor Reuben. He cared so deeply about what other people thought of him. "I didn't tell Sadie a thing about John and Linda Sue." She'd only told the girls that Reuben needed a little cheering up, and maybe he didn't need to know that.

His lips twitched. "She doesn't know I left Sugarcreek in disgrace?"

Fern wanted to growl. Was he purposefully refusing to see the truth? No one in Sugarcreek thought of it as a disgrace. "She is giddy that you shook her hand. Most girls think you are wonderful handsome. They would never in a million years guess that you had been disgraced." Fern didn't mean to let the sarcasm creep into her voice, but for sure and certain Reuben was thick sometimes.

Reuben nodded thoughtfully. "And you won't tell her, will you?"

"Of course not. I wouldn't dare spill such a deep and horrible secret."

Her exasperation was lost on him. "*Denki.* I want people here to like me."

If he'd quit frowning so hard, they'd like him just fine. If he would let go of his grudge and forget his heartache, they'd fall in love with him. Reuben was a magnet that drew people to him. Certainly he'd have no trouble winning over the entire knitting group if he wanted to.

Fern furrowed her brow. She wasn't altogether comfortable with the thought of the knitting group fawning over Reuben Helmuth. He needed friendship, not admiration.

Her galoshes made a squishing sound as she walked toward the orchard and encountered some mud. "I've come to help you dig."

Was it her imagination, or did his face relax a little? Maybe it was the galoshes. Nobody could hate a poor girl in clumsy, too-big-for-her galoshes. "I don't need help."

"I am a *gute* digger. Remember when I helped you and John dig post holes?"

"You drove sticks to mark where we were supposed to dig. You didn't even pick up a shovel."

Fern thumped her shovel into the dirt to show him she knew how to handle it, then crossed one foot over the other. The shovel went about an inch into the ground. She and Reuben both stared at it. An inch deep wasn't going to convince him of anything. She lifted the shovel again and drove its sharp edge down with all her might. Two inches was an improvement. He had to concede that it was an improvement.

He almost smiled. Almost. Probably just her imagination playing tricks.

She propped her free hand on her hip, just to look more determined. "I've shoveled a lot of manure in my day, and you know that when I want to tag along, there's nothing you can do to stop me."

"Your *mamm* is in Ohio. You can't run tattling to her if I say no."

"I can whine. I know how you love my whiny voice."

He snorted. "I've really missed hearing the dogs howl when you screech."

"I haven't screeched for years."

"Oh really? The memories haunt me every night."

Fern laughed at the mischievously tortured expression on his face. Even as unhappy as he was, Reuben was an incorrigible tease. "So," she said, "why are we digging trenches?"

He didn't even try to argue. "You think you can be of much use in my *dawdi*'s galoshes?"

"Of course. Digging is more about arm strength than the size of my boots."

He rolled his eyes. "You always think you know more than you do."

"*Ach, vell.* We have something in common."

His eyes were going to roll out of his head if he wasn't careful. "See that puddle over there?"

Fern looked to where he was pointing. Four peach trees stood in a slight depression in the ground, and water pooled at the base of each tree.

"It's only an inch or two deep," Reuben said, "but standing water like that will kill the roots as sure as drought. I think one of the trees is already dead. I'm digging a trench to see if I can get some of the water to drain off and save the rest of those trees. They'll be in bloom in a few weeks unless there's a late frost."

"Does that happen very often?"

"*Jah.* Mostly nobody tries to grow peaches this far north, but Mammi loves them so Dawdi planted this orchard for her. They don't usually get much fruit unless the spring is mild. In bad years, Dawdi pulls out the smudge pots. Sometimes they help. Sometimes they don't."

She pointed to the good-size trench he'd started several feet away from the orchard puddle. "You're digging up to the water."

"So it's not such a muddy job until the very end."

"I'll start on the wet end," she said.

He opened his mouth to protest.

"I've got galoshes," she said. "And we'll knock into each other if I start at your end."

"That's why it's a one-man job."

"Stuff and nonsense. I want to help."

Fern sloshed into the shallow puddle and started digging so her trench would eventually meet up with Reuben's. It was a wet, almost futile job. As soon as she shoveled out a little dirt, muddy water moved in to take its place. Soon not only were Felty's galoshes covered with mud, but the bottom four inches of her hem were soaked. She didn't mind the dirt—she'd had worse on the pig farm—but Reuben kept glancing at her.

Huffing in exasperation, he stopped digging, took off his work gloves, and handed them to her. "Here. You're going to get a blister."

"So are you."

"My hands are calloused. I don't get blisters anymore." He gave her a partial smile. "A girl with hands soft enough to knit needs a pair of gloves."

Fern put on Reuben's gloves, not because she needed them, but because it made him happy to do nice things for her. It had been that way ever since she was a little girl. They soon fell into an easy rhythm, shoveling dirt out of the trench and depositing it on the low ground of the orchard where the water was starting to dwindle. "*Denki* for fixing my bike the other day," she finally said, unwilling to let a perfectly good opportunity for chitchat go to waste.

"How is your ankle?"

"I'll have a scar I can brag about."

"Next time, wear shoes," he said, before pressing his lips together. Reuben knew very well why Fern didn't wear shoes most of the time. At least he knew enough to be embarrassed about his slip of the tongue, but he hadn't hurt her feelings. So Fern's family was poor. There was no shame in that, even if Reuben thought there was.

Suddenly, he hissed and shook his hand as if he'd touched something hot.

"What happened?" Fern said.

He grimaced. "Nothing. I got a sliver from the shovel handle."

She leaned her shovel against one of the trees, hung her gloves at the V of two branches, and slogged toward him. "Let me see."

He shoved his hand into his pocket. "It's nothing. I'm fine."

"I feel responsible because I was wearing your gloves."

He took a step backward. "It's a little sliver. It'll work its way out yet."

Fern scrunched her lips together so she wouldn't smile. "You're such a baby."

"I am not."

"I remember when you got a hangnail and wouldn't let anyone so much as touch it. Then you got an infection and had to see a doctor," Fern said.

"You made me cookies."

"I'm not making you cookies for a sliver."

Reuben tucked his injured hand tightly under his arm. "I don't need your help with a sliver. It will work itself out."

Fern pitched her voice into a high whine. "Mamm, Ruby won't let me take out his sliver."

He may have smirked, but the whine always worked. In resignation, he held out his hand and let her take a look. "It's right at the surface of the palm," she said, grinning at him. "It would be nothing to pull it out with my fingernail."

He drew his hand away as if she'd offered to cut it off. "*Nae*, don't touch my sliver."

"Come on, now," Fern said, trying to capture his hand while he waved it above his head. "Be a big boy, and let me get it."

"Uh-uh. It will hurt."

Fern giggled. "You are a *buplie*, a baby." She stepped close enough to wrap her arms around him if she had to. If he wanted to wrestle, she'd oblige him.

Looking down at her upturned face, he hardened to stone, and his arresting blue eyes seemed to pierce right through her skull. And what was that enticing smell? She expected him to smell like sweat, but he smelled more like tea tree oil and a clear spring day. Fern drew in a long breath. She really should move away and quit sniffing.

"That scarf makes your eyes look so brown," he said.

Fern's tongue stuck to the roof of her mouth. Anna's scarves might be as powerful as she said they were.

Taking advantage of Reuben's momentary stillness, Fern grabbed his wrist and pulled it toward her. He briefly pulled back and then gave up. "Don't hurt me."

"It's going to hurt worse if you leave it in."

"You can't know that for sure." He squeaked like a mouse when she probed around the sliver and tried to work it closer to the surface.

"Hold still and try not to cry. I've about got it."

"I want my gloves back." He flinched as she scratched back a layer of skin. "Ouch. You promised to be gentle."

She looked at him out of the corner of her eye and curled her lips. "I never said that."

By digging her fingernails lightly into his palm, she was able to grab the small sliver and pull it out. A little blood filled the space where the sliver had been.

She gave him back his hand, and he examined it with a pout on his lips. "It's bleeding."

Fern couldn't help teasing him with a grin. "You really are a baby."

She turned to retrieve his gloves, and he grabbed her wrist and tugged her close to him. "Wait, Fern," he said, his face within inches of hers. Her lungs stopped working and she felt so light-headed, she thought she might faint right there in the middle of the orchard. In Felty's boots. Slowly, almost with a caress, Reuben took his thumb and swiped it lightly across her cheek. "You have a little mud right there."

She pressed her fingers to her cheek where he had touched her. Her hand came away with a gooey dab of mud on it. Reuben grinned so wide she could see his molars. "*Vell,*" he said, "you have a little mud *now.*"

"*Ach!*" Fern squealed in righteous indignation.

Reuben folded his arms across his chest and chuckled. "It looks pretty good on you."

Fern's growls mixed with her laughter as she tromped to the shrinking mud puddle, picked up a fistful of mud, and flung it in Reuben's direction. Reuben didn't even have to duck. The mud sailed over his head like a bird. His smirk enticed her to try again. She waded to the muddiest patch of the orchard and picked up another handful of mud, but her galoshes were no match for the thick goo at her feet. She threw the mud in Reuben's direction and stepped right out of one of her galoshes. Reuben easily dodged her throw and laughed all the harder.

Fern gasped as her bare foot sank into the cold mud and squished between her toes. She always seemed to be getting herself into scrapes. She wouldn't be surprised if she was stuck forever. Putting all her weight on the one foot still inside her galosh, she tugged her other foot out of the mud. Thrown off balance, she kicked her foot up into the air, sending a shower of mud ahead of her. Reuben wasn't expecting that. He jumped back too late and got pelted by a thousand drops of muddy rain.

"*Ach*," he grunted.

Despite her ice-cold foot, Fern laughed as she watched him try to brush the mud from his shirt, his arms, his hair. "You look like you have chicken pox."

He glowered at her in mock displeasure. "You can't throw, but I underestimated the power of your foot. You'd probably be *gute* at soccer."

Felty's galosh made a satisfying squishing sound as Fern tugged it from the mud with her two hands. She'd have to go wash her foot and come back. She couldn't put a mud-caked foot into Felty's boots. It would be gritty forever after. "I'm going to wash my foot," she said, as she limped away with one shoe off and one shoe on. "You can use my gloves while I'm gone."

"They're my gloves," he said.

Fern swatted an imaginary fly. "You should have been wearing them. You wouldn't have gotten a sliver."

"Will you be coming back?" Reuben said, wiping the grime from his face.

Fern's heart did a little skip. Did she detect eagerness in his voice? "Oh, I'll be back. I haven't been nearly annoying enough today."

He seemed to remember that he didn't like her all that much. "I wouldn't say that."

Chapter Seven

Reuben slid out of the buggy with Fern close behind him. Even though the afternoon was a little chilly, the gathering at the minister's house had spilled out onto the front lawn. Some of the boys were playing volleyball in short sleeves, oblivious to the cool temperature. Girls sat on the front porch with their arms wrapped around their knees or stood in little clumps watching the volleyball game and trying to stay warm. Why did girls always stand in clumps? A team of Percheron horses would be useless to pull them apart.

Fern squeezed his elbow. "This is going to be fun."

Reuben frowned so hard, he was in danger of pushing his lips right off his face. "I don't know why I let you talk me into this."

"Because you've been living like a hermit at Anna and Felty's house for three months. You need to get out and meet people, make some friends if that's even possible."

"Thanks for the encouragement."

Fern nudged him forward. "Look. Nobody knows about your little difficulty. You'll be fine."

"My little difficulty? Your brother ruined my life."

Fern was all smiles as she looked over the crowd of young people milling about the front yard. "I wasn't talking about that. I meant the little difficulty you have with pride. Try not to let it show."

Reuben scowled, but Fern didn't even flinch. He wouldn't have been able to wipe that aggravating smile from her face with an eraser. "I'm starting to regret letting you tag along."

"*I* invited you. Remember?"

He trudged slowly up the sidewalk. "I wish that you and your self-righteousness would have stayed home."

Her eyes flashed. "And miss out on my chance to embarrass you in front of all *die youngie*? Not a chance. Besides, you had to pick me up. I didn't have a ride, and we both would have been embarrassed if I'd had to bring my bike." She nudged him with her shoulder and knocked him off the sidewalk. "Don't you worry. I'll watch out for you, big brother, and make sure you don't make a fool of yourself."

"Maybe I don't want to be seen with you."

"Well, I don't want to be seen with you, but I'm willing to make the sacrifice for your sake. You need friends. You need butterflies and daisies and happiness in your life. I'm here to help."

Reuben shook his head. "I need your help like I need another set of wisdom teeth."

"Exactly."

Even though he was grumpy about being at the mercy of John's little sister, Reuben followed her into the yard like a puppy. Fern had been in Bonduel for an even shorter time than Reuben, but apparently she had made an effort to get to know some people. At least she was friends with the members of the knitting group.

He trailed a step or two behind her as she headed straight for one of those formidable clumps of girls standing in the yard. Oh, *sis yuscht.* His throat swelled up and he thought he might choke, but what could he do but follow? He didn't have any male friends in Bonduel. He had been so wrapped up in his own shame and embarrassment, he hadn't made an effort to be friends with anybody. He realized now that was probably a mistake. He was likable, and he should try to get to know some people. Nobody ever had to find out about Linda Sue.

Reuben relaxed slightly when Sadie Yoder turned around and smiled like a sunrise when she saw him. "Fern," she said, "you convinced Reuben to come."

Fern grabbed Reuben's sleeve and tugged him forward, irritating him to no end. He didn't need Fern's help to talk to girls. "Reuben is a wonderful-*gute* volleyball player," Fern said. "But he hasn't played for months. I insisted he come so he doesn't get rusty."

An attractive blush painted Sadie's cheeks. "He doesn't look rusty to me." All six girls in Sadie's little clump gazed at Reuben and giggled softly. It was just like it had been before he'd started dating Linda Sue. Girls thought he was good-looking and tended to disintegrate into giggles whenever he came near. John had teased him about it constantly.

Reuben smiled but not too wide. He didn't want to appear overconfident, and he certainly didn't want a lecture from Fern about humility. It wasn't his fault he was handsome.

The girl next to Sadie divided her gaze between Sadie and Reuben as if she very much wanted to meet

Reuben but very much craved Sadie's approval. She was short and plump with black hair and a petulant gleam in her eyes. She sort of turned up her nose at Reuben, but he sensed it wasn't personal, as if everyone and everything offended her to one degree or another. She hooked her elbow around Sadie's and tugged. Sadie took the hint, even if she was a little snippy about it. She nudged the other girl's arm away and drew her brows together in annoyance. "Don't get impatient, Esther. Reuben just got here." She rolled her eyes at Reuben, as if he were in on the secret that friends were such a bother sometimes. "Reuben, this is Esther Shirk. She's in the knitting group too."

"Sadie's the only one in the group who's really met you." Esther frowned at him as if it were his fault.

Sadie lifted her chin. "Well, one of us had to meet him, and we wouldn't have picked you. You're the worst knitter of us all."

Esther stuck out her bottom lip. "I am not. Didn't you see how far I got last time?"

"How far you got?" Sadie said, the sarcasm dripping from her lips like honey from a hive.

Fern stepped directly in front of Sadie and pulled another girl forward. Reuben wiped his hand across his mouth to hide a grin. Fern had cut Sadie off without saying a word or making a scene. No wonder everyone back home loved her. She didn't pussyfoot around problems but handled them with grace and sensitivity so no one got their feelings hurt. "Reuben, this is Lorene Zook," Fern said.

Lorene was plain with an unusually large mole on her chin. Her expression flashed with good humor, as if she were someone who liked to laugh. "Be nice, Sadie," Lorene said. "Esther's supposed to be your best friend." She turned a bright shade of red. "Nice to meet you, Reuben. I was getting impatient having to wait my turn."

Reuben smiled. Lorene was the eager type he expected when he met new girls.

"But you are definitely worth waiting my turn for," Lorene said before erupting into a fit of laughter that no doubt could have summoned every dog in the county. Reuben was so startled he flinched and took a step back. He'd never heard anything quite like Lorene's cackle before.

Fern watched Reuben out of the corner of her eye. He could just see her mouth forming into a frown, no doubt getting ready to chastise him if he showed any sort of reaction to Lorene's ducklike, ear-splitting laughter. He was almost insulted that Fern would worry. Reuben may have been shocked to his core, but he was smart enough to hold his tongue.

Fern was shuffling people back and forth faster than money was exchanged at a horse auction. From the clump, she pulled two identical girls forward. "This is Clara, and this is Carolyn Yutzy."

The twin sisters were tall brunettes. The twin in the blue dress wrapped an arm around Fern's shoulder. "I can't believe you got it right. People usually can't tell us apart until they've known us for a while. Even our *dat* can't tell us apart from a distance."

Esther smirked. "I still can't tell you apart."

"It's easy," Sadie said. "Carolyn has a little freckle on her right earlobe."

All the girls leaned in to get a better look at Carolyn's ear.

"I've never noticed that before," Esther said, pouting as if they'd kept a big secret from her.

Fern curled her lips into that cute grin that had attracted more than one boy's attention in Sugarcreek. "They just look different to me. Clara's eyes are rounder and their mouths are different shapes."

"I am impressed you noticed," Clara said. She turned and eyed Reuben. "I'm Clara, in case you're mixed up already."

Both sisters peered at him with interest, but they didn't act desperate or overeager—not that Reuben minded overeager. Sadie and Lorene were enthusiastic, but at least they didn't treat him like a leper. They thought he was attractive because they had no idea he'd been humiliated in Sugarcreek. He intended to keep it that way.

"How long are you staying with your grandparents?" Carolyn said.

Reuben flashed a charming grin, and the clump of girls seemed to collectively lean closer to hear his answer. "I might find a place of my own and stay forever. Everyone has been very kind, and the girls here are wonderful pretty."

That comment drew an appreciative murmur from the clump, and he noticed more than one girl blushing profusely.

Carolyn smoothed her hand down the front of her dress. "Fern has been a *gute* influence. This is the first time you've come to a gathering in the three months you've been here."

Reuben glanced at Fern, who gave him a smug smile, as if she were responsible for his very existence. "Fern knows how to pester people."

"Don't I know it," Esther said, as if she were complaining about the weather. "She got both Sadie and

Eva Raber to join the knitting group, and Eva would rather die than talk to anybody yet."

"I was happy to join," Sadie said, as if it was very important for Reuben to know how excited she was to be in the group.

"Tell us about your family, Reuben," Carolyn said. "Do you have brothers and sisters?"

Except for Fern, all the girls gazed at him as if he had an answer to every question in the Bible. "I have six brothers and two sisters. I'm the oldest but one."

"His *dat* is a minister," Fern said, as if she were taking credit for it.

Reuben could have hugged her for saying that. Girls were always more welcoming if your *dat* was rich or was one of the elders in the church. Reuben's *dat* was both. It was how he'd been able to catch Linda Sue's attention in the first place.

Sadie's smile grew wider. "My *dat* is the bishop."

Sadie was pretty and interesting *and* her *dat* was the bishop. This gathering was getting better and better.

"So your *dat*'s the bishop," Esther said. "That doesn't make you any more important than the rest of us."

Sadie pursed her lips. "I never said it did. I only mentioned it because me and Reuben have something in common."

"Do you want to farm when you move to Bonduel?" Clara asked.

Reuben casually brushed some imaginary dust from his shoulder. "If I move to Bonduel, I don't know what I want to do."

"My *dat* has a dairy," Sadie said.

For someone who seemed to want Sadie's approval, Esther seemed more like an adversary than a friend. She practically scowled at Sadie.

Sadie eyed Esther with irritation. "What's wrong with that?"

Did Esther ever have a pleasant word for anybody? "You want Reuben to know you're rich, that's what."

"Just because we have a dairy doesn't mean we're rich."

"You have four employees and three new solar panels on your roof," Esther said. "You're rich."

"There's nothing wrong with being rich," Fern said. "You can help the poor with your money." She smiled at Reuben as if she didn't mind so much that he was rich, even though she chastised him all the time for it. "Reuben's *dat* is very generous. He gave the church a lot of money when one of the children had a heart transplant. Reuben is just as unselfish. Once he paid for fabric so a girl could have a new dress for her sister's wedding."

Reuben's eyes met Fern's, and his insides felt all jumbled together. How did she know about that, and why was she so eager to praise him?

Esther, who frowned on Sadie's riches, seemed excessively pleased that Reuben had money. She lifted her eyebrows and studied him as if he were up for auction. Lorene and Sadie had similar reactions while Clara and Carolyn nodded to each other with matching expressions on their matching faces.

What was Fern up to? "Reuben is a *wunderbarr* volleyball player, and he sometimes trains horses for *Englischers*. He's very *gute* with the animals, and he knows how to swim. He saved me from drowning when I was ten."

"*Ach, du lieva,*" Clara said. "What happened?"

"It was nothing," Reuben said, starting to feel sheepish about Fern's admiration.

"Nothing?" Sadie said. "You can't say saving Fern's life was nothing."

"I'd gone in too deep," Fern said, her smile sending a pulse of warmth through his veins. "My brother didn't even notice when I sank under the water. Reuben swam out and pulled me in to shallower waters. I coughed and sputtered and spit water all over his face. He didn't even complain."

Sadie and the rest of the girls gazed at Reuben as if he'd done something truly heroic. He'd only been fourteen, just a kid, and Fern had floated too far from the shore. She'd never been a *gute* swimmer, and always tried to do all the things Reuben and his friends did, even when Reuben knew she couldn't. She could have killed herself several times over the years if he hadn't watched out for her. Somebody had to do it.

When the silence dragged on for a second too long, he realized they were waiting for him to say something. "Fern was like my little sister. I always watch out for family."

Fern's eyes sparkled, as if she liked that answer very much. Reuben liked that sparkle very much. Until Christmas Eve, Fern had always seemed to be able to make him smile, no matter how bad a mood he was in. He'd always liked that about her. But when John had stolen Linda Sue right out from under his nose, Fern's smiles had seemed more like gloating, and her good-natured teasing felt as if she was throwing salt on his wounds.

Carolyn looked from Reuben to Fern and back again. "It's a compliment that Fern thinks highly of you. Fern is as good as they come."

Reuben didn't want to contradict Carolyn when they'd only just met, but Fern didn't think that highly of him. A week ago, she had chastised him for being proud and resentful.

He studied Fern's face. If she disliked him so much, why was she was helping him out, making sure the girls knew all his *gute* qualities so he didn't have to tell them himself? He wanted them to like him, to respect and admire him like everyone used to back in Sugarcreek. But if he'd told them all that stuff about himself, they would have thought he was bragging. Fern had done him a favor. A big favor.

Maybe she didn't dislike him so much.

A wiry *fraa* opened the front door of the house and stepped out onto the porch. "Pretzels are fresh out of the oven," she called.

Sadie gave Reuben an inviting smile. "*Cum.* Edna Kiem makes the best pretzels. You can't truly say you've been to Bonduel unless you've tasted them."

"Then we'd better go get them while they're hot," Reuben said, surprised at how eager he was to be charming and likable and friendly.

Lorene laughed. *Oy*, anyhow, she almost broke his eardrum. "We'd better hurry, or the boys will finish them off."

Sadie's smile faltered at Lorene's laugh, but she pressed on. "I'll introduce you to some of the boys. Matthew Eicher is always looking for *gute* volleyball players."

"I'm coming with you," Esther said. Everything sounded like a true burden to her. "I know all the boys too. I can introduce you as well as Sadie can."

Reuben let himself be led along by Sadie and Esther, plus the other knitting group members. They all wanted to go into the house in a clump, it seemed. Reuben was glad he had a clump to belong to, even if it was a clump of girls. Sadie had said she'd introduce him to some boys. Maybe he'd make a new best friend tonight.

He glanced behind him. Fern was leaning with her back against the tree, watching him walk away with her knitting group in tow. She folded her arms and flashed him a smile. She seemed truly happy that he'd made a few friends but not inclined to tag along. He'd told her that he didn't want to be seen with her. Hadn't she known he was just being contrary? He wouldn't really consider leaving her out.

Reuben stopped and turned around. The clump of girls stopped too and looked at him as if waiting for instructions. "I'll be right back," he said, as he jogged to the tree Fern was standing against. "You can't say you've been to Bonduel until you've tasted Edna Kiem's pretzels. I brought you along with me. You can't avoid me now."

She cocked an eyebrow. "I thought you didn't want to be seen with me."

"I've gotten kind of used to you tagging along after me. It won't seem like a gathering if you don't make a pest of yourself."

Fern slowly pushed herself from the tree. Her eyes danced with amusement and exasperation. "I'd hate to disappoint you, Reuben Helmuth."

"*Jah.* I am the richest boy in town. You want to stay on my *gute* side."

She cuffed him on the shoulder. "That's going to be tricky. You don't have a *gute* side."

"*Ach*," he said in mock indignation. "Be careful what you say, or I won't let you have a pretzel."

She made a show of clamping her lips together and

nodding obediently. "I'll be careful, but only because I'm starving. And you'd better be nice or I'll have to tell them about the greased pig. It won't be pretty."

He raised his eyebrows. "I'll give you an extra dollop of jam for your silence."

"Okay, but you better hope it's raspberry."

Chapter Eight

Reuben tried not to get too excited as he oiled the leather on Dawdi's buggy. He hated to admit it, but he was really starting to like knitting day. Fern sometimes came early and often stayed late, and always came outside for a visit with Reuben, no matter how bad the weather was or how occupied he was with chores. She said she liked helping him with whatever he was working on and didn't mind the hard stuff. She was stronger than most girls and definitely not afraid of work.

He frowned to himself. He was comfortable around Fern, but he'd be wise to keep his distance. She was John's sister, after all, and if John could so easily betray a friend, there was no telling what Fern could do. Reuben's chest tightened. Maybe it was unfair to Fern to think of her like that. Since she'd been in Wisconsin, she'd been nothing but honest and forthright with him, even when her opinions were completely wrong. At least she wasn't afraid to tell him what she thought.

He shouldn't punish Fern for John's sins. She'd always been a *gute* friend to him, even if John hadn't. Reuben wiped his hands and tossed the rag on

Dawdi's workbench. Why was he even thinking of Fern? She was like a kid sister to him and certainly not the reason he liked the knitting group. Every time the knitting group met, one pretty girl after another would come outside to talk to him, as if they'd planned it or something. They didn't know about Linda Sue, so they didn't act sorry or embarrassed for him. They just wanted to talk. Sadie had said they all wanted to get to know him better.

Sadie was very pretty, with yellow hair and sky-blue eyes. She didn't smile as much as Fern did, but her *dat* was the bishop and he owned a large dairy. The best thing about Sadie was that she was very interested in Reuben. Before he'd started dating Linda Sue back home, lots of girls had been interested. When it came to what girls were thinking, Reuben never had to guess. They fawned over him. That was all there was to it.

Except for Fern.

She acted as if he were an annoying brother she needed to keep in line. Reuben swiped his hand across his mouth. Fern was John's little sister and the daughter of a pig farmer. What did she know?

Why did Fern pop into his head while he was thinking of Sadie and all the other appealing girls in the knitting group—like the Yutzy sisters? They were wonderful nice. He liked that they were tall, maybe even a little taller than Fern. Reuben was six foot three. He towered over the short girls.

He pressed his lips together. Linda Sue was short. He hadn't minded so much a few months ago.

Lorene and Esther weren't bad either. Lorene's laugh could have stopped traffic on the highway, and Esther didn't have a nice thing to say about anything, but at least they didn't know about John and Linda Sue and couldn't feel sorry for Reuben. Things were starting to look up.

He'd had a *gute* time at the gathering last week. Not only was the knitting group extremely welcoming but three or four of the boys seemed eager to be his friend, even though he was older than most of them. They'd been impressed with his volleyball and ping-pong skills.

Edna Kiem, the *fraa* who made delicious pretzels, had told him he was too old and too good-looking not to be married yet. She didn't have to tell him that piece of bad news. If it hadn't been for John King, Reuben would have been married this fall.

Gmay had been different this week too. He had tried to be friendlier, and two or three of the boys in the district had invited him to sit by them. Maybe people here would come to admire him the way they had in Sugarcreek before Linda Sue dumped him like a stinky diaper.

The barn door swung open, and Reuben felt sort of warm around the edges as Fern strolled into the barn. Her smile seemed to light up the entire space, and her bright eyes always held some sort of happy memory. She was wearing her brown dress today, and her eyes looked like two vats of bittersweet chocolate. Besides her church dress, Fern had two dresses to her name. The brown one and a navy-blue one. Reuben couldn't decide which he liked better.

She looked pretty good for an annoying kid sister.

He furrowed his brow. With that apron tied around her waist, she also looked extra skinny. "Are the Schmuckers feeding you anything? Or are you just a picky eater?"

She smirked. "What are you talking about?"

"You look like you're wasting away."

"I eat. I even had one of your *mammi*'s cookies the other day."

He smiled. "At least you're willing to try new things."

"How are our babies doing today?" she said, coming close enough that he could count the freckles that dusted her nose and smell the sharp scent of clean soap that always hung about her.

He cleared his throat and turned toward the long worktable where their latest project sat. "A few of the marigolds have begun to sprout, and the tomatoes too."

They'd filled eggshells with peat and vermiculite and propped them up in some egg cartons, then planted marigold, tomato, and bachelor button seeds in the shells. When it got warm enough to transplant everything outside, they wouldn't even need to take the seedlings from the eggshells. The roots would spread out on their own and into the soil.

It was a *gute* thing that Mammi made something she called Eggs Benefit almost every morning for breakfast. They had plenty of eggshells for planting.

Fern fingered the tiny, pointy leaves that were just coming up from the tomato seeds they'd planted. "It was genius to plant them in eggshells."

Why did it please him so much to see Fern happy? "That is the first compliment you've ever given me."

She laughed and cuffed him on the shoulder. "It is not. I give you plenty of compliments. At the gathering last week, I said you were a wonderful-*gute* volleyball player."

"You scolded me for almost killing you when I spiked it."

"You did almost kill me. I wanted to make you aware in case you wanted to try it again." She picked up the watering can from the table and gave the marigolds a little drink. "*Denki* for seeing that they get enough sun. That can't be an easy job."

Reuben nodded, pasting a forlorn look on his face. "I stand here all day, moving the table with the sun shining through the window. I only stop to eat when the sun goes down."

Shaking her head, Fern gave him an indulgent smile. "I'm sure you do. I hope I don't find you in here one day, weak from starvation, still pushing that table back and forth across the floor in search of the sunlight. I'd feel very guilty if you died for our tomatoes."

Two weeks ago when Reuben had suggested they start seeds for the garden, he had known it would be something Fern would enjoy. He hadn't even wondered how long she was planning on staying in Bonduel, or if she needed to get back to Sugarcreek to help with the family farm. She had told him she was going to stay until he had forgiven John, but she'd have to go home sometime. Her family needed her help on their farm, as well as the money she brought in with outside work.

Maybe he should pretend to forgive John for Fern's sake. She couldn't afford to stay here indefinitely, even if Reuben had pledged never to forgive her brother.

Of course, he didn't want Fern to leave anytime soon—not that he especially wanted her to stay, but she would want to see her tomatoes and marigolds blooming in Anna's garden. It would make her very happy.

Reuben took a couple of steps from Fern and turned his gaze away. She could leave anytime she wanted, as far as he was concerned. What did he need with an auburn-haired fireball lecturing him about forgiveness and compassion every time she opened her mouth, even if it was a nice mouth, most often curved into an irrepressible smile? It was almost as if she liked him no matter what he did or said. She smiled at him when she should have been angry. She laughed even when he was trying to be rude. He didn't know whether to admire that quality or be offended that she never took him seriously.

"What will you be doing today while the knitting group knits?" Fern said, bending over to examine the egg carton that was supposed to be sprouting bachelor buttons. "You know you're always welcome to join us."

Reuben smirked. "I don't think so. Girls in big groups see a boy as an intruder. I wouldn't dare."

Fern gave the bachelor buttons some water. "Then what will you be doing while we knit blankets for all the poor children in the county?"

"I'm planting peas."

Fern's eyes sparkled. "One spring my *mamm* planted peas, and the rooster scratched every one from the ground and ate it."

"I don't wonder that your *mamm* did not take that well." Fern's *mamm* didn't stand for any nonsense, even from a chicken. Come to think of it, Fern was quite a bit like her *mamm*. She didn't put up with a lot of nonsense from anybody. Reuben found it aggravating.

"Mamm had spent the last of our weekly grocery money on those seeds. So she chopped off that rooster's head, took the peas out of his stomach, and replanted them. We had roast chicken for dinner."

Reuben chuckled. "The other chickens learned a valuable lesson."

The barn door creaked open, and Dawdi came strolling into the barn. This morning, he'd already milked the cow, fed the chickens, and gathered eggs for breakfast. Dawdi did more in an hour that most *Englischers* did all day, even as old as he was. His wrinkles piled up on themselves when he smiled. "*Gute maiya*, Fern. Have you come to do some knitting?"

"*Jah*," Fern said, glancing at Reuben as if he was supposed to know some secret about the knitting group. "We are making baby blankets for the hospital."

"You must be wonderful eager to get those blankets done," Felty said, eyeing Reuben with the same look on his face that Fern wore. "You meet three days a week. Your pile of blankets is going to be wonderful tall."

Fern nodded. "We hope so. Many people need a *gute* blanket. A blanket can be such a comfort. It can make you forget about your troubles and forgive the people who have wronged you. It can make you feel loved and accepted and not so sad anymore."

Fern was putting a lot of stock in a blanket. But Reuben wasn't a knitter, and Fern knew a whole lot more about blankets than he did.

Dawdi picked up one of their eggshell pots. "I knew it wouldn't take these tomatoes long to sprout. Reuben pushes this table back and forth, back and forth all day, chasing the sun from the upper windows. He's very dedicated to your plants."

Fern gave him a smile that might have knocked over a fourteen-year-old schoolboy. It was a *gute* thing Reuben was not a schoolboy. He wasn't about to be knocked over by Fern King. "Reuben has always been very kind to me," Fern said. "Even if he is a little cocky."

She had to throw that in there, didn't she? Fern was incapable of saying something nice about him without trying to cut him down to size at the same time, always delivering her criticism with a stunning smile. Today, she was too aggravatingly adorable to make him mad. A wisp of curly, auburn hair had escaped from her *kapp*, and it dangled temptingly at the nape of her neck, just begging Reuben to touch it.

He stifled a chuckle, folded his arms across his chest, and gave Fern his I'm-barely-putting-up-with-you look. Her smile only got wider. "If I weren't cocky, I'd be boring, and girls don't like boring."

"That's true," Dawdi said. "I attracted your *mammi*'s attention with the license plate game. We used to sit by the stop sign on the highway and watch for license plates every Saturday. Annie had never known such excitement."

Reuben couldn't help himself. He reached out, curled the errant lock of Fern's hair around his finger, then let it go, *boing*. Fern's eyes glinted with surprise and amused exasperation as she pressed her fingers to her neck and tucked the wisp of hair under her *kapp*. Reuben watched it disappear with regret.

She fumbled with her words for a moment. "The . . . the license plate game?"

"Dawdi plays the license plate game every year," Reuben said, "trying to find all fifty states before December thirty-first."

Dawdi pulled a small spiral notebook from his trousers pocket and showed it to Fern. "It's only April, but I've already found twenty states. Of course, I always get the easy ones first. One year after Christmas, I had a driver take me to Milwaukee to finish my list. We found Nevada and Rhode Island parked right next to each other. I almost shouted right out loud I was so excited." He tucked the notebook back into his pocket. "Canadian provinces are extra credit. That's the kind of excitement we get around here."

"I'll keep my eyes open," Fern said. "We probably see more plates in Ohio than you do up here."

Dawdi smoothed his fingers down his white beard. "*Jah.* It's true. I've considered moving to Florida for that very reason. Disney World is loaded with plates. Or Yellowstone Park. I hear you can find every license plate in one day there. But the harder they are to find, the more the excitement builds through the year."

"I'll start carrying a pen and paper wherever I go," Fern said.

"It only counts for my license plate game if I see the license plates personally," Dawdi said, "but you can always start your own game."

Fern nodded. "Looking for license plates and knitting baby blankets will keep me wonderful busy."

Dawdi thumbed his suspenders. "That reminds me. Ben and Emma's little one is sick today, and Anna went to see what she could do to help. She said to put you in charge of the knitting group, and the girls told me to tell you they are starting the timer. I don't know what that means, but Esther Shirk seems pretty huffy about it. Her nostrils started flaring, so I thought I'd better deliver the message."

Fern snapped to attention. "We can't have flaring nostrils. We must keep all foreign objects off our blankets. Are you coming in, Felty?"

"*Nae.* I steer clear of the knitting group."

Fern's lips twitched. "Are you afraid we'll teach you how to knit?"

Dawdi waved his hand in Fern's direction. "*Ach*, I already know how to knit, but I'm not very *gute* at it. Anna only asks me to knit pot holders when it's an emergency. When she was trying to find a husband for our granddaughter Mandy, Anna was giving away a dozen pot holders a week. It took three of us to keep up with all the boys who came around. Two boys returned my pot holders because they had unraveled. They wanted their money back, and they hadn't even paid for them." Dawdi stroked his beard. "I stay away from the knitting group because women clam up when a man's around, and Anna can't solve people's problems if she doesn't know what they are."

Fern brushed the dirt off her hands and sighed. "*Ach, vell.* They've set the timer. I should be going. I'll come out after we knit and help you plant peas."

Reuben tried not to wilt like peach blossoms in a late frost. "Dawdi said he would help me." There would be nothing for Fern to do after knitting group.

Dawdi scrunched his lips together and glanced at Fern. "I have some bad news. I won't be able to help with the peas. I'm meeting some friends in town. I can't solve anybody's problems unless I know what they are."

"I don't mind planting the peas," Reuben said.

Fern smiled at him. "And I don't mind helping when the knitting group goes home."

Reuben nodded, determined to plant extra slow so there would be something for Fern to do when she came out. It made her happy to be helpful, and he liked it when Fern was happy. She was like family, after all.

Fern practically skipped out of the barn. Was that girl ever grumpy? Maybe she was being extra cheerful to make up for his sullen mood the last three months. He *had* been sullen and angry and downright unpleasant to be around, but maybe all that was coming to an end. The community in Bonduel was wonderful nice. He could have some friends here.

Reuben helped Dawdi hitch up his small two-seater buggy and watched as he drove down the hill with his jacket collar tucked around his chin. Reuben grabbed a hoe, a shovel, the seeds, and some gardening gloves and tromped to the garden. Dawdi had a nice size plot with at least a quarter acre of raspberries and plenty of room for a long row of tomatoes and several other vegetables.

Reuben started tilling up the soil with his shovel, forming a long furrow for water to drain. He'd string twine when he finished planting so the peas would have somewhere to climb. The ground was moist and heavy, but it was no match for Reuben's shovel. Mammi and Dawdi would get a *gute* crop of peas if Reuben had anything to say about it.

Almost as if the knitting group had some sort of plan, Sadie appeared from around the side of the barn at exactly ten minutes after nine o'clock. Reuben glanced up and smiled. Sadie looked very pretty in an emerald-green dress and crisp, white *kapp*. One of her two front teeth was slightly crooked, and it made her smile interesting and sort of playful. She smiled at him now like a scholar on the last day of school, and he suddenly felt very glad that he had left Sugarcreek. He could start fresh here in Bonduel where no one thought he was a fool and no one whispered about him behind their hands.

"Sick of knitting already?" Reuben said, flashing her one of his best smiles.

"I like being in the knitting group, but I don't particularly enjoy knitting. At least I'm better than Esther. She is hopeless." Sadie tiptoed around the muddiest places in the garden until she was standing on the dirt clods Reuben had just turned over. "To tell the truth, I'd rather be out here with you."

"I'm sure you're a fine knitter."

"Mamm says knitting is a waste of time. Nobody ever got a husband because they were a good knitter."

Reuben wasn't so sure about that. Dawdi was constantly praising Mammi's knitting.

"It's better to know how to cook," Sadie said. "I will have to make you my pineapple upside-down cake. All my friends say it's the best dessert anyone in Bonduel makes." She lowered her eyes modestly. "Not that I'm bragging. I would never brag about my cooking skills."

"I'm sure your friends are telling the truth. It's not bragging if it's the truth."

Sadie smiled in satisfaction. "Getting ready to plant something?"

"Peas."

"A *gute* cool-weather crop."

"*Jah*. They aren't likely to freeze even this early in the season."

Sadie nudged a clod of dirt with her foot. "We plant peas every year. Being the bishop, my *dat* is always getting called away from home, so my brothers pick the peas, and my *mater* and sisters and I shell them. We sit out on the porch in the evening and watch the sunset while we shell. Then we freeze them for eating in the winter."

"I'm sure your *dat* is busy. My *dat* gets called away plenty."

"Do you have a big farm?" Sadie asked.

Reuben shrugged. "*Nae*, it's small. My *mamm* and *dat* sell essential oils. They're some of the top distributors in Ohio."

"So that's why your *dat* is so generous."

Reuben's smile wilted, and it was only with great effort that he kept it in place. At the gathering, he had wanted Sadie and the other girls to know that his family was rich, and he was glad Fern had been the one to tell them. No one could have accused him of bragging. So why did he suddenly feel embarrassed that Sadie knew?

You feel superior to everyone because your family is so rich.

Just because Fern thought so didn't make it true. He wasn't superior to anybody, but he had to admit that sometimes his family's wealth tempted him to be proud. They did a lot of good in the community, and people were in awe of their generosity. Maybe it wasn't such a *gute* thing that Sadie knew about it. Her admiration would only tempt his pride.

"Many families give money to the church," he said, concentrating on his digging. "We're not more special than anyone else."

Did he really believe that? Why had Fern made him doubt himself when he'd never doubted himself before? He wouldn't have been having this conversation if it weren't for Fern. She should go back to Sugarcreek and leave him in blessed peace.

"You saved Fern from drowning once," Sadie said.

"And anyone can see that you are an extra special young man. You're just being humble."

There. Even Sadie recognized his humility. He wasn't proud, and if Fern had trouble believing it, that was her problem, not his.

"I try to be a godly man," he said, hanging his head low over his shovel. Anybody could see how hard he tried just by looking.

"I know you are. That girl in Sugarcreek was a fool for letting you go, but it was our *gute* fortune, all the same."

Reuben's tongue swelled up like a wet sponge. "What girl in Sugarcreek?"

"Your girlfriend," Sadie said, as if she were discussing the group's latest knitting project. As if his heartbreak had been as important as a three-year-old newspaper. "She's obviously not very smart to break up with a wonderful-*gute* boy like you."

He gritted his teeth to keep from biting Sadie's head off. "How do you know about that?"

It was a stupid question. There was only one way she could have known about Linda Sue.

Sadie's eyes filled with concern, and she took a step closer. He obviously wasn't doing a very *gute* job schooling his expression. "We all know about it, and we all agree that it's nothing to be ashamed of. You're the minister's son, and your family is important in the community. We're on your side, Reuben. Fern started the knitting group so we could cheer you up."

Reuben was on fire. He couldn't tell which was hotter, his anger or his embarrassment. Without another word to Sadie, he drove his shovel into the dirt, left it standing there, and stormed to the house.

"Reuben, I didn't mean to offend you," Sadie said

as she chased him across the lawn. "We're all more than happy to help."

Reuben stomped up the porch steps and shoved open the front door so hard, it crashed against the wall behind it. The members of the knitting group snapped their heads around and stared at him as if he had a moose in tow. He glared at Fern, because she was the one responsible for all his troubles. "I don't appreciate being talked about behind my back, I don't need your pity, and I don't want to be cheered up."

Fern didn't even flinch. She expelled an exasperated sigh and had the nerve to smile at him. "We're trying to knit here, Reuben. And we've set certain rules about the timer that not even you can break."

The fire seemed to consume him. How dare Fern be so flippant with his feelings? Linda Sue had broken his heart, humiliated him in front of his friends, and forced him out of Sugarcreek. He refused to let Fern laugh about it. "The knitting group is over," he said. "Everybody go home, and don't bother coming back."

The twins' eyes were as round and wide as cereal bowls, and Lorene looked as if she were about to burst into tears and cry all over her half-finished blanket. After hearing Lorene laugh, Reuben had a feeling he didn't want to hear her cry.

Esther narrowed her eyes. "What about our blankets, Reuben Helmuth?"

"Finish them at home," Reuben said. "I want you all out."

A woman who looked to be in her early thirties set down her needles, gave him a look that could have withered Fern's tomato seedlings, and started gathering up her knitting supplies. "*Cum*, Eva," she said. "Some young people never learned their manners."

The mousy girl sitting next to her immediately stuffed her knitting into a canvas bag, keeping her eyes downcast as if she was terrified to look anywhere but the carpet.

Fern finally lost her smile and replaced it with a look of forbearance, as if Reuben were a two-year-old throwing a tantrum. He wanted to snarl at her. That girl's feathers couldn't be ruffled with a heavy-duty rake. "You'll do no such thing, Dorothy, Eva," she said. "This isn't Reuben's house. He can't throw us out."

He doubted himself for half a second, wondering if he had any right to tell people to leave his *mammi*'s house, but that look on Fern's face pushed him beyond second thoughts. "This isn't your house either," he said. "And I live here."

Fern stood up, folded her arms, and seemed to dig her heels into the floor. "We're not leaving."

Sadie, who had followed Reuben into the house, shook her head. "I don't care what you say, Fern. I'm going. I won't stay where I'm not welcome. Besides, I hate to knit. I don't know why I even said yes to your group."

Sadie helped Esther put away her yarn, and the two of them stomped hand in hand out of the house. Esther gave Reuben a little grunt of displeasure as she walked past. He pretended not to hear her.

The twins each took one of Fern's hands. "It's okay," Clara—or Carolyn—said. Reuben wasn't close enough to see any earlobe freckles. "We'll see you at *gmay*."

Fern seemed to droop. "I'm sorry. I've never known him to be this rude."

The stricken look on Fern's face made Reuben's confidence trip all over itself before falling flat on its face. Much as he hated to admit it, Fern was right. He'd never been so rude.

"Sometimes Reuben lets his pride get in the way of his heart," Fern said, talking to the twins, but eyeing Reuben as if he were the most pitiful creature in the world.

He lifted his chin until it nearly pointed at the ceiling. He was doing the right thing. He wouldn't let Fern make him feel guilty. She only thought she had the moral high ground.

Carolyn—or Clara—nodded as if she knew more about Reuben than he did. "He'll get over it. It just takes some boys longer to grow out of stupidity."

Reuben ground his teeth together until they squeaked. He couldn't stand when people talked about him like he wasn't in the room. It was what Linda Sue and John had done that last night. And he wasn't stupid. He was furious, and that was Fern's fault. He was perfectly justified in dissolving the knitting group, since it was organized solely for him in the first place. Now that he knew what they were up to, there was no need for them to try to cheer him up.

The twins left as if the house was on fire, followed by Lorene and the two women Reuben didn't know. They all passed Reuben as if he might reach out and pinch them as they went by.

The room emptied surprisingly fast, and Reuben and Fern were left on opposite sides, staring at each other in sharp silence. The silence would be much nicer without skinny Fern standing in it. "You go too, Fern. I never wanted you here."

Unsmiling, Fern stood where she'd planted herself, but despite everything, her eyes still gleamed with a small spark of sisterly affection. Reuben tried to swallow the hard lump in his throat. He didn't need to hear Fern say it to know he'd really messed things up this time, but Fern, of all people, wouldn't be allowed to scold him.

"How could you?" she said.

"How could *you*?" he said. "You lied to me."

She pursed her lips together and shook her head. "I never lied. I told the girls you needed cheering up. For all they knew, it was because your dog got run over by a car."

"You told them Linda Sue broke my heart. Sadie said so herself."

Fern smiled as if she felt sorry for poor, *dumkoff* Reuben Helmuth. "Lorene has a pen pal in Sugar-creek. Daniel and Treva's daughter Ina. Lorene brought a letter to knitting group today and read it to us. There was nothing I could do after that, even if I'd wanted to."

Ach, du lieva. That one little detail he'd neglected to get made all the difference in the world. Reuben felt so sheepish, he was probably shedding wool, but he knew better than to think Fern was completely blameless. "You wanted the rumors to spread."

"They're not rumors, Reuben. They're the truth, and who cares if people know? You're so wrapped up in your problems that you can't see I'm trying to pry you out of the tiny box you've put yourself in."

"But now they know how humiliated I was."

Fern crossed the room, took Reuben by the hand, and led him to sit at the table. Her touch made him feel worse and worse. "That's what I mean about a little box, Reuben. Lorene read her letter, and every-one agreed that Linda Sue was *deerich* for breaking up with you. No one felt sorry for you. No one thought you'd been humiliated. They all talked about how much they like you and want to see you happy." She sat back in her chair and studied him with those chocolate-brown eyes, truly concerned that he'd just made a complete fool of himself. "They probably don't think so anymore."

The balloon that was Reuben's confidence withered until it was a wrinkly little blob of rubber. When had he lost all sense of reason? His stomach sank to his toes, and the bile rose in his throat. He propped his elbow on the table and buried his face in his hand. "*Ach*, Fern. What have I done?"

She wrapped her fingers around his wrist. "It's going to be okay."

"*Nae*, it isn't. I was rude, and now they hate me."

"You're hurting. We all understand you're hurting."

"I'll have to move to Montana and start over again," he said.

"Maybe not. The knitting group can be saved." She pulled his hand from his eyes and stared at him until he surrendered and met her gaze. "I'll help you fix it, if you want me to."

Reuben breathed out a long sigh. "Why would you want to help me? Isn't your first loyalty to your *bruder*?"

"It is," she said. Her nose crinkled when she smiled, but she wasn't mocking him. "But how silly of you to think I'm being disloyal to John by helping you. I want you two to be friends again and so does John."

Reuben's throat felt gravelly, as if he'd swallowed a handful of sharp remorse. "Did you know John was in love with Linda Sue?"

Her eyes pooled with her own regret. "Not at first, but at Communion last fall I saw something that made me wonder. Linda's eyes followed John everywhere he went, and he seemed to orbit around her like steel to a magnet. He knew how mad I was at him for keeping it from you, but he didn't have the courage to tell you. In December I threatened to tell you myself if he couldn't do it. He would have done anything to save your friendship."

Reuben grunted. "*Jah.* Sure he would have."

"But is there any use crying over spilt milk?"

"Right now, I want to know how I can fix the knitting group before they have me shunned and run out of town."

Fern lifted an eyebrow as if she thought he was being ridiculous. "No one is going to shun you, but a few of them might give you the cold shoulder."

"It doesn't matter. I'm not going to stay long enough to find out."

Fern stood up and pulled three of Mammi's ginger snaps from the cookie jar. She poured a glass of milk and brought the milk and cookies to the table. "It's going to be okay, big *bruder.* Eat a cookie."

Reuben picked up a cookie and bit into it, savoring the satisfying scrape against his teeth. Nothing was as comforting as one of Mammi's homemade cookies. "You should be happy. I've been dragged to the depths of humility. You can't accuse me of pride anymore."

Fern gave him that you're-being-ridiculous look again. "You're confusing regret with humiliation, Reuben. And you *should* regret how you treated the knitting group. It was horrid. But you can ask forgiveness and make amends." She stole a drink of his milk. "And contrary to what you believe, I'm not happy when something bad happens to you." She turned her face from him. "You just ruined everything. It makes me want to cry." Her eyes turned moist, and her sniffle sounded very much as if she was thinking about crying.

Reuben didn't like that at all. "Hey, Fern. Hey," he coaxed, nudging her chin with his finger so she'd turn her eyes to him. He gave her a half smile. She tried to smile back. "Have a cookie?"

She giggled and wiped at her eyes. "*Nae, denki.*"

"I'm the one who just cleared the room with my temper. If there are any tears to be shed, I should be the one doing it."

"*Jah*, you should."

He leaned back in his chair. "And that's why I'm moving to Montana."

"You don't want to move to Montana. I hear the wind blows all the time."

"There's lots of Amish in Florida. I could go to the beach."

Fern's smile looked like a scold. "You're not going to run away until you've fixed things with the knitting group."

Reuben slumped his shoulders as his guilty conscience slugged him in the chest. "How do you suggest I do that?"

"It's not going to be easy, and it may involve some groveling."

Reuben frowned harder. "I was rude. I'll do what I can to make it right, but I'd rather not grovel, if it's all the same to you."

Fern pinned him with a critical eye as if trying to determine whether he was truly serious about repentance. She picked up one of his cookies and tapped it against the table like a gavel. "You can't avoid the groveling, because the first person you've got to apologize to is your *mammi*."

Chapter Nine

"She's here," Reuben said, doing his best to look cheerful as he finished stringing twine between two stakes.

Fern, maneuvering in Felty's boots as best she could, stepped over the row they had just planted and gazed past the barn and down the lane. A silver car lumbered up the lane with a cute little Amish woman in a white *kapp* in the passenger seat. Anna was back, and Reuben was about to get very uncomfortable.

Fern brushed the dirt off her hands and smiled reassuringly at Reuben. He dreaded the thought of his *mammi*'s disappointment, but it had to be done. "*Cum,*" she said. "Sooner than later is always best."

Reuben squinted and fingered the small scar in his eyebrow. "You don't have to come, if you don't want. You had no part in my temper tantrum."

Fern twisted her lips into a silly grin. "You're very brave, but I'm afraid without me, you'll mess it up and be worse off than before."

He raised his scarred eyebrow and studied her face

as if he were thinking about it. "Mammi will never take you seriously in those boots."

"These are Felty's boots. She thinks they're adorable on me."

"Adorable and floppy. You're going to break your neck someday."

She didn't mean to prove Reuben right, but she turned and stumbled over a dirt clod, nearly losing her balance and her dignity at the same time. Grinning smugly, Reuben slipped his hand into hers and tugged her forward.

Ach, du lieva.

She wished he wouldn't do that. He thought of her as a little sister, but it never felt quite brotherly when he took her hand. She shook her head. Her daydreams had been nonsense six years ago when she was a moony fourteen-year-old. They were still nonsense. Reuben was handsome and lovable, but he was proud and impetuous and too *gute* for a pig farmer's daughter. She'd given up on her daydreams years ago.

Reuben slowed his pace so Fern could keep up in her wobbly boots. "We've been digging and planting for two hours, and I still haven't figured out what to say to Mammi except 'I'm sorry.'"

"It will be fine. Anna would never hold a grudge against her favorite grandson."

"Mammi has more than fifty grandsons," Reuben said. "I'm not even in her top ten, especially after I tell her what I've done."

They approached the car as Anna climbed out, wearing a hot-pink sweater and dragging a large canvas bag behind her. Fern liked the sweater even though it wasn't the traditional Amish black. Maybe she'd gotten special permission from the bishop to wear pink. Anna's face lit up at the sight of Reuben and Fern. She leaned over so she could see the driver through the window. "Peggy, this is my grandson Reuben and his friend Fern. Fern is a knitter, and Reuben has done nothing but fret for three months. But he seems to be getting better."

Reuben curled his lips. He loved his *mammi* very much, and Anna never meant harm to anybody. He took her bag and slung it over his shoulder.

Anna waved to her driver through the open window. "Good-bye. Thank you for the ride."

"I hope the little one feels better," Peggy said.

"She will. It's a mild case."

The car did a three-point turn and drove down the hill. Though she was as spry as a sixty-year-old, Anna took Reuben's arm and let him lead her up the porch steps and into the house.

Fern followed them and left Felty's boots on the porch. She'd come out later and clean them off.

Reuben helped Anna take off her sweater, then hung it on the hook by the door. "*Denki*, Reuben dear."

"How is little Sarah?" Reuben asked.

"Chicken pox is miserable, but she's young, so she doesn't have a bad case. She screamed like a raccoon through her oatmeal bath, but then she settled down and let me read her a book. Then every *mater* in the neighborhood brought her children over to play."

"On purpose?"

Anna nodded. "They all want their *kinner* to get chicken pox so they don't have to get the shot. There were children running amok all through the house. Mind you, I don't mind noisy children. I had thirteen of my own, but Sarah is sick and Emma very nearly pulled her hair out. Andy Schmucker climbs on everything, and Mary Kiem eats her boogers." Anna shuffled to the fridge and pulled out a can of biscuit dough. "I think I'll make Spam Pinwheels for lunch. How does that sound?"

"Delicious," Reuben said, and Fern marveled at Reuben's ironclad taste buds. "But you've had a long morning." He strode to the kitchen and took Anna's arm. "Why don't you sit and rest yourself for a minute. You just got home."

Anna waved him away. "I'm not tired, and you two look hungry. I can always see it in the eyes when someone needs to eat. I've got a sense about such things." She peeled some of the paper covering from the biscuit can and made Fern jump when she smacked it against the corner of the counter. There was a pop, and biscuit dough began to seep from the seams in the can.

Fern swallowed hard. No matter how empty her stomach was, Spam Pinwheels sounded about as appetizing as oyster and water chestnut salad. Could she pretend to have a stomachache? She wouldn't have to pretend once she ate them.

Anna pulled the dough from the can one triangle at a time and smashed each one onto a cookie sheet. "How was knitting group? Did Eva finish her blanket? She was the furthest along."

Reuben frowned and glanced at Fern. "That's what I wanted to talk to you about."

"You wanted to talk to me about something?"

"Maybe you should sit down," he said.

Anna stopped squishing triangles and peered at Reuben over her glasses. "Oh dear. Is it serious? Did Esther tie a knot that Dorothy couldn't untangle? Did she throw her yarn at someone? I was afraid she'd do that from the very first. She is a lovely girl, but she does have a bit of a temper."

"*Nae*, nothing like that, Mammi," Reuben said. "I'm the one with the bit of a temper."

Anna looked increasingly puzzled as Reuben took her greasy hand and led her to the table. "Did Dorothy quit? She's very patient, but Esther could try the patience of Job."

"*Jah*," Reuben said, pulling a chair out for Fern and then sitting down next to his *mammi*. "Dorothy quit the knitting group. And Lorene and Sadie and everybody but Fern."

Fern smiled to herself. Reuben had confidence she'd stick with him, even though there was no point to a knitting group with one member.

The crisscross pattern of wrinkles on Anna's forehead congregated around her eyebrows. "How many knots did Esther tie?"

Reuben cleared his throat and scooted his chair forward and then back and then sideways so it ended up where he'd started. He wasn't comfortable, but Fern was proud of him. Despite his strange taste for Anna's cooking, she knew how hard it was for him to eat humble pie. "They quit because of me, Mammi."

Anna's wrinkles started bumping into each other. "How many knots did you tie?"

Reuben looked at Fern as if she could give him the right words.

"There was a misunderstanding," Fern said.

Reuben nodded so enthusiastically that he nearly fanned up a breeze. "*Jah*, a misunderstanding."

The worry lines on Anna's face kept getting deeper. "Did the egg timer break? It was a very *gute* one from Lark Country Store. If anyone knows his gadgets, it's Felty."

"Mammi," Reuben said, scooting his chair in a dozen

different directions. "The knitting girls found out about Linda Sue, and I thought they felt sorry for me. I thought maybe they were poking fun at me behind my back yet. There's no excuse for it, but I lost my temper. I told them all to go away and never come back. They went."

"Even Dorothy? She loves to knit."

"Even Dorothy. She told me I didn't have any manners, and she was right. I'm ashamed of myself, Mammi, and I hope you'll see it in your heart to forgive me."

Anna pressed her lips together as her gaze traveled to the ceiling. She blinked rapidly, as if clearing any thought of tears from her eyes. "Of course I forgive you, Reuben. You're wrapped up in yourself and you don't think things through very well, but you're my grandson and I couldn't love anybody better. But what about Esther's blanket? She'll never finish it for the hospital. And how will we ever get you a wife if you throw perfectly nice girls out of my house?"

"I didn't throw anybody out—"

Anna's agitation compelled her to stand up and pace the small space between the fridge and the kitchen counter. "What about Fern? She was hoping the knitting group would cheer you up, and I know she really wanted to give some blankets to the hospital. Think of all those babies who will have to go home wrapped in nothing but newspaper."

"I don't think they do that anymore," Reuben said.

Anna came back around the counter, plopped herself far from Reuben and next to Fern, and patted Fern's cheek. "Poor Fern. She's the only member of the knitting group. Everyone's gone except Fern."

Reuben glanced at Fern and made her heart hop like a grasshopper. "Except Fern. She is the only one who stayed, even though she had every reason to leave."

Anna eyed Fern as if an idea had just occurred to her. "Fern, you're a very pretty girl, and you have a very thick skin to put up with Reuben."

Fern smiled. "Not at all. Everyone loves Reuben." She grimaced as if she'd just eaten a lemon. "*Vell*, almost everybody. The knitting group isn't so fond of him right now, but there is still hope. We have a plan to make it all better."

Anna tilted her head as if that improved her hearing. "What plan?"

Fern studied Reuben out of the corner of her eye. The penance would have to be grand to make amends to Anna. Fern had to act now, and Reuben would simply have to go along with it or lose his *mammi*'s favor forever. "Reuben feels terrible about what he did."

Reuben nodded earnestly. "I do."

"So in honor of you and the knitting group, he will learn how to knit."

Anna lit up like a sky of a thousand stars. "He will?"

Reuben lit up like a bonfire doused with gasoline. "I will?"

Fern stared him down with all the force of an annoying little sister. "He will, and he will personally knit a blanket for the hospital. A pink one."

Anna clapped her hands together, leaned over the table, and gave Reuben a loud smack on the cheek. "You always were one of my favorite grandsons," she said. "Titus and Mark are the only ones who know how to knit."

Reuben was probably giving Fern a very stern lecture in his head, but he wouldn't dare say anything that would make his *mammi* unhappy. She gave him the biggest grin she could stretch her cheeks around. He smiled back through gritted teeth.

Anna sat back down and squeezed Fern's wrist. "I never thought I'd see the day. Isn't it *wunderbarr*, Fern?"

"*Jah.* I have a feeling Reuben is going to be a very dedicated knitter. The babies won't get newspaper from him, for sure and certain."

Anna sighed mournfully. "I'd invite him to join the knitting group, but there isn't one anymore."

"Don't worry about that," Fern said. "Reuben and I are going to do everything we can to get the knitting group back together."

"I can't wait to see what you've got in mind," Reuben said. Fern was doubly impressed. To spare Anna's feelings, he kept any hint of sarcasm out of his tone.

Fern pursed her lips to keep from laughing at the suspicious yet powerless expression on his face. She wasn't a cook, but when she was finished with him, he'd eat crow, humble pie, and several of his own words. She didn't intend to put him down, humiliate or embarrass him, but this was for his own good and he knew it. He'd gone too far with the knitting group, and he'd fix it.

Like it or not.

Chapter Ten

Reuben trudged several feet behind Fern as she glided over the flagstones that led to Sadie Yoder's front door. It was his own fault that he'd been reduced to begging forgiveness. He'd gotten himself into this and he'd take his medicine like a man, but he still approached Sadie's door like a scholar on the first day of school.

If it hadn't been for Fern, he didn't think he would have been able to do this. She felt confident that the knitting group would forgive him freely and welcome him into their circle of friends in Bonduel. She assured him that he would be able to live a very long time in Bonduel without shame attached to his name.

And she'd come up with a pretty *gute* plan—if it worked.

What would he do without Fern?

She got halfway up the steps before turning to give Reuben a sympathetic look. "Don't look so forlorn. It's going to be okay."

"She'll slam the door in my face, and I'll be forced to move to Montana."

Fern smirked. "I hear it's very pretty there, and they have famous potatoes."

He joined her on the porch. "That's Idaho. Montana is Big Sky Country."

"How do you know that?"

"Dawdi's license plate game. You can learn a lot when you pay attention."

Reuben stamped his feet on the porch as if removing snow from his boots, even though there wasn't any snow and he wasn't wearing boots.

Fern nudged his arm with her shoulder. "Sadie is a wonderful-nice girl."

"I'm sure she is. Her brother Tyler is married to my cousin Beth."

Fern puckered her lips and looked sufficiently impressed. "I didn't know you knew each other."

"We don't really. Our family went to the wedding, but I don't even remember Sadie being there—but don't tell her I said that. I'm hanging by a thread with her already."

"I don't think she remembers you either. She's never mentioned it."

"Of course she remembers me." He spread his arms wide. "Who could forget this face?"

Fern giggled. "We all try very hard to forget, but it's like a nightmare that keeps coming back."

He let his mouth fall open. "You're just saying that because you think my head is too big, but I know what you really think of me."

She pumped her eyebrows up and down. "Do you?"

Before he could prepare himself, Fern knocked on the door—a determined, forceful knock that said,

"Reuben is here, and you *will* give him a chance to explain himself."

At least that's what it said to him. Sadie might think it sounded like a pathetic Sugarcreekian standing at the door hoping for a crumb of kindness.

A short, plump woman with Sadie's eyes and good humor in her face opened the door. She took one look at Reuben and wrinkled up like a prune. The knitting group had only been disbanded this morning, but Sadie had obviously told her *mater* everything. Nobody was going to be happy to see Reuben at her door.

"Fern and Reuben," she said, saying Reuben's name like he was the smashed half of a dill pickle sandwich. "*Vie geht*? Have you come to see Sadie?"

"*Jah*, if we could," Fern said, sensing that Reuben couldn't get his mouth to work properly yet.

"*Cum reu*, then," she said. She left them on the landing, lifted her skirts, and trudged down the stairs of their split-level house. Reuben smelled something savory cooking in the kitchen upstairs and heard faint voices floating up from downstairs. Where did they hold *gmay* when it was their turn? The levels would make it impossible to spread out, unless they spread all the way down the stairs.

Sadie's *mater* came up the stairs and kept going up into a room behind the living room that was probably the kitchen. "She'll be right up."

Fern smiled as if the excitement was just too much to contain. Reuben twitched his lips and shook his head in exasperation, which only made her smile wider.

With a pinched face and short steps, Sadie strolled

up the stairs with her hand wrapped around her other wrist, studying Reuben's face while trying to seem as if she wasn't looking at anything in particular. "Hello, Fern," she said.

Oh, *sis yuscht*. She wouldn't even acknowledge him. He didn't know why he'd hoped for anything different. He'd been very rude. "Sadie, I came to apologize for how I acted this morning. I was rude and mean and I hurt your feelings, and I'm sorry."

Sadie shrugged and stared at a spot just above Fern's ankle. "You didn't hurt my feelings."

Fern reached out and wrapped her fingers around Sadie's arm. "It's okay, Sadie. Reuben knows he was horrible."

"Really horrible," Sadie said, shifting from one foot to the other.

Reuben nodded. "Really horrible, and I am very sorry. There is no excuse for what I did or said. It's just that I left Sugarcreek because I was so ashamed about Linda Sue. I was afraid that if any of you found out about it, you'd make fun of me or feel sorry for me, and I'd be humiliated all over again."

"What made you think we'd make fun of you?" Sadie said. "We're not mean like that."

"I know that now, and that's why I'm sorry about what I said. I know I made you very upset, and you had every right to be." When she didn't respond, he knew he'd have to eat the whole piece of humble pie, even if he gagged on it. "I am a terrible person, unworthy to even talk to people like you and Esther."

Sadie folded her arms and leaned against the wall behind her as some sort of dam seemed to break. "I was just trying to be friendly, and you almost bit my head off. When we left Huckleberry Hill, I almost cried, I was so upset. Esther says we should never speak to you again and I've half a mind to do it."

"It wasn't your fault," Reuben said. "I take full responsibility."

Sadie was just getting started. "The knitting group was a very bad idea." She looked at Fern. "I know you meant well, but Esther can't knit, and the timer didn't work half the time, and Dorothy Miller thinks she knows everything when I'm just as *gute* a knitter as she is. Esther is coming over tonight, and we're going to burn our blankets to protest that you can't yell at us like that. It's nothing for Esther to burn her blanket. She barely has five rows, and her stitches look like a bowl of pink spaghetti. My blanket was almost done. Any baby would have been proud to be wrapped in one of my blankets, and I'm not bragging. Clara told me so herself."

Fern decided to rescue him. She was obviously better equipped to handle a very irritated girl. She slid her arm around Sadie's shoulder and led her to sit on one of the steps. "You have brothers, don't you, Sadie?"

Sadie smirked and looked away, as if it was a painful subject. "*Jah*, I have brothers. Joseph Elmer hogs the food at dinner and teases me all the time, even when Mamm gets after him."

"Then you know how boys can be. One minute they pull your hair and the next minute they're helping you lift heavy milk cans. Sometimes, we just have to forgive them for being so thick, because we love them anyway."

Sadie shrugged. "I suppose you're right."

Fern smiled at Reuben as if she didn't think he was

so incorrigible after all. "Reuben is a wonderful-nice boy who wishes he hadn't lost his temper."

"I'd give anything to take those five minutes back," he said.

Fern glanced at him as a signal that maybe he should keep his mouth shut. He would mess things up, and she could handle things just fine.

He buttoned his lip.

"Reuben thinks Linda Sue humiliated him. You know how some boys get when their pride is threatened."

Sadie nodded. "Joseph Elmer won't ever admit he's wrong. He'll take it to his grave that I can run to the far pasture and back faster than he can."

Fern nodded. "So maybe you could see it in your heart to give Reuben another chance."

"Maybe," Sadie said.

"He wants to make it up to you," Fern said.

Reuben nodded. "I want to make it up to everyone."

Sadie stared at Reuben for another second or two as if she were deciding how many chances to give him. "Do you?"

He knelt down on one knee so he could be closer to her and gave her the smile that never failed to charm the girls—old or young. "I do. Tell me what you want me to do."

Sadie's lips twitched as if she was trying not to smile. He'd gotten to her. He could see her melting before his eyes, the lines of reproof softening around her mouth, her eyes pooling like bowls of mush. He added a wink to sweeten the offer. No girl could resist "the wink."

"Well . . ." she said, looking at Fern and then back

to Reuben. "I suppose I should be a *gute* Christian and show forth forgiveness. But don't tell Esther."

Reuben couldn't hold back a genuine smile. He really wanted the whole knitting group to like him again. "*Denki*, Sadie. You don't know how much that means to me."

Sadie returned his smile with a brilliant one of her own. "I shouldn't have let it upset me. Everybody does things they regret."

"Some of us worse than others," Reuben said, taking Sadie's hands, standing up, and pulling her with him. He then reached out a hand and tugged Fern to her feet. She gave him a half smile—probably meaning to scold him for winking at Sadie. Some girls took the winking the wrong way. But he'd had to do it. He'd been desperate.

His heart swelled like dough in a bread pan at the feel of Fern's hand briefly in his. Fern wasn't the least bit cross, but she always gave him her opinion, even without saying anything. He liked how contrary she could be sometimes.

"I really don't want to burn that blanket," Sadie said. "What would the babies do?"

Reuben shoved his hands into his pockets. "So what can I do to make amends for being so ornery?"

Sadie twisted one of her *kapp* strings and batted her eyelashes. "*Ach*, you don't need to do nothing. You've apologized and that's enough for me."

"You have such a kind heart," Reuben said, "but I won't feel right until I've done something to show how sorry I really am. Isn't there something I could do for you?"

Sadie curled one side of her mouth. "I hate to even ask. . . ."

"Go ahead. I really want to help."

"*Ach, vell,* Joseph Elmer and I are supposed to paint the picket fence this week. You could come help if you want, but don't feel like you have to."

Reuben nodded. "That is a wonderful-*gute* idea. I would love to help."

Sadie seemed more than a little pleased. "Okay. Joseph Elmer will say I just want to get out of painting, but he can talk all he wants. I don't care." She raised her brows. "Can you come tomorrow morning at nine?"

Reuben looked at Fern. "What do you say, Fern? Do you want to come help?"

Both Fern and Sadie seemed to wilt. "Fern doesn't have to come," Sadie said, sort of stumbling over her words. "You're the one who got mad at the knitting group."

"You'll have to paint the fence without me," Fern said. "I've got other things I need to do."

Reuben furrowed his brow. "What?"

"Just other things."

Sadie recovered her enthusiasm. "I don't mind painting with just the three of us, and Joseph Elmer might still be milking at nine. We can paint it ourselves." She took a step closer. "Just you and me." She nibbled nervously on her bottom lip. "But don't tell Esther."

They walked off the road so far north that Reuben wondered if Esther lived in Canada. In the middle of the woods in Canada. He stopped and peered through the trees. Fern turned around and watched him. "How do they get to church without a lane?" he asked.

Fern grinned and shrugged. "Maybe they like to walk."

"Through five feet of snow in the winter?"

They only took a few dozen more steps when Fern pointed ahead. "There it is. Not much farther now."

When they hadn't been able to find a lane leading to Esther's house, Reuben had parked Dawdi's buggy on the side of the road, and they'd started walking. It was going to be dark soon. He'd rather not hike back through the woods at night. Lord willing, Esther wouldn't want a long apology.

He caught up with Fern and pointed out a tree root so she wouldn't trip over it. He didn't want her to fall and hurt herself, especially if it meant he'd have to carry her back to the buggy. "Why can't you come with me to Sadie's tomorrow?"

She never seemed to be without that smile. "Do you want me to?"

"Of course I want you to. You know how to say things so I don't offend everyone in sight."

"You've never had that problem before."

"I seem to have lost my ability to make anyone like me," he said.

Fern cocked an eyebrow. "Oh, I'd say you are as charming as ever with the girls. You just have to get your confidence back." She stopped and pinned him with a reproachful eye. "Although after a little awkwardness, you seemed just fine at Sadie's."

"Winking at Sadie might have been a little fresh, but it did the trick. She forgave me."

"And you filled her with all sorts of expectations." Her smile faded slightly. "Are you prepared to meet them?"

"What expectations? I didn't promise anything."

"I know winking or smiling at a girl doesn't mean anything to you, but she might think you like her. She might get her hopes up only to find out that you have no affection for her at all." Her faded smile died completely.

"Hey. Hey," he said, nudging her chin with his finger. "It's okay. I don't think Sadie will read quite so much into a wink."

She immediately reattached her smile, and he knew she was okay because a mischievous gleam sparked to life in her eyes. "You silly goose. Of course she will. Most girls are like that, and you are very *gute*-looking. It's just a friendly warning."

"You think I'm handsome?"

"And too big for your britches." She started walking double-time toward the house.

He jogged to catch up with her. "You still haven't told me why you can't come to Sadie's with me tomorrow."

Her lips curled into a tease. "You don't want to paint the fence by yourself?"

"The job will go faster with two. Three if Sadie helps. Why can't you come?"

Her steps faltered only briefly. Or maybe he'd imagined it. "I got a job Tuesdays, Thursdays, and Saturdays."

"Tuesdays, Thursdays, and Saturdays?"

"So I wouldn't miss the knitting group. Thanks to you, that was completely unnecessary."

Fern's family needed every penny she and her siblings could bring in. It couldn't have been easy for her to be away from home. It didn't surprise Reuben at all that Fern had found a job. It did surprise him that she hadn't told him about it.

He jogged backward, facing her as she pressed forward toward Esther's house. "Why didn't you tell me? What kind of a job?"

"You never asked," Fern said. "And it's a secret. I'm working for the police as a spy."

"You are not. What job?"

She shook her head and trudged persistently ahead. "It's just a job, and I'm getting paid well, and I'm not telling you."

She gave him an aggravating smile, and he knew he wasn't going to get anything out of her. She often made him want to tear his hair out in frustration. "Well. Then. Spend some of that hard-earned money on food, why don't you?" He'd never known Fern to be a picky eater, but she didn't like Mammi's cooking. Maybe she didn't like Barbara Schmucker's cooking all that much either. "You'll waste away if you're picky."

She pursed her lips to stifle a smile. "I don't particularly like oysters. That doesn't make me picky."

That was true enough. He'd seen her eat seven different kinds of pizza, fried tomatoes, and Brussels sprouts swimming in butter. She loved Big Macs at McDonald's, and she always cleaned her plate at mealtime. Maybe she was too busy to eat, what with the knitting group and a job. It kind of irritated him that she didn't take better care of herself.

Esther's house sat in heavy shade amid a forest of trees. Three forsythia bushes bloomed bright yellow, like campfires against the house. Reuben heard a comfortingly low hum and turned to see two beehives standing in a sunny clearing not twenty feet away. Esther seemed to live in the middle of nowhere.

The house faced south, and off to the left a lane meandered through the woods. That was the way they should have come, but Reuben had no idea where the lane ended up.

Reuben knocked on the door. Fern widened her eyes, sufficiently impressed by his show of bravery. He had a feeling that asking Esther's forgiveness was going to be much less pleasant than a visit with Sadie, but he would face whatever Esther threw at him. And he wouldn't wink at her under any circumstances—unless it was an emergency.

The door sounded like it hadn't been oiled in about forty years. Reuben could practically hear the rust flaking from the hinges and falling to the floor when the door opened.

Well . . . it didn't exactly open. He could see Esther just inside the door, but she barely cracked it four inches, as if she was expecting a band of robbers. Maybe she thought Reuben was going to yell at her or expected Fern to march into her house and criticize her knitting. "What do you want?" she said, bringing her mouth close to the crack so they could hear her better.

Reuben blew air out from between his lips. It was plain that Esther was the resentful type. He'd have to be patient and sweet and tricky. "Esther," he said, "I've come to apologize for how rude I was to you this morning."

Esther puckered her lips. They were the only part of her face Reuben could see very well. "You don't need to apologize to me. I've got a thick skin yet. Go apologize to Sadie. She nearly cried her eyes out after we left. We're burning our blankets tonight just to prove how mad we are."

Reuben glanced at Fern. Sadie said not to tell Esther about the fence or the blanket. Was he not supposed to tell about the apology either? "I . . . I already apologized to Sadie."

Esther opened the door three more inches. It screamed in protest. "Why did you go to Sadie's first? Do you like her better?"

Reuben had no answer for that, but Fern did. "Sadie lives closer to Huckleberry Hill," she said, and Reuben did the calculations in his head. He didn't think that was exactly true, but Esther's house certainly seemed farther when you had to walk. Maybe Esther wouldn't think about it too hard.

Esther's mouth tightened resentfully, and she narrowed her eyes in Fern's direction. "You should have let me go first in the rotation. Sadie's gotten more than her fair share of time with him."

Reuben didn't know why Esther was turning her irritation on Fern, but he wasn't going to let her do it. "I don't want to talk about Sadie," he said.

Esther tilted her head and opened the door another inch. "You don't? Why not?"

"Because I came to see you and ask you to forgive me for how rude I was."

"You were mean. When you first came to Bonduel, I told Sadie not to get her hopes up. She gets overly excited about a *gute* face. But you don't fool me, Reuben Helmuth."

"I don't want to fool anybody," Reuben said, trying to keep his frustration from showing on his face. Maybe he should try the wink.

Esther stuck out her chin. "*Gute*, because I won't be fooled."

Was it his imagination, or was that gap between the

door and the doorjamb getting wider? "I know you have a *gute* heart, Esther, and you'll forgive me if you can."

"I always give a boy the benefit of the doubt when he deserves it. But you did nearly make me cry my eyes out this morning."

Reuben nodded earnestly. "I feel terrible about that, and I want to make amends for being so rude. What can I do?"

Esther wrapped her thumb around her chin and tapped her lips with her index finger. "You want to make amends?"

She wanted him to grovel. He'd grovel. He had no one to blame but himself. "More than anything."

"Maybe there's hope for you yet," she said.

"I hope so."

She opened the door a tiny bit farther and gazed up at the sky. "It will be dark soon. You can come back tomorrow and wash my dog. He smells like feet."

He couldn't come back tomorrow. He was helping Sadie paint a fence, and Esther wasn't supposed to know about it. Besides, when he came back to Esther's, he was coming back with Fern. Something told him it would be very unpleasant being alone with Esther and her stinky dog. He looked at Fern. "Wednesday?" he mouthed.

Fern gave him a sweet grin and a slight nod, then turned to Esther. "It wonders me if we could come on Wednesday."

Esther's lips drooped, and her forehead lined up like a freshly plowed field. Her frown went all the way to her scalp and probably beyond. "My dog smells really bad." She squinted like an old man who'd lost his glasses. "And so does your sin, Reuben Helmuth."

Oy, anyhow. Esther wanted him crawling in the dirt. But he had to keep reminding himself that he deserved it. No matter that he was rich or pious or the son of a minister, he needed to repent. Fern smiled at him as if she knew he could do it. She'd see just how humble he could be. He slid his straw hat off his head and lowered his eyes as he fingered the brim. "I want to wash your dog better than he's ever been washed."

"It's a girl," Esther said.

"Better than *she's* ever been washed," Reuben said. "But I can't come until Wednesday. Can you ever forgive me for that?"

Okay. Maybe he was laying it on a little thick, but short of winking at her, he didn't know what else to do.

The lines around Esther's lips seemed to relax. "Come on Wednesday at noon. Come hungry, and don't be late"

Come hungry? Okay. Anything Esther wanted. "Okay. Wednesday at noon."

"But it might not be good enough," Esther said.

Reuben bent his head closer and raised his eyebrows. "What?"

"Just washing my dog might not be enough to make up for all the pain and hurt you've caused me. I've been crying all morning, you know."

He swallowed whatever lump of pride was still stuck in his throat. "I'll keep coming back until you say it's enough."

She might have thought about maybe cracking a smile. "*Gute.* I have three dogs and two horses."

Fern pointed to the lane that seemed to wander farther into the woods. "Does this lane hook up with the road? Reuben can spend more time washing your dog if he doesn't have to walk."

Esther eyed both of them as if they were incredibly *dumm*. "It connects with North Street right past our mailbox. Just look for the giant mailbox with a green ribbon tied on the post. Mamm says that mailbox could hold a hundred-pound hog. You can't miss it."

"*Denki*, Esther," Fern said, with a genuine smile. "You are a wonderful-nice girl to help Reuben out like this."

Esther's lip twitched smugly. "I've always tried to be *gute* to my fellow man and woman. I have a very forgiving nature when people say they're sorry."

"*Denki*," Reuben said. "I am very grateful."

Esther swung the door closed until all they could see was her right eye. "Don't tell Sadie," she said.

Reuben didn't know what to say. Surely Esther and Sadie would have to have a talk about it sometime. "Okay," was all he could muster.

"I'm still burning my blanket," Esther said, giving Reuben what must have been the stink eye. He couldn't be sure. He couldn't see much of the rest of her face. She slammed the door, and even though it had been open only three inches, the force rattled the front window. The forsythia bushes trembled with fear.

Reuben let out the breath he didn't realize he'd been holding, and Fern sighed and grinned at him as if they'd just been to the amusement park and ridden the roller coaster. "At least one of us is enjoying herself," he said.

Her giggle sounded as if it had been waiting a long time to escape. "You're so cute."

Reuben groaned. "No boy wants to be told he's cute."

"It's just that you're so sincere and so kind, and

these girls can't help but like you. It's going to be like taking candy from a baby."

"It hasn't felt that way so far."

As they strolled along, she reached up and laid a hand on his shoulder. It was a sisterly gesture, and Reuben liked how comfortable he felt next to her. "You're doing even better than I could have hoped."

"Meaning you thought I would really mess it up?"

Laughter always seemed to trip so easily out of her mouth. "*Nae*, but I was afraid I might have to smooth things over more. You really are a wonder, Reuben Helmuth."

He didn't know why, but her praise made him feel better somehow, as if her approval was the only thing that mattered. "Don't tell me that. You'll tempt me to pride."

"You're already proud. A word or two from me isn't going to make much difference."

It made more difference than she realized. Reuben had just realized it himself.

In the fading light, they ambled through a grove of aspens, with their stark white bark and fuzzy spring buds. Reuben smiled. "Do you remember that time when you, Katie, and Lavina hiked too far into the woods and carved your initials into that big aspen tree?"

Fern turned her face from him, but he could see the hint of a blush on her cheeks. "Mamm thought we were lost and sent you and John to find us. I got in big trouble for hurting the tree and using Mamm's *gute* paring knife."

"You carved F and H." Reuben chuckled. "Me and John never did figure out who H was."

Fern's eyes sparkled with mischief. "John was sure it was Henry Beiler."

"Was it?"

"Henry Beiler used to chase me at recess and try to kiss me. I kicked him in the shins once. It wasn't Henry."

"Then who?"

She fingered her *kapp* strings. "I'll never tell."

Reuben grabbed her hand and pulled her to a stop. "Is it someone you still like, maybe?"

She slipped her hand from his grasp, turned, and kept walking. "Maybe."

Reuben wasn't ready for the pang of annoyance that poked at his gut. It shouldn't surprise him that Fern had a boy waiting for her at home—she probably had eight or nine boys waiting for her—but he knew without even having to know who they were that none of them were good enough for Fern. She might have been a poor pig farmer's daughter, but she was pretty and fun and aggravatingly, adorably cheerful. Reuben made a mental list of all the boys in Sugarcreek. None of them measured up.

"Don't settle for just anybody," he said, trying to keep his tone light, even though it was Fern's future they were talking about. She shouldn't throw it away on someone unworthy of her.

With half-lidded eyes, she seemed to skip over the ground, moving farther and farther away as he tried to keep up. "*Ach*, you don't have to worry. H is very nice."

Reuben caught up and loomed over her like a storm cloud. "Is he?"

"Oh, *jah*," she said lightly, as if she didn't even care that H might be her future husband. "He's in wonderful-*gute* shape. He rides his bike to the RV factory every day, where he works scraping glue off toilet seats. He comes home and clips his nose hairs every night but never combs his hair because it's just too long and gets tangled in his fingers."

Reuben drew his brows together until they were nearly touching. He never heard of an Amish boy with long hair.

She tripped lightly over the damp ground, and the lovesick lilt in her voice was unmistakable. "He's very handsome, even with the wart, and he doesn't smell as bad as some of the boys in the *gmayna*." She raised her eyebrows as if she were teasing him. "He had my name tattooed on his arm. It's next to the tattoo of the spider crawling out of a skull. Isn't that romantic?"

Reuben's mouth fell open. There were no words. For sure and certain he'd talk her out of that boy right quick. "Just a minute, Fern. No almost-little-sister of mine is going to get mixed up with a stinky tattooed boy."

She looked at him in wide-eyed innocence, batted her eyelashes, and started to giggle. *Ach, du lieva.* He didn't know whether to growl or shout for joy. She was teasing.

He folded his arms and gazed at her in mock indignation. "You had me all worked up for nothing."

"I'm glad to know that you still like me enough to get worked up about something."

"I like you fine, but sometimes, I can't stand you."

Fern smiled like she always did when he said something like that. Nope. He couldn't ruffle that girl's feathers. "I think you were a little jealous until I mentioned H's wart."

"I didn't want you hanging around a boy with tattoos. I was afraid he'd get you to try a cigarette, and I wouldn't want to see you addicted."

Fern laughed. "He probably would have convinced me to get a tattoo. I'd get a butterfly on my ankle."

"You wouldn't, and you won't."

"If I wore stockings all the time, you'd never know."

He curled one side of his mouth. "Too bad you go barefoot so often. You'd never be able to hide it." They started walking again. Reuben was eager to beat the sunset. They wouldn't be able to find their way in these woods when it got dark. "You still haven't told me who H was. Or *is*."

Fern concentrated very hard on the path in front of her. "*Was*. He loves someone else, and I'm not in love with anybody."

"Well, *gute*, because I would never take another boy's girlfriend to dinner."

"You're taking me to dinner?"

"McDonald's."

"*Ach*, Reuben, I can't afford McDonald's."

"I'm taking *you* to dinner. That means it's my treat."

Her face lit up like a fast-food heat lamp. "Can I get a Big Mac?"

"Two Big Macs and a large fry."

"And lemonade? I love lemonade."

He could never say no to that face. He didn't even want to.

Chapter Eleven

Esther had not been lying. Her dog was the stinkiest thing Fern had ever had the misfortune of smelling. Sweetie Pie smelled worse than Anna Helmuth's oyster and water chestnut salad or her deviled Spam sandwiches. Sweetie Pie smelled like skunk, rotten tomatoes, and dog poop. Fern gladly let Reuben get close to the dog. She would stand aside and hold the soap bottle and the garden hose.

Sweetie Pie was a large, yellow dog with curly fur and paws the size of saucers. And she absolutely, positively did not want to take a bath.

Fern giggled and held her nose as Reuben chased Sweetie Pie around Esther's front yard and finally caught her by the neck. Half hugging, half coaxing her, he dragged Esther's dog to the washtub and lifted her in. Poor Reuben! After being that close to the dog, he was going to stink to high heaven. Fern might have to spray him down before they were finished.

"Keep hold of her collar or she'll run away," Esther called from her perch on the camp chair she had brought outside to sit on. It was clear she had no intention of helping Reuben and Fern wash her dog.

Reuben was doing penance, and Esther intended to enjoy it.

"I've got her," Reuben said, trying to catch his breath as he clutched Sweetie Pie's collar and wet her fur at the same time. He looked up and nearly knocked Fern over with the force of his smile. Despite the stinky dog, he was in a very *gute* mood. "Can I get a little water over here?"

Fern shook her head even as she took a few steps closer to the washtub. "I'd rather not get too close to the smell."

"She's wonderful ripe," Reuben said.

"She killed a skunk last week," Esther said. "The whole house smells bad."

Making a mental note not to set foot in Esther's house, Fern let the ice-cold water splash over Sweetie Pie's fur. Sweetie Pie tried to shake it off. Reuben held her firm. Fern poured a generous amount of soap over the dog's back, and Reuben worked it into a lather with his free hand.

"Get his belly too, Reuben," Esther called. "Haven't you ever washed a dog before?"

"Never," Reuben said, smiling as if he'd just discovered his new favorite hobby.

"I used to wash the hogs when we took them to auction," Fern said.

Reuben wrapped his fingers around Sweetie Pie's tail. "I should have helped you all those years. I can tell I've missed out on a lot of fun."

Fern poured more soap on the wiggly dog. "Except hogs mostly hold still, and they don't smell half as bad."

He glanced behind him at Esther and winked at Fern. "*Denki* for coming today," he said, quietly enough that Esther couldn't hear. "I don't think I could have managed this alone."

"I don't mind, but I don't know if I'll want to sit next to you on the way home. You're going to smell like something dead and rotting."

He chuckled and ran his soapy hand down one of Sweetie Pie's front legs. "Don't complain, or I'll give you a hug and share my good fortune."

Reuben had picked her up this morning in Anna and Felty's courting buggy, a two-seater, open to the air. She'd probably be able to endure the smell temporarily.

Fern had made sure to be waiting for him in front of the Schmuckers' house when he'd arrived this morning. The less Reuben knew about her living situation, the better. She was already quite low in Reuben's estimation because of John and Linda Sue. It would be better if Reuben didn't know how much further she'd sunk. She was in Bonduel to cheer Reuben up. She couldn't have any influence on him if he found her repulsive. She was low enough already, thank you very much.

The same went for her new job. Let Reuben guess all he wanted. She'd never tell him that she was being paid to scrub toilets. There was only so much a boy could endure.

Sweetie Pie was a fluffy ball of fur and foam. Reuben had even scrubbed her ears. "Okay, Fern," he said. "You can spray her down."

"Don't spray too hard," Esther called. "She's got very delicate skin."

Fern and Reuben shared a private smile. If Sweetie Pie had sensitive skin, Fern would like to see what Esther thought was tough. That dog looked like she could eat garbage for breakfast and come out licking her chops. "Step away from her so you don't get wet," Fern said, holding her hose at the ready.

"She'll get away if I let go. You'll just have to do your best to miss me."

She raised an eyebrow. "And you trust me with that job?"

He made a face. "*Nae.* Not really."

"You're already wet," Esther said. "Sweetie Pie will run straight for the compost pile if you let go, and she'll be dirtier than when you started."

Reuben nodded to Esther and then looked daggers at Fern with a grin twitching at his lips. "Remember, I'm bigger than you. Any mischief and I'll get even. It would be wonderful chilly in a soggy dress."

Fern pretended to think it over. Much as she would have liked to dowse Reuben with her hose, it was only April and there was still a taste of frost in the air. She didn't want Reuben to catch a cold, and she certainly couldn't afford to get sick.

She stepped closer and let the water trickle down Sweetie Pie's back while Reuben rubbed her fur and wiped the soap away. They did his head and his legs, working together like a team of well-trained horses. Reuben's long, deft fingers splayed along Sweetie Pie's back and up across her neck. Fern's hands ached with the cold water. His must be freezing. Fern loved Reuben's fingers. They were attached to strong and competent hands and hard, muscular arms. Reuben might be stuck-up and rich, but he wasn't lazy or soft like many of the *Englisch* boys who did nothing but sit in their basements and play video games all day. Reuben knew how to work, and he had the arms to prove it.

Reuben held tight to Sweetie Pie's collar but stepped as far away as he could as Fern gave the dog one last rinse. "Okay," she said. "You can let go."

Reuben released the dog, and she immediately jumped out of the washtub.

"Look out!" Esther squeaked. Showing more life than she had all morning, she leaped from her camp chair and ran into the house.

Sweetie Pie trotted up to Reuben as if she wanted a pat on the head, gave him a smile, and shook herself from head to toe. A rainbow of water droplets flew from Sweetie Pie's fur, soaking everyone and everything in its wide arc, but mostly Reuben, who sucked in his breath, wrapped his arms around his head, and tried to jump out of the way. Fern ran for the trees, but water drops pelted her like rain.

"*Ach, du lieva,*" she cried as the cold water trickled down her neck and stole her breath away.

The rain stopped falling, and she turned to see Reuben swiping water from his face, which had gotten wet despite his best efforts. Water dripped from his dark hair and trickled down his neck, and his shirt, which had already gotten wet from Sweetie Pie's bath, was completely soaked. He grinned at Fern and shook the water from his hands. "*Denki,* Sweetie Pie," he said, sounding very ungrateful and giving the dog a token pat on the head.

Sweetie Pie gave him a "you're welcome" bark before trotting into the woods, no doubt to undo all the work Reuben had just done.

It was no wonder that dog smelled like three days of garbage.

Fern smoothed her hand over the front of her apron. It was damp but not dripping. The back of her dress and apron were damper, but she had been far enough away to avoid the drenching Reuben had received. A drop of water fell on her cheek, and she pressed her hand to her head. Her scarf was the wettest thing on her. She tugged it off her head, wrung it out, and knotted it back in place around her hair.

She looked up to see Reuben studying her intently, with an unreadable expression on his face. He quickly averted his eyes as if he shouldn't be looking, but she saw a grin playing at his lips as he tried to wring out his shirt while still wearing it.

"Did you get soaked?" he said.

"Not as badly as you did. I'm damp."

He swiped his wet, unruly hair out of his eyes. "You're going to get cold."

She loved how he watched out for her, even though he was in much worse shape than she was. "You're going to freeze."

Esther opened her front door just wide enough to stick her head out. She obviously didn't like cracking that door any farther than she absolutely had to. "I told you to watch out. Sweetie Pie always shakes the water off after a bath."

"I'll remember that," Reuben said, his lips twitching with a stifled grin.

"You need to clip her hair next," Esther said. "And then do the other dogs and my horses." Fern had only known Esther for a few weeks, but she could tell that ordering people around gave Esther a great deal of pleasure. She seemed to enjoy being in charge, and she plainly loved being in charge of Reuben.

Esther wasn't likely to let Reuben off easily or soon. He might be toiling for Esther all summer. He had promised Esther that he'd work until Esther was satisfied, but it made Fern a little irritated that Esther would take advantage of his *gute* heart.

Reuben smiled, not at Esther, but at Fern—a private smile that said he knew exactly what Esther was doing. "Have you got clippers?"

Esther finally dragged herself out of the house and shut the door. "You can't clip Sweetie Pie now. She's all wet." For the first time since Fern had known her, Esther seemed to be uncertain of herself. She wrung her hands as if she didn't know what to do with them and sort of peered at Reuben out of the corner of her eye. "You'll have to come back tomorrow."

Fern clamped her lips together and tried not to let her eyes widen in surprise. Esther, in her own abrasive way, was interested in Reuben. Fern's heart did a flip, and she felt as if one of her brothers had just given her a good shove. She had a wonderful-strange way of showing it, but Esther liked Reuben.

Of course she did.

Fern didn't know why it surprised her. Reuben was handsome and good-natured and as fun as a whole litter of puppies.

Reuben was looking at Fern as if expecting her to say something. Had he asked a question? "Can you come tomorrow?" he said.

As Fern expected, Esther wasn't enthusiastic about Fern tagging along with Reuben. "She doesn't need to bother. I can help you clip Sweetie Pie."

Well. Maybe Fern *wanted* to tag along. She always had at home when Reuben and her brother went on adventures and she hadn't wanted to be left out. But the decision was Reuben's. If he wanted to clip dog fur alone with Esther, Fern shouldn't interfere. Although Esther was abrasive and blunt, Fern couldn't be absolutely sure that Esther didn't strike Reuben's fancy. She didn't like the thought of Reuben and Esther together, but if that was what Reuben wanted, Fern would stay away—no matter how her chest tightened at the thought.

Reuben did a *gute* job of looking disappointed. "I can't come tomorrow." His face lit up, as if a *gute* idea had just landed on him. "I can come on Friday with Fern. It will go faster with three of us."

Fern had told Reuben that she worked Tuesdays, Thursdays, and Saturdays. She had blocked out Monday, Wednesday, and Friday because of the knitting group.

Her heart did a little dance that it had no business doing, and she immediately tamped down any excitement that might be brewing there. This didn't mean he wanted to spend time with her. How silly of her to entertain that idea for even a second. He didn't want to spend time alone with prickly Esther, that was all. Poor Esther. It seemed her hopes for Reuben were in vain, at least for the time being. Reuben might still fall in love with her, but he'd have to do it with Fern standing by. But he didn't seem to mind.

Esther shrugged, as if she didn't know how to argue with that. "Okay. Come on Friday at nine and don't be late. I hate it when people don't get here when they say they're going to get here."

"Maybe we can clip the other dogs before we wash them."

Esther tilted her head to one side. "That sounds like a *gute* idea. We can clip together while Fern washes."

Fern sighed to herself. She'd washed enough pigs in her day. She could wash Esther's dogs, no matter how bad they smelled or how wet she got or how badly her knees ached. She'd do it for Reuben. She was already far from home, eating tuna fish for dinner almost every night. What was one more sacrifice for his happiness?

More than anything, she wanted him to be happy. It was why she was in Bonduel in the first place, to convince Reuben to forgive John, forget Linda Sue, and come home. His smiles gave her reason to hope.

He needed to come home.

Reuben dumped the water from the washtub and Fern rinsed it with the hose. Reuben took both the hose and the washtub to the small barn behind Esther's house. Esther's *dat* worked construction and didn't do any farming to speak of. They had a barn to keep the horses and the cow but little cleared land. Fern glanced at the trees in the near vicinity of Esther's house. Holes dotted the bark of the surrounding maples. It looked as if the Shirks tapped their trees for sap. Fern's family did the same thing on the few sugar maples on their property to make maple syrup. Every little bit of income helped.

By the time Reuben returned from the barn, Fern's teeth were chattering. Her overall state of dampness and the raw, chilly taste of spring in the air was a bad combination. It would be a very cold ride in the open-air buggy for both of them, and they still had several more visits to make.

Reuben tapped his straw hat onto his head, still dripping from Sweetie Pie's attack. He smiled at Esther as if he'd spent a very pleasant time in her company. "We will see you on Friday then."

Esther seemed to grow grumpier the closer the time came for Reuben to leave. "I hope you don't think that washing my dogs is going to make full amends for yelling at me. You can plan on many more chores before I'll see fit to offer my forgiveness."

"Of course," Reuben said, more cheerfully than Fern would have answered. "I want you to be satisfied."

Esther was the youngest in her family, which partially explained her eagerness to give Reuben several jobs. She probably had responsibility for most of the chores around the house. Of course, it was plain that getting Reuben to do her chores was simply a side benefit of having him at her house so she could spend time with him. Fern had to give Esther credit. It was a *gute* plan.

"You really made a mess of washing my dog," Esther said. "I hope you're better with the horses."

Reuben sidled close to Fern and took the bottle of soap from her hand. She'd been so wrapped up in his smiles that she'd forgotten she still held it. He handed the soap to Esther. "Do you have a blanket I could borrow?"

Esther frowned and shuffled her feet back and forth when Reuben got close. "Now?"

"I promise I'll bring it back on Friday."

"Okay, I suppose." Esther ducked into her house and returned with a gray blanket that had to be made of wool or some other itchy material. She handed it to Reuben, who thanked her as if she'd given him one of her kidneys.

Fern hopped onto the buggy seat and watched Esther watch Reuben climb up beside her with the precious blanket over his arm. He settled in his seat, then draped the blanket over Fern's shoulders. Despite Reuben's ice-cold fingers, warmth tingled across her skin when his hand brushed against her arm. His eyes seemed extra bright against his ruddy cheeks as he tucked the blanket up around her chin. "There," he said. "That should help a little."

A hint of something sour like pickle juice traveled across Esther's face. "You're getting my blanket wet."

"Lord willing, I will bring it back completely dry," Reuben said.

"You are very kind to let me use your blanket," Fern said. She glanced at Reuben and cleared her throat. Her voice sounded rough all of a sudden.

Reuben waved to Esther one last time. "See you Friday," he said, as he snapped the reins and prodded Felty's horse to a walk.

"Don't be late," Esther called. Did she have that tight of a schedule?

The horse pulled the buggy down the bumpy lane that meandered through the woods as if it led nowhere in particular. "It doesn't seem fair that you got the soaking, and I get the blanket," Fern said.

"You were shivering so hard back there, I felt the earth move."

Fern grinned. It wasn't fair, but she was glad she had it. These days, she never felt warm enough. Still trembling violently, she clenched her teeth to keep them from knocking into each other. She'd rather not need to see a dentist.

He glanced at her, his face a mixture of amusement and concern. "You need to get your head warm. Have you got a dry scarf?"

Fern snaked her hand from beneath the warmth of the itchy blanket and slid the scarf off her head. Reuben's eyes wandered briefly to her hair before he looked away and seemed to concentrate hard on the lane ahead. Fern had never minded being a redhead, even though John taunted her that most boys found the color *hesslich*, homely. She'd never let it bother her. John had no room to be smug. His hair was flaming carrot orange while hers was more the color of dark maple leaves in late fall. Reuben had never teased her about her hair, but that didn't mean he liked it. And right now, for some ridiculous reason, it mattered very much that he did.

Self-consciously, she fingered the errant strands of hair at the base of her bun. Did Reuben think red hair was pretty? And why in the world did it matter?

Still her heart sank at the thought that Reuben preferred black or brown hair to red. Golden-blond Sadie Yoder hair was probably his favorite color. Who could compete with blue eyes and blond hair? She cleared her throat and pushed away any thought of feeling sorry for herself. Who even wanted to compete?

Fern reached into her apron pocket and pulled out the prayer covering she had put there this morning. She'd brought it because they were planning on visiting some of the other members of the knitting group today, and a visit in a scarf wouldn't do. Since it had been in her apron pocket, the *kapp* was also a little damp but much drier than the scarf. After removing the pins she'd stuck into the *kapp*, she placed it on her head, tucking in the hair as best she could. With skill born of years of practice, she pinned it securely into place.

She tugged the blanket up around her ears. Esther's blanket was almost as prickly as Esther was. The rough fibers tickled Fern's face, and she crinkled her nose to avoid a sneeze. "Do you want to share?" she said, knowing he'd say no, but thinking she should offer anyway.

He glanced at her again and raised his hat. "I'd rather air dry. It's quite refreshing with the wind blowing through my hair."

"It's not doing much blowing. I think it's frozen to your head."

They reached the end of the lane that connected with the country road that led straight into Bonduel. Reuben looked right, then left. "Do you want me to take you back to the Schmuckers' house to change clothes? I don't want you to catch cold."

She absolutely did not want him to take her back to the Schmuckers' house to change. The less he knew about her situation there, the better. "It's almost half an hour out of our way, and if you want to see the rest of the knitting group today, we'll have to go a little damp." She sniffed the air. "And a little stinky."

He lifted an eyebrow. "Are you talking about me?"

"You smell like wet dog."

"Will it make a difference?"

"Dorothy probably won't let you in her house."

"It might be the shortest apology ever." Reuben took a deep breath as if bracing himself for bad news, or at least burdensome news. "Where to?"

With her teeth still clamped together, Fern pointed in the direction of Eva's house. "Cheer up. I think we're past the worst of it."

Reuben tapped his finger to his lips. "Let's see. Eva hasn't ever talked to me before, so she's not likely to talk to me ever again. The twins will shoot dirty looks at me from two different directions, and Dorothy thinks I have no manners. I can't say as I agree that we're past the worst of it."

"You're not going to chicken out on me, are you?"

He grew momentarily serious, as if such an idea were unthinkable. "I wouldn't do that. I'm not like some people. I have to make this right."

Fern pretended to be interested in some yellow wildflowers along the side of the road. She knew exactly what Reuben thought of "some people," but it was good of him not to say her brother's name out loud. She swallowed the lump in her throat. "*Ach, vell*, you're coming along nicely with Esther."

"Coming along nicely with Esther? She criticized the way I filled the washtub. I don't think I'm ever going to satisfy her."

Fern shook her head. "I wouldn't be too sure. I think she likes you."

Reuben pumped his eyebrows up and down and plastered a mischievous look on his face. "They all like me."

Fern loved that silly grin of his. "You are insufferable." She cleared her throat. "For sure and certain, Sadie likes you. Is she happy with her fence?" Fern watched Reuben out of the corner of her eye. Maybe she'd be able to tell if he liked blond hair better than red by the expression on his face.

His smile was too wide, and Fern thought it was extremely unfair that boys were always drawn to the blond girls. "She likes her fence so much, she invited me back to paint her chicken coop."

Chicken coop? Whoever heard of painting a chicken coop? "Did she say how many things you have to paint before she'll forgive you?"

"*Ach*, she's already forgiven me, but I want her to like me. She's the bishop's daughter. If Sadie decides she likes me, then I know I can fit in here. All *die youngie* will accept me if Sadie's my friend."

Fern eyed him with a scold on her lips. "I'm sure Sadie would be happy to know you're only painting her chicken coop so she'll let you into her circle of friends."

He nudged her with his elbow. "It's not just that, Fernly. She's wonderful pretty, and she laughs at all my jokes."

"What boy could resist that?" Fern said, giving her voice a lighthearted lilt, even though she suddenly felt dull and heavy. It wasn't fair. What was so special about blond girls and bishops' daughters anyway? Her shoulders drooped. She knew exactly what was so special to Reuben. He craved importance and acceptance, and he thought they were the same thing. Nothing would make him happier than to marry the bishop's daughter and be the richest, most important, best-loved man in the community.

"Sadie helped me paint the fence, and then she gave me a pineapple upside-down cake as a thank-you. She's a very *gute* cook."

Fern didn't realize she was strangling the blanket until she looked down at her hands. Her knuckles had turned white. Loosening her grip, she sat up straighter. It was *wunderbarr* that Reuben had found someone to take his mind off Linda Sue. Maybe Sadie would make him happier than he'd ever been with Linda Sue. If Reuben was happy, Fern was happy. She sighed.

Reuben glanced in her direction again. "Are you okay? I can still turn around. You need dry clothes."

Fern shrugged the blanket off her shoulders and shook off whatever listlessness had suddenly overtaken her. "It won't do any good trying to stall for time.

You're going to see the rest of the knitting group today whether you like it or not."

A doubtful grin formed on his lips. "Okay," he said. "But don't blame me if you catch pneumonia."

Fern unpinned her black apron, slipped it off, and raised it in her hand like a flag. It flapped in the wind behind her as Reuben drove down the road.

"What are you doing?"

"I'm letting my apron dry out. At least one of us should be presentable when we show up at Eva's house."

"It won't matter. She's not likely to say a word."

Eva's house was right off the main road, with two large warehouses and a sizable garden behind and to the side. Eva's *dat* fixed plumbing and refrigeration systems on *Englischers*' motor homes. They had a phone inside one of the warehouses and a shed outfitted with two solar panels to heat water for their home.

"It doesn't look as if they use the front much," Reuben said, as he pulled into their wide driveway.

"Let's try the back first."

Reuben parked the buggy behind the house. They could hear someone hammering away at something inside one of the warehouses.

Fern jumped down from the buggy and pinned her apron into place. Reuben came around beside her and peered hesitantly toward the house. "Do you think she'll talk to me?"

"You're too handsome. She might faint."

He scrunched his lips to one side of his face and rolled his eyes. "That's not what I mean."

Fern pressed her lips together as she saw three faces staring at them from the upstairs window. "In truth, you'll probably scare her to death."

"What should I do?"

Fern expelled a puff of air from between her lips. "*Vell*, it's your apology to make, but it wonders me if I should talk to her first."

Reuben nodded eagerly. "I'll wait right here, and when Eva says it's okay, wave me over."

"Wave you over? What does that mean?"

"You know. Motion for me to come, and I'll come."

Fern couldn't stifle the grin that wanted to escape. "You mean you'll take orders from Fern King?"

He narrowed his eyes in mock irritation. "Don't get uppity about it."

Fern marched up to Eva's back door and knocked firmly three times. They obviously knew she was coming, and she heard what sounded like a stampede of cows inside. They were racing down the stairs all together. She hoped no one tripped in their haste.

A stocky, unkempt boy, probably a little younger than Fern, slowly opened the door. His round face was pocked with acne scars, and he had Eva's chestnut-brown hair and hazel eyes. His face was bright red. Had he been stricken with a case of heat rash? Or perhaps he had overexerted himself tromping down those stairs.

She suddenly felt embarrassed that she had probably seen him at *gmay* but hadn't really noticed him. Her only excuse was that she had been squarely focused on Reuben for so many weeks, she'd barely made an effort to get to know anybody else.

Of course, Eva's brother looked like someone who didn't want to be noticed, even if Fern had tried.

He stood at the threshold with his gaze downcast, as if completely unable to meet Fern's eye or say one word to the girl at his door. Behind him, four younger children stood staring silently at Fern like statues in a museum. They had planted themselves among the muddy boots lined up along the wall and between the coats and hats that hung on hooks above their heads. They stood with their backs against the wall, blending in with the boots and coats as if they were each assigned to a place like one of the sweaters. The mudroom, which was more like a mud hall, ended at a closed door, which probably led to the kitchen.

Fern paused, thinking that someone might ask her in. Nope. The young man seemed more likely to quietly shut the door on her than invite her into the house. She would have to take matters into her own hands. "Hello," she said, flashing her I'm-not-going-to-bite-you smile, which was very much like her regular smile with a little extra honey and syrup. "I'm Fern King, a friend of Eva's."

"*Jah*," he said, before clamping his lips together as if he were shocked that such a thing had come out of his mouth.

"Is Eva home?"

The boy, undoubtedly Eva's brother, looked back at one of the children standing against the wall, and she immediately scooted down the hall and out the door at the end of it. Was she going to fetch Eva? It made sense that if no one in your family said anything, you'd have to learn how to use hand signals and the smallest of gestures to communicate. Since it seemed that none of them said more than absolutely necessary, the Rabers probably had their own unspoken language just to make things easier.

Fern glanced over her shoulder at Reuben, who leaned against the buggy with his arms folded across his chest. He gave her a bewildered expression, as if he were afraid Fern might be standing on the porch until dinnertime. She smiled back and tried not to laugh. She seldom saw Reuben at a loss for what to do.

Never lifting his gaze from the floor, Eva's brother shifted his weight from one foot to another. Would he be more comfortable if she tried to have a conversation with him or simply stayed quiet? She wasn't sure about him, but the silence was too much for her. "Are you Eva's brother?"

He nodded. "Johnny."

"I have a *bruder* named John. Isn't that *wunderbarr*?" She didn't really know if the fact that John and Johnny shared names was *wunderbarr*, but she felt the need to have enough enthusiasm for both of them.

Without a word—well, Fern hadn't expected anything else—Johnny turned and disappeared down the hall, leaving the door open and his siblings holding up the wall to his left. With great effort, Fern held her smile firmly in place. Johnny had obviously had enough small talk.

Of the Raber children who remained, one—a boy in his early teens—faithfully studied his fingernails, tapping his toe as if keeping time with the seconds dragging by. The two girls—who looked younger and less lively than Johnny—watched Fern with interest, but couldn't seem to work up the courage to say anything to her.

"I'm Fern," she said, hoping someone, anyone, would speak. Her visit was beginning to feel like a funeral.

The taller of the two girls managed a faint smile. "I'm Martha, and this is Toby and Priscilla."

"Eva is a wonderful-*gute* knitter. Do either of you knit?"

"I don't knit," Toby said, as if it should be obvious.

Martha pressed her lips together and regarded Toby the way a big sister often looked at an annoying little brother. "We all like to knit. All the girls." She emphasized "girls" as if knitting was too *gute* for the boys.

After a long pause, Fern realized Martha wasn't going to say more, but she couldn't stand by and let them descend into bleak silence once again. "What do you like to knit?"

"Blankets and such."

"I like to quilt," Priscilla volunteered.

Fern nearly fell backward with surprise. "I like to quilt too."

Eva, with Johnny and the other little sister in tow, opened the door at the end of the hall and ambled in Fern's direction. She gave Fern a worried frown, but was brave enough to close the distance between them. Using that mysterious, unspoken language, she turned to her siblings and shooed them out of the hall. They shuffled into the adjoining room as if they were sad to go. As if they had truly been enjoying the lively conversation.

Eva fidgeted with the neckline of her dress, hooking her fingers over the seam and tugging gently, as if it were too tight. "Johnny said you wanted to talk to me."

Fern motioned toward the buggy. "*Jah*. You see, we feel really bad about—"

Eva gasped, snatched Fern's arm, and yanked her over the threshold. Panting heavily, she slammed the door and pressed her hand against it. "Reuben Helmuth is out there!" she said, as if a tornado were standing by the buggy instead of a handsome boy.

Fern did her best to act as if Eva hadn't just turned hysterical. "*Vell*, yes. He came to apologize for what he did at the knitting group on Monday."

Eva's eyes filled with horror, as if she'd just been assigned to recite a speech for the school program. "Apologize?"

"*Jah*. He was very rude."

"Apologize to me?"

"He's very sorry," Fern said, not sure what else she could say to help Eva understand why Reuben was waiting patiently outside. "He's a little smelly, but he doesn't have to come in if you'd rather not."

Eva tugged both her *kapp* strings as if she wanted to pull her *kapp* over her eyes and shut out any boys who might want to make apologies. "He can't. I don't know what to say. I think I'd rather die."

Coming from anyone else, Fern would have thought these words were just overly dramatic, but when Eva said she'd rather die, Fern believed her. Eva was a nervous little thing, and the thought of talking to a boy probably made her want to throw up.

"What if he stays right where he is and you open the door and let him yell his apology to you?"

Eva pulled one of her *kapp* strings so hard, the stitches popped and the string tore off. Okay. No yelling of apologies. "I'm sorry he stinks, but he really wants to ask your forgiveness. Could he come in?"

"Can't I just forgive him from a distance?" Eva said.

It was probably the best Fern was going to get. "Are you sure? He was pretty mean."

Eva nodded so hard her one-stringed *kapp* nearly flew off. "For sure and certain. Tell him I forgive him but to please never come over again."

Fern cupped her hand around Eva's elbow. "Are you okay? I'm sorry I made you so upset."

Eva leaned back against the door, probably as a precaution in case Reuben tried to break in. "I'm not upset. I'm just shy. Mamm says it's okay to be shy as long as I get a husband." She frowned until three deep lines appeared between her brows. "I don't think I want a husband if I have to talk to him."

Both Lorene and Eva needed to marry someone deaf. Were there two such men in Bonduel? "It can be wonderful frightening."

"Too frightening for me."

Fern squeezed Eva's hand in hopes of lending her a little comfort. What would life be like if she were afraid to talk to people? "I will tell Reuben you forgive him. You won't have to say a word. Is that okay?"

"*Jah.* Tell him."

"But do you really forgive him, or do you just want him to go away?"

Eva paused, as if she'd finally realized what Fern had come for. "He scared me right out of my wits yet."

"I know, and I scolded him but good."

A ghost of a smile might have crossed Eva's lips. "I wish I was brave enough to give a boy what for."

Fern grinned, remembering how much she'd enjoyed it. "He deserved it."

"He did."

"What can Reuben do to make amends for his *hesslich* behavior?"

Eva seemed to back away, even though she was standing against the door. "*Ach,* I don't want him to do nothing. I'd rather just forgive him."

Fern nodded. "I understand. He'll be happy that you accepted his apology without his ever having to make it, but if you ever think of anything he can do . . ."

"Wait." The lines between Eva's eyes could have been

plowed there. She twisted her homeless *kapp* string around her finger. "Could you do something instead?"

"What?"

"Would you do something to make up for Reuben?"

Fern shrugged. "I suppose, as long as Reuben doesn't care. What do you have in mind?"

Eva wrapped her fingers around Fern's wrist and pulled her farther away from the kitchen door as if she feared her siblings might be listening in. It was quite possible they were. Fern's lips twitched with amusement. You could always count on your siblings to stick their noses in your business. "I want you to take a buggy ride with Johnny," Eva whispered.

"A . . . a buggy ride?"

"I'll have him pick you up tomorrow at seven."

Surely her ears were playing tricks on her. "Are . . . are we talking about your brother Johnny?"

"*Jah.* He thinks you're pretty, and he wants to take you on a buggy ride."

Fern had a vivid imagination, but in her wildest dreams she couldn't imagine Johnny wanting to take her anywhere. He seemed too shy to be alone with a girl, let alone carry on a conversation. It would be like riding around town with a baked potato. "But he's so young. Why would he want to go on a ride with me?"

Eva eyed Fern as if she had spinach stuck in her teeth. "He's twenty-two. Aren't you twenty?"

Fern cringed. *Oy,* anyhow. She shouldn't put her foot in her mouth like that. "He seems so young at heart, I guess."

"He'll pick you up at seven tomorrow night."

"*Ach,*" Fern said. "I have to work."

"At seven?"

"I work late." Long days on the job were the only

way to clear her Mondays, Wednesdays, and Fridays. She needed the money, but her primary purpose for being here was Reuben. She couldn't make him all better if she worked six days a week.

"Then what about Friday night?"

Fern had hoped to spend some time with Reuben on Friday teaching him how to knit, but it would have to wait. If this was all it took to convince Eva to forgive Reuben, Fern would gladly do it. She mentally mapped out all the things she and Johnny could talk about. Was he interested in hogs? Did he like red hair?

She smiled as if she were eager to spend an evening talking to herself. "Friday night at seven."

Eva gave Fern what passed for a smile. She wasn't all that prone to smile, so Fern appreciated the effort. "*Denki*, Fern. I know he'll be thrilled."

Given that he couldn't form a complete sentence in her presence, Johnny might not be so much thrilled as mortified, but he'd probably feel some deep emotion associated with Fern, whether it was terror or elation or irritation.

It was something, anyway.

Eva lowered her voice even further. "You don't have to fall in love with him."

"Okay. I'll keep that in mind."

"He needs to learn how to be with a girl. I don't want him turning out like *mein bruder* Melvin."

"I don't think I know Melvin."

Eva cringed as if she'd bit into a green cherry. "He lives on the edge of town with no one for company but his dogs and cows and chickens. And he's thirty years old. Mamm says there's no hope for him."

"I see." Fern nodded. "I'll be waiting in front of Barbara and Wally Schmuckers' house at seven sharp."

"They say Barbara Schmucker is crazy," Eva said.

Fern didn't want to share any sort of opinion about Barbara, even if she had one. "Maybe she's just shy."

Eva seemed taken aback. "Maybe she is. I never thought of that. It's very sweet of you not to judge. People shouldn't judge."

"I agree." Fern sidled toward the door. "I should be going. Reuben will be eager to hear you've forgiven him."

Eva stayed far away from the door, for sure and certain not wanting Reuben to catch a glimpse of her. "Don't forget Friday night."

"I won't," Fern said. "Tell Johnny I'm looking forward to it."

Making sure Eva was out of sight, Fern carefully shut the door behind her and sighed. What would Johnny think when his sister told him she had scheduled a buggy ride? Would he be upset or excited? She hoped neither. She knew already that she wasn't interested in Johnny, but a boy like that, who never got any notice from girls, might take her kindness the wrong way.

She bit her bottom lip. There seemed little danger of his falling in love with her after one buggy ride. She was only a pig farmer's daughter, after all. Surely Johnny Raber was setting his sights higher than that.

That thought made her feel better. At least she wouldn't have a broken heart on her conscience when she returned to Sugarcreek.

Standing next to the shed, Reuben seemed to be engaged in a very serious conversation with Eva's *fater*. Reuben caught sight of Fern, shook Eva's *dat*'s hand, and jogged toward her with a wide grin. "Did you know that Vernon Raber heats his water with solar panels? They have plenty of hot water for bathing, but they also run pipes under the floor that heat the house. Isn't that *wunderbarr*?"

"No more woodstoves," Fern said.

"*Jah.* No chopping and hauling wood or risk of fires. I've got to tell my *dat* about this."

Fern raised her eyebrows. "You should come back to Sugarcreek and talk to him face-to-face."

Reuben shoved his grin off his lips and shook his head. "Still up to your tricks, I see."

She shrugged. "It was worth a try."

"What did Eva say? Can I go in and apologize?"

Fern formed her lips into a definite no. "You must promise never to come here again."

"Why? What did she say? Is she still mad at me?"

Fern smiled at the disconcerted look on Reuben's face. He really did want to put things to rights. "She says she forgives you but would be very upset if you actually tried to apologize to her. She wants you to go away immediately, and she'll offer her forgiveness from a distance. She's very shy and just a little frightened of you."

"Frightened?"

"Don't let it give you a big head. She's scared of boys in general, the ugly and the good-looking ones."

She motioned toward Reuben when she said "ugly," and he grunted his indignation. "I know I'm handsome. You can't talk me out of it."

She rolled her eyes. "It's a wonder you can stand to be in the same room with yourself."

"It's hard, but I'm so *wunderbarr*, there's no one I'd rather spend time with."

She cuffed him on the shoulder. "Every fool enjoys his own company."

He chuckled. "A fool or a very wise man." Taking her elbow, he boosted her into the buggy and laid the blanket over her legs. "So Eva is satisfied with my— your—our apology?"

"She wants one thing in return." She hesitated. Reuben was going to laugh, and it didn't seem right that he should laugh at Johnny's expense. At her expense. "She wants a buggy ride for her brother Johnny."

Reuben puzzled that out for a few seconds as he hefted himself into the buggy and picked up the reins. "She wants me to take her brother on a buggy ride?"

"She asked me to make amends for you by letting Johnny take *me* for a ride."

"You didn't do anything wrong," he said.

"I'm sure my parents would tell you differently. I can be obstinate when I want to be."

"Don't I know it. But you shouldn't be punished for something I did."

"It's the only thing Eva wants," Fern said. "I don't see much harm in it if it helps ease your conscience. Eva says he thinks I'm pretty."

Reuben's eyebrows loomed like storm clouds over his dark eyes. "Of course he thinks you're pretty."

What did he mean by "of course"? Fern didn't think she was pretty by any stretch of the imagination. Reuben was just being silly now.

"How do we know he'll bring you home at a decent time? He may not know how to handle horses well. You could get killed in an accident. How can I be sure he'll treat you well? What if he talks you into a second ride and a third? No good will come of you getting friendly with Eva Raber's *bruder*."

"It's only one ride, and then you'll be off the hook with Eva."

He snapped the reins, and the horse jumped forward. "Sorry, Rhubarb," he said, relaxing his arms and giving the reins a little slack. "I don't like it."

Fern's pulse hummed through her veins. "It's going to be fine, Reuben."

He pinned her with a stern eye, as only a big brother could. "Mind that you don't fall in love."

"Why?"

"I just don't want you to, that's all. I've got enough to worry about without you chasing after some boy."

It made sense. He'd taken on the role of big brother, and there was nothing a big brother disliked more than a boyfriend. At least she thought so. Fern had never had a boyfriend, so she had never seen John be stupid about one.

She laid a hand on Reuben's arm. "I won't fall in love with Johnny Raber. It's just one ride, and then you can stop worrying about Eva."

His jaw quit twitching. "Okay, but if he asks you for a second ride, I want you to turn him down. There's no reason to get his hopes up."

Fern did her best to keep the tease out of her voice. "Oh, for sure and certain I'll turn him down. I'd rather meet at the lake. It's much easier to kiss a boy when you're not sitting in a buggy."

She heard the telltale scrape as Reuben clenched his jaw. He'd break a tooth if he ground his teeth any harder.

Chapter Twelve

If Clara and Carolyn had a brother anywhere close to Fern's age, Reuben thought he might put a stop to the whole apology thing. He couldn't risk Fern falling in love with one of the knitting group member's brothers. Even though he didn't know any of them, they weren't *gute* enough for her.

Clara and Carolyn Yutzy's house was three down from the Rabers', but this being Amish country, that was still half a mile away. Unlike the Rabers', the Yutzys' house sat back from the road with a circular gravel driveway and room for parking buggies and cars. Fern didn't need to tell Reuben which house the twins lived in. A modest, hand-painted sign pointed the way. YUTZYS CANDY SHOPPE, CLOSED SUNDAY, PLEASE HONK.

Fern jumped from her seat before he'd even come to a complete stop. Didn't she ever get tired? Or discouraged? Apparently not. Maybe she was anticipating a buggy ride with Johnny Raber, and her excitement made her giddy.

Reuben clenched his teeth until they screeched. The twins better not have brothers.

"*Cum*," Fern said, when she turned to notice that Reuben was still sitting in the buggy. "Their peanut-butter-chocolate drops melt in your mouth."

"Will they give us a sample?"

"Sometimes they give out free tastes, but you yelled at them on Monday. They'll probably charge you double."

He grunted in Fern's direction and gave her the stink eye, which only made her laugh, but he didn't mind. He loved the sound of Fern's laughter, except when it came at his expense.

The Yutzys' small candy shop was attached to the house and had screened windows on three sides. A placard hung on a hook next to the door. OPEN. IF NO ONE IS HERE, KNOCK ON THE FRONT DOOR. The screen door creaked and rattled as Fern pulled it open. They both stepped inside, and Fern flinched when the door slammed ear-splittingly behind them. The candy shop was deserted and dim, as if no one had been in there for months.

Two tables sat in the middle of the room surrounded by smooth white shelves lining every wall. The shelves were empty except for half a dozen jars of raspberry and dandelion jelly in the corner and three tubs of divinity stacked on top of each other. Several tubs of peanut-butter-chocolate drops sat on the table with a stack of crispy rice treats and a basket of assorted colors of lollypops.

April couldn't be considered tourist season yet. This was probably all they could sell in an average week before the summer rush. Reuben examined a tub of peanut-butter-chocolate drops. Maybe there wasn't a summer rush. Sugarcreek teemed with *Englischers* during the summer, but Bonduel was off the beaten path in northern Wisconsin. Maybe there were no tourists.

There was a small window between the candy shop and the white kitchen where they must have made candy. Fern slid the window open and stuck her head into the kitchen. "Hello! Clara? Carolyn? Is anybody home?" She turned and grinned at Reuben. "*Englischers* honk when they come to buy. The Yutzys listen for the honk."

"Should I go outside and try to sound like a car?"

Fern giggled. "It couldn't hurt. Or we could follow the instructions and knock on the front door."

Reuben turned at the sound of approaching feet. Clara—or Carolyn—practically danced into the kitchen and burst into a grin when she spied Reuben and Fern through the interior window. *Vell,* her smile was most likely for Fern. Reuben still hadn't apologized for his behavior on Monday, and Carolyn—or Clara—probably hated the very sight of him. It was an attitude he was sort of getting used to.

Sure enough, Clara's—or Carolyn's—smile faltered when she caught sight of Reuben. He gave her a half-hearted, humble, I'm-so-ashamed-of-myself wave and tried to look contrite—not that he had to try very hard. He really was sorry for how he'd behaved and for sure and certain wanted to make things right.

"Fern! It's so *gute* to see you." Clara—or Carolyn—stepped through the small door to the side of the window and gave Fern a warm hug. She glanced at Reuben almost as an afterthought. "And, Reuben, you are always welcome to buy anything you want."

"*Denki*, Clara," he said, hoping against hope he'd

chosen the right name. Nothing impressed a girl so much as if you remembered her name.

Fern's eyes danced in amusement. "It's Carolyn, Reuben. Look at the eyes."

Reuben cringed. He'd have to learn to tell the difference between the twins if he didn't want to be continually offending them. Although, something told him they didn't get offended easily. Clara and Carolyn seemed like level-headed, reasonable girls who wouldn't hold a grudge. They were both exceptionally kind to Fern, whom they hadn't known very long, and that told Reuben all he needed to know about what kind of girls they were.

Carolyn laughed. "You look as if your puppy just died, Reuben. It's okay. People mix us up all the time." She studied Reuben's face and drew in the corners of her mouth as if she was trying not to smile. "So," she said, lacing her fingers together, "you've come to apologize."

Reuben glanced behind him as if someone might be looking over his shoulder giving Carolyn all the answers. "How did you know?"

Carolyn let her smile escape. "I saw Sadie and Esther yesterday. Separately, of course. Sadie doesn't know that you have apologized to Esther, and Esther doesn't know that Sadie hasn't burned her blanket. Clara and I figured you'd work your way around to us yet."

Might as well get to it, then. "I'm really sorry about how I acted."

Carolyn swatted away his apology. "Wait and say it to both of us at once. Clara wouldn't want to be left out." She went back through the small door to the candy kitchen and cupped her hands around her mouth.

"Clara, come down. It's Fern and Reuben." A dimple pressed deeply into her cheek as she picked up a blue porcelain bowl and passed it through the open window. "Have a taste. It's white chocolate and almonds."

Reuben grinned at Fern. He was going to get his sample after all. He took a piece of the silky white chocolate from the bowl and popped the whole thing into his mouth. It melted like soft butter on a hot day, leaving a crunchy almond and a sweet, creamy taste on his tongue. "Mmm, this is *appeditlich*. I could eat this for breakfast, supper, and dinner everyday."

Carolyn seemed pleased with his praise but not overly impressed with Reuben in general. "The peanut-butter-chocolate drops are still the most popular."

"They're my favorite," Fern said, licking a hint of white chocolate from her fingertips.

Carolyn came back through the door, retrieved two tubs of peanut-butter-chocolate drops from the table, and handed one to Reuben and one to Fern. "Fern, yours is free. Reuben, you have to pay."

Reuben let his mouth fall open in mock indignation. "Would it make any difference if you let me apologize first?"

Carolyn's lips twitched with a hint of amusement. "*Nae.* Someone with as big a mouth as you should pay. It will keep you humble."

Fern tried to press the tub into Carolyn's hand. "I can't take these. That's four dollars of lost profit."

"Four dollars?" Reuben said, acting as if Carolyn had just asked for his firstborn child. "You expect me to pay four dollars?"

Carolyn folded her arms and stood in front of the table so Fern couldn't put the peanut-butter-chocolate drops back on the stack. "No arguing. I know how things are." She gave Fern a pointed look, as if the two of them knew something Reuben didn't.

Reuben pulled some money out of his pocket, muttering under his breath with a tease in his tone that told Carolyn he wasn't really all that put out about it. Fern had said that the Yutzys' peanut-butter-chocolate drops were delicious. He didn't mind paying for them. He'd been planning on buying something, just to soften up the Yutzy sisters for his apology.

He counted out his money and laid the bills in Carolyn's hand with exaggerated care. "Here's eight dollars for both Fern's and mine."

Fern threw back her head and seemed to be growling and laughing at the same time. "Oh, *sis yuscht.* I'm fine without a box of peanut-butter-chocolate drops."

Carolyn crinkled the dollar bills in her hand and arched an eyebrow. "He can afford it. I'm happy to let him pay."

Fern surrendered and let herself smile. "Okay. I'll let Reuben pay. He needs the blessings." All three of them laughed, and Fern shook a finger in Carolyn's direction. "But no more trying to give away half your store. Kindness won't pay your bills."

"Yours either," Carolyn said, and it sounded like a scold.

Clara marched into the shop. "*Ach, du lieva.* Oh, my goodness," she said, giving Fern a hug identical to the one Carolyn had given her. Keeping her arm securely around Fern, Clara turned and eyed Reuben. "So, you've come to apologize, ain't not?"

Reuben shook his head in resignation. There was nothing like the gossip network in an Amish community. Talking about the neighbors was one of the most exciting things Amish folks did. "I hope you've been looking forward to my visit."

"Lorene is furious that you haven't apologized to her yet. You've already been to Sadie's house and washed Esther's dog," Clara said. She wrinkled her nose. "And you smell like it."

Fern drew her brows together. "We washed the dog only this morning. How did you know?"

"Esther told Lorene you were coming."

Reuben nudged his hat to the side and scratched his head. "Maybe I should buy another tub of peanut-butter-chocolate drops for Lorene."

Carolyn moved so that Fern was between her and Clara and draped her arm around Fern's shoulders, twining her arm with Clara on the other side. The Yutzys looked as if they were ready to defend Fern from an attack. Fern smiled almost as if she was surprised by their affection.

"So, Reuben Helmuth," Carolyn said, "what have you to say for yourself?"

"*Ach, vell,* you know why I'm here." He took off his hat and tapped it against his leg. "I said some terrible things on Monday, and I lost my temper because I jumped to conclusions I shouldn't have. I'm sorry. I'm usually a wonderful-*gute* boy. People in Sugarcreek like me." He lowered his eyes as the thought of what he'd lost hit him like a shovel to the head. "Well, they *used* to like me."

"They still like you," Fern said, handing Reuben a peanut-butter-chocolate drop as if that would make his humiliation all better. She glanced at Carolyn. "He doesn't know what he's talking about. Everybody adores Reuben."

"I don't wonder that they do," Carolyn said, nodding as if she knew everything about everything. "So you've washed Esther's dog and painted Sadie's fence."

"*Jah*, and I want to do something for you to make up for how rotten I was. I'm hoping you'll see fit to forgive me and maybe not think so badly of me anymore."

Carolyn tightened her arm around Fern's shoulder. "Fern likes you, and I trust her opinion over most anybody's."

Reuben slumped his shoulders. "That doesn't make me feel better. Fern likes everybody."

"I'm not picky," Fern said with a teasing grin.

"You really shouldn't lose your temper like that if you want to have any friends," Clara said.

Fern popped a peanut-butter-chocolate drop into her mouth. "It was very unlike him. Reuben is usually so good-natured. Linda Sue broke his heart but good, and he's been in a bad mood for four months."

Reuben wanted to protest. Linda Sue had broken up with him, but the humiliation of being replaced by his best friend was what had put him in a bad mood. He caught a glint of light in Fern's eyes, and suddenly his reasons seemed a little shallow. How deeply, really, had he been in love with Linda Sue?

Because a broken heart wasn't the reason he had left.

Did Fern sense that? Is that why she didn't ever seem that sorry for him whenever they talked about Linda Sue?

Carolyn still sported her know-it-all expression. "It's plain you and Linda Sue weren't the right match."

Reuben squinted at Carolyn in confusion. "What do you mean? Do you know her?"

Carolyn practically dripped with smugness. "*Nae*, but I think there are other girls better suited to you right here in Bonduel."

Fern pursed her lips. "Like Sadie Yoder. She's the bishop's daughter."

Carolyn nodded slowly. "Maybe."

Reuben didn't like the direction of the conversation. No one was going to plan his life for him. If he married Sadie or Eva, or heaven forbid, Esther, it would be his own doing, not because some silly girls schemed to match him with the most likely *maedle.* He pretended he hadn't even heard Fern's last words. "Is there anything I can do to make up for hurting your feelings?"

"You didn't hurt my feelings," Carolyn insisted.

"Or mine," Clara said. "And we forgive you."

Carolyn nodded. "It takes a strong man to admit he was wrong, especially to a bunch of girls." She studied Reuben's money, still clutched tightly in her fist. "Though there is something you can do."

"What do you mean, Carolyn?" Clara said. "We don't have a dog."

Reuben said a silent prayer of thanks. No dogs. "I'm willing to brush your horse."

Carolyn took her arm from around Fern and smoothed Reuben's dollar bills out flat in her hand. "We want you to come to the shop every week and buy something for Fern."

Fern's eyes popped even wider. "Me? Why me?"

"You're willing to put up with Reuben. For that, you deserve a pound of peanut-butter-chocolate drops every day."

Reuben didn't protest. Fern had always stuck by him, even when he lost his temper with the knitting group. Even when he'd been humiliated in Sugar-creek. His heart leaped into his throat and made it hard to swallow. Besides his extremely lovable grandparents, Fern was his one constant. She deserved three pounds of peanut-butter-chocolate drops a day.

"It would be my pleasure," he said, smiling at Fern so she knew he really meant it.

She smiled back, and she seemed to glow like the full moon on a clear night.

"You don't really have to buy me something from the candy shop every week," Fern said as Reuben pulled the buggy up to the fabric shop. She pushed her lips doubtfully to one side of her face and looked at him sideways. "Four dollars is a lot of money."

He set the brake and gave her his most reassuring look. "I don't mind, Fern. Carolyn is right. You deserve mountains of candy every week. Besides, I'll be okay. I've got a down line, you know."

She rolled her eyes. "*Ach*, stop with the down line. All I ever hear about is your down line."

He chuckled. "As a matter of fact, I never talk about my down line."

She sighed. "I suppose you don't. It just seems that way because it looms so large in your life."

Reuben didn't even argue. Fern loved teasing him about his money, but her needling didn't bother him. Three years ago, his *dat* had helped Reuben start his own essential oil distributorship. Reuben had made enough to put a hefty sum in the bank to buy his own home and farm when he got married. He'd been looking at property just outside Sugarcreek when Linda Sue had announced she was in love with John King. Bitterness filled his mouth. John King couldn't even afford to buy his own courting buggy.

Fern's gaze flicked to his face and then away. "You really don't have to do it. The twins forgive you anyway."

Reuben swallowed the gravel in his throat and gave

her his best big-brother smile. "I don't mind. You need some meat on those bones."

A water spigot stood in the yard over an empty plastic tub. Reuben turned on the water and filled the tub halfway so Dawdi's horse could have a drink. It had been a long day for Rhubarb too. He led the horse, buggy and all, to the water and let her drink. Propping his hands on his hips, he peered at the fabric shop attached to the main house. "So this is where Dorothy works?"

"I think she is the owner. Her *dat* added on to the house so Dorothy could have some income of her own." Dorothy was over thirty years old. Maybe she'd given up on finding a husband.

"Let's go then," Reuben said, motioning for Fern to lead the way into the shop. He depended on her to soften Dorothy up. He depended on her to soften everybody up.

A bell above the door tinkled cheerfully as Reuben and Fern strolled into Dorothy's fabric shop. Pillars of fabric lined every wall in every color Reuben could imagine for a Plain dress. The dark blues and greens and burgundies were the most plentiful, but there were plenty of other, brighter colors, like pink, baby blue, and purple. Fern would look very pretty in that bright, sunny yellow. The lavender fabric would bring out the gold flecks in her eyes. In the middle of the room sat a table with a wide, green cutting board, several pairs of scissors, and something that looked like a pizza cutter. There were also two racks full of tiny shirts, pants, and dresses already made for babies and toddlers. A quilted wall hanging hung behind the squatty counter where the adding machine sat waiting to ring up purchases.

Dorothy was nowhere to be seen. The businesses here didn't likely get much but local buyers. No wonder Dorothy didn't think it necessary to stand in her shop all day when the customers were sparse.

Fern ambled around the perimeter of the shop, fingering fabrics, sometimes stopping to press one against her cheek to test its softness. She sighed as her hands found a collection of plump fabric that was probably for quilt making. It didn't look like dress fabric. "*Cum*, Reuben. Feel how soft this is. Mary Mast in Sugarcreek made a blanket for her *buplie* out of this. It's like a cloud."

Reuben put down the pizza cutter and walked over to the far wall. "It's wonderful soft," he said.

"It doesn't sound like you mean it."

He shrugged. "I've never taken much of an interest in fabric."

"You would if you had a blanket like this. You would float away to sleep and never wake up freezing in the middle of the night."

They both snapped their heads around as the front door opened and the bell tinkled. Dorothy craned her neck to see around the rack of baby clothes. "Fern?"

"*Jah*. And I brought Reuben with me."

Reuben took a step to his right so Dorothy could see him, and he wasn't surprised when her mouth sort of crinkled like a prune. "Do you need some fabric?"

Reuben took three slow steps forward and held out his hands in a gesture meant to communicate that he'd come in peace, just in case she was concerned he'd start yelling. "I've come to apologize."

Dorothy didn't seem impressed. "Why?"

"Because I lost my temper and hurt your feelings."

Dorothy's laughter escaped as a single, thunderous

snort. "You'll have to try a lot harder than that to hurt my feelings. Boys like you aren't worth the trouble of getting worked up about."

Reuben hadn't expected Dorothy to throw wide her arms and give him a hug, but did she really think he wasn't even "worth the trouble"? He was a pretty nice boy when people got to know him. Even Fern, who scolded him for being proud and self-righteous, thought he was a pretty nice boy.

Fern came to his rescue once again. "What Reuben means is that he is sorry for being so rude on Monday, and he wants to apologize."

Dorothy balled her fists and propped them on her hips. "Well, get to it then. As you can see, I'm wonderful busy."

Reuben looked around the empty shop with its neatly lined bolts of fabric. It seemed not one thread was out of place. But he was here to apologize, not argue with Dorothy Miller about if she was truly busy or just wanted to get rid of him. He already knew the answer. "I am sorry for how I behaved on Monday, and please don't blame my *mater* or my grandparents. My *mamm* taught me better than that."

Fern was truly turning out to be his greatest ally. "He . . . he was distraught about his girlfriend and acted in a way that he never has before."

Reuben nodded his sincerity. "Or ever will again, and I want to know if there is anything I can do to make it up to you."

"What do you mean?"

"I washed Esther's dog and painted Sadie Yoder's fence to show them how truly sorry I am. Is there something I can do for you?"

Dorothy folded her arms and stared at Reuben so

long, he was afraid she'd fallen asleep with her eyes open. She was probably dreaming up some outrageous penance like making him knit blankets for every *buplie* at the hospital or milking a thousand cows with his feet. He just hoped Dorothy didn't have a smelly dog. There was only so much odor a boy could take before people started shunning him. Essential oils couldn't cover up a bad stench.

The longer she stood there, the less pronounced the lines around Dorothy's eyes appeared, and her mouth seemed less and less like a prune. Her gaze traveled back and forth between Reuben and Fern as if she were making up her mind about something. "Have you eaten today?"

Um. Maybe she wanted to put Tabasco sauce on the tip of his tongue or watch him swallow a whole bar of soap. "I had two plates of my *mammi*'s Eggs Benefit this morning." That had been one filthy dog and five hours ago. His stomach growled at the thought.

Dorothy didn't seem the least bit interested in what Reuben had eaten for breakfast. "What about you, Fern?"

Fern's expression was partially obscured by a fold of mint-green fabric she was studying in front of her face. "I've eaten nearly a third of a tub of peanut-butter-chocolate drops."

"Not good enough." How could Dorothy make three words sound like a lecture? "*Cum* to the house," she said, already halfway out the door. "I'll make sand-wiches and *kaffee*, and we'll have a talk."

Dorothy left the door open behind her, and Reuben turned to Fern. "She wouldn't think of poisoning me, would she?"

He loved how she laughed at all his jokes, even if

they were as limp and bland as week-old celery. "She wants to talk. That is a *gute* thing."

They followed Dorothy around the side of the house where she opened a screen door and led them into her kitchen, or rather her family's kitchen. Her fabric shop was attached to her family's home. A cut of forest-green fabric was spread across the table with a pattern piece pinned over the top of it. Dorothy folded the pattern into the fabric and slid it off the table. "My latest project," she said, placing the fabric on the cupboard near the fridge. "My niece is starting school in September, and I'm making her a new dress. She's growing like a weed out of her old ones." She lifted a blue-checked apron from the hook behind the door and quickly tied it on. "Now, Fern, let's see. You need something hardy and warm to stick to your ribs. Do you like grilled cheese?"

Fern glanced at Reuben. "Is grilled cheese okay with you?"

Dorothy grunted her disapproval. "I don't care what Reuben wants. Do you like grilled cheese?"

Fern gave Reuben a lopsided, apologetic grin. He shook his head slightly. So Dorothy didn't particularly like him. Fern shouldn't feel bad about it. "I love grilled cheese," Fern said.

"And tomato soup?"

"With milk?"

Dorothy pulled a loaf of bread from the cupboard. "Of course."

"My favorite," Fern said.

Dorothy insisted that Reuben and Fern sit while she fixed grilled cheese sandwiches and tomato soup. Reuben's mouth started watering when he smelled the rich aroma of *kaffee* in the pot on the stove. Dorothy didn't like him, but by the smell of it, she knew how to make *gute kaffee*. That talent made up for a lot of short-comings.

"We're thinking of maybe getting the knitting group back together," Fern said. Maybe she was hoping that would soften Dorothy up.

Dorothy turned one of the sandwiches on the griddle. "*Ach.* I don't mind about the group. I was doing it as a favor to Anna, but I don't especially enjoy knitting. I'd much rather quilt, to own the truth."

Dorothy laid a plate of three grilled cheese sandwiches, each cut in half, on the table, then came back with bowls and the pot of soup. She poured the *kaffee*, and Reuben thought he'd gone to heaven as steam rose from his hot mug. He still felt a little damp. Strong *kaffee* would warm him to the bone. Fern needed *kaffee* too. He wasn't altogether sure her teeth had ever stopped chattering.

After Dorothy sat down and they said a silent prayer, Dorothy ladled soup into the three bowls and Fern and Reuben helped themselves to a sandwich. Reuben bit into his and nearly sighed out loud. Dorothy had used two different kinds of cheese and bits of bacon. It was almost as *gute* as Mammi's Spam, olive, and mayonnaise casserole, and that was saying something.

Dorothy sipped on her *kaffee* and didn't touch either her soup or a sandwich. "Now, Reuben. You say you want to make restitution for acting like a five-year-old the other day. Are you serious about that? Because if you're not willing to do what I ask, then I'm not going to bother asking."

Reuben swallowed hard. She was going to ask him to milk the cows with his feet, he just knew it. "I'm serious." He really wanted everyone in Bonduel to like him, even stern Dorothy Miller.

She gave him the once-over with her gaze and must

have decided to believe him. "What I'm about to tell you—and you too, Fern—is a secret. I can't have you repeating it. The gossips would have a heyday if they found out."

Reuben swallowed harder. "Okay," he said. His agreement sounded more like a question. What had he gotten himself into?

"I have five sisters and three brothers, and I'm smack dab in the middle of the family. It hasn't been easy. I'm thirty-four years old yet, and I'm the only one who isn't married." She took another sip of *kaffee*. "Reuben, I want a husband, and you are going to help me."

Reuben accidentally inhaled his sandwich. Wheezing and coughing, he very nearly choked and died in Dorothy's kitchen. Fern gave him five *gute* slaps on the back before he could speak. He wanted Dorothy's forgiveness, but he drew the line at marrying her. It was too much to ask. Surely Dorothy could see that. "Doro . . . Dorothy," he sputtered. "I'm flattered that you would think of me, but I can't marry you. I don't want to hurt your feelings, but you're too old for me."

Dorothy turned bright red, and Reuben was sure her eyes would pop out if someone tapped her on the back real hard.

"I'll milk a thousand cows with my feet," he blurted out, for fear she'd have a stroke sitting there at the kitchen table.

Fern clapped her hand over her mouth, and Reuben could hear the high-pitched rumble of laughter stuck in her throat. Why was Fern laughing? There was nothing funny about a middle-aged woman wanting to marry him.

Dorothy banged her *kaffee* mug down on the table with such force, *kaffee* jumped from the mug and splattered in an interesting polka-dot pattern on the tablecloth. "Reuben Helmuth," she said, with an indignant click of her tongue. Before she launched into the lecture Reuben knew was coming, she glanced at Fern, caught her breath, and pressed her lips together into a tight line.

Fern's laughter spilled out of her mouth like water babbling in a brook, and Dorothy couldn't seem to resist. Her rigid expression cracked, then crumbled, as she too exploded into hysterical laughter.

Reuben's gaze darted from Fern to Dorothy and back again. He'd obviously missed out on the joke.

"Fern warned me that you thought very highly of yourself," Dorothy said. Tears ran down her face, and her sigh came from deep within her throat. "*Ach, du lieva*, I haven't laughed that hard since my brother Benji stuck a quarter up his nose and couldn't get it out."

Reuben leaned back in his chair and cocked a very annoyed eyebrow. "You're not asking me to marry you?"

Dorothy giggled and swiped her hand across her eyes. "*Nae*, but that look on your face was worth a thousand proposals." She patted Fern's hand. "*Ach*, Fern. I like him—in spite of himself."

Reuben didn't know if that was a compliment, so he kept his mouth shut. Best not to say anything he'd have to apologize for later. He did not like to be laughed at.

Fern laid her hand over his, and her smile had such affection in it, he almost forgot what had irritated him. That smile of hers could coax the sun to rise and warm the very air around him. For the thousandth time, he found himself grateful that she had come to Bonduel.

Even though he didn't need her here, she had a way of smoothing out the rough spots.

Then again, if she'd never come, he wouldn't be sitting in Dorothy's kitchen trying to negotiate an apology. He frowned. Was Fern his saving grace or a wonderful nuisance?

Dorothy picked up her napkin and dabbed at the spots of *kaffee* on the tablecloth. "There is a bachelor I've had my eye on for a decade."

"A decade?"

Dorothy sent him a prickly stare that should have given him a rash. "Try getting someone to ask you on a drive when they won't even talk to you, Reuben Helmuth. I've tried everything I know to get him to notice me, but nothing is working. He's as silent as the grave, and I'm getting desperate."

Dorothy was a patient woman. If Reuben had been in the same situation, he would have been desperate about eight years ago. "So you want me to ask this person to propose to you?"

"Well, stuff and nonsense, you can't go charging in like a bull in a china shop. I want him to take me on a ride, then maybe bring me some eggs from his chickens, then ask me to go fishing or take me out on the lake in a canoe. I'll make him a cake, and he'll hold my hand." She took another sip of *kaffee*. "I'd like a wedding by September."

Reuben tried to smile, but he couldn't manage more than a grimace. "It wonders me how I'm going to talk him into holding your hand."

Dorothy crumpled her napkin in her fist. "*Ach, du lieva*, Reuben. If you prime the pump, I'll do the rest. Melvin just needs a little nudge to get things moving."

If Dorothy had been trying to attract his attention

for ten years, Melvin would need more than a nudge. He'd probably need a whole can of axle grease and a crowbar.

Fern's ears seemed to perk up. "Melvin Raber?"

"Do you know him?" Reuben said. How was it that he had been in Bonduel three months longer than Fern, and she knew so many more people?

Fern shook her head. "He's Eva's *bruder*. I've never met him, but she's worried he'll die a bachelor."

"He turned thirty last month," Dorothy said. "A little young, but my *mamm* is always telling me I seem younger than thirty-four. My *dawdi* was twenty years older than my *mammi*. They were happily married for fifty years, and she died first."

"What if I can't get him to budge?" Melvin had stood firm for more than a decade. Who was Reuben to think he could unstick him? More to the point, who was Dorothy to think Reuben could unstick anybody?

Fern reached over and clutched Reuben's forearm. "We've got to try, Reuben. The future happiness of two families is at stake."

The pressure kept mounting. First a quality paint job on Sadie Yoder's fence, now the happiness of an entire generation of Rabers and Millers. Reuben nodded, more to reassure himself than Dorothy. "I'll do what I can, but I don't want you to get your hopes up."

Fern bloomed like a brilliant orange poppy. "*Ach*, Reuben. That's wonderful kind of you."

"Ask your *mammi*," Dorothy said. "She and Felty have found matches for at least a dozen of your cousins." She picked up the last half a sandwich on the plate and handed it to Fern. "You'd better eat this, or it'll go to waste."

Mammi and Dawdi had a reputation for sticking

their noses into family members' love lives. It was a wonder that they hadn't tried to match him up with somebody yet. But Dorothy was right. His grandparents might at least have an idea of what he could do.

"Don't feel bad if you fail," Dorothy said, "which you probably will." She obviously didn't have much faith in him. He didn't blame her. "I will still forgive you for being rude and forgetting your manners. From the first time I saw you, I didn't expect much."

It was a *gute* thing Reuben had just swallowed the last bite of his sandwich. He would have choked for a second time. Did Dorothy always speak her mind? Would Melvin be happier being a bachelor? Of course, Fern spoke her mind, but whenever she scolded him for being proud or self-centered, there was always affection behind it, and he never took it real hard. Would he ever make friends with that kind of disapproval from Dorothy? He decided to ignore her kick in the teeth. "I will do what I can with Melvin yet."

Dorothy studied his face and nodded. "Warn me if he's going to come over so I can make him a cake." As if she were finished with the conversation and ready to have him gone, Dorothy gulped down the rest of her *kaffee* and plunked her mug decidedly on the table. "Now. Fern, I made some *gute* mozzarella that I want to send home with you as well as a loaf of seven-grain bread. What about apples? Do you have apples?"

Fern's gaze flicked in Reuben's direction as she hopped to her feet and cleared the bowls and plates. "I don't have apples," she said, as if she didn't really want to talk about it. Reuben furrowed his brow. Did she like apples? He couldn't remember.

"They've been in the root cellar all winter," Dorothy said, "but they still have plenty of vitamins." She filled a bag with the cheese, the bread, and a few apples, plus four oatmeal-raisin cookies from her cookie jar. Dorothy must have recognized how thin Fern was looking.

If Fern would eat more of Mammi's perfectly *gute* food, she wouldn't be near as skinny. It was her own fault for being a picky eater.

Dorothy stood at the door as if she wasn't going to allow Reuben and Fern to leave. "Remember. No telling anyone about this."

"We won't make a peep," Fern said, locking her lips with an invisible key and tossing it behind her back.

"Find out what his favorite color is and favorite pie and also favorite animal."

"His favorite animal?" Reuben said.

"You never know when that information might come in handy."

Maybe Reuben should just send Melvin a question-naire. It might speed things up a bit. Dorothy had been waiting for ten years. She'd probably be grateful if she didn't have to wait another decade.

Chapter Thirteen

Fern glanced at the bird clock that hung in Anna's kitchen. She still had more than an hour before she had to leave. There was plenty of time to teach Reuben how to purl. She turned her gaze to Reuben and grimaced inwardly. She'd taught Reuben how to hold the needles correctly, but he still held them in his fists as if his fingers were as thick as cucumbers. When it came to knitting, he truly was a lost cause. But Anna would be heartbroken if Fern didn't at least attempt to teach Reuben how to knit. If he could manage to make a pot holder, Anna would probably be satisfied.

Fern bent over her own knitting. A pot holder might take Reuben weeks. Lord willing, Anna would figure out for herself that Reuben was not meant to knit and release him before he accidentally started a fire or something.

Not that anyone could conceivably start a fire with yarn and a pair of knitting needles, but Reuben's attempts at knitting would surely bring some sort of disaster upon them.

Fern and Reuben sat on the sofa, where Fern could

guide every stitch Reuben made. Anna had her own knitting gathered about her in the rocking chair, and Felty sat in his recliner reading *The Budget*. Anna hadn't asked him to join their little knitting party, and he hadn't offered.

Fern laid her knitting in her lap. She shouldn't have brought it. Keeping Reuben from tangling his fingers into a knot commanded all her attention. "Wrap the yarn around the back needle," she said, showing him how to scoop up a new loop for the hundredth time, irritated that when her fingers brushed against his, the touch tingled all the way up her arm. Reuben dominated far too many of her thoughts lately. Why should she care that he spent time with Sadie Yoder or smiled at the Yutzy twins as if they were his closest friends? Whom Reuben liked was none of her business. She was in town to help him forgive John and convince him to come home.

How could she let the mere touch of his skin against hers or a bright, heart-stopping smile send a shiver snaking down her spine?

They both laughed when Reuben's entire first row slipped from his needles and landed on Anna's dog, Sparky, who was napping at Reuben's feet. Reuben stared down at his sorry attempt at knitting. "I think we can rightly say that I have made a blanket for Sparky." Even though it was obvious he wasn't going to learn to love to knit, he smiled at her, his eyes alight with something deep and warm.

Fern's heart thudded beneath her ribs. Reuben would do anything for his *mammi*. It was one of his best qualities.

"You're coming along just fine," Anna said, slipping into the voice *mammis* reserved for hopeless grandchildren whom they loved no matter how bad they were at knitting. "You've only been knitting for twenty minutes, and you're already better than Esther Shirk."

"You are very kind, Mammi," Reuben said, plucking his hopeless little strand of yarn from Sparky's fur. "But I'm not better than anybody."

"And that's okay," Anna said. "You're only a failure if you quit trying. No matter how long it takes, Fern is going to teach you to be a knitter. She'll probably have to spend several hours a day sitting right next to you on that sofa." Anna let out the slack of a ball of yarn in her bag. She knitted so fast, her fingers fairly flew off her hands.

Fern tried not to think about spending hours sitting on the sofa next to Reuben. He'd probably much rather be painting Sadie Yoder's chicken coop or eating Clara Yutzy's peanut-butter-chocolate drops. Why would he want to spend time with the pig farmer's daughter who cleaned toilets three days a week?

"Do you think the knitting group will get back together again?" Anna said, glancing at Fern as if they shared a secret. "Reuben could join us. You said you've been to see Esther and Sadie."

Reuben took his eyes off his knitting and dropped a stitch. It didn't matter. He dropped stitches whether he had his eyes on his knitting or not. "I apologized to both of them. Then I painted Sadie's fence and her chicken coop yesterday and washed Esther's second dog this morning."

Esther's dog Zipper had been much easier to wash than Sweetie Pie had been. Zipper couldn't have weighed more than eight pounds and was as cooperative as Sweetie Pie was contrary. Though the hem of Reuben's trousers had gotten damp, Fern hadn't gotten wet at all. It had been a much more pleasant ride home.

"And both Sadie and Esther have forgiven you?" Anna said.

"Sadie has," Reuben said, with a conviction that ruffled Fern just a bit. Why was he so sure about Sadie? "Esther hasn't decided that I've completely made it up to her yet. She might not come back to the knitting group." Reuben studied his *mammi*'s face doubtfully. "She burned her blanket."

Anna shrugged. "*Ach, vell.* It was quite a mess. In *gute* conscience, I couldn't have given it to one of the babies in the hospital anyway."

Reuben cheerfully knitted away, as if he weren't making a mess of his own blanket. "But Sadie likes me. She invited me to come back next week to see how the dairy works, maybe milk some cows with her and her brothers."

Fern eyed Reuben. He was pleased with himself— that was certain. Painting the chicken coop must have gone very well yesterday.

Well. *Gute.*

Reuben had been wallowing in self-pity long enough. He needed friends. He needed acceptance. He needed someone to help him forget Linda Sue. Fern was very grateful, even though she couldn't seem to swallow past the lump in her throat. Reuben would soon be back to his full glory—back to a time when the bishop's daughter was his girlfriend and he was the most popular and well-liked boy in the district. She couldn't wait.

Anna must have been very happy to see her plan working so well, even if the knitting group never met again.

Fern cleared her throat. "On Wednesday, Reuben apologized to the twins, and I apologized to Eva."

"Eva was a *gute* addition to the knitting group," Anna said, "even if I knew deep down inside that she and Reuben wouldn't work out."

Reuben looked up from his tangled yarn. "What do you mean by that, Mammi?"

It would do no good for Reuben to know that the knitting group was just a ruse to find Reuben a wife. "I'm going on a ride with Johnny Raber tonight," Fern blurted out in hopes of diverting Reuben's attention.

It worked. His frown of concentration disappeared, replaced by something grumpier. "*Ach.* I forgot." He sighed in resignation. "It's my fault."

"I don't mind."

Anna's frown matched Reuben's. "You're going for a ride with Johnny Raber? That will never do. I was hoping you'd spend the evening with us helping Reuben with his blanket or his pot holder or whatever it is he's making."

Fern had a feeling that Anna would not be able, in good conscience, to give Reuben's blanket to an unsuspecting baby. "You will have to take over for me, Anna."

Anna shook her head. "It has to be you and only you, Fern. I've chosen you specifically for this. You're so much more patient than I am about such things."

Fern couldn't imagine anyone being more patient than Anna Helmuth. "I'm sorry. Eva doesn't want Johnny to turn out like her brother Melvin."

"And she thinks one buggy ride is going to cure him?" Anna said.

"I think she's hoping one ride will lead to another and another and maybe a gathering or a *singeon*," Fern said, ignoring the probing look coming from Reuben's direction.

"And will it?" Felty said behind his paper. He had a way of inserting himself into the conversation when no one thought he was listening.

"Will it what?"

"Lead to another ride? Johnny is as shy as a church mouse."

Fern's lips twitched upward. She sort of liked that concerned look on Reuben's face, as if he cared whether or not she'd go on another ride with Johnny. "Well, I don't know. I do enjoy talking as much as I want without the inconvenience of being interrupted."

Reuben cracked a smile and shook his head. "I'd feel better if I knew you weren't looking forward to it."

"Of course she's not looking forward to it," Anna said. "She'd rather be here knitting with us."

"Of course she would," Reuben said, with the slightest hint of hope in his voice.

"That's why we need to reunite the knitting group." Anna set her knitting on her lap and held up her fingers as she counted. "Sadie, Esther, Clara, Carolyn, and Eva. What about Lorene?"

"I've talked to Lorene too," Reuben said, nodding at Fern.

"You went by yourself?" she said.

"*Jah*. Yesterday after I finished Sadie's chicken coop."

Fern felt dull and tired. She'd been at work all day yesterday, and Reuben had needed her.

"I went to see Lorene before her anger boiled over. Clara and Carolyn said she was pretty mad."

Fern didn't know whether to be proud of him for

having the courage to go by himself or cross with him for doing something that they'd only done together.

"I took her a tub of peanut-butter-chocolate drops."

"That was smart of you," Fern said. "How did she react?"

"She answered the door and pulled me into the house as if I was one of the family. Before I could say a word, she told me she'd forgiven me days ago and would I like to meet her family? She introduced me to three brothers, two sisters, her cat Sally, and her *mamm*. Then she took me outside to the barn where we met her *dat*, two other brothers, her chickens, and her horses. She gave me a tour of the barn and invited me to dinner." Reuben paused to take a breath. "And, she wants to start the group again as soon as possible."

"Lorene is such a *gute* girl, even if she's not the girl I have in mind." Anna picked up her knitting. "What about Dorothy? I know she's older and just comes for the knitting, but you still need to apologize to her. If I'm the heart of the knitting group, then Dorothy is for sure and certain the brain. Or maybe she's another heart." Anna wrinkled her brow. "Although I tend to think of Fern as the second heart. Or maybe Fern is the true heart as everything depends on her. But what about Dorothy? I know she took the breakup of the knitting group very hard. She'd rather knit than do just about anything else."

Well, not exactly. Dorothy would be perfectly content if the knitting group never met again. "We've been to see Dorothy. She was very gracious," Fern said.

Reuben abandoned his knitting. He probably found it hard to think about two problems at once. "Mammi and Dawdi, I need your help. Dorothy asked me to do something for her, and I don't know quite how to go about it."

Anna nodded. "She wants you to find her a husband."

Fern's eyes widened at the same time Reuben's did. "How did you know?" she said.

Anna waved her knitting needles in Fern's direction. "Every girl wants a husband."

Felty folded his paper down so they could see his face. "Every man would want a wife if all the girls was like you, Annie-banannie."

"Now, Felty," Anna said. "Dorothy has just as much sense as I do, and she's almost as *gute* a cook. Surely there's someone who can see what a catch she is."

"She has her eye on Melvin Raber," Reuben said. "And Fern says he's as shy as his brother Johnny."

Felty fingered the beard on his chin. "Melvin Raber just as soon throw up as talk to a girl. I know. I seen him do it once."

"He likes my rice, bacon, and apricot salad," Anna said. "I took some to him when he had a cold last fall, and though he never says much, he was truly speechless."

"Dorothy is willing to bake," Fern said.

Anna inclined her head toward Reuben. "To make a match, you have to be sly, and you must either do a lot of baking or a lot of knitting."

Felty's paper crunched as he crinkled it into his lap. "We should leave poor Melvin be. Nobody likes throwing up. Maybe he doesn't want to marry."

"But Dorothy does," Anna said, "so we've got to make Melvin see reason. He could stop himself from throwing up if he really wanted to. This is a *gute* project for Fern and Reuben to work on together."

"But what can we do?" Reuben said.

Warmth spread down Fern's arms. Reuben said "we." He depended on her, even if he had gone to Lorene's by himself.

Anna pursed her lips, deep in thought. "I don't think we should stoop to deceit, but what about a little trickery?"

"Is there a difference?" Fern said.

"Dorothy could lose her buggy wheel right in front of Melvin's house in a pouring rainstorm. He'd have to help her fix it."

Reuben frowned. "But, Mammi, I've never seen a buggy wheel just fall off."

Anna nodded. "*Jah*. We'd have to be clever. And we'd have to wait for a rainstorm. *And* Melvin would have to be at home."

Felty didn't seem so sure. "It's a wonderful-*gute* idea, but it would risk Dorothy getting hurt. I don't think she would be willing to break her neck in the name of love."

Anna smiled eagerly at her husband. "I think she would."

Felty's eyes brightened as an idea seemed to light upon him like a bird. "Melvin plays the license plate game."

"Now, Felty dear. How is the license plate game going to help Melvin and Dorothy?"

"Leave that to me and Reuben," Felty said. "All I know is that Virginia is for Lovers, Alabama is the Heart of Dixie, New Mexico is the Land of Enchantment, and Ohio is the Heart of It All. That's romantic enough for me."

For Fern too. She couldn't wait to see what Felty had in store.

Chapter Fourteen

Reuben knew it was wicked of him, but he'd never wished so hard that the minister would end his sermon and let them all out of church half an hour early. It would never happen, but he could hope, couldn't he?

Gmay had never seemed so long—not on the day he'd been baptized two years ago and surprisingly, not even on the day after Linda Sue had broken up with him. It had been all Reuben could do not to tap his foot impatiently during *"Das Loblied."* The *Vorsinger* must have sensed his restlessness, because he had cast a frown at Reuben and taken the song even slower.

Reuben couldn't help it that curiosity had made him antsy. Fern sat among the women and girls to his right. The Burkholders' great room was a wide space, so the men and women weren't facing each other this time, and he couldn't get a *gute* look to see if she had a dreamy expression on her face or if her eyes were glazed over with infatuation. It wasn't likely that she'd fallen in love with Johnny Raber after one buggy ride, but for some reason, the possibility had Reuben stewing.

It didn't help that Johnny Raber was sitting right behind him, his shoulders rounded and his eyes dull and lifeless like they always were, no doubt gloating that he'd spent Friday night driving Fern around when she should have been home with Reuben knitting a blanket or a pot holder or a mitten. Reuben didn't like it one little bit, and he couldn't wait to corner Fern after services and make sure she hadn't promised her hand in marriage to Johnny Raber.

Reuben sat between Aaron Glick and Matthew Eicher, boys in the district he'd made friends with at one of the gatherings. Matthew was popular with the girls because of his golden hair and shocking blue eyes. Aaron had a girlfriend but was wonderful fun to be around when he was in a *gute* mood. Aaron and Reuben had gone fishing last week before Reuben had painted Sadie's chicken coop. They'd caught enough fish for both of them, and Mammi had made her famous Trout Mango Stew.

Reuben shifted on the bench. The minister was talking about the Sermon on the Mount and being our brother's keeper. That's all Reuben was trying to do with Fern. She was far from home and someone needed to watch out for her. On Saturday night, he'd even considered going to the Schmuckers' house and waiting for her to come home from work, but he had decided against it because he didn't know when she got home or if she would think he was being nosy.

If only she'd told him where she worked, he could have gone to visit her there. Why was it such a big secret? Did she work for an *Englischer*? Around here, that was very likely, and it was nothing to be ashamed about. Lots of the Amish worked out, and Fern hadn't been baptized yet. He wouldn't think less of her for that. Besides, though she hadn't said so, he knew her family needed the money. With the Schmuckers feeding her and giving her a place to stay, she was probably sending most of her earnings back home.

Reuben leaned forward and sneaked a peek to his right. He could just make out Fern's profile among a sea of girls. She sat with the twins on one side and Lorene Zook on the other, watching the minister intently, as if she was listening. She probably was, which was what Reuben should have been doing, but he couldn't pull his thoughts from that buggy ride. Johnny Raber might be more charming than he appeared.

Surely he was at least as charming as a mailbox.

Finally services ended, and Reuben bolted too eagerly from his bench to help set up tables, keeping Fern fixed in the corner of his eye. She helped with the food, dishing peanut butter and cheese spread into smaller bowls, slicing bread, and looking especially radiant today with her drab brown dress and bright, sparkling eyes. Her *kapp* always seemed to be barely able to contain her unruly curls, and there were always a few spirals that escaped and teased Reuben to reach out and touch them. He pressed his palms against his trousers and rubbed up and down vigorously to stop his fingers from tingling.

"*Cum*, Reuben," Aaron said, pointing to the table nearest the window. "Sit by us. Lily said she would serve us first."

Of course Reuben wanted to sit with Matthew and Aaron and his other new friends in the district, but he was wonderful itchy to talk to Fern too. The minute fellowship supper was over, he would find her. He could only be patient for so long.

He positioned himself so he had full view of the

kitchen and Fern. She picked up a platter of bread and passed it down one of the tables. Reuben pressed his lips together. Johnny Raber seemed to be waiting for her to emerge from behind the counter. He followed her down the rows of tables like a puppy hoping someone would drop a morsel of food. Reuben clenched his teeth as Fern turned to Johnny and gave him one of her nicest smiles, as if she was very happy to have him tag along after her. His face felt like it was on fire when she said something and Johnny said something back.

Reuben unclenched his fist. It shouldn't irritate him that Fern was just being friendly. Fern was the friendliest person he knew. Of course she'd try to be nice to Johnny Raber. As a Christian, she was supposed to be nice to everybody.

Reuben couldn't really follow the conversation at the table. Matthew was talking about the time he did donuts with his buggy in the parking lot at the Lark Country Store, and Aaron wanted to plan a fishing trip on the Wisconsin River during the summer.

The minute he finished his last bite of bread, Reuben jumped to his feet, stuffed his plate in the garbage can, and made a beeline for Fern, who was sitting next to Clara Yutzy—or Carolyn. Fern looked up and smiled at him as if maybe she wasn't in love with Johnny Raber. Relaxing a little, he smiled back and slowed his steps. He didn't want her to think she was under attack.

Before he could say a word to Fern, Sadie seemed to appear out of nowhere. She and Esther positioned themselves between Reuben and Fern, an obstacle Reuben couldn't simply knock over. They hadn't done it on purpose, but Reuben almost groaned, all the same. Hearing all about the buggy ride with Johnny Raber would have to wait. Keeping Sadie happy was more important. If he truly wanted to fit in here in Bonduel, he needed to be close with the bishop's daughter. Unfortunately, Esther was the bishop's daughter's best friend. Reuben had to get on her *gute* side too.

"Reuben," Sadie said, her smile as bright as a sparkler on the Fourth of July. "How are you? We sure miss the knitting group, don't we, Esther?"

Esther squinted in Reuben's direction as if in warning. "I don't miss it. I hate to knit. Good riddance yet."

Reuben had been given strict instructions from Sadie that Esther never be told about the fence and the chicken coop. He'd been given strict instructions from Esther that Sadie shouldn't know about the dog washing. How the two of them could be friends and keep such secrets was beyond Reuben's comprehension.

Reuben pretended to keep his attention focused squarely on Sadie as he glanced furtively in Fern's direction. She had turned her back on him, and she and the twins were clearing off their table. Hopefully she wouldn't go very far before he had a chance to talk to her.

Sadie glanced behind her in Fern's direction. "Esther, go get two dishrags. We should help wipe tables."

Esther lifted one side of her lip in disgust. "I'm not your servant."

Sadie sighed loudly and gave Reuben a look of patient forbearance. "Just go, Esther. It's silly for both of us to go fetch a rag when you can just as well get one for both of us."

Esther looked daggers at Reuben before slouching away, as if it were somehow his fault that her best friend wanted to get rid of her. It probably was.

Sadie leaned closer and lowered her voice. "You're still coming tomorrow, aren't you?"

"*Jah*," he said, unable to keep his eyes from another glance at Fern. "I want to see the dairy."

"It's growing bigger every year. The *Englisch* love the organic. My *dat* hired two new workers last week. He can't keep up on the work with only him and my *bruders*. He bought two new milking machines too. We'll soon be one of the largest dairies in the state. We already give more money to the church than anybody in the district." She drew her brows together. "I mean, I think we do. Dat hasn't ever come right out and said it. That would be proud."

"I understand," Reuben said. His *dat* gave lots of money to the church as well. But Sadie was right to keep it to herself. It was proud to talk about such things.

"I feel true charity for the poor," Sadie whispered. "We all must do what we can." She folded her arms and motioned toward Fern with her head. "Some girls can't even buy new shoes. I'm glad my *dat* takes *gute* care of us."

Reuben kept his expression steady and eyed Fern's shoes. They were black lace-up vinyl shoes, coming apart at the seams in one or two places, but they still seemed serviceable. Fern didn't wear shoes most other days, unless it was chilly, but Reuben thought the bare feet were kind of cute. He didn't especially like that Sadie looked down on Fern for her shoes, but he had to admit that Fern's *dat* couldn't afford to buy her new shoes. He was a pig farmer. He could barely afford to feed his family.

"I hope I never have to scrape and struggle for money the way some people do," Sadie said. "That's why I am happy to know your *dat* gives so much to the poor like my *fater* does. If we don't have our Christian charity, we are nothing."

Reuben was happy that he didn't have to struggle for money, wasn't he? So why did he feel so low when he peered at Fern? Did Sadie think she was better than Fern because of her money? Did he?

Before he had time to take a *gute* look at his own shortcomings, Esther returned with two soapy dishrags and handed one, dripping wet, to Sadie.

Sadie took the rag but jumped back from the dripping water, making sure her scuffless, expensive church shoes didn't get wet. "Esther, don't you know to wring them out first? I can't wipe up with this."

"Go wring it out yourself if you're so persnickety," Esther said, making no attempt to save her own shoes or her dress. Drops of water and soap streaked the front of her white apron. "I'm going to wipe tables."

Sadie sighed another great sigh in Esther's direction. "If you did things right the first time, I wouldn't have to redo them." Holding her rag straight out in front of her, she smiled at Reuben. "Good-bye," she said, giving him a barely perceptible nod that said, "I'll see you tomorrow, and my shoes are going to be just fine."

Reuben waved to her as she moved away from him, then snapped his head around to look for Fern among the crowd of women and girls tidying up. He growled softly. She'd disappeared. If she'd gone behind the house to kiss Johnny Raber, Reuben didn't know if he would be able to keep his temper.

He headed for the door while shaking that *deerich* thought from his head. Fern wasn't the type of girl who gave out her kisses like lemon drops. She was sweet and cheerful but not inclined to flirt.

He stepped out onto the porch and shielded his eyes from the bright May sun. There she was, strolling down the Burkholders' lane heading for the road. He felt as if he'd swallowed a piece of glass. She was going to leave without talking to him? As if they weren't even friends?

The Schmuckers hadn't come to *gmay* today. Had she walked all the way here by herself? Anger pressed against his chest. Was she planning on walking all the way home? What was she thinking? It was nearly three miles. Surely Mammi and Dawdi wouldn't mind if they drove her home in the buggy. It irritated him that Fern hadn't asked.

"Fern!" He jumped off the porch and jogged down the gravel lane until he caught up with her.

She turned around, and he thought he saw a glimmer of something deep and forlorn in her eyes before the expression disappeared and was replaced by a breathtaking smile. How did she do that?

It took him a second to gather his scattered thoughts. "I can take you home."

With that smile still in place, she shook her head. "I don't mind walking."

"But why walk when you have a chance to ride with the best-looking boy in Sugarcreek *and* Bonduel put together?"

She didn't laugh like he expected her to. "There are better-looking boys, and I can walk."

He studied her face. He might have been overly sensitive, but something seemed amiss. "Is something wrong?"

Her smile faltered, but only for half a second. "I'm glad you are making some friends. I want you to be happy here."

"But?"

Her hesitation was so subtle, someone who didn't know her well might have missed it. "But nothing. You're much happier than when I first came here. Remember? At that first *gmay*, you sat on that bench like a lump of slime and glared at me."

"A lump of slime?" he repeated.

"*Jah.* You were that unpleasant."

He tilted his head so she'd meet his eye. "You're my friend too, you know. Even if you are from Sugarcreek."

Her mouth twitched at one corner. "I'm sure you'll get over it."

"Over what?"

"You won't need me much longer. Sadie and Esther and Matthew Eicher will take *gute* care of you. Aaron Glick and Serena are both wonderful nice."

What was she talking about? He would always need her. His gut twisted like a wrung-out dishrag. She couldn't stay in Bonduel forever. "This place is growing on me," he murmured.

She narrowed her eyes. "Or you could come home."

He looked out at the pasture that ran alongside the lane. "I guess maybe I could."

Her smile returned with full force and a hint of surprise. "You think maybe?"

He kicked the gravel at his feet. "I don't know. It doesn't hurt as much as it used to, but maybe that's because I'm not there to see John and Linda Sue parade around like a couple, rubbing it in my face every time we see each other."

"John would never do that. You know he feels as bad as you do."

"*Nae*, he doesn't," Reuben said, with less conviction than he used to feel on the subject. "Maybe there isn't room for all three of us in Sugarcreek anymore."

"Sugarcreek is a big place." She always tried to coax him out of a bad mood by teasing him. "Even for someone with as big a head as you."

"*Ach*, a big head? I've half a mind not to invite you over for knitting tomorrow night."

She giggled. "You'll never finish that blanket without my help."

"Pot holder. I've changed it to a pot holder. It will go faster."

Fern shook her head as if she thought he was incorrigible. "No new mother wants to take her baby home wrapped in a pot holder."

"Maybe if it's a preemie." He reached out and tugged at one of her errant curls. "Will you come? Tomorrow night to give me a knitting lesson?"

Fern touched her fingers to the base of her neck. "*Jah*, but only because I wouldn't want to disappoint your *mammi*. She's got her heart set on you learning how to knit."

He shook his head. "She's going to be very disappointed."

"Don't give up yet. I still have hope for you."

Warmth spread inside his chest. Fern never gave up on anything.

A buggy crammed with children came slowly down the lane. "*Cum*," Reuben said, leading her to the pasture fence and leaning against it. "I want to hear all about the buggy ride."

Fern grabbed the wooden post and boosted herself to sit on the top rail. "It rained a little, but Johnny brought two umbrellas."

"What did he say?" *Did you fall in love with him? Are you going for another ride? Why was he tagging after you like a puppy at the fellowship supper?*

Fern grinned. Did she have an inkling how irritated he'd been about the whole thing? "He didn't say much at first, but I was patient. He finally opened up."

"Finally opened up? You mean you had a conversation?" Of course they had. Fern could make a porcupine feel comfortable.

Fern nodded. "He has a dog named Blue, and he works as a lumberjack. He likes to hunt and fish, and his mother is on a diet."

Reuben cocked an eyebrow and tried to look happy that Fern hadn't spent the buggy ride in silence. "Anything else?"

Fern blushed. Reuben didn't like it. A girl was interested in a boy if she blushed when she talked about him. "He asked if he could take me home from the next singing."

"What did you tell him?" Reuben said, disgusted that he couldn't seem to catch his breath.

"Don't take this the wrong way," Fern said, biting her bottom lip. "Johnny is a wonderful-nice boy, but I am probably the first girl who's been nice to him, the first girl he's said more than two words to besides his sisters. Boys like that tend to think they're in love even when they're not."

"Of course he's in love with you. Who wouldn't be?"

She widened her eyes and formed her lips into an

O. He didn't know why that took her by surprise. "You think so?" She seemed to think better of smiling, and her lips sagged into a frown. "You don't think it's proud of me to say that?"

"It's obvious he's in love with you. He couldn't keep his eyes off you today."

"I want you to know that I don't think I'm better than him or anything like that, but I'm afraid if I keep being nice, he'll think I'm interested, which I'm not."

Reuben could have jumped up and down and shouted "hallelujah." He'd known from the very beginning that Fern and Johnny weren't right for each other. "What are you going to do?" he replied, without a hop, skip, or a jump.

"I don't want to *not* be polite, because he really is a nice boy and I don't want to hurt his feelings."

"And because you are incapable of being unkind to anyone."

She slumped her shoulders. "Maybe I should just ride home with him. He'll eventually take the hint that I don't love him back."

Reuben adamantly shook his head. "You'll be standing in front of the bishop on your wedding day before Johnny takes the hint. At that point it would be quite inconvenient to tell him how you really feel."

"Maybe I'm making a big deal over nothing. It's likely he's simply glad to have a friend who's a girl."

"*Nae.* I saw how he looked at you. He's already in up to his neck. The further you let it go, the harder he'll take it."

Her frown etched itself into her face. "But I hate hurting his feelings."

"Tell him you're riding home with me. I don't mind taking you, and he'll think you and I are coupled up."

"He'll be very sad," she said.

"Not as sad as on the night he proposes to you, and you have to turn him down."

"I suppose you're right."

He folded his arms across his chest in hopes she'd see his muscles flex. "I'm always right."

She rolled her eyes. "And always arrogant."

He growled and chuckled at the same time. "You adore me just the way I am."

"How fortunate for you that I'm hard to get rid of." Fern's eyes came to life with an idea. "I could help Johnny find another girl. Nothing mends a broken heart like a diversion." She paused, grinned sheepishly, and giggled. "Anyway, I think that might work for Johnny."

"You want to play matchmaker to Johnny, and I'm supposed to be matchmaker for his *bruder* Melvin—the two most timid, girl-shy boys in Wisconsin. We've got our work cut out for us." Getting Melvin to talk to Dorothy seemed downright impossible.

"What is Felty planning for Melvin and his license plates?"

"I'm not sure. He said he had to talk to his *Englisch* friend Ken. Ken gives tours of the area to *Englisch* folks who want to see the Amish. That's all I know of Dawdi's plan. He told me to be ready to go as soon as he gives the signal." Reuben winked at Fern. "I don't know what the signal is, and I don't know what I need to do to get ready. I'm going to fail miserably."

"With Anna and Felty helping you out, you have nothing to fear. I hear tell they are the best."

"When I was a boy, I truly believed my grandparents could do anything. I hope they prove me right," Reuben said.

"For sure and certain they will." Fern turned her face to the cloudy sky. "I need to go. It looks like rain."

Reuben wrapped his hands around her waist and helped her down from the fence. His thumbs came troublingly close to touching each other in front. Fern was getting altogether too skinny. Why did she have to be such a picky eater? "Don't worry about the rain. I'll drive you home and then come back for Mammi and Dawdi."

She smiled as if she was surprised he'd remembered his offer. "Okay. But you should drop me off a little way from the house. Barbara gets terrible headaches, and any little noise sets her off."

Reuben didn't see how buggy wheels and horse hooves could make that much noise, but if Fern wanted to be dropped off away from the house, he'd oblige her. From a few things he picked up from Mammi and Clara Yutzy, he'd gotten the impression that Barbara Schmucker was a fussy, difficult-to-please *fraa*. If it made her grumpy to have a buggy pull up in front of her house, Reuben would stay far away.

Sadie came running down the lane, and Fern glided backward toward the main road. "Reuben, I'm glad I caught you," Sadie said, pausing to catch her breath. "Mamm wants you to stay for dinner tomorrow night after I show you around the dairy. After that the family is playing Scrabble. Can you stay?"

A chance to spend time with Sadie's family—the bishop in particular—was too *gute* to pass up. He looked at Fern, but he didn't know why. He didn't need her permission. "Of course I can stay. But I'll warn you. I haven't lost a game of Scrabble since I was twelve."

Sadie clapped her hands. "Wonderful *gute*." She

seemed to remember Fern was there, even though Fern was slowly drifting backward. "I hope you don't mind, Fern. Mamm didn't give me permission to invite anyone else."

Fern pressed a smile onto her lips, all the while moving farther and farther down the lane. "I don't mind. It will be a *gute* chance for Reuben to get to know your family better."

Reuben wanted to smack his palm into his forehead. He'd forgotten all about knitting with Fern. "*Ach*, Sadie," he said. "Fern and I are knitting tomorrow night."

Sadie made a face as if his words tasted bad in her mouth. "Knitting? What are you knitting?"

Reuben forced a carefree smile. He shouldn't have said anything. What would Sadie think of a boy who knew how to knit? "Mammi was very sad when I broke up the knitting group. I thought it would make her happy if I learned to knit."

Sadie smiled. "You're a very thoughtful grandson, but can't you make the knitting lessons another night? Scrabble is so much fun at our house. Joseph Elmer is a terrible player, and he misspells almost every word he tries. Dat keeps the dictionary close."

"We can knit another time," Fern said, now almost ten feet down the lane.

"*Jah*," Sadie said. "There's always time to knit."

"Okay." Reuben furrowed his brow at the unnecessarily cheerful expression on Fern's face.

"Okay," Fern said. She smiled and waved and smiled some more. "We'll knit again real soon."

"Okay," he said again, waving back and feeling as if he'd forgotten something. Fern turned her back on him and skipped down the road as if she was being chased by lightning.

Sadie's excitement was a pot of jelly boiling over on the stove. "Mamm always makes caramel popcorn for Scrabble night. It's so good you will die, but don't tell Esther. She'd only be jealous for no reason and then I'd have to spend three hours talking her out of being mad that she didn't get any popcorn." Sadie shielded her eyes and gazed into the sky. "It looks like it's going to make down hard. Come inside, and I'll tell you all about the *Englischer* I met yesterday who sells essential oils. She knows your *dat.*"

"Okay," Reuben said, which seemed to be the only word his mouth could form at the moment. A large hole opened up in the pit of his stomach. He wanted to play Scrabble with Sadie and the bishop, but he'd brushed Fern off like a piece of lint from his shirt.

Something hard and heavy like a semitruck plowed into him. He'd not only cancelled knitting night, he'd forgotten about his offer to drive Fern home. A drop of rain slapped him in the face as he followed Sadie back into the house.

Chapter Fifteen

The sheer number of spindly trees and unruly bushes in Melvin Raber's yard made it seem as if the forest was trying to smother Melvin's house. It was a *gute* place for someone who wanted to go unnoticed. Reuben pressed his lips together. Dorothy might want to marry Melvin, but it was clear by his unfriendly yard that Melvin wanted to be left alone. Reuben couldn't see a single crocus or daffodil, not to mention a tree in bloom. Flowers seemed to be forbidden on Melvin's property. It didn't bode well for a romance to blossom.

Dawdi led the way to Melvin's porch, where a screen door looked to be more rust than door, and Reuben walked headlong into a cobweb. He scraped it off his face before any spiders decided to hitch a ride as well. The sun had set about half an hour ago, and soon it would be too dark to see the porch or the house. At least the car idling in Melvin's driveway had headlights and a tiny light in the back to illuminate the precious license plate.

Dawdi had said the whole plan would work better in the dark. Dorothy lurked in the backseat of the slightly pink Cadillac. It was better if Melvin couldn't see her from his front door. Not that he would be able to see her anyway. The bushes were so thick between the driveway and the house that Reuben hoped they'd be able to find their way out.

Dawdi knocked on Melvin's door, and Reuben found himself wishing Fern had come, even though it was a Tuesday and she had to work—at whatever job she had to work at. He depended on Fern to know just what to do in situations like this. But Dawdi had been right to want to leave Fern out of it. Melvin would never open his door if she were standing on his porch. According to Dawdi, he frightened too easily.

Still, Reuben wished he could have talked to her after what happened at *gmay* two days ago. He should have followed after Fern in his buggy and taken her home, but Sadie's *dat* had enlisted him to help load benches into the wagon and he couldn't have said no to the bishop, especially since the bishop also happened to be Sadie's *dat*.

Even though Fern didn't work on Mondays, he hadn't seen her yesterday either. He'd spent all day with Sadie looking at her cows and walking around the dairy. Reuben's cousin in Sugarcreek had milking machines, so Reuben knew how to use them. He'd joined in the afternoon milking, helped clean up after the job was done, set Sadie's table for dinner. It was almost as if he were part of the Yoder family—or they wanted him to be.

Reuben's gut clenched, and he ground his teeth together. What was wrong with him? Sadie was everything he could want in a girl—even better than Linda Sue, if he were being honest with himself. Sadie's family had money, and Sadie was ever so much prettier.

There was no reason he should feel so discontented about being with Sadie. Fern would tell him he was just being proud. That's what she always told him.

The door opened with an eerie squeak just as Reuben had expected it would. The cobwebs, the rusty door, the knobby trees were all a little spooky. Did Dorothy really want to marry Melvin Raber? He was a hermit at thirty years old.

Reuben didn't know what he'd expected, but it wasn't the intelligent, if ordinary, looking man who answered the door. Melvin's walnut-brown hair hung over his ears in the traditional Amish fashion, with bangs neatly trimmed to an inch above his thick brows. He was clean shaven, as most unmarried Amish men under forty were. If an Amish bachelor reached the age of forty, the elders allowed him to grow a beard like the married men.

Melvin did meet Reuben's expectations in at least one way. Lowering his eyes, he stood safely behind the tight screen door and fidgeted with his suspenders.

"Hello, Melvin," Dawdi said, tapping his palm against the screen in an attempt to get Melvin to look up.

Melvin's eyes flicked to Dawdi's face and then back to his own feet. "*Gute maiya*, Felty."

"This is my grandson Reuben, from Sugarcreek."

Melvin briefly lifted his gaze before letting it fall again. "Nice to meet you, Roger."

"Reuben," Reuben said, immediately chastising himself. What did it matter if Melvin got his name right when the least mistake could spook Melvin like a horse?

Dawdi didn't seem to notice that Melvin could barely string a sentence together. "I know this is strange, to see us this time of night, but we thought you'd want to see something very exciting that Dorothy found."

Melvin squinted through the screen door. "Dorothy?"

"Dorothy Miller," Dawdi said. "You know her? That wonderful-pretty girl who lives on First Street with the fabric shop?"

Melvin scratched his cheek. "*Jah.* I know Dorothy."

"She knows you like the license plate game and brought something for you to see. It's parked in the driveway." When Melvin didn't seem inclined to do anything but stand there, Dawdi said, "Do you want to come out and take a look? You'll really like it."

Melvin fell silent—well, more silent—and Reuben half wondered if he had fallen asleep. Was Dorothy sure about wanting to marry Melvin? She *had* said she was desperate.

"What do you think?" Dawdi said.

"Okay." The door slowly swung open, and Melvin stepped out onto the porch.

Dawdi motioned for Reuben to lead the way, and he shoved branches out of his path as he went. Melvin's yard needed a chain saw and an ax. They slogged through the jungle to the car, an old Cadillac that Dawdi's friend Ken saw while filling his car at a Shawano gas station. The car's owner, Haku Kalani, had been more than happy to help Ken, especially when Ken promised his wife she'd get to meet some Amish people.

Haku and his wife, Nora, sat in the front with Dorothy waiting in the back, ready to jump out as soon as Melvin appeared—or ready to pounce, as the case may be.

The car's headlights were bright enough to light the way once they reached Melvin's brick driveway.

Melvin followed Reuben to the passenger side of the car. Dorothy opened the door and slipped slowly out of her seat, as if she knew any sudden movements might send Melvin back to the safety of his house. "Hi, Melvin," she said, with a subdued smile and a tone that would have coaxed a badger to trust her.

Melvin tensed so quickly, Reuben could almost hear his spine stiffen. He didn't say a word in reply as his gaze darted between Dawdi and Dorothy.

Dorothy hesitated only for a second before stepping behind the car and pointing to the license plate. "Felty says you play the license plate game."

Melvin shuffled around to the back of the car as if Dorothy was leading him to his doom. He took a look at the license plate, and the wary expression on his face shifted ever so slightly. "Well," he said, scratching the stubble on his chin with four curled fingers. "Well."

Dorothy clasped her hands together in front of her. "Felty says it's rare. I wanted you to see it."

Melvin transferred his weight from one foot to the other. "Well."

"Do you like it?" Dorothy said, budding hope making her seem ten years younger.

Melvin scratched his chin again and glanced at Dorothy. While his posture was still rigid, his forehead didn't look so much like a plowed field anymore. "That's really something."

"I've never seen a Hawaii license plate before," Reuben said, fearing they'd descend into uncomfortable silence if he didn't keep the conversation going.

Melvin kept scratching his chin, which must have been extremely itchy. "It wonders me how they got it all the way from Hawaii."

Melvin had actually uttered a complete sentence in front of a woman. Reuben looked at Dawdi in surprise. Dawdi nodded back as if he'd been expecting it all along. Dawdi had warned him not to underestimate the power of the license plate game.

Dorothy seemed more surprised than any of them. "Haku told me all about it. He lived in Hawaii until his company transferred him to California. They shipped his car over on a boat. He and his *fraa* drove to Wisconsin for a vacation." Dorothy motioned to the front of the car where Haku and Nora sat patiently and quietly. They'd been warned Melvin might be a little timid. "Would you like to meet them?"

Melvin took three steps backward as if he were going to make a run for it. "*Nae, denki.*"

Dorothy's eyes flashed with something akin to panic. She knew she'd made a mistake asking Melvin to reach far outside the little box he'd put himself in. "Oh, they didn't expect to talk to you. They just came to show you the plate."

Dawdi patted his trousers pocket where he kept his small notebook. "We both got Hawaii tonight."

Melvin took one step forward, like maybe he was thinking he didn't have to run away. "I saw Rhode Island three weeks ago at the lake."

"*Ach, du lieva,*" Dawdi said. "I need to do more fishing."

"I'll keep looking," Dorothy said. "Lord willing, we can find all fifty this year."

Dorothy had just made herself part of the game. It was wonderful clever of her.

Melvin gave Dorothy a nearly, almost, barely kind of smile, as if he didn't know quite what to make of her—

as if he were too stunned to form any coherent thoughts.

Dorothy's confidence seemed to grow when Melvin actually made eye contact. She went around to the side of the car, opened the door, and pulled out the rectangular cake carrier she'd held on her lap since they'd picked her up. "I brought you a cake, Melvin," she said, giving no other explanation. She couldn't very well tell him that she hoped the way to Melvin's heart was through his stomach and she hoped Melvin would bring her eggs from his chickens and hold her hand and propose before September.

Melvin could only swallow so much in one day.

When he seemed not to know what to do about it, Dorothy foisted the cake carrier into Melvin's hands. "It's pineapple upside-down cake. I didn't know what kind was your favorite, so I guessed." She looked daggers at Reuben as if it were his fault she didn't know what kind of cake Melvin liked.

Reuben grimaced sheepishly. It probably was his fault. Dorothy had asked him to find out.

"I like pineapple," Melvin said, holding the carrier away from his body as if it might explode.

"Well, aren't you going to invite us in to have a piece?" Dawdi was as sharp as a tack and cool under pressure.

"Uh." Melvin was again at a loss for words.

Dawdi tapped on Haku's window, and Haku rolled it down. "Thank you for the ride, Haku," Dawdi said. "We are going in the house to have a slice of cake with Melvin, and then he'll take us home."

Haku's dark face accentuated the bright white of his teeth. "No problem, Mr. Helmuth. It is my pleasure."

"You'll still come to dinner tomorrow night?" Dawdi said.

Haku grinned at his wife. "We wouldn't miss it."

Melvin stepped away as Haku backed his car out of the driveway. "My table is piled high," Melvin said, holding the cake in one hand and scratching his chin with the other.

"How high?" Dorothy said, with that look in her eye that said she was willing to move mountains.

Melvin opened his palm and touched a spot at the level of his waist.

Dorothy pushed her sleeves up past her elbow. "Leave that to me. You're going to want a taste of this cake." With a spring in her step, she led the way as if she already lived there, and Melvin, Dawdi, and Reuben followed close behind.

Too bad Fern couldn't have come. She loved cake, and Reuben would have seen to it that she ate at least two pieces. But even more than the cake, she loved seeing people happy.

And Reuben loved seeing her that way.

Chapter Sixteen

Fern swiped her arm across her face to get rid of the moisture that kept seeping from her eyes like a leaky faucet. Here she was, wrist deep in toilet water, hungry, and tired, and she couldn't come up with anything better to think about than Reuben Helmuth?

She quickly swabbed the toilet bowl and sprayed down the rest of the toilet. The sharp smell of disinfectant stung her nose and made her eyes water even more. *Gute.* At least she was crying over something useful.

Even though she bristled at the thought of Reuben finding out, Fern didn't really mind scrubbing toilets or mopping floors, and they paid her ten dollars an hour for the gas stations and twelve dollars an hour for the offices. Working six hours a day cleaning gas station bathrooms and six hours a day cleaning doctor and law offices, she was able to send almost four hundred dollars a week home to Mamm and Dat. Dat didn't hound her to come home so much when she sent that kind of money their way. It was almost cheaper for them if she was gone.

Sending money home didn't leave a lot of money for groceries, but Fern didn't mind going hungry for Reuben's sake. Her parents need never know that the Schmuckers weren't feeding her a bite. The bread and cheese Dorothy had given her last Wednesday had lasted nearly a week, and she ate Anna Helmuth's cooking when she was extra hungry.

Dorothy had offered Fern a job on Friday afternoons at the fabric shop though she couldn't afford to pay her, except in food. Because people in the community considered Dorothy an old maid, they paid her little attention—as if she didn't matter because she didn't have a husband. But Dorothy noticed everything. Food was the best thing she could have offered Fern. Dorothy had once been friends with Barbara and Wally Schmucker's daughter Lisa before she'd left the church to marry an *Englischer*. Dorothy knew a lot more about Barbara Schmucker than most people did.

But Dorothy was sensitive to Fern's dignity, so she had offered her a job instead of a handout. Her friends here in Bonduel knew Fern didn't want a handout, no matter how poor she was, so they helped with what they could and left the rest to *Gotte*. Most of them didn't know how bad it was at the Schmuckers', but some of them suspected—Dorothy was more conscious of Fern's troubles than anybody.

Fern sniffed back her tears. How could she feel sorry for herself when she had three *gute* jobs and a place to sleep? Some people had none of those.

Juana, the tiny Mexican lady who cleaned offices with Fern, stuck her head in the stall and gave her a kind smile. "You okay, Fairn?" Juana spoke almost no English, but she was sweet and motherly and never without a smile on her face.

Fern got on her feet and flushed the toilet one more time for good measure. "*Sí, Juana. Yo bueno*," she said.

Juana's eyes lit up at Fern's attempt to speak Spanish, even though Fern knew about six Spanish words and her accent was terrible. Juana wrapped her latex-gloved hands around Fern's waist and gave her a warm hug. She couldn't have been more than four-foot-ten. It was as high as she could reach. "You good. No cry," she said. "Boys are *stupido*."

How in the world did Juana guess that Fern was crying over a boy?

Maybe that was the only thing girls ever cried over.

Fern nodded and gave Juana a quick squeeze. "Boys are *stupido*," she repeated, wishing she actually believed it. It would make things easier if Reuben wasn't worth the trouble. She picked up her spray bottle and moved to the next stall.

She had purposefully avoided Reuben since *gmay* on Sunday when she had run all the way to the Schmuckers' house without stopping, her tears mixing with the rain that ran down her face. Even when she had been an irritating little tag-along as a child, Reuben had always kept an eye out for her. He'd helped her up when she tripped and made sure she never fell too far behind, even when John and the other boys tried to run fast enough to lose her.

Sunday was the first time Reuben had purposefully neglected her. He'd let her walk home by herself in the rain, and he hadn't even cared.

Fern put all her emotion into spraying the toilet. She made herself stop when disinfectant puddled on the tile floor. She was a girl who cleaned toilets, and a pig farmer's daughter. She had never really deserved

Reuben's kindness, so why did the lack of it hurt so much now? He was forging his own way, making friends, finding love again. Couldn't she be happy about that?

Why did the thought of Scrabble with Sadie Yoder make Fern ill? She could just imagine Reuben with that heart-stopping smile on his face, eager to make a *gute* impression on Sadie's parents, laughing and joking, maybe even calling Sadie a pet name like Fernly or something equally as silly. She couldn't blame him for canceling knitting lessons to be with Sadie, but that didn't mean she had to like it.

But she *should* like it. Wasn't this exactly what she had wanted to happen? If Reuben was happy, Fern was happy. She'd been tagging after him long enough. It was time to leave the poor boy alone and get out of his way.

She wanted to believe that if she stayed away long enough, he'd come looking for her, which wouldn't be a *gute* thing, considering where he might find her.

Maybe it was time to go back to Sugarcreek.

Her throat tightened, and she blinked back more tears. She couldn't go home yet. She needed to help Reuben wash Esther's third dog tomorrow. And then there was the benefit haystack supper on Friday night. And she had promised Anna she would teach Reuben how to knit.

Reuben didn't need her for that. Sadie was a better knitter than Fern would ever be.

Fern scrubbed her rag across the toilet seat as if she could wipe the porcelain off if she pressed hard enough. Reuben was going to be okay. She wanted him to come back to Sugarcreek, but now that he and Sadie were coming along so well, that seemed less likely than ever.

Her breath hitched in her throat.

She should go home.

Still. She wanted her brother and Reuben to be friends again, even if Reuben never came back to Sugarcreek. She wanted John to apologize to Reuben and Reuben to say out loud that he forgave John. She had to do that one last thing.

For Reuben's sake.

Then she'd go home.

A tear escaped her eye and plopped into the toilet.

"You okay, *chiquita*?"

"*Jah.* I'm okay."

But she'd never be able to breathe again without that hitch in her throat.

Chapter Seventeen

Reuben tapped the broom across the cement, trying to keep the floor at least partially swept up halfway through the benefit haystack supper. He stole another glance at Fern, who was dishing up rice at the far table. As if she sensed his gaze on her, she lifted her head and smiled at him. Even from across the warehouse, she almost knocked him over.

And what was it about her lively eyes that always made him catch his breath?

She wore a cheery light blue apron over her brown dress that brought out the cinnamon highlights in her auburn hair and made her eyes look extra chocolatey. She was the prettiest girl in Bonduel, even though she was from Sugarcreek, Ohio.

Johnny Raber wasn't the only boy in Bonduel who had taken notice of Fern King, though he was the most obvious about his admiration. Two boys sat at one of the long tables eating haystacks and glancing at Fern every few seconds, while Marty Lambright and Abe Kauffman loitered near the open door to the warehouse, keeping an eye on Fern and the other girls serving food. Johnny Raber hovered near Fern, not daring to speak, but not straying far from her. He stood four feet behind her while she served food to *Englischers* and Amish.

Reuben raised an eyebrow at Fern and motioned to Johnny with a slight nod of his head. She took a quick look behind her and turned back to her rice, her face glowing with an attractive peaches-and-cream blush. She eyed Reuben, pursed her lips together, and shook her head slightly, as if to warn him not to do anything to humiliate poor Johnny Raber. He grunted his indignation, although she was too far away to hear it. She knew him better than to think he'd do anything to embarrass Johnny. Reuben liked to tease Fern, but he wouldn't do it at Johnny's expense.

"I'm driving you home tonight," he mouthed.

She stared at him with a puzzled look on her face. "What?" she mouthed back.

Reuben leaned his broom against the wall and pointed to Fern, then to himself, then pantomimed opening a buggy door and jiggling some reins to get the horse moving.

Fern's mouth formed into an O, and she peered doubtfully at Reuben before her attention was pulled away by a plump *Englischer* wanting a scoop of rice.

Reuben frowned. He deserved her hesitation. He'd told her he would take her home last Sunday and failed her, and he hadn't seen her once this week to apologize. She'd sent him a note on Wednesday morning telling him she couldn't come with him to wash Esther's dog because she'd been able to pick up an extra shift at work.

What kind of shift? He still didn't know.

Thursday was another day at work for her, and as of

a week ago, her Fridays were spent at Dorothy Miller's fabric shop dusting shelves and cutting fabric for customers. If Reuben didn't know better, he'd think she was avoiding him. But that was silly. Fern had never been able to resist poking her nose into his life. Surely she'd want to know how things were coming along with Sadie.

Wouldn't she?

He scowled so hard, his face hurt. He was wonderful mad at himself for canceling the knitting lesson. The more he considered his behavior, the more ashamed he felt about it. Fern might have been an underling in Sugarcreek, but she didn't deserve to be treated like she was expendable when he got a better offer.

He hadn't seen Fern this week at all, but he'd seen Sadie three times. She just kept finding excuses for him to come over. First it was the dairy and a game of Scrabble. Then on Tuesday he'd helped her inspect cow hooves, and on Thursday, they'd gone to a bonfire at the lake with a few of *die youngie*.

Reuben snatched up his broom and turned his face away so he couldn't see Fern, not even in his peripheral vision, though he wasn't sure why it mattered. Even if she saw him frowning with his whole face, she wouldn't guess that he was thinking that Sadie had neglected to invite Fern to the bonfire last night. Of course, with her work schedule, she might not have been able to come. That was probably why she hadn't been invited.

Reuben swept so hard, he was soon sending up a cloud of dust. He relaxed his grip on the handle and ambled farther away from the tables. No one wanted their food seasoned with dirt.

The benefit haystack supper was being held in one of Vernon Raber's big warehouses. Since the Amish didn't buy health insurance, a haystack supper was one way they raised money to help pay for medical expenses of district members. The Burkholders' little girl needed leukemia treatments. They hoped to raise two thousand dollars. Reuben had come early in Dawdi's two-seater buggy to help set up tables, and Mammi and Dawdi were coming later with Reuben's cousin Moses, his wife Lia, and their son.

Dorothy Miller strolled into the warehouse clutching a notebook to her chest and smiling as if she'd just awakened from a nice dream. She practically twirled over to the tables where the food was being served and said hello to everyone, waving her fingers in greeting and getting plenty of grins in return. Her gaze swept over the eating tables, and when it lighted on Reuben, she seemed to burst. Glancing this way and that as if hoping no one noticed her, she rushed toward him. Was he going to need to defend himself with the broom?

"Reuben Helmuth," Dorothy said in a loud whisper when she came closer.

"*Guten Owed*, Dorothy," Reuben said, not even bothering to lower his voice. He didn't see any reason for secrecy.

She looked behind her and motioned for Reuben to edge closer to the wall. He followed, mostly because he didn't think it would do much good to be contrary. "I never thought I'd say this in a million years, Reuben, but you are a genius."

Dorothy's compliments always sounded suspiciously like insults. "*Denki*?" he said.

Dorothy beamed in triumph. "Melvin was waiting for me outside."

"Just now?"

"When I got here. He wanted to show me Arizona. He found it parked on the street when he came for the fellowship supper."

"That's wonderful *gute*. Is Arizona a hard one?"

Dorothy grimaced. "It's not about the plate, Reuben. Melvin talked to me. Voluntarily."

"He wanted to show you the license plate."

"That's not all. We walked all the way down the street looking at the license plates parked along the side."

Reuben didn't dare mention that cars were parked along the street, not license plates. Why risk Dorothy's good mood? "So, he took you on a walk."

"And," Dorothy said, pausing as if the next thing she had to say would change Reuben's life. "We found Kentucky. Melvin told me to be sure to write it down." She turned her notebook over so Reuben could see "Kentucky" and "Arizona" written across the top of the first page. "It's more words than he's said to me in ten years, Reuben, and I owe it all to you."

"Not me. Dawdi thought of the idea."

"But you thought to ask your *dawdi*. I don't know how I'm going to thank you."

Reuben couldn't help but grin. "Don't thank me until there's a wedding."

Dorothy hugged her notebook. "Two weeks ago, I wouldn't have dared hope. Maybe your coming here wasn't such a bad thing after all, even though your temper broke up the knitting group and you strut around like a rooster."

"*Denki*?" he said again, unable to keep that question

mark out of his voice. Dorothy didn't really like him, but she was trying to be gracious in her own untactful way. Probably.

She pressed her lips together and eyed Reuben, nodding as if she had him all figured out. "And even though she came of her own choice, it's been a trial for Fern."

How could any of this have been a trial for Fern? Reuben was the one who'd been hurt—and by Fern's brother, no less. Fern's coming had given her a break from slopping hogs and shoveling manure. She had a nice place to stay, a steady job, and a tub of peanut-butter-chocolate drops every week. The best part for her was that nobody in Bonduel knew how low on the social ladder she and her family were. In Sugarcreek, she was an underling. In Bonduel, she was just Fern King, likable, smart, and pretty.

"I don't think Fern would consider it a trial."

"Not that she'd show," Dorothy said. "She's too cheerful by half. It's hard to see how bad she's hurting on the inside."

How bad she's hurting? She might feel bad about John and Linda Sue, but Dorothy didn't know anything. Reuben had known Fern for almost her whole life. He knew her better than anyone else in Bonduel. "Fern is fine."

Dorothy flicked her wrist in his direction. "I'll take *gute* care of her. It's the least I can do for all you've done for me. And your *mammi* and *dawdi* are watching out for her too." The lines bunched around her eyes. "But mark my words. You can only neglect the tree so long before it starts to wither."

"I'll remember that," Reuben said, pretending he

knew what she was talking about. He'd rather not see her roll her eyes a third time.

She rolled her eyes anyway. "See that you do something about it." Dorothy tucked her notebook into the bag slung over her shoulder. "I want to make Melvin a cake in honor of Arizona. What do they eat in Arizona?"

"I don't know. Cactus maybe."

Dorothy squinted. "Hmm. Like prickly pear?"

"I don't know. I've never seen a prickly pear before, except in books."

"I have a recipe for a fancy pear tart, but pears aren't in season yet and I don't think it will work with canned pears."

"He'd probably be happy with a nice snitz pie."

Dorothy eyed him as if he had tried to brush his teeth with the broom. Okay, maybe she didn't think so highly of him, even if she'd just called him a genius. "A snitz pie? Reuben Helmuth, what does a snitz pie have to do with Arizona?"

Reuben shrugged. "Nothing, but everybody loves snitz pie."

"I can't risk everything on a snitz pie. I made a pineapple upside-down cake in honor of Hawaii. I've got to think of something to go with Arizona."

"Maybe you could make a blue cake in honor of Kentucky, the bluegrass state."

She thought about it for a second. "I hoped you'd have more to say for yourself, Reuben Helmuth. I'll have to figure this out on my own." She turned her back on him and headed to the food table. Fern greeted her with a delighted smile, and they stood shoulder to shoulder to serve rice.

Reuben shook his head and grinned. He'd never get Dorothy's full approval.

But he wouldn't lose sleep over it.

Johnny Raber had moved from behind Fern to one of the tables stationed in full view of the serving table where he could watch Fern and eat his haystack at the same time. Fern needed to put a stop to this before Johnny's heart was broken beyond repair.

Sadie, Esther, and Serena Hoover strolled into the warehouse and let their eyes adjust to the dimness. Matthew Eicher, Aaron Glick, and three or four other boys followed close behind. Reuben pressed his lips together. As the bishop's daughter, Sadie should have been helping with the haystack supper from the very beginning. And what about the rest of his new group of friends? Maybe the most respected folks in this community didn't help with haystack suppers and such. Maybe they left the work to people who weren't quite so important.

He leaned his broom against the wall. He wanted to be one of the important people. Maybe he shouldn't be sweeping.

Reuben glanced at Fern across the wide space between them. She'd never looked prettier, serving rice, smiling with even the slightest of provocations, greeting people, and radiating the light of *Gotte* on her face. Of course he should be sweeping. Who was he to think he was more important than anybody else? Fern had scolded him for just such thoughts many times.

"I was an hungered and ye gave me meat. Inasmuch as ye have done it unto the least of these my brethren, ye have done it unto me."

Sadie and her friends moved in unison like a flock of sparrows. She saw Reuben and came straight at him. A small part of him was glad he wasn't holding the broom, but another part of him felt an immediate twinge of guilt for being glad.

Sadie had her elbows hooked between Esther and Serena. Esther stared at him with hooded eyes, as if she wasn't sure if she should be friendly because he'd washed her dogs, or unfriendly because she didn't want Sadie to know he'd washed her dogs. Sadie and Esther should probably have a long talk. Reuben wasn't happy about being the secret each of them kept from each other.

"Reuben, we've been looking everywhere for you," Sadie said.

He couldn't help but stand a little taller. Sadie considered him part of her group. "For me?"

"*Jah*," Matthew said. "My *dat* bought a new horse, and we're going to go try her out."

"Did you bring your courting buggy?" Sadie said.

"It's not really mine. It belongs to my *dawdi*."

Aaron nodded. "Felty's horse is fast. We want to race."

"There's a *gute* place on this side of the lake we like to go," Sadie said. "We do buggy races there all the time."

Reuben's heart knocked against his chest. If he could win a buggy race, he'd be better liked than Matthew or Aaron. Sadie would likely fall in love with him on the spot. He smiled so wide, his ears probably slid upward. "Rhubarb is fast. And I just cleaned the buggy."

Sadie looked as if she might float off the ground with excitement. "Then let's go."

Reuben gazed at the crowded tables. "Don't we need to stay until supper's over and help clean up?"

And Fern. His heart sank. He'd told Fern he'd take her home.

Matthew eyed him as if he were an ignorant child. "That's the old folks' job. Don't you want to have some fun?"

His heart sank even further. He shouldn't have said anything about cleaning up. Sadie and her friends obviously felt no need to stay, and his mentioning it only made him look foolish. But what could he do? Fern was counting on him to take her home. He wouldn't let her down a second time. "Of course I want to have some fun. But I'll warn you, Dawdi's horse used to run races. She never lost."

Matthew grinned. "We'll just see about that."

"Come on, then," Esther said. "All your talk is wasting daylight."

"Do you mind if I invite Fern? She'd love to see a buggy race."

Matthew nodded. "As long as she cheers for me."

Reuben didn't miss the look Sadie gave Serena, and his heart scraped the pavement as he realized what it meant. Sadie didn't want Fern to come.

But how could that be? Fern had been the one to invite Sadie to the knitting group. Fern was pretty and smart and unfailingly kind to everyone. What didn't they like about her?

"We might not have enough room for Fern," Serena said.

"She can ride over there with me," Reuben said.

Sadie smiled and batted her long eyelashes. "I sort of wanted to ride with you."

"We can make room," Aaron said. At least the boys seemed willing to include Fern.

The excitement of a race couldn't keep Reuben

from sinking and sinking until he could have seen eye to eye with the ants crawling along the warehouse floor. Sadie didn't want him to bring Fern, that much was obvious, but Fern was his friend and things seemed to always go better when Fern was around. Besides, she'd wind up accidentally engaged to Johnny Raber if Reuben didn't take her home. He fastened on his most charming smile for Sadie. "Fern can ride with Matthew. That leaves me with room for one more."

She didn't react the way he thought she would. She nibbled on her bottom lip and pressed her frown deeper into her face. But whatever her problem with Fern, she didn't say anything, so Reuben figured he had her reluctant agreement.

"I'll go get Fern and meet you outside," he said. "Don't leave without me."

"For sure and certain," Matthew said. "I want a *gute* race. Aaron's horse is as slow as cold tar."

Matthew and the other boys slipped out the door at the back of the warehouse while Sadie stood immovable and waved her friends away. "I'll catch up."

Esther puckered her face into that sour look Reuben had seen many times. "You always think you're so important, Sadie."

Sadie returned Esther's look with a nasty one of her own. "Just go. Reuben and I will be right out." With her palm down, she wiggled her fingers to shoo them away.

Esther's look turned from sour to deadly, but she and Serena obeyed. Sadie watched silently as her friends marched across the warehouse and disappeared out the back door. After they were gone, Sadie grabbed Reuben's broom from its perch against the wall and started sweeping. Sort of.

"Reuben. We need to have a talk." She swiped the broom along the floor in small, halfhearted strokes as if looking busy would make their conversation seem less suspicious. Less suspicious to whom, he couldn't guess.

"Could we talk on the buggy ride over to the lake? I don't know how long they'll wait for us."

"They'll wait, and what I have to say is wonderful important." She paused and pinned him with a serious gaze. "You have a kind heart, Reuben. It's one of the things I like best about you, and I wouldn't want you any other way, but don't you think you've stretched your kindness far enough?"

"What do you mean?"

"You have done more than your duty with Fern. You've been nice to her and have let her tag along when you go places. You drive her everywhere, and Lorene says you buy her treats at the Yutzys' candy shop every week. You've done her a *gute* service, and no one can expect any more from you, especially since her *bruder* stole your girlfriend."

Reuben tensed like a rubber band around a shoe box. "That's not Fern's fault. She's trying to convince me to forgive him."

"*Ach*, believe me, I know the whole story. Lorene has a pen pal in Sugarcreek who says the bishop is none too happy about his daughter marrying the son of a pig farmer." Sadie stopped sweeping altogether as her gaze darted about the warehouse. She lowered her voice. "Lorene's pen pal says that Fern and her family aren't *worthy* of you, Reuben. She says your family is the richest in the district." Sadie leaned closer to whisper. "It wonders me why you were ever friends with Fern's *bruder*."

Because John was the best of friends.

The tension pulled even tighter. Fern and her family were what the Amish called underlings. Of course, such a word was uttered in hushed tones because no one wanted to admit that they treated some of their neighbors with less than Christian charity, and no one wanted to be accused of pride, though pride was at the heart of it. Underling families were never completely accepted by the rest of the community. Their opinions didn't count for much in the church— no matter how upstanding they were—and their children had a difficult time finding someone to marry.

Every muscle in his jaw clenched. Would Sadie reject him because of Fern? It wasn't a very nice thought to have, but he might as well face the truth. He hadn't wanted Fern here in the first place, and if she was holding him back, he should tell her to go home.

The catch in his breath pulled his thoughts up short. If it hadn't been for Fern, he'd be sitting in Dawdi's barn right now wallowing in his pity. If it hadn't been for Fern, he wouldn't have found his smile. If it hadn't been for Fern, he never would have met Sadie, never would have gotten the chance to start rebuilding his reputation.

But did his relationship with Fern put all that at risk?

Something sharp and ragged stabbed at his heart, and he hadn't the courage to look to see what it was.

He cleared his throat. "Fern is . . . Fern is my friend."

"I won't deny that Fern is a nice, pleasant girl, but don't you see?" She took the drastic measure of giving his arm a little tug to move them both farther from the people sitting at the nearest table. "If you want to make a *gute* impression on people here in Bonduel, you don't want them to think that you and Fern are close. She is more Johnny Raber's kind of people. Let her stay with her own kind."

Reuben's thoughts felt like they'd been picked up by the wind and scattered around the countryside. John and his other friends in Sugarcreek had always tried to keep Fern from tagging after them. Even when he had been ten and eleven years old, Reuben hadn't felt good about abandoning her—she had been just a little kid, after all. He'd always watched out for Fern, and it hadn't seemed to hurt his standing in the community, even though the Kings were underlings.

But now, things were different. He'd been humiliated in Sugarcreek, and he stood on shaky ground in Bonduel. Some sacrifices would have to be made. Again, that guilt attacked him as if it were eating him from the inside out. He held his breath until the feeling subsided. "Okay."

"Okay?" Sadie said doubtfully.

"I just need to go tell her I'm leaving."

Sadie pressed her full, rose-petal lips together. "Why?"

"I promised her a ride home."

Sadie had gotten her way. She burst into a smile. "I'll meet you outside."

Reuben took the broom from Sadie and dragged it with him to the serving table. Fern's smile made him feel so low, he could have licked the dirt off the warehouse floor.

"You're doing a *gute* job with the sweeping," she said. "The floor is staying nice and clean."

Dorothy dumped a spoonful of rice onto an *Englischer*'s plate with a flick of her wrist. "Stuff and nonsense. My two-year-old nephew could sweep better than that. Reuben's just pushing the dirt around."

Reuben tapped his knuckle on the table as if he'd made an appointment. "Uh, Fern?"

Fern raised her eyebrows. "*Jah?*"

When it came right down to it, he couldn't look her in the eye. "I'm going out with Sadie and some of the others for a while, but I'll be back to take you home."

He glanced up to see that she'd plastered her smile into place. "*Ach.* Okay. Have fun."

Dorothy gave Reuben a look that could have made a cow dry up. With her sticky spoon still in her hand, she wrapped an arm tightly around Fern's shoulder. The rice stuck to the spoon like glue. "He won't have near as much fun as we will. Vernon Raber has three big sinks and a wall-mounted sprayer in back. We're going to be washing dishes the fancy way."

Fern seemed to be trying to muster enthusiasm for the wall-mounted sprayer. "*Jah.* I'm excited to try it out. I've washed dishes with a hose before but never a sprayer."

Reuben flashed a weak smile. "It would have come in handy with Esther's dogs."

He must have said the wrong thing, because Fern gave up even trying to smile. "*Jah,* Esther's dogs," she said, looking down at her spoon as she prodded it into the rice. "I will see you at *gmay* then."

Gmay? Gmay was over a week away. What was she thinking? He planned on seeing her plenty of times before then, including when he took her home tonight. Sadie need never know how he spent his time when he wasn't at her house painting something. He rested his hands on the table and leaned across the large pan of rice. "I'm coming back to take you home."

She waved her spoon casually in front of her, as if she couldn't care less what he did. A single grain of rice flew off her spoon and landed on Dorothy's shoulder. "Don't worry about it. I don't mind walking."

Dorothy looked horrified at the very thought. "You're not walking. It's almost three miles." The skin on her forehead aligned itself into nice rows as she raised her eyebrows. "I'll ask Melvin to take you home."

"No need," Reuben said, annoyed that Dorothy was trying to take over when he'd already solved the problem. "I will be back in one hour."

Dorothy gave him a significant look. "Maybe you should stay away on purpose. It will give me another chance to talk to Melvin."

"I told Fern I would take her home, and I'm taking her home."

Fern's eyes flashed with something akin to anger. "I'll walk. I don't want to be a burden on anyone."

Reuben scowled. Sadie had put him in an awkward position, which in turn had put him in a bad mood. Couldn't these girls understand the sacrifices he was making for them? "You're not a burden, Fern."

She shoved her spoon into the rice and folded her arms across her chest. "It's plain to see I am."

"Well, I'm taking you home anyway."

Fern seemed to wilt like a poppy in the heat. She sighed and pressed three fingers to her forehead. "*Cum*, Reuben," she said. She motioned for him to step to the side, and she came around the table to meet him. "I know," she said, swallowing hard and studying the ragged shoes on her feet, "I know you feel like you have to watch out for me, but you are getting along so well with Sadie and the others. I'm in the way. I don't want you to sacrifice what you have here because you feel guilty about me."

He wanted to adamantly disagree with her, but

considering that was why he wasn't inviting her to the buggy races, he couldn't say much at all. Could he have felt any lower? Fern didn't want him to feel guilty, but he couldn't feel anything but. Was he doing the right thing? Maybe he should tell Sadie to go without him and stay here and help Fern do dishes. But if he did that, he might never be accepted by Matthew and Sadie and their group. Then he'd be no better off than if he moved back to Sugarcreek. Or Montana.

The lump in his throat nearly choked him. "I don't feel guilty. I'll be back to drive you home."

The light in her eyes was completely extinguished. "Lord willing," she said, as if she didn't really care whether he'd be back or not, as if she just wanted to shut him up and make him go away.

Oh, *sis yuscht*. Girls were so irritating.

It was late. Too late for much hope. The Bonduel roads were deserted. All Reuben could hear was the *clip-clopping* of Rhubarb's hooves on the asphalt and his own labored breathing as his frustration increased with every passing second. He jiggled the reins and tried to relax enough to keep a blood vessel from popping in his neck. No matter how big of a hurry he was in, he couldn't feel good about making Rhubarb go faster. She was plenty tired after running her heart out in two races.

For the tenth time, he pulled his watch out of his pocket and tried to read the face by the sliver of moon overhead. He shouldn't have let Sadie talk him into staying for the bonfire, but many of *die youngie* from the district had been there and Sadie had wanted him to get to know everyone better. It had become obvious as the evening wore on that Sadie had wanted to get to know him better as well. She hadn't left his side as they'd roasted marshmallows and played volleyball on the cold beach.

It didn't matter that Reuben loved volleyball or that Sadie had paid so much attention to him. He hadn't enjoyed himself one little bit. All he did was watch the sky grow darker and darker and hope that Fern had thousands of dishes to wash.

Taking Sadie home had given him a chance to spend some private time with her, but it had also taken him half an hour farther away from the Rabers' house, and the private time had only made him feel worse about everything. Sadie was smart and cheerful and pretty, but she was immature and demanding and had a bit of a mean streak, especially to *die youngie* she thought were below her—the underlings, like Fern. Plain and simple, Sadie Yoder was a snob. Reuben didn't find it a very attractive quality. He needed her to get him into her circle of friends, but he squirmed every time Sadie said something disparaging about someone in the district, as if she were the judge of all things good and acceptable.

How could Fern accuse *him* of being a snob when he didn't behave anything like Sadie Yoder? He sucked in a hard breath. He'd let Sadie talk him into excluding Fern because she wasn't "*gute* enough" and had gone off with his new friends, leaving Fern to do up the dishes. He hadn't even bothered to be back like he said he would.

Now who was the snob?

Self-reproach clamped around his chest like a vise as he squinted harder to read his watch. Surely Fern was still there, washing dishes and visiting with Dorothy.

Surely Johnny Raber had given up hovering over her and gone into the house. Surely Fern would wait for him after he'd assured her that he would return to take her home.

Rhubarb pulled the two-seater buggy beneath a street lamp, and Reuben took a look at his watch. 10:17. His heart thudded so hard he could feel his pulse clear to his teeth. Lord willing, Fern would still be there. She just had to be there.

The warehouses loomed like shadowy square mountains up ahead. There wasn't a flicker of light to be seen anywhere on the property, not around the outbuildings or inside the house. Like as not, they'd all gone to bed. With a low growl, Reuben jumped out of the buggy and tested the warehouse doors just to be sure. They were closed tight.

Somebody might as well have kicked a hole through his chest.

He was going to be sick.

Fern never asked for help, even when she needed it. When she was a young teenager, she had once walked to his house in the snow with bare feet because her sister had needed to borrow her shoes. She had always been so eager to tag along with Reuben and John that she often hid scraped knees or cuts so they wouldn't make her go home for a Band-Aid. Once when they were climbing trees, she scraped her leg on a branch and Reuben only noticed it when he saw blood dripping down her ankle an hour later. And of course there was the time when she nearly drowned because she didn't want the boys to know she had gone out too far.

Reuben felt so ashamed of himself, he almost couldn't breathe. He'd always watched out for Fern, and he'd abandoned her for Sadie Yoder and the chance at popularity.

He pressed his palm against the warehouse door and tried to catch his breath.

But he couldn't just neglect Sadie Yoder either. They had been getting along so well. Because of Sadie, the others, like Matthew and Aaron, had accepted him. The bishop even seemed to approve of him. He couldn't just give that all up, could he?

Besides, it was almost as if Fern hadn't expected him to be back in time to take her home. She had told him he didn't need to worry about her. Maybe she didn't really care.

That made him feel momentarily better. Fern didn't really care that he hadn't been here, and Dorothy would have seen to it that she got home okay. He frowned. Dorothy or Johnny Raber. Fern said she didn't want to get Johnny's hopes up, but she might have accepted a ride home from him if she didn't have another way.

Panic wrapped itself around Reuben's throat as an even worse thought hit him. What if Fern hadn't let Johnny take her home? What if she had decided to walk?

She was just *deerich* and headstrong enough to set out by herself in the dark.

With racing pulse, he jumped into his buggy and snapped the reins. What if she'd fallen into a ditch or gotten herself tangled in a barbed-wire fence? What if she'd been hit by a car?

Peering into the darkness ahead of him, he guided Rhubarb along the route Fern would have most likely taken if she had walked back to the Schmuckers. He squinted into every depression along the side of the road and studied every Fern-sized shadow along the way.

He didn't see her, but that didn't mean he hadn't missed her.

With his nerves pulled tight as a wire, he pulled up to the Schmuckers' house. With the exception of a street lamp standing guard a few dozen feet down the road, it was as dark as the Rabers' place had been. If Fern had made it back safely, she had long since gone to bed. He sat in horrible suspense. Should he assume that Fern had made it home and come back tomorrow?

He shook his head. He couldn't assume anything. If Fern was in trouble, he had to help her, even if it meant waking up the whole neighborhood. Why was she so prone to put herself at risk? If she were any other girl, he could have felt sure that she would have found a ride home.

Reuben secured the reins and stepped down from the buggy. Fern had said something about noise giving Barbara Schmucker a headache. He'd have to risk it. He wouldn't get a wink of sleep until he knew Fern was safe, and it would go a long way toward assuaging his guilty conscience.

He'd gone about halfway across their weedy yard when he encountered a clothesline that nearly took his head off. He ducked just in time, and his arm brushed against a damp piece of clothing hanging there.

Thank the *gute* Lord for that street lamp. It gave him barely enough light to see by. Crumpling the fabric in his fist, he held it close to his face. If the dark wasn't playing games with his vision, it was a light blue apron. It was damp, which meant someone had worn it recently. This had to be the one Fern had been wearing at the haystack supper, which meant that she'd made it home safely.

Reuben was relieved enough to think about maybe thanking Johnny Raber for taking Fern home—*if* he had taken her home. It was better than imagining she'd walked all the way by herself in the dark—but just barely. Fern was too smart to accidentally fall in love with Johnny Raber out of gratitude, wasn't she?

Reuben let out a breath he'd been holding for what seemed like an hour. Fern was okay, and tonight, that was all that mattered—Johnny Raber or no Johnny Raber.

With a smile playing at his lips, he fished around in his pocket and pulled out a four-inch strand of pink yarn he'd stuffed in there during knitting lessons. He tied it around one of the apron strings. Lord willing, Fern would notice it and know he'd been here. He had meant to drive her home. That had to count for something.

Everything would be right as rain soon enough. He still felt bad for leaving her to fend for herself, but he'd make it up to her, and he didn't even need to wonder if Fern would forgive him. She always did.

Thank the *gute* Lord for that.

Chapter Eighteen

If Fern didn't have to be so careful with her shoes, she would have given her bike a swift kick and thrown it into the ditch. She'd gotten off the bus after a long Saturday at work and hadn't ridden her bike ten feet down the road when one of the pedals had fallen off and the tire had exploded and flattened like a pancake. She threw back her head and growled to the sky. *Gotte* must be trying to tell her something, though what He wanted to communicate was a mystery.

She tried to set the kickstand, and the bike tumbled to the ground. She didn't even care anymore. There wasn't much more damage she could do to the thing. Having last seen her pedal bouncing toward the underbrush along the side of the road, she tiptoed gingerly into the weeds to avoid puncturing her shoe with a sticker or a sharp rock. The escaped pedal sat innocently among a flock of purple wildflowers. She picked it up and tossed it into the basket on the front of the bicycle. Maybe she could convince Reuben to put it back on for her.

A shard of glass stabbed into her heart. She wasn't

going to ask Reuben to do anything for her ever again. He had his life, and she had hers.

It was a mistake to think of Reuben at a time like this. She'd been forcing him from her thoughts all day. Tonight, she needed all her energy to walk this rusty old bike home. It was nearing sunset already, and if she didn't hurry, she'd be forced to walk home in the dark for a second night in a row. She truly regretted buying that three-dollar lock for her bike. Someone would be doing her a favor if they stole it.

And three dollars bought a lot of French fries at McDonald's.

She reached down, grabbed the handlebars, and pulled her bike to standing. The handlebar caught on her dress and ripped a small hole in the hem. She gasped at the sheer injustice of it all. Three dollars wasted on a bike lock when she could have bought a spool of thread and maybe even a needle.

Her eyes stung with tears. *Oy*, anyhow, she felt sorry for herself.

At home, Mamm would never have let Fern wallow in self-pity. Wallowing was for the hogs, she always said. But Mamm wasn't here, and Fern had two miles to walk before she got home, where nothing waited to greet her but an empty lunch box and two bottles of water. She had two miles to wallow all she wanted to, and no one would be the wiser.

She quit fighting it and indulged all the tears she'd been saving up.

The bike squeaked in about seven different places as she pushed it along the side of the deserted road. It sounded as if it were crying with her. The noise was oddly comforting, as if the bike, at least, had an idea of what she must be going through. It had started squeaking again about a week ago, and Reuben hadn't noticed that it needed oiling. Reuben hadn't noticed much of anything lately, except for Sadie Yoder and her lovely yellow hair.

A quiet sob escaped Fern's lips. She'd never been a loud crier, and she didn't intend to start now, no matter how violently her heart was breaking.

Okay then. Reuben would never pry the truth out of her, but she was honest enough to admit it to herself. She loved Reuben Helmuth. She had loved him deep down even when she had pretended not to. Since she had been six years old, she had never stopped loving him, even when he and Linda Sue had practically been engaged.

To a six-year-old girl who had never gotten much attention from anybody, Reuben was her protector, her guardian angel, and even at that young age, she had loved him for it. She had loved him the first time he took her hand and escorted her around the ice, even though he surely had better things to do than babysit John's pesky little sister. Part of the reason Fern had tagged after John and his friends so persistently was because she loved nobody better in the whole world than Reuben Helmuth, even though he was four years older and even though she knew she wasn't good enough for him.

Reuben had always possessed that rare combination of kindness and confidence that endeared him to everybody. He'd cheerfully put Band-Aids on her skinned knees, taught her how to skate and throw a softball. He'd saved her from drowning and paid for fabric so she could have a new dress for her sister's wedding. Before they'd come to Bonduel, he had never treated Fern as a bother or a nuisance. Unfortunately, he'd been so considerate and patient that he'd made himself downright irresistible.

When Reuben had started *rumschpringe* at age sixteen, Fern had cried herself to sleep, knowing it was only a matter of time before he forgot all about her and fell madly in love with someone—someone who was not a pig farmer's daughter. Someone who didn't have red hair and splatters of freckles all over her nose.

When he had started dating Linda Sue, Fern very nearly talked herself out of loving him. Her friend Katie had told her it wasn't sensible to pine over an impossible dream, and Fern had made up her mind to quit being foolish. It was a *gute* thing that Reuben was stuck-up and rich. She found it easier to pretend to be indifferent when she focused on his flaws.

She'd done an admirable job of remaining indifferent until he had yelled at the knitting group. How could she not love someone who needed her so desperately?

She shouldn't have come to Bonduel. She shouldn't have let herself have even a glimmer of hope. She shouldn't have let her emotions overrule her common sense. She had a very full basket of "shouldn't haves," but it didn't change the truth that she loved Reuben Helmuth like crazy, even crazier than Barbara Schmucker was.

She loved him even though he had never loved her. Even though he hadn't wanted her to come to Bonduel. Even though he was proud and self-centered and more concerned about pleasing Sadie Yoder than about telling the truth.

She had a whole plate of "even thoughs." If only she could eat "should haves" and "even thoughs," her stomach wouldn't feel as empty as a dry well.

So what if Reuben had made his way to the Schmuckers' house eventually last night? The pink yarn tied to her apron was proof that he'd at least cared enough to stop by, but that didn't make up for lying about taking her home or saying he'd be back in an hour. She'd been so upset that she'd refused rides from Dorothy, Johnny Raber, and even Anna and Felty. Anna had been beside herself that Reuben wasn't there to take Fern home, but Fern had pretended that she didn't care. Anna might have even been convinced.

But now her shoe had a hole in it and her bike was broken, and she didn't even have enough money for a candy bar. Her stomach growled just thinking about it. She'd trade her shoes and the bike for a Big Mac right now. She let go of one handlebar and pressed her palm against her belly button. Soon she'd be able to touch her backbone.

She made the mistake of smoothing her hand down the front of her apron and heard the stiff paper envelope crackle in her pocket. In the midst of her bike and boy troubles, she had almost forgotten about the letter, even though it weighed her down like a bag of stones. She gazed down at her pocket, and a tear dripped off her nose. *Gute.* She needed to wallow good and hard.

Two weeks ago, she'd sent a letter to her parents with two hundred dollars cash stuffed inside. The letter had never made it to Sugarcreek—no doubt stolen somewhere along the way or lost in the mail. She knew it was risky to send cash in the post, but she couldn't afford to open a checking account, let alone pay for checks, so she thought she could get away with sending cash as long as she prayed real hard over it first.

It hadn't worked.

She slid her hand into her pocket and wrapped her fingers around Dat's letter. She could practically hear him yelling all the way from Sugarcreek. Two hundred dollars lost due to her carelessness. Her parents needed that money to buy feed. She could have used that money to feed herself. Now, she'd have to send every last penny to Mamm and Dat in a money order. She couldn't very well afford a money order either, but it was better than losing everything.

She'd gotten herself into a pickle for sure and certain.

Oh, *sis yuscht*. She stopped so fast, a cloud of dust rose up in front of her. Reuben's buggy—or rather Felty Helmuth's buggy—was parked on the road right in front of Barbara Schmucker's fancy white mailbox with the ivy twining up the post. Her heart pumped so hard, it was like to break her ribs.

What was he doing here? Was he sitting in Barbara Schmucker's parlor having a cup of *kaffee*? Had he wandered back to the barn and discovered her sleeping quarters?

She exhaled a very long breath when Reuben appeared from behind one of the oak trees at the front of the Schmuckers' yard, eyeing her tentatively with his hands stuffed in his pockets. He didn't know the Schmuckers. Maybe he hadn't wanted to disturb them and so hadn't knocked on their door. She could only hope.

She must have looked a sight. Her apron was smudged with dirt, her face couldn't have been much cleaner, and her hair was likely sticking out in all directions from the scarf she'd tied on this morning to keep it in place.

She quickly swiped the tears from her eyes. She shouldn't have indulged in the wallowing. Wallowing always got her into trouble.

The second Reuben realized her predicament with the bike, he frowned and jogged down the road to meet her. Fern held her breath. Reuben Helmuth was surely the most handsome boy she had ever and would ever lay eyes on. It was pure truth, and she was sensible enough to be honest with herself, even though she'd never be good enough for him.

"Fern," he said, gifting her with a bright smile before turning his gaze to her hopeless bike. He got down on one knee and ran his hand halfway around the flat tire. "You're going to need a new tube."

"*Jah.* I figured." She tried her best to smile, partly to mask the fact that she'd been crying but mostly because she didn't have the heart to give Reuben the cold shoulder. Sadie and Esther, Matthew Eicher and Serena were the very friends Fern wanted for Reuben. Being admired and well-liked made Reuben happy, and more than anything, Fern wanted him to be happy. Her broken heart—which was entirely her own fault—meant less than a gnat splattered against a windshield.

"You lost a pedal."

She pointed to her basket. "It's in there."

He stood, retrieved the broken pedal, and turned it over in his hand. "I'll need a few tools to fix this. You didn't happen to save the bolt?"

The bolt was somewhere between here and the bus stop. "It's gone."

"We can find one to fit." He studied her face as if he

were afraid of what he might find there. "You've been crying."

"You'd cry too if your pedal fell off and your tire exploded. It's two miles from the bus stop." She wasn't about to tell him the real reason for her tears.

His smile slid off his face, and he looked as if he'd never be happy again. "Fern, I'm wonderful sorry about last night. When I got back to the Rabers' house, you were already gone. I came here to be sure you'd made it home safe. Did you see the yarn?"

She couldn't muster more than a poor excuse for a smile, and she couldn't meet his gaze. "*Jah.* I saw it. *Denki* for being concerned."

"I wanted to come over this morning and apologize as soon as possible." He tilted his head in an attempt to get her to look him in the eye. "But I didn't want to make you late for your job at the stables shoeing horses."

Her lips twitched upward. "Nice try, but I'm not going to tell you where I work. It's none of your business."

"Oh, don't you worry. I'll find out soon enough, Fernly." When she didn't react to his teasing, he huffed out a frustrated breath. "Fern. Will you . . . will you please look at me?"

Reluctantly, she lifted her gaze to his face, trying very hard to look excessively cheerful and carefree even though she really wanted to bawl her eyes out.

His frown sank deeper into his face. "Fern, I'm wonderful sorry about last night. I should have been there to take you home yet. I said I would, and I let you down."

"I told you last night that I wouldn't need a ride home. It wasn't important. You don't have to apologize. I was fine."

Some stormy emotion traveled across his face. "Did Johnny take you home?"

"Of course not. Johnny is a sweet boy. I would never want to give him the wrong idea about how I feel. You gave me that advice."

He seemed to want to smile and scowl at the same time. He settled for pressing his lips into a rigid line. "And it was *gute* advice. But you had to ride home with somebody. Dorothy?"

"*Nae*. She rode home with Melvin."

He raised his eyebrows. "How did she manage that?"

"She asked Melvin if he could drive me home, and when I said I didn't need a ride, Melvin offered to take her home. They were talking about license plates as they drove down the driveway."

Reuben shook his head. "Melvin is becoming downright sociable."

"Who would have thought license plates could bring two people together like that?"

Narrowing his eyes, Reuben folded his arms across his chest. "Please don't tell me you walked home."

"Okay. I won't tell you."

He looked so ferociously irritated, it wouldn't have surprised Fern if he'd started growling like a bear. Why was he so mad? If he hadn't wanted her to walk, he should have been there to drive her home.

She bit back something bitter she was tempted to say. She had no right to expect anything of him. This was what she wanted. If Reuben was happy, she was happy. Although right now, he didn't look very happy.

"Why didn't you ask my grandparents? They came, didn't they?"

"Anna and Felty offered to take me home, but I

couldn't let them. The Schmuckers' house is so far out of their way."

"*Nae* it isn't."

Anna had been quite concerned about leaving Fern at the warehouse, but Fern had assured her she'd find a way home. She hadn't told Anna that the way home was her own two feet. Anna wasn't at all happy that Reuben had disappeared, and she kept shaking her head and saying, "That boy," as if Reuben were an incorrigible sixth grader. Reuben would have to double down on his knitting lessons or his *mammi* might never smile at him again.

Reuben was still scowling at her. *Ach, du lieva.* Why did he care so much that she had walked home? "Your *mammi* invited me for dinner tomorrow."

The line between Reuben's brows smoothed out. "*Gute.* She's making olive loaf. It's one of my favorites."

Fern swallowed her misgivings. The food didn't matter. It was an invitation to go and eat someone else's food, and Anna's cooking was better than nothing. She made all her recipes with love, and Fern would be ungrateful to turn up her nose. She was so hungry, she'd eat a bowl of sawdust if it had chocolate sauce drizzled over the top.

Reuben stared at her with a serious look on his face, then reached out and smoothed a piece of hair from her cheek. She clenched her teeth to keep a shiver from traveling down her spine. "Fern, I'm sorry you had to walk home last night. You shouldn't walk home in the dark."

"I was fine."

He shook his head. "I'm not blaming you, though it sounds like it. I wasn't there to take you home. Will you forgive me?"

She forced a wide smile onto her lips. If Reuben was

happy . . . "There is nothing to forgive, but I'll forgive you if you quit pestering me."

He nodded and twitched his lips doubtfully. "Am I a snob?"

Okay. She appreciated the change of subject, no matter how abrupt. "Why ask me? You already know what I think."

"You think I'm proud."

She didn't have to try so hard for a smile now. This was a conversation they'd had many times. She liked teasing him, and he usually didn't mind the teasing. "And a snob."

He groaned. "A snob like Sadie Yoder?"

Fern took a step backward. He wouldn't paint her into a corner no matter how much practice he'd had at painting lately. She refused to say a word against Sadie. "You think you're better than everybody, but at least you're nice about it."

"That doesn't make me feel better."

"It's not supposed to. It's supposed to make you uncomfortable."

"Then it's working," he said. "I'm sorry for being a snob."

"You can't help it."

"I should have invited you to come with us last night."

"It was better that you didn't," Fern said. "I would have hurt your chances with Sadie and her friends. Nobody wants an annoying little sister tagging along."

She could tell he wanted to argue, but he kept his mouth shut because she was right. Sadie liked Reuben. She wouldn't have been happy about Fern coming along.

Reuben kicked at the gravel at his feet. "I want to be accepted here. I want Sadie and the others to like me."

"How could they not? You're handsome and fun and rich. Everything a girl could want in a boy." She gave his arm a sisterly pat. "They have welcomed you with open arms, Reuben. I can tell. You can be very happy here, even if I'd rather you come back to Sugarcreek and be happy there. I know John and Linda Sue hurt you, but maybe in time you'll learn to look past it."

He shrugged and shifted his feet. "I suppose it doesn't hurt so bad anymore."

She eyed him suspiciously. Was he telling the truth? That was more than he'd ever admitted to her before.

"But it feels strange to go back," he said. "I can buy a piece of land, do some farming, and manage my down line from here."

She couldn't keep the hurt from her voice. She'd been expecting this, but it still ached in the pit of her stomach. "What about the people in Sugarcreek who love you? Your parents, your siblings, your friends. Don't their feelings count for anything?"

"They've gotten along fine without me for almost five months."

Fern felt her face get warm. "How could you possibly know that? How can you know what other people are thinking? Don't you even care?"

She wanted to take him by the shoulders and shake some sense into him. Things were coming along well for him in Bonduel, but there were a lot of people in Sugarcreek who needed him desperately. Was he so blind that he couldn't even see it?

Her head started spinning. If Reuben didn't know how badly his family in Sugarcreek needed him, then he truly was a selfish, proud, stupid boy.

Reuben's voice sounded fuzzy. "Fern? Are you all right? Fern?"

His strong arms shot out to grab her as everything went black.

Had she fainted? Her head spun in several different directions like a yard full of pinwheels. Was she still standing or had she fallen over?

"Stay still, *heartzly*." Reuben's low voice sounded like a caress against her skin.

Yep. She had fainted, and she was still unconscious. Reuben would only have called her *heartzly* in her dreams.

Groaning softly, she lifted her hand to her forehead and opened her eyes. Reuben's face was mere inches from hers, and he didn't seem inclined to pull away. His expression was saturated with concern as he tightened his arms around her. She sat on the ground while Reuben knelt beside her, keeping her upright with his firm embrace.

"Did I faint?"

"About fifteen seconds ago. Hush. Don't try to talk."

The last thing she needed in her already frazzled state was to be this close to Reuben Helmuth, who smelled so *gute*, it should probably be against the *Ordnung*. She tried to push away from him so she could stand up, but he only pulled her closer. If she didn't give up the struggle, he'd persist in drawing her dangerously close to his heart.

"You'll fall over if you try to stand just yet. I'd rather not see you hit your head."

She slid her hand across her forehead and willed her head to stop doing somersaults. "*Ach.* I've never fainted before."

"Shh. Take some deep breaths. I wish I had some peppermint oil handy."

She let herself relax against him. Lord willing, Sadie wouldn't happen by this way and see Fern King in her boyfriend's arms. "This isn't proper."

He didn't jump up and away from her like she half expected him to. He didn't even flinch. "Are you sick?"

She shook her head, which made the spinning start all over again. Another small groan escaped her lips.

His warm fingers set her skin on fire as he brushed away another errant lock of hair. "You've been working too hard, Fernly."

"I didn't have time to eat lunch today." Or money. She hadn't had money for breakfast either, but he didn't need to know that. "The walk home made me a little light-headed yet."

His breath tickled her ear. "Don't skip lunch anymore. I can feel all your ribs. You should eat. Why haven't you been eating?"

She closed her eyes and let her hand fall to her side. "You told me not to try to talk."

He gave her a good-natured growl. "You're not eating enough, and you're working too hard on that sheetrock business."

She giggled and shifted her weight so she could sit up. He relaxed his hold on her. "It takes long, hard hours to make a business successful."

He chuckled before pinning her with an anxious look. "Are you dizzy?"

"Not anymore."

"You need something to eat."

She nodded. "I'll make sure to eat something as soon as I can." That wasn't a lie. She might have a few leftover peanut-butter-chocolate drops she could suck on until dinner tomorrow at Anna and Felty's.

He rolled his eyes. "That's not good enough. I'm taking you to McDonald's for a Big Mac and a large fry. Two Big Macs if you're nice."

Fern's heart all but melted. Reuben might be a snob, but he always remembered how much she liked Big Macs. It was one of the reasons she loved him. She clamped her eyes shut and refused to cry. She was a gnat. Nobody cared about a gnat's feelings.

"Can you stand?"

"I think so."

Reuben took her elbow and helped her to her feet. Holding on to his arms, she took three deep breaths and tested out her knees. He didn't let go as he led her to his buggy and made sure she settled securely in her seat. He grinned like a cat as he took a chunky green crocheted afghan from the floor of the buggy. "My *mammi* made this and told me to keep it in my buggy just in case," he said, spreading it over her lap and tucking it around her legs. "It's not all that cold out here, but you just fainted, so I'm not taking any chances."

He kept one eye trained on her as he climbed into the buggy and picked up the reins. "To McDonald's we go," he said as he prodded the horse to a trot.

Fern's stomach growled in enthusiastic approval. She hoped Reuben planned on paying, because if not, she'd have to settle for a glass of water and some ketchup packets. Her stomach would not be happy.

Chapter Nineteen

Once they finished brushing the horse, they'd have to brush Fern, or take a hose to her. Her brown dress was covered in horse hair. Esther's dogs had stunk to high heaven, and her poor horse hadn't been brushed for a very long time.

Fern worked on brushing one side of Fluffy, the big black horse, and Reuben worked on the other. Fluffy stood perfectly still, occasionally neighing her approval as Reuben and Fern brushed her from head to toe. It was a *gute* thing Reuben had brought two dandy brushes, because Esther didn't have any. Someone needed to have a talk with Esther's *fater* about taking better care of his animals. Reuben would ask Dawdi to do it. He had a real heart for the animals, and he was *gute* at hard conversations like that.

Esther sat on the high, narrow ledge between the stalls, content to let Reuben and Fern work while she chomped on a piece of bubble gum, occasionally blowing huge bubbles to pass the time. Reuben was starting to wonder if earning Esther's forgiveness was worth the trouble. He'd washed all three of her dogs—two with Fern's help—mucked out Esther's small barn, milked her cow twice, and repaired her buggy. There was no end in sight to the chores. For sure and certain, Esther would have him coming back every week for forever if she thought she could get away with it.

Every time he left Esther's house, she warned him that he'd better come back and do more work if he wanted to receive her forgiveness.

He felt bad about losing his temper at the knitting group, but the way he figured it, he'd made amends several days ago. Esther was just using him to get out of her own chores. He wanted to help her out, he really did, but his sense of fairness told him he'd done his part.

Still, if he kept Esther happy, she would in turn put in a good word for him with Sadie. He needed Sadie's approval if he wanted to make a name for himself in Bonduel. He'd have to keep coming around to Esther's until he'd secured his place as an important person in the community. Then the servitude would cease.

He hoped it didn't take too long.

"You missed a spot," Esther said. "You've got to brush all the way down."

Fern leaned her head to the side and peeked at Reuben from behind Fluffy's neck. Her smile seemed a little sad, but it still lit up the dim barn like a brilliant sunset. Reuben's heart did a flip. He almost looked forward to working at Esther's when Fern came with him. She carried her own sunshine with her, even on cloudy days.

He studied her face until she stepped back and resumed brushing her side of Esther's horse. Something had been different about Fern ever since that Sunday after *gmay* when he had let her walk home by herself in the rain. It felt almost as if she was in mourning even though nobody had died. She was wonderful *gute* to everyone and almost as cheerful, but her brown eyes held a look of sadness that Reuben wasn't quite sure how to get rid of.

He couldn't shake the feeling that he was responsible for that look, but he didn't know what he might have done. *Ach, vell,* that wasn't entirely true. He could think of a lot of things he'd done lately that he shouldn't have, but Fern had never held his mistakes against him. She was the most forgiving soul he knew, and among the Amish, that was saying something. And she had been willing to come to Esther's today to help brush the horse that had probably never been groomed in its life.

Reuben knew he was risking Esther's displeasure, but he just had to say something. "Esther, how often do you brush Fluffy?"

"I never brush her. I get too close to horse hair, and I sneeze something wonderful. That's why I'm having you do it. My *dat* was getting impatient for it to be done."

He clenched his teeth and determined to keep his temper. "Esther, your horse needs to be brushed every day. She could get all sorts of diseases without proper care."

Esther shrugged. "We've had her for three years, and she's never took sick a day in her life."

He swallowed a heavy sigh. "Then I guess *Gotte* has been looking out for her." Dawdi would have to talk to Esther's *dat*. Reuben would not get far with Esther.

"She's a wonderful-pretty horse under all this hair,"

Fern said from the other side of Fluffy. She sneezed twice in succession.

Reuben stood on his tiptoes to look over Fluffy's back. "You okay?"

Fern dabbed at her nose with her forearm. "Right as rain. I just had a little tickle."

Esther stiffened. "Shh. Quiet."

Reuben froze. He heard a horse and buggy drawing up outside Esther's house.

"Who is that?" Esther asked, as if Reuben or Fern must know who had just ridden into her yard.

Reuben shrugged. "You expecting someone?"

"Of course not," Esther hissed. She let herself down from the stall door and peeked out the small window. Gasping like a leaky bicycle tire, she ducked beneath the window, got down on her hands and knees, and motioned wildly for Fern and Reuben to do the same. Reuben stayed on his feet. He was standing in the stall. No one could see him from the window. Fern, with raised eyebrows and a quirky grin on her lips, retreated to the safety of the wall behind Reuben and pressed her back against it.

Reuben winked at Fern. "Is it the police?"

"Don't be ridiculous," Esther scolded, whispering loudly enough that Reuben's deaf uncle could have heard her. "It's Sadie. She doesn't know you've been coming around to court me."

Reuben's lungs seized up as if Fluffy had sat on his chest. Did Esther say "court"?

Maybe he'd heard her wrong.

Fern's mouth dropped open, and her eyes were as round as saucers. She clapped her hand over her mouth, but whether it was to stop a horrified laugh or a terrified scream, Reuben couldn't begin to guess.

Okay, it was plain from Fern's reaction that he hadn't heard Esther wrong. She'd said "court," and something told him that was exactly what she had meant.

He was in big trouble.

Esther cracked open the door as if she were planning on sliding out like a pancake. "Stay here, and don't make a sound. I'll get rid of her." She squeezed out the door and slammed it behind her.

Fern looked dazed and confused and slightly uneasy, as if she'd just woken up from a dead faint. "Oh, *sis yuscht.*"

Reuben returned her dazed look with a horrified one of his own.

"You're . . . you're not courting Esther, are you?"

He coughed as if her question had choked him. "How can you even ask that?"

She let out a sigh, which sounded a great deal like relief, grinned, shushed him loudly, and tiptoed so close he could smell her clean scent. "You're supposed to be quiet," she whispered. "And why does Esther think you're courting her?"

"A wild imagination?"

Fern giggled softly. "You're handsome, nice, and a very *gute* dog washer. It's probably wishful thinking."

"You forgot *proud,*" he said, flashing her a self-deprecating smile.

"*Jah.* Everything a girl could want." Fern twirled her finger around a lock of hair that had escaped from beneath her scarf, then tucked it behind her ear.

Reuben clenched his fists. "Quit doing that."

"Doing what?" she whispered back.

"That thing you do when you smooth your hair behind your ears. It drives me crazy."

"Why?"

"We can't afford to be distracted right now. We've got to figure out a way to break the news to Esther that I'm not courting her and that her horse needs to be brushed more than once a decade."

"I think you're just going to have to come right out and tell her," Fern said.

Her face was within inches of his, and he couldn't think of anything else but that her skin looked as pale and smooth as vanilla bean ice cream. "Tell her what?" he mumbled.

"Tell her that you're not courting her." She crinkled her nose. "Unless you want to court her, then I suppose you don't have to tell her anything."

"Of course I don't want to court her, but if she gets mad at me, she might convince Sadie and the others to leave me out of things."

Fern looked away as if she had something very important to see on the far wall. "Like buggy racing."

He shouldn't have said that. Every time he thought of the buggy races, it felt like a sliver stuck in his heart. There was no telling how the memory affected Fern. "You're right. Esther might be angry, but I can't let her go on anticipating a wedding."

"It would be terrible if she did."

"How long do you think we'll have to hide in here?" Reuben said, after a long minute of just staring at Fern while she stared at the far wall.

"Did they go in the house? We could sneak out while they're in there."

Reuben chuckled. "I don't know why we're being so

secretive. Sadie will be suspicious the minute she sees Dawdi's buggy. Esther would have to be very clever to explain the buggy."

Fern smiled. "You're right. It's only a matter of time."

Reuben started brushing Fluffy's hind end. "If we're stuck in here for a while, we might as well make the most of it."

"*Jah*," Fern said. "If Esther chases you off or Sadie invites you to a picnic, we ought to finish with Fluffy first." She disappeared around the other side of the horse and sneezed again. "Esther could stuff a small pillow with all the horse hair we've collected."

"Don't suggest it to her."

They heard two very loud voices just as the door swung open, and Sadie marched into the barn as if she was on the attack. The door made a wonderful racket as it slammed against the back wall. Sadie obviously meant business.

"Reuben? What are you doing here?" she snapped, as if he'd been caught sneaking around a bank after hours. Her nostrils flared, and her face was about three different shades of bright pink.

He didn't quite know how to explain himself without making Sadie madder than she already was. So he opted for the simplest answer. "I'm brushing Esther's horse."

She narrowed her eyes. "Why are you brushing Esther's horse? And why didn't you tell me you were coming over?"

The answer he wanted to give was that it was none of Sadie's business how he spent his time, but he'd rather not see her turn purple. He stepped away from

Fluffy and toward Sadie. "I've been working to make amends for breaking up the knitting group."

Sadie eyed Esther with disgust. "That was almost three weeks ago. What do you think you're doing?"

Esther stuck out her bottom lip in a very impressive pout. "Reuben hurt my feelings wonderful hard. It's going to take a lot of time to see clear to forgive him yet."

Frowning mightily, Sadie folded her arms across her chest and tilted her head to one side. "You expect me to believe that? Why didn't you tell me Reuben has been coming over here?"

"I didn't want a lecture about forgiveness," Esther said, lifting her chin so high, it nearly pointed to the ceiling.

Sadie turned on Reuben like an angry cat. "Why didn't you tell me?"

Reuben's heart sank. For sure and certain, she'd think twice about inviting him to the next buggy race. "Esther asked me to keep it a secret. I took it as part of my punishment."

That explanation didn't seem good enough for Sadie. "I don't care what Esther asked. You should never keep secrets from your girlfriend."

Esther drew in a breath as if she were trying to suck in all the water in Lake Michigan. "You're not his girlfriend. I'm his girlfriend."

Ach, du lieva! Reuben's tongue stuck to the roof of his mouth. Was this really happening? How could he go from having no fiancée one minute to having two girlfriends the next?

He glanced behind him at Fern. She'd turned

deathly pale, her lips pressed together and eyes round with apprehension.

Sadie's eyes grew wider than Fern's, and she huffed and puffed at Esther like the big, bad wolf. "You are not Reuben's girlfriend. He's been to my house several times. Dat invited him to dinner, and he's played Scrabble with my family. My *dat* has already given his approval."

Reuben thought he might throw up. What exactly had Sadie's *dat* given his approval for?

Esther stepped forward until she was nearly touching noses with Sadie. "He's washed my three dogs and brushed my horse and fixed my buggy."

"Only because he feels obligated," Sadie said.

Esther grunted her indignation. "He ate a whole pint jar of my famous pickled red beets."

Well, not exactly. He'd given them to Fern, and Fern had eaten them.

Reuben could practically see the smoke coming out of Sadie's ears. "Oh, really? You told me you hated Reuben and that you hoped he went back to Sugarcreek."

"That was before I changed my mind," Esther said. "Reuben loves me. He works our farm like Jacob in the Bible worked for Rachel."

There was no way Reuben would keep coming to Esther's for seven years. He took a few steps back and moved next to Fern. Maybe they'd keep on fighting and forget he was in the barn. He couldn't begin to untangle the knot Esther and Sadie had tied.

Sadie's look could have made Dawdi's beard fall off. "Why don't we just ask Reuben about that?"

Both girls turned in his direction and glared at him. He swallowed hard. So much for the plan of sneaking out when they weren't paying attention. He hoped Fern had some ideas, because he couldn't begin to know how to make both girls happy.

"Reuben," Sadie said.

He half considered bolting for the door before she could say another word. It would be better for him if they just kept guessing. Forever.

"Tell Esther who your girlfriend is," Sadie said, arching an eyebrow and pasting a smug smile on her face. Of course she was confident. She was good-natured, pretty, and the bishop's daughter. She had to know that she was more appealing than Esther. She also knew how much time Reuben had been spending at her house. Had he made a horrible mistake?

His mind raced for a solution to this mess. He needed Sadie's friendship in order to be truly accepted in Bonduel, but he couldn't pretend she was his girlfriend when she wasn't. Sadie had her *gute* qualities—even Esther had some *gute* qualities, though he couldn't think of any at the moment—but Sadie was also snobby, self-centered, and mean-spirited. There was a chance she'd grow out of that, but he didn't want to wait to find out.

Surely Fern would help him out of this. She was a girl. She knew how girls' minds worked. He glanced at her, hoping she'd take the hint and say something sensible that would make everything all better.

Fern stood like a stone with her arms braced around her waist, her lips clamped so tightly together, he'd need a crowbar to pry them open. He couldn't begin to guess what she was thinking, but he had a sinking feeling that she would be no help at all. The only thing Reuben was sure of was that he couldn't lie to Sadie or Esther, and he certainly couldn't lead them on, no matter the consequences. Linda Sue had lied to him, and Reuben would at least be honest about his feelings.

He swallowed hard again, which did nothing to stop him from stuttering. "I . . . I . . . I'm sorry, but can't the three"—he motioned to Fern—"four of us just be friends?"

"Friends?" Esther said, scrunching her lips as if he'd just asked her to eat horse manure.

Sadie looked no less horrified, except that her eyes pooled with tears. "What do you mean, *friends*?"

Fern didn't fail him after all. "I think what Reuben is trying to say is that he doesn't want to have to limit his circle of friends by singling out just one girl."

That wasn't what he was trying to say at all, but it would do for now.

Sadie slapped a tear off her cheek. "I don't see how you have anything to say about it, Fern. You want Reuben for yourself."

Reuben stepped forward before Sadie started gnashing her teeth. "Now, Sadie. That's not true. Fern just wants to be my friend too."

"Friendship with her isn't going to get you anywhere," Sadie said, as the tears streaked down her face.

Reuben frowned. His friendship with Fern was the only thing that had kept him afloat in Bonduel. "Sadie, I know you're angry—"

"Angry?" she sobbed. "I'm not angry. I'm hurt. All this time, all that painting. I thought you liked me."

"I thought you liked me," Esther said. "You borrowed my blanket."

Reuben stepped between Sadie and Esther and awkwardly patted them both on the shoulder. "I do like you. We've been getting along wonderful well."

Sadie mopped up her face with the hem of her apron. "You've flirted with me for weeks. Everybody thinks you're my boyfriend. Everybody."

"I never did," Esther said, folding her arms and refusing to look at either of them.

"I won't be friends with you," Sadie said. "I'm either your girlfriend or nothing."

All the hard work he'd done over more than a month was about to crumble, but he couldn't lead Sadie on the way Linda Sue had led him on. And there was no chance that things with Sadie would get better. He couldn't overlook the kind of person she was deep down. He couldn't excuse the way she treated people like Fern. He could only hope that she'd still accept him into her group. But by the way she looked at him, acceptance didn't seem likely.

He pushed up his hat and scratched his head. "Please, Sadie. Don't be like that. I don't want to go steady, but that doesn't mean we can't be friends."

The leaky dam Sadie had been trying to hold back suddenly broke. She cried as if her heart were breaking. "You told me you might stay in Bonduel. I beat you at Scrabble, and you helped my *dat* milk cows. You made me believe you wanted to marry me."

He hated to tell her that he had let her win at Scrabble. That girl couldn't have won a game of Scrabble if she was playing against herself. Reuben didn't know what else to do but that awkward patting thing again. "I . . . I'm sorry, Sadie. I was trying to be friendly."

Sadie sniffed back her tears. "You're such a liar, and I'm done shedding one more tear over you. It serves you right." She turned up her nose at him and strutted out of the barn.

"What about me?" Esther said. "I'll still be your girl-friend."

Reuben would have laughed if the whole thing hadn't been so absurd. Poor Esther. "I just want to be friends with you too."

She seemed to chew on his words for a second. "I still expect you to come every week and clean something."

"Esther," Sadie yelled from outside, "we are never speaking to Reuben Helmuth again. Either of us."

Esther narrowed her eyes and practically hissed at Reuben. "That's right. We're never talking to you again." She took one step toward the door, then turned back around and came closer. "But you can still come over every week," she whispered. "I'll leave a note with your chores. Don't tell Sadie."

Chapter Twenty

Fern's stomach felt as if she'd swallowed a watermelon-sized rock. Even though she practically had to force-feed herself during dinner, she often had no idea where her next meal was going to come from, so she couldn't justify being picky. Or ungrateful. Anna Helmuth might not be a very *gute* cook, but the love she put into her cooking made even the corn casserole with rice and raisins go down easier.

Fern had eaten two helpings of everything at the table and only stopped when she truly couldn't stuff another bite into her mouth. Anna had made crispy, crunchy, burned corn dogs, corn-rice casserole, banana-tomato bread, and green Jell-O with pickles for Sunday dinner. Fern had smeared half an inch of butter and huckleberry jelly on her bread, and the jelly had covered the taste of tomato well enough—well enough that Fern had been able to eat two pieces without gagging. She had separated the pickles from the Jell-O while Anna wasn't looking, shaken the runny, green gelatin from each one, and popped them into her mouth. She liked pickles. And Jell-O. But not necessarily swimming together in a bowl.

Still, Anna had outdone herself, and Fern was incredibly grateful. Today was in-between Sunday, and because they didn't have *gmay* with a fellowship supper afterward, Fern often went hungry on in-between Sundays.

"That was a wonderful-*gute* dinner," Fern said, easing onto the sofa and picking up her knitting.

Reuben swept while Felty finished wiping the table. Then Felty hung the dishrag on the faucet, came into the great room, and sank into his recliner. "The queen of Africa never ate that good, Annie-banannie," he said, picking up his newspaper and settling in to read it.

Anna dried her hands on the dish towel hanging from the fridge handle. "*Denki*, dear. I made all of Reuben's favorites hoping it would cheer him up."

Without looking up, Reuben emptied the dustpan and returned the broom to the closet. "There's nothing wrong with me, Mammi. I don't need cheering up."

Anna looked at her grandson as if she didn't believe a word he said. "Stuff and nonsense. You've been moping around for days, acting like your dog died."

"I don't have a dog."

"No wonder you're so depressed."

Reuben tried so hard to smile, he looked as if he were in pain. "I'm okay, Mammi. I just . . . I just don't know what to do about my life. I'm thinking of moving back to Sugarcreek."

Anna's eyebrows moved up several inches on her forehead. "Moving back? *Ach*, *vell*, we will miss you something wonderful, but I know your *mamm* has been wanting you back. We can't be so selfish as to keep you to ourselves."

"I'd miss your cooking, Mammi. Nobody cooks like you do."

Fern looked up from her knitting and studied Reuben's face. Reuben was considering moving back? He must be feeling lower than Fern had expected. Of course he felt low. He had only been trying to do the right thing by Esther and Sadie, and he'd gotten into trouble that he didn't deserve.

On Wednesday at Esther's barn, Fern had felt truly sorry for Reuben and secretly overjoyed at the same time. Esther had jumped to several conclusions about their relationship, and he'd been forced to set her straight. But Fern had half feared, half expected Reuben to declare his love for Sadie right there in front of Fern and Fluffy. It would have broken Fern's heart, but it would have cemented his place as the most important young man in Bonduel.

Sadie may have been sorely disappointed, but Fern had gone home and cried herself to sleep in relief.

It was selfish to feel glad that Reuben didn't love Sadie, but Fern couldn't help it. Her heart would break completely when Reuben got married. Lord willing, he would marry someone nice like Linda Sue, who didn't think she was better than other people simply because she was the bishop's daughter.

Fern might feel better about his marrying if it was to someone nice.

But probably not.

The immediate problem was how to cheer Reuben up when at least two Bonduel girls hated his guts.

On Friday night, Reuben had taken Fern to the gas

station mini-mart for a sandwich, and they'd passed a park where Sadie and some of *die youngie* were roasting hot dogs—with marshmallows and chocolate and without Reuben. Though he hadn't said a word, the sight of Matthew and Aaron and the others laughing and having fun without him had made Reuben very unhappy.

Fern patted the sofa and motioned for Reuben to sit. He needed to practice his knitting if he was ever going to finish that pot holder. She gave him a teasingly innocent look. "When do you want to come home to Sugarcreek? I have a bus schedule."

Reuben expelled a heavy sigh and picked up his knitting. Fern didn't know if the sigh was because she'd mentioned Sugarcreek or because he had to knit. "You've been pestering me to come home ever since you got here."

She grinned at him. "It sounds like it might have worked."

He smiled back and made her heart jump around like a drop of water on a hot griddle. "You've worn me down."

Anna's knees creaked as she planted herself in her rocker. "Much as your *mamm* misses you, I don't think you should give up on Bonduel just yet. Fern has so much more to teach you about knitting. And if you get bored with that, she could start you on crochet."

Reuben threw Fern a sideways grin. "I don't think I'll ever get bored with knitting, Mammi."

"You're such a dear boy. Who would have thought that one of my grandsons would have taken so naturally to it?" Anna rocked back and forth while she let out some slack in her ball of yarn. "It wonders me why Esther and Sadie are so cross with you. You're a handsome boy with a nice head of hair and *gute* teeth."

Of course Reuben was handsome and likable. That was why Esther and Sadie were so cross.

Fern glanced at Reuben out of the corner of her eye. With his tongue sticking out and his eyes narrowed in concentration, he held his knitting needles like a toddler learning to use a spoon. His knitting was hopeless, but he'd do anything to make his *mammi* happy.

Fern felt so heavy, she thought she might sink into the sofa. *Oy*, anyhow. Reuben broke her heart every second of every day. She didn't know how she would bear it when he married. She could hardly bear it now.

"I suppose *gute* hair and nice teeth aren't enough," Reuben said.

Anna shrugged and seemed to let all the air out of her lungs. "I don't wonder that nothing is *gute* enough for Esther. She's grumpy, and you wouldn't improve her mood even if you proposed. But Sadie Yoder comes from a wonderful-*gute* family. Her *bruder* Tyler is just about the finest boy you'll ever meet. She's too nice to hold a grudge."

No matter how *gute* Tyler Yoder was, Fern didn't believe Sadie was that nice. Sadie had forgiven Reuben for yelling at the knitting group, but she wouldn't be so ready to forgive him for making a fool of her. It was going on five months, and Reuben still hadn't forgiven John for making a fool of him. Fern couldn't see Sadie being less self-centered than Reuben was.

After the scene at Esther's barn, Reuben had been unhappier than ever. He never smiled, and their last knitting lesson on Friday had been conducted in almost complete silence, because Reuben hadn't been in the mood for chitchat.

"I found some beautiful blue yarn at the store yesterday," Anna said, seemingly oblivious to all the gloom in the room. She was the only one still enthusiastic about Reuben's knitting. A thousand tangled balls of yarn wouldn't have been able to dim her excitement. "When you finish that pot holder you're working on, you should make a baby blanket. You are coming along so well, and they're so eager at the hospital."

If they saw Reuben's pot holder, they wouldn't be so eager.

"Okay, Mammi. I'd love to try a blanket," Reuben said, with that resignation in his voice he always got when they talked about knitting. He was too kind to discourage his *mammi*, but everybody knew the pot holder was a lost cause. A blanket was out of the question.

"Of course Reuben is coming along well, Banannie," Felty said from behind his newspaper. "He learned from the best."

"Now, Felty. I can't take any credit for Reuben's success. Fern is the one who's been teaching him."

Fern wasn't about to take any credit. Her one pupil hated to knit and got his fingers tangled every time he picked up his knitting needles.

"Fern is a *gute* teacher," Reuben said, "but I am a poor learner."

"You're coming along very well," Anna insisted. "And don't let anyone tell you otherwise."

They settled into a comfortable silence as Felty read the paper and the other three concentrated on their knitting with varying degrees of success.

Reuben stifled a groan, and Fern leaned closer to see what mess he'd made of his knitting. "Here," she said, showing him what he did wrong while trying not to notice how *gute* he smelled. "It goes over instead of under."

A loud knock on the door made Fern flinch. Reuben, more than happy to leave his knitting behind, jumped up and answered it. Sadie's brother Joseph Elmer stood in the doorway, holding an envelope in his hand and looking quite put out.

"Joseph Elmer," Anna said. "What a wonderful-*gute* surprise."

Joseph Elmer looked as sour as dandelion tea as he shoved the envelope in Reuben's direction. "Sadie wanted me to bring this *immediately*." He obviously felt he had been greatly imposed upon by his sister.

"*Denki*, Joe," Reuben said, glancing doubtfully at Fern. Fern returned his look with an uncertain one of her own. Sadie had sent him a note? This couldn't be good.

"Won't you come in?" Anna said even as Joseph Elmer clomped down the porch steps and out of sight.

"I guess not," Felty said, still engrossed in the newspaper.

Reuben shut the door and stared at the envelope in his hand as if deciding whether or not to open it. Had Sadie decided to forgive him? Or had she wanted to vent her indignation in a letter?

It was none of her business, but Fern itched to get her hands on that letter all the same. The Helmuths would probably be shocked if she jumped to her feet and ripped the letter out of Reuben's hand. It would almost be worth the looks on their faces if she got a chance to read it.

"Are you going to open it?" Anna said.

Dear Anna. She was always thinking of others.

Reuben gave Fern a doubtful smile and carefully, too slowly, slid his finger along the top edge. He pulled out a yellow note card and read it silently, furrowing his brow as he slid it back into the envelope.

Fern wanted to strangle him. Couldn't he see she was going to choke on her curiosity?

Dear Anna came to her rescue again. "What did she say? Is she coming over? I could whip up a nice bread pudding with my leftover tomato-banana bread."

Reuben's lips twitched upward, and Fern thought she might sink into the depths of despair. If the letter made Reuben happy, it could only mean one thing. Sadie had seen it in her heart to forgive him.

Chapter Twenty-One

Fern's stomach lurched violently, and it wasn't because she was hungry. Dinner at the Helmuths' had only been two hours ago. Something didn't feel right about the singing tonight. Why would Sadie invite Fern when Sadie had made it plain that she didn't especially like her?

Anna sat in the front with Felty, and Reuben was with Fern in the back. Fern couldn't very well tell Felty to turn the buggy around and drive her home. She frowned and glanced at Reuben. He'd been all smiles since this afternoon when Sadie's note had come.

Fern had tried her best to be happy for Reuben. If Sadie really wanted to be friends again, everything in his world would be set to rights once more. With Sadie's approval, he would be as popular as ever. Maybe Sadie had realized there were advantages to having Reuben as a friend. Maybe she wasn't ready to give up hope that he'd fall in love with her. And maybe that was why Fern's stomach was doing flips. She hated to even think it, but given enough time together, Reuben was bound to fall in love with Sadie.

Fern sighed to herself. She'd given up hope of a relationship with Reuben a long time ago. It was none of her business whom Reuben chose to love. She was being selfish, plain and simple.

She should be jumping up and down for joy. Reuben would be happy at last.

So why was she finding it so hard to even sit up straight?

She forced herself to give him a teasing smile. "We're almost there. Whatever you do, don't hold Sadie's hand in public. You want to stay on her *dat*'s *gute* side."

He curled his lips upward and fidgeted with Sadie's note. Fern didn't think he'd put it down since Joseph Elmer had delivered it. "But what does it mean?" He read it out loud for the fourth time. "*Reuben, I really want you to come to the singing tonight, and please bring Fern. I need to talk to both of you.*"

Fern pushed her smile wider until her lips hurt. "Isn't it obvious? She wants to be friends again." With both of them? Not likely.

The buggy rounded the corner, and the Miller home and Dorothy's fabric shop came into sight. Fern's heart sank even lower. Sadie, Esther, and Serena were clumped under the big oak tree on the west side of the house with Matthew Eicher, Aaron Glick, and five or six other young people. It didn't look like an ambush, but Fern's whole body tensed anyway.

When the buggy rolled onto the gravel driveway, Sadie looked up from her conversation and waved enthusiastically. Maybe not an ambush. Maybe a welcoming party. So why had Fern been invited?

Anna caught her breath and waved back. "You see,"

she said, wobbling forward when Felty stopped the buggy. "I told you Sadie was a nice girl, and you're a very *gute* catch."

Reuben's irritating enthusiasm seemed to dim. "I want to be her friend, but I hope I made it clear not to expect anything else. I don't want to marry her."

"Of course you don't, dear," Anna said, winking at Fern before reaching over the seat and patting Reuben on the leg. "Sadie is not the one."

"And Annie should know," Felty said. "She's made more matches than Noah on his ark."

Felty slid out of the buggy and helped Anna down after him. Reuben went out next and gave Fern a hand down. Frowning, he lingered over her hand for a few moments before letting go and stepping away. He glanced in Sadie's direction. "I'm going to wait and let Sadie come to me. She's the one who needs to apologize this time."

Fern could only nod. It wasn't in Reuben's nature to grovel, but he wanted to get back in Sadie's good graces something wonderful. No matter what the note said, something told Fern Sadie wasn't going to be the one to apologize.

Melvin Raber and Dorothy Miller stood on the sidewalk intently studying a wire-bound notebook with pens in hand.

Fern nudged Reuben with her elbow. "Look. You've done a lot of *gute* here. I don't wonder that Sadie still wants to be your friend."

Reuben's gaze traveled in Dorothy's direction. His eyes danced at the sight of Dorothy and Melvin with their heads together, engrossed in conversation. "The license plates was Dawdi's idea."

"And you had the *gute* sense to ask my advice," Felty said.

Dorothy burst into a smile and waved at the four of them with her whole arm. She said something to Melvin, and they both headed toward Fern, Reuben, and Reuben's grandparents.

"How are you, Melvin?" Felty said, shaking Melvin's hand.

"I have a license plate question," Melvin said, with his eyes downcast and his hands crossed awkwardly in front of him. No matter how much he liked Felty or Dorothy, Melvin was still painfully shy.

Obviously sensitive to Melvin's distress, Dorothy hooked elbows with Fern and nodded to Reuben. "We'll go over here and visit so you can have some privacy." Fern couldn't imagine anyone needing privacy to talk about license plates, but Dorothy was sweet to make things easier for Melvin.

Reuben glanced in Sadie's direction before he, Fern, and Dorothy strolled around to the other side of Felty's buggy, out of sight of Melvin and the grandparents. "I don't want him to be uncomfortable," Dorothy said. "He's not staying for the *singeon*. He just wanted to consult me about license plates." Dorothy's cheeks were apple red. Without warning, she gave Fern a breathless hug. "Melvin found Texas this morning, but he wanted my advice as to whether it was acceptable to play the license plate game on the Sabbath. I told him if my *dat* and *mamm* can play Scrabble on the Sabbath, he can very well play the license plate game." She clasped her hands together over her heart and lowered her voice. "Oh, Fern. I used to think he was so quiet, but now we talk about everything. Yesterday we spoke for nearly half an hour about why Pennsylvania is the Keystone state. He saw Idaho last week, and I made him my famous Funeral Potatoes. He said they were so delicious that it was a shame to save them only for when someone dies."

Fern squeezed Dorothy's hand. "I'm wonderful happy for you."

"I owe it all to you two." Dorothy patted Reuben's arm. "I'm sorry I didn't like you very much when we first started the knitting group. I don't know that I like you all that much now, but you gave Melvin the nudge he needed and I'll never forget that."

Reuben sprouted a crooked grin. "*Ach, vell.* I hope I'll grow on you."

"Maybe," Dorothy said. "But I wouldn't count on it, not unless you stop walking around with blinders on and start noticing things."

He looked to Fern for some help. Dorothy was a little hard to figure out sometimes.

"We will keep sending license plates your way when we see them," Fern said with the express purpose of diverting Dorothy from the fact that she didn't like Reuben all that much.

"Please do. We always need license plates." Dorothy reached into the bag slung over her shoulder, pulled out a granola bar, and handed it to Fern. "Are you coming in, or are you going to stand out here and sing from the yard?"

"We're coming in," Fern said. "Save us a seat."

"I will, unless Melvin decides to stay. He might want me to sit across from him."

Fern shook her head in mock horror. "Don't save us a seat. We'd never in a million years want to upset the plan."

The three of them walked around the buggy.

Melvin, Felty, and Anna seemed engrossed in a very important conversation about Mississippi. Dorothy joined them, leaving Fern and Reuben to fend for themselves. A warm breeze played at Fern's bonnet strings as she watched Anna and Felty visit with Melvin and Dorothy. Reuben's grandparents had a way of making everyone feel loved, even the people who didn't deserve it, like Fern. It didn't matter what happened tonight, Anna and Felty would still love her. At least she could find some comfort in that.

Fern looked to the small group of Sadie's friends congregating around the tree and felt sick to her stomach. She shouldn't have agreed to come, no matter how badly Sadie wanted to see her. "Do you want to talk to Sadie now or later?"

Reuben took a deep breath. "Before the singing starts." He pumped his eyebrows up and down. "The suspense is killing me."

In any other circumstances, standing in any other yard, Fern might have laughed. She couldn't even muster a smile. "Let's go then, before you have a heart attack." She hesitated when she realized that it wouldn't help Reuben's chances with Sadie if he were seen with Fern. She stopped in her tracks. "You go over. I'll count to twenty and follow."

Reuben pursed his lips as his brows drew closer together. "Are you sure?"

"Sadie doesn't like me very well."

He thought about it for too long, which told Fern all she needed to know. "*Nae*. We came in the same buggy. We're standing together in the yard in plain sight. She already knows we're friends."

Fern would have protested, but she really wanted to hear the first words that came out of Sadie's mouth, in case Sadie was feeling nasty instead of forgiving. She let Reuben lead the way as they marched across the lawn. Reuben might have been going to a triumphal reunion, but Fern felt like she was marching to a funeral.

Matthew Eicher must have been telling a funny story, and *die youngie* laughed as if they were having a wonderful-*gute* time. Sadie stood with her back against the tree flanked by Esther and Serena. Even though Matthew was talking, it was clear that Sadie was the center of attention. And why wouldn't she be? She was by far the prettiest girl in Bonduel, and her *dat* was the bishop. Everyone loved Sadie, except for maybe Fern, and Reuben would say that Fern was just jealous.

Sadie glanced up, and Reuben caught her eye and waved. She waved back as if she were obligated to acknowledge him but would rather not. Then she tapped Esther on the shoulder and whispered something in her ear while Esther smiled as if she'd been saving it up for a long time.

Reuben tensed beside her. "Maybe she's not as eager to talk as she sounded in her note."

Fern's mouth went dry. "She seemed happy about it five minutes ago." Did Sadie plan to punish Reuben for hurting her feelings? Or was she glad to see him but felt she had to be subtle about it so as not to draw attention to herself? Did she want Reuben's friendship or his humiliation?

Fern's stomach dropped to the floor. Either way, this evening was not going to turn out well for her. She shouldn't have come, no matter how badly Reuben needed her.

Fern ignored the pang in her heart and squared her shoulders. She was nothing if not durable. Hadn't she endured many worse things in her life? She couldn't think of a single one at the moment, but surely there were bigger problems than a heart shattered into a million unfixable pieces and her hopes and dreams spilled on the floor like an overturned bucket of nails.

"Fern!" Sadie exclaimed, as if she had just noticed her. She pushed herself from the tree and threw out her arms. Was she going to hug Fern? She'd never been that friendly before.

Jah. She was going to hug her.

More in shock than anything else, Fern stood as stiff as a stone pillar and let Sadie pull her into an embrace. "I'm so glad to see you," Sadie said, taking her by the elbow and dragging her toward the group of young people. "I have a big surprise."

Sadie left Reuben to follow or not, and Fern couldn't help but think she'd done it on purpose. It wasn't too hard to guess what game she was playing. Indignation oozed out of Sadie's pores like sweat. She was out for revenge. The hostility made Fern shiver, even as Sadie squeezed her elbow and pulled her forward.

The small group parted as Sadie led Fern into the midst of them. Right in the middle of *die youngie* stood her brother John with his hands out and a grin stretched across his face. "Hullo, sis."

Fern gasped and launched herself into John's arms. "You said you weren't going to come."

He laughed as he squeezed the stuffing out of her. "I changed my mind. Dat sent me to fetch you home, and"—he paused and glanced past Fern to Reuben, who stood apart from the group looking as if someone had smacked him in the head with a stick—"I came to make things right."

Fern pulled herself from John's grasp, torn between her joy at seeing her *bruder* and that look on Reuben's face, as if she'd somehow betrayed his trust. She flashed a hopeful look in his direction and mouthed his name.

Sadie had somehow managed to get behind Reuben, and she nudged him forward into the little circle created by *die youngie.* "Look, Reuben," she said, obviously pleased with herself. "Your former best friend."

Reuben eyed Fern with a mixture of pain and longing on his face, as if he ached to forgive his best friend but had dug his heels in too deep to actually do it. Fern's heart hurt for both of them. It was plainly written in the tortured lines of his face that Reuben wanted to reconcile with John—but not like this, not with all these people here—not if it meant that Reuben would have to grovel in front of the people he wanted to impress the most. His broken heart was not a circus sideshow.

But Sadie had turned it into one.

"Reuben's girlfriend, Linda Sue, fell in love with John," Sadie announced, looking as smug as a flat-nosed cat. "John and Linda Sue are engaged, but Reuben refuses to forgive John. Isn't that the most pettiest thing you've ever heard?"

Nae. Not the pettiest thing. Reuben's resentment didn't even come close to Sadie's jealousy.

Fern would put a stop to it right now. "What's between John and Reuben is between them alone. This is not the time or place."

Sadie wasn't about to be deprived of her triumph. She folded her arms and smiled at Fern as if she were the stupidest person in the world. "You're such a sweetie, Fern, and so sensitive, but why not settle it now?"

Esther nodded eagerly, like a butcher sharpening a knife just before sticking a pig. "We want to see Reuben open his heart to Jesus and forgive John for taking his girlfriend."

Reuben's eyes flashed with anger, and Fern could almost hear his spine stiffen as he drew himself up to his full, impressive height. He focused his gaze—not on Sadie or even John—but on Fern. His withering glare knocked the wind right out of her. "John didn't take my girlfriend. He stole my girlfriend. He sneaked around behind my back even while Linda Sue and I were dating. He lied to my face, and I believed him. I thought he was my best friend."

"We never meant to hurt you," John said, but few words were ever more wasted. He'd said them so many times, they almost had no meaning. It was the reason Fern had come to Bonduel in the first place. Reuben had to be coaxed, and John couldn't have known that his apology served no purpose except to make Reuben feel weak and humiliated.

Reuben scowled. "Hurt? I wasn't hurt. I was betrayed by the two people I trusted most in the whole world. I'll never forgive you for that."

"Did you hear that?" Sadie said. "Reuben refuses to forgive, and yet for weeks he flirted with me and Esther at the same time."

"He made me think he wanted to marry me," Esther whined.

Sadie blinked back some very large alligator tears.

"Me too. I thought he was going to propose. He didn't care one lick about breaking both our hearts."

Matthew Eicher looked downright concerned. "I don't know how they treat girls in Sugarcreek, but in Bonduel, we don't lead them on like that."

"That wasn't the way it happened," Fern said, because Reuben had fallen silent, and she wasn't about to let Sadie get away with making Reuben look wicked. "Reuben was trying to be nice. You must have misinterpreted—"

"He washed all three of my dogs," Esther said, as if that proved he loved her.

A storm raged on Reuben's face. He took a deliberate step away from Fern as his eyes flashed like lightning. "I don't need you to defend me."

Fern caught her breath. She'd never heard such disdain coming from his mouth, as if he despised her even more than he hated John and Linda Sue. A sharp and ragged piece of ice pierced her heart. Did he really hate her that much?

Fern couldn't seem to catch any sort of breath as Reuben glared in her direction. He didn't want her help. He didn't want her here. Hadn't he plainly told her so weeks ago?

In concern, John turned his eyes to Fern. Fern shook her head slightly. John could charm the quills off a porcupine, but his interference would only make things worse.

With a nod of his head, Reuben motioned in Sadie's direction. "I painted your fence, but I never said anything about marriage."

Sadie turned up the tears, and Serena put a protective arm around her. "I showed you around the dairy," Sadie said, managing to sob and gloat at the same time.

Sadie's dramatics were very impressive. "We played Scrabble with the whole family. You worked hard for my *dat*'s approval. Don't pretend you didn't. You acted as if you wanted to marry me, all the while leading Esther on at the same time. I thank the *gute* Lord that He showed me your true character before it was too late."

Esther nodded. "Linda Sue is much better off with John."

Annoyance dripped from Sadie's expression as she glanced at Esther. "What I was going to say is . . ." Sadie surveyed the curious faces around the circle. *Die youngie* stood at rapt attention, even as Felty and Anna visited with Dorothy and Melvin, seemingly oblivious to the storm brewing not thirty feet away. "I don't wonder but Linda Sue saw who Reuben truly was and was overjoyed to escape."

"My *bruder* is the best of men," Fern said, unable to hold her tongue. "But Reuben is just as *gute*. He spent hours painting your chicken coop."

"And flirting," Sadie said, turning up her nose. "Linda Sue is blessed to have found John, even though he is who he is."

Even though he is who he is.

Nobody had to ask what Sadie meant by that. John and Fern were the children of a poor pig farmer. Fern knew what people thought of her family.

Reuben clenched his jaw so tight, Fern could hear his teeth grind together. Sadie's meaning hadn't escaped him. Sadie wanted to make it clear that she thought Reuben was lower that John King. It was probably the most cutting thing she could have said to him, and Fern had no argument against it. She knew what people thought of her. She had tried to pretend that

Reuben didn't believe the same thing, but it was plain by the horrified look on his face that he had absorbed every word.

Her throat tightened, and she bit back bitter tears. She wouldn't cry. Crying was Sadie's trick, and an unfair and deceitful one at that.

Sadie wiped her eyes and sniffed in Reuben's direction. "You can't even see fit to forgive your own best friend."

Fern gazed around the circle. Matthew and Aaron acted as if they didn't know what to do or whom to believe. Serena looked as self-satisfied as a cat. Fern hadn't invited her to join the knitting group, and she probably felt justified in hating everyone from Sugarcreek. Too bad Fern hadn't even known Serena existed when she had started the group. Esther's mouth puckered as if she'd eaten a whole lemon, and she stood with her hand propped on her cocked hip, gloating with her whole body. It was plain that she hadn't yet guessed that if she treated him poorly, Reuben wouldn't be over again to do her chores. She'd find out soon enough.

"Reuben," John said, reaching out to lay a hand on Reuben's shoulder.

Reuben was having none of it. He stepped away from his best friend.

John pulled back his hand as if Reuben had tried to bite it. "Reuben, I truly am sorry for what happened. I would be so grateful if you would forgive me. And so would Linda Sue."

A hole gaped open in the pit of Fern's stomach. Couldn't John see how humiliated Reuben already was? She wanted to yell at him for being so stupid.

Maybe he thought this was his one and only chance to make a face-to-face apology.

He'd get no forgiveness now.

"Let's go somewhere to talk about this privately," Fern said, without hope that Reuben would agree. His expression was already fierce and hard, as if he was set in stone and would not be moved.

"You should forgive him, Reuben," Matthew said. He was trying to be helpful, but every word, every frown from one of *die youngie* only served to cut Reuben's legs out from under him. Reuben was stubborn and proud—in a good way. He wouldn't stoop to apologize when it was clear that Sadie only wanted his humiliation served cold on a platter.

"*Jah*, you should," Sadie said.

"This isn't the time or the place," Fern said again, making her voice loud and insistent. She would not stand by and watch Sadie beat Reuben down.

Johnny Raber stepped forward and nudged two people aside. "Fern is right," he said. "This is a *singeon*. Not a confession."

Fern's heart galloped along her rib cage. Johnny would have rather danced a jig than say anything out loud. He never spoke a word unless it was absolutely necessary. She nodded at him, hoping he saw the deep gratitude in her eyes. Johnny Raber was awkward and shy, but he was also a very kind boy.

"No better time for Reuben to clear his conscience," Sadie said. Fern wanted to poke Sadie with a pin. Sadie knew Reuben wasn't going to forgive John in front of everybody. In fact, she was counting on it.

Fern folded her arms to keep from bursting with indignation. "Let he who is without sin cast the first stone," she said. "Reuben yelled at the knitting group

almost a month ago, and Esther still can't let it go."
She pointed to Sadie. "And you won't forgive Reuben
for not wanting to marry you." Fern was so angry her
hands shook. It only made it worse that Sadie was
eyeing her with barely disguised disdain, as if Fern was
a spoiled child throwing a temper tantrum. "You'd
rather embarrass him in front of everybody."

"I'm not embarrassed," Reuben said, clenching his
fists as if he were trying to squeeze all the blood out of
his palms.

Fern could feel the heat and rage radiating from his
body even from four feet away. She had to get him
away from here. "Reuben, we need to—"

He looked away, as if he couldn't stand to lay eyes
on her. "Don't, Fern. Just don't."

Fern couldn't breathe past the lump in her throat.

"I don't care what any of you think," Reuben said,
"and I never will. Gossip all you want. I don't have to
explain myself to anyone."

Without looking back, he pushed his way through
the small group of young people and took off across
the lawn.

Fern glanced at John, and the pain in his eyes must
have matched hers. "Stay here," she said. She could
usually talk Reuben down from one of his bad moods,
and John's presence would only make Reuben hostile.

Vell, more hostile than he already was.

Sadie tossed one of her bonnet strings over her
shoulder. "I told you he would refuse to humble himself. We're better off without him."

Fern peered at Sadie and shook her head. She felt
sorry for someone so pretty and yet so spiteful. "Shame
on you, Sadie Yoder," she said, before turning her back
on all of them. She could hear Sadie protesting loudly

that she'd done nothing wrong. Fern followed Reuben as he walked quickly past Anna and Felty, who were still visiting with Melvin and Dorothy.

"Reuben, dear, where are you going?" Anna called.

Reuben paused long enough to answer his *mammi*, in the most bitter tone Fern had ever heard. "I'm leaving Bonduel, and good riddance."

Anna furrowed her brow. "But what about your knitting?"

Reuben clenched his teeth as if he was chewing on his resentment. "I hate knitting, Mammi. It's a waste of time, only fit for old women and spinsters who don't have anything better to do with their lives." Reuben turned and stalked down the lane toward the road.

Anna caught her breath and tears pooled in her eyes, but Reuben was long gone before he saw what damage he had done. As much as Fern wanted to go after Reuben, she couldn't leave Reuben's *mammi* in such a state. She took Anna by the hand. "I'm sorry, Anna. It's no excuse, but Sadie was very rude to Reuben, and he isn't thinking straight."

Felty put his arm around Anna's shoulder, pulled a handkerchief from his pocket, and handed it to her. "There, there, Annie girl. He had no call to say that to you."

Anna dabbed at her eyes. "Reuben is a *gute* boy, but he's had a very hard few months. No matter what he says, I know deep down in his heart he loves to knit."

"I knew I was holding back my full approval for *gute* reason," Dorothy said.

Melvin nodded but didn't seem inclined to remark further.

Fern gave Anna a quick hug. "I'm sorry to leave you, but I need to catch up with him."

"*Jah*," Anna said, cheering up considerably. "Reuben needs you, Fern. You're the only one, even though he can't see past the nose on his own face."

Fern stole a glance in Sadie's direction. She and three or four of *die youngie* had their heads together, no doubt talking about how concerned they were for Reuben's soul. John stood off from Sadie's group with Matthew and Aaron and some of the others, looking as if he didn't know what to do with himself. Fern pressed her lips together and nodded to John. The singing was about to start. She'd come back for him. Reuben needed her more than ever. She wouldn't abandon him, no matter how badly he thought he wanted to be left alone.

Reuben had disappeared from sight around the bend in the road. She'd have to run to catch up with him. She walked as quickly as she could in her long dress until she rounded the bend. Reuben was a couple of hundred feet ahead, walking fast. Fern had always been speedy. As long as he didn't start running, she could catch up with him in a trice. She picked up her skirts and ran, being careful to make as little noise as possible. He might break into a sprint if he heard her coming up behind him.

If he heard her, he chose not to do anything about it. "Reuben," she panted as she slowed to a walk along-side him. "Where do you think you're going?"

He didn't slacken his pace or look at her, but his frown hardened like mud on a hot day. "Montana," he said.

"Walking all the way?"

He stopped so quickly, his shoes scraped against the asphalt. "Go home, Fern."

She couldn't bear what she saw in his eyes—deep,

painful regret and hot, barely controlled anger. Fern felt like weeping for him, but the last thing he wanted was her pity. "You know what an annoying tag-along I am. You can't shake me that easy."

The muscles in his jaw twitched fiercely. "Why can't you just leave me alone?"

"I want to help."

"Help?" He narrowed his eyes. "They hate me. They all hate me. I don't need any more of your help."

"They don't hate you."

"You heard Sadie. She thinks I'm no better than a pig farmer."

Fern drew her brows together. Reuben couldn't have known how much the derision in his tone hurt her. "Being a pig farmer isn't so bad."

"That's because you don't understand how people really see you."

A heavy weight pressed against Fern's chest as if Reuben had shoved her against a wall and held her there. "How . . . how do they see me?"

Reuben growled as if frustrated with himself, took off his hat, and scrubbed his fingers through his hair. "What I mean is, if it hadn't been for you, Sadie and Matthew and Aaron might have wanted to include me with their friends instead of thinking I'm a nobody who can only make friends with other nobodies."

His words stung as if he had lashed her across the face with them. "You think I'm a nobody?"

He shook his head, and resentment saturated his expression. "Befriending John has brought me nothing but grief."

Fern took a shallow, shuddering breath. She *was* a nobody, and all the wishing and smiling and kindness in the world would not change that fact. Or change the way Reuben saw her.

Her family was poor and they kept smelly pigs and worked in the mud and slop all day long, but they gave as much as they could to the church and tried to be *gute* Christians. Her *mamm* was always called upon to tend sick babies, and more than once her *dat* had helped raise a barn or bring in someone's crops.

Her parents were *gute* people, and she'd never heard an unkind word from her siblings, even John, who as a boy had found Fern very tiresome.

Surely Reuben didn't think ill of her family. It was Fern herself he couldn't stand. He thought he lowered himself by even talking to her, and she couldn't contradict him. Who was she compared to Reuben Helmuth or Sadie Yoder? She was a pig farmer's daughter who lived in a barn, cleaned toilets, and didn't even have enough money to keep herself fed.

"I'm . . . I'm sorry, Reuben. I didn't know." Didn't know how much her presence had hurt him. Didn't know how ashamed he was to have her as a friend. Didn't know how much he despised her.

He kicked the gravel at his feet. "Go home, Fern, and leave me in peace."

Putting his hat back on, he turned away from her and walked slowly down the road, his head bowed, his shoulders slumped. She didn't try to stop him. She couldn't have moved in his direction if she'd wanted to.

He was so much better off without her.

Her heart felt as if someone had scrubbed it raw with a steel wool pad. She finally admitted the truth to herself. Reuben didn't love her. He didn't even like her. How foolish to have let herself hope.

She took one last look at Reuben as he put more and more space between them. She would always love his unrestrained smile, the playful tease of his voice, and the way his eyes flashed with fire when he got angry, but she couldn't be responsible for his happiness anymore. She was holding him back from the person he could be, from the friends he could make.

No wonder he couldn't stand the sight of her.

Fern stumbled down the road as if someone else was doing the walking for her. Every breath felt like a sledgehammer to her chest, every heartbeat a slash with a very sharp knife.

She would fetch John, and they'd ride the bus home together. They'd done all they could have done to gain Reuben's forgiveness. She'd given him fifteen pounds and two months of her life. He certainly didn't want her to give any more. Besides, Mamm needed her home. They had John and Linda Sue's wedding to help plan and bridesmaids' dresses to make. She didn't have time to nurse a broken heart.

Her hands felt like ice and her cheeks were clammy and moist by the time she walked back into the Millers' yard. Everyone had gone inside except one person sitting on the porch gazing earnestly in her direction.

Johnny Raber. Was he waiting for her?

She still couldn't seem to catch her breath as she forced her feet to carry her across the lawn and up the porch steps. "Johnny," she said. "You didn't have to wait."

"I wanted to make sure you got back okay. Reuben sometimes leaves you behind."

Jah. He sometimes did that.

This time, he'd left her behind for good and left her heart in tatters at his feet.

Her vision went fuzzy, and her knees buckled. Johnny reached out his hand as the blackness overtook her.

Chapter Twenty-Two

Reuben sat in the barn on a prickly bale of hay cradling his head in his hands while the propane lantern hissed at him like an angry mob. He'd walked the six miles back to Huckleberry Hill and had been too agitated and hot to go into Mammi and Dawdi's house. The barn was cooler, but Iris the cow wasn't much for conversation, and he didn't really want to be alone with his thoughts. They were admonishing him sorely for his pride.

He'd made a complete mess of everything tonight, and he didn't know how he would ever make it right. He should have known better than to fall for Sadie's dirty trick, but he'd been so eager to be accepted by her friends that he hadn't thought it through very well, and he hadn't expected Sadie to be quite so vindictive. She was the bishop's daughter. Hadn't she been taught better than that? Mammi said that her brother Tyler was the best of men. Maybe Sadie would turn out all right in the end, but she certainly had some growing up to do.

He'd ruined his chances with Sadie, but surprisingly,

that didn't seem to matter all that much anymore. Sadie was well liked by *die youngie*, but why would he want to be friends with someone who was so nasty to sweet Fern King?

Reuben pressed his fingers into his forehead. How could he find fault with Sadie for treating Fern badly when he had been more than *hesslich*, ugly to Fern himself? He ached to unsay every cruel word he had said to her tonight. The second he'd said them, he had wanted to snatch them back, but his all-important pride had gotten in the way. He hadn't wanted to humiliate himself more than he already had.

But Fern hadn't deserved his anger or his harsh words. What had she done but stand by his side and help him through his grief? What had she done but be his friend even when he hadn't been very likable? He'd called her a pig farmer's daughter as if it were an insult. Oh, *sis yuscht*. He'd been wonderful mean tonight.

He needed to apologize. Now. Fern shouldn't go one more minute without knowing how deeply sorry he was for what he'd said. He stood up and almost as quickly sat back down. It was getting late, and he had no transportation but his legs. If Mammi and Dawdi got home soon, he could take the buggy to the Schmuckers' house. Or he could start walking now. He had to talk to Fern—had to make her smile, had to hear her reassurance that she was still his friend.

He caught his breath with the sudden realization that Fern's friendship was the most important of his whole life.

Reuben gazed up at one of the barn's high windows. It was pitch dark outside. Even if Mammi and Dawdi came home right now, Fern and the Schmuckers would be in bed. No matter how desperate he was to talk to Fern, he'd have to wait until morning.

A half smile curled at his lips. Fern didn't work on Mondays. He'd show up at the Schmuckers' house first thing in the morning and take her to McDonald's for a Sausage McMuffin. She loved Sausage McMuffins. He'd said things to her that he wouldn't have said to his worst enemy. He'd buy her two Sausage McMuffins so she knew he was sincere.

A twinge of anxiety pulled at his gut. What if she didn't want to go with him anywhere? What if she refused to talk to him?

He shook his head. Fern would forgive him in a heartbeat. She knew what a headstrong, stubborn boy he was, and she persisted in being his friend. She'd probably forgiven him already.

Reuben heard the muffled thud of horse hooves on gravel. Mammi and Dawdi were finally home. He frowned. He'd have to apologize to Mammi too. He'd insulted every woman who'd ever picked up a pair of knitting needles.

A sprinkling of raindrops fell on Reuben's shoulders as he pushed the barn door open. Mammi slid from the buggy, waved and smiled at Reuben, and tromped into the house while Dawdi drove the buggy into the barn. Maybe Reuben didn't need to apologize to Mammi after all. She seemed as cheerful as ever.

Dawdi gave him a grunt and a nod, and in silence they unhitched the buggy together. Reuben led Rhubarb to her stall, kind of hoping that Dawdi wouldn't mention the *singeon* or the fact that Reuben had missed it because of a temper tantrum.

"I'm sorry you couldn't make the *singeon*," Dawdi said, raising an eyebrow as if he were getting ready to scold his short-tempered grandson, "especially after you were specially invited by Sadie Yoder."

Reuben took the brush from the hook in the stall and started brushing Rhubarb's neck, hoping Dawdi would appreciate his thoughtfulness and maybe not be so cross about his inexcusable behavior. "I'm sorry I lost my temper, Dawdi. As soon as I brush Rhubarb, I'll go in and apologize to Mammi. I know I hurt her feelings."

"Not tonight," Dawdi said. "You can tell her you're sorry in the morning." With the wrinkles deepening around his eyes, he pointed at Reuben. "Wait here. I'll be right back."

Dawdi left the barn, and when he didn't come back right away, Reuben decided to finish brushing the horse. Dawdi might have gone into the house and forgotten that he'd left Reuben in the barn.

Once he finished the horse, Reuben decided to muck out the stall. Might as well make hay while he had nothing better to do. He had a lot of fences to mend, and after Fern, Mammi and Dawdi were next on the list. They had been so kind to him, and he'd been grumpy and surly and hard to live with. The guilt squeezed his chest like a vise. He couldn't have made a bigger mess if he'd planned it.

He didn't get very far mucking out before Dawdi came back into the barn carrying a pillow, two blankets, and a plate of cookies. "I'm afraid you'll have to sleep here in the barn tonight," Dawdi said.

Ach, du lieva. Reuben propped the shovel against the wall and took the pillow from Dawdi. "I'm sorry. Mammi must be wonderful upset."

Dawdi waved away Reuben's apology. "*Ach.* Your *mammi* has forgiven you already. She knows you only lashed out because Sadie Yoder is a pill."

"I never meant to be disrespectful about Mammi's knitting."

Dawdi nodded. "She'd just as soon let you sleep in our house for the rest of your life. But I can't allow anyone to treat my sweetheart like you treated her tonight. I want you to sleep in the barn and think about how a boy should talk to his *mammi*."

Reuben already felt terrible, but Dawdi's words knocked the wind right out of him. He had never felt more ashamed in his life. He thought he had sunk pretty low when Linda Sue broke up with him, and even lower when Sadie had humiliated him in front of *die youngie* tonight at the singing, but this . . . this was truly his lowest point. After months of moping because John and Linda Sue had embarrassed him, it had taken a smack upside the head with Dawdi's wisdom to make him realize. What other people did to him could never bring him as low as what he did to other people.

Why had he not understood this months ago?

"In the morning, I'll expect an apology for your *mammi* and a change of heart for *Gotte*," Dawdi said. "The measure of a man isn't how popular he is with his friends, but how he treats those who have nothing to give him."

Reuben bowed his head. He had crammed his heart into a tiny little space, trying to make himself fit in a place that left no room for anyone but himself and his own selfish desires. He stumbled to the hay bale and practically fell into it. "*Ach*, Dawdi. I don't even deserve to sleep in the mud."

Dawdi chuckled. "Now, now, there. You're not as wicked as all that. You haven't a lazy bone in your body, and you praise Annie's cooking to the sky."

"I love Mammi's cooking. That doesn't make me a *gute* man."

"*Nae*, but you finish chores before I even know they need to be done. You bring me back a little gift every time you go to the market, and you made a valiant effort at knitting because you knew it would make your *mammi* happy." Dawdi stroked his horseshoe beard. "And then there's Fern."

Reuben's heart leaped at the sound of her name.

"You watch out for her like she was one of your sisters. You've fixed her bike four times, taken her to McDonald's, and given her rides home from gatherings."

Not as many rides home as he should have. "Who wouldn't do nice things for Fern? She's always doing something for someone else. She never thinks of herself."

"Sadie Yoder wouldn't. Or Esther Shirk. They think Fern's an underling."

Reuben nodded, unable to speak with the lump sitting at the base of his throat.

"What do you think?" Dawdi said, pinning Reuben with an intense blue-eyed gaze.

"I . . . I think Fern is *wunderbarr*." And thick-skinned. And pretty. And smart and feisty. He adored feisty girls.

"Even though she's a pig farmer's daughter?"

Reuben's heart pounded an uneven rhythm. "Even though."

Dawdi gazed at Reuben as if inspecting his soul for damage. "Then maybe a change of heart isn't far away."

It was as far away as ever. Reuben had too many flaws, and Fern was painfully aware of every one. But his weaknesses never seemed to bother her. Why else would she keep coming back for more?

Dawdi laid the blankets beside Reuben on the hay bale and ambled backward. "If you get cold, come in for another blanket, but it looks to be a warm night yet."

"I'm wonderful sorry."

Dawdi thumbed his suspenders. "I know. You're forgiven. But could you do me a favor and not tell your *mamm* I made you sleep in the barn? She wouldn't understand, and I'd rather not offend my daughter-in-law."

"I'm as silent as the grave."

Dawdi left, and Reuben hung the shovel on the hook. He'd finish mucking out tomorrow when he wasn't so weary and when it wasn't the Sabbath. Even though Reuben was bone-tired, as if he'd worked the fields all day, he wouldn't sleep a wink. He had too many sins to think upon.

The propane lantern still hissed like so many people scoffing at him, but this time they were chiding him for being proud and hotheaded. Reuben pulled five hay bales from the stack and laid them in a row, long sides together. It would be a prickly bed, one to remind him of his mistakes every time he rolled over.

Someone knocked on the barn door, and for a second, Reuben's heart soared at the hope that Fern had come to check on him. He could apologize and maybe make her smile. He longed to see that smile again.

The door creaked open, and Fern's brother John stepped hesitantly into the barn. Reuben's first impulse was to scowl, but then he remembered that what other people had done to him wasn't as important as what was in his own heart.

Fern would have wanted him to open his heart to her brother, and Reuben owed Fern a lot. He'd do it for Fern's sake.

And for his own. He'd been holding on to a grudge for far too long.

With wide, uncertain eyes, John took a few steps into the barn, obviously unsure of the welcome he'd get, if he got one at all. "Felty said you wouldn't mind if I came out here. I hope he wasn't joking."

John had always been skinny. As a teenager, he'd been a collection of long limbs, hands too big for his arms, feet that arrived at church five minutes before he did. He had filled out a little since Reuben last saw him, but he still had the same playful, good-natured cast to his expression, as if every day were a new adventure and every stranger was a friend waiting to be made. His eyes were like Fern's, soft brown and kind, with a hint of mischief at the corners.

"I know it's late," John said, "but I hoped you wouldn't mind."

Every muscle in Reuben's body tensed as John walked farther into the barn as if he planned on staying for a while.

"I'm sorry about what happened at the singing. I wouldn't have gone if I had known what Sadie was going to do."

Reuben nodded. "I know you better than that. You never would have knowingly agreed to shaming me."

John raised his gaze with a hopeful light in his eyes. "Do you? Because Linda Sue and I never wanted things to turn out the way they did. We never wanted you to leave Sugarcreek or feel like you'd been betrayed by two of the people you love the most. It happened so quickly that we didn't rightly understand it ourselves. We never meant to hurt you."

"Whether you wanted to or not, it hurt just the same."

John scrubbed his hand down the side of his face like he always did when he was upset. "I know. I'm sorry, Reuben. I love Linda Sue to the bottom of my soul. If someone stole her from me, I don't know that I would ever be able to breathe again, and that's what makes me so ashamed. I'm a hypocrite to be asking your forgiveness, because I could never forgive you if you did the same to me."

Reuben studied John's face. Up until five months ago, seldom a day had gone by without Reuben and John seeing each other. Their houses were not half a mile apart, and John often came over for dinner or dessert, while Reuben had gone to John's house more than once to help with the hogs or to bother one of John's younger siblings, usually Fern. He had loved that John was always game for anything. They had fished and hunted, dived into swimming holes they had no business diving into, and played softball and volleyball in Reuben's backyard. Almost every *gute* memory Reuben had included John and Fern.

Reuben closed his eyes and let the memories wash over him like a soothing balm. He'd been away long enough to gain some valuable and painful perspective— with Fern's help. Thank the *gute* Lord for annoying, persistent Fern King.

Ach. He'd been so proud, and his love for Linda Sue had been as flimsy as tissue paper. He hadn't loved Linda Sue as much as he'd loved the idea of her and what she could do for his standing in the community.

He hadn't left Sugarcreek with a broken heart so much as wounded pride.

Reuben's heart pounded against his rib cage as if it were trying to escape. John King was his best friend.

And Reuben wasn't mad at him anymore.

He gasped as the weight of five months sloughed off his shoulders like scales off a snake, and he found himself wishing he hadn't held on to it for so long. His embarrassment didn't matter. It was in his own head and nowhere else.

This new awareness was Fern's doing, of course. Everything came back to Fern. She'd been working on him for weeks, prying the lid off his pent-up emotions, teaching him how to breathe again. And Reuben had barely even noticed.

John stood with bowed head and rounded shoulders beneath the light of the propane lantern.

"I want my best friend back," Reuben said, reaching out and pulling John in for a bracing hug.

John resisted momentarily—probably expecting Reuben to throw him to the ground and stomp on his head—then he wrapped his long arms around Reuben and squeezed the air out of his lungs. "But do you forgive me?" John said, with that cocksure tone that Reuben had sorely missed.

Reuben chuckled. "You better hope so, because your wedding won't be half as fun if I decide not to come."

John grew momentarily serious. "We do want you to come."

"I'll try to clear my schedule."

"Fern will be glad. She's always had the worst crush on you."

Reuben's gut clenched. Fern had long since grown

out of her girlish crush, but what must she think of him tonight? For the hundredth time, he wished he could go back and make it right. Maybe he could. "John, are you staying at the Schmuckers' with Fern? Do you think she's still awake?"

John grinned sheepishly. "I'm staying with the Yoders."

"Sadie's house?"

"*Jah.* I wanted to surprise you and Fern, so Anna and Felty got me in touch with Sadie's *bruder* Tyler. He's married to your cousin."

"*Jah,* I know."

"The Yoders are a wonderful-nice family," John said. "Even Sadie was nothing but welcoming when my bus arrived last night. I should have been suspicious that she was so happy to see me."

Reuben smiled wryly. "You couldn't have known."

"I'm sorry," John said. He would have been more believable if he hadn't chuckled softly. "There's no one quite so clever as a girlfriend out for revenge."

Reuben raised an eyebrow. "Don't be so smug about it. My relationship with her wasn't how she made it out to be."

"I don't doubt it."

"But did you see Fern home after the singing? Do you think she's still awake?"

John frowned. "Didn't Felty tell you? She wasn't feeling well and went home before the singing started. I don't wonder that she went right to bed."

"Wasn't feeling well?"

"She fainted before she even crossed the threshold of the house."

Something heavy settled in the bottom of Reuben's gut. "Fainted?"

"*Jah.*"

Reuben tried hard to suck in some air as his throat tightened painfully. She'd taken ill right after she'd tried to talk some sense into him, right after he'd yelled at her and called her a pig farmer's daughter as if it were a dirty word. "What happened?" he said. "Is she okay?"

"A boy—I can't remember his name—Johnny some-body, caught her and lowered her to the step before she fell. She wasn't out but five seconds, but it shook us all up pretty bad."

Reuben did his best not to scowl. Fern should take better care of herself, and she should know better than to faint in front of Johnny Raber. He'd get his hopes up.

"She's wonderful skinny, Reuben. Has she been eating enough?"

"Probably not." Even though he took her to Mc-Donald's occasionally and bought her a tub of peanut-butter-chocolate drops every week. Reuben wanted to kick himself into next Sunday. For sure and certain Fern hadn't fainted because she was hungry. She had fainted because Reuben had been *hesslich* and mean. "Did you drive her home?"

"Johnny—I wish I could remember his last name—offered to take her home, and since I didn't have a buggy and don't know how to get to the Schmuckers' house, I thought it would be okay. She was white as a sheet, but she wouldn't let me come with her. She wanted me to enjoy the *singeon*, though after the spectacle Sadie made, I wasn't in any kind of mood."

He furrowed his brow. "I should have gone with her, but she was pretty adamant."

Reuben wanted to give John a stern lecture about having more care for his sister, but he had no right to admonish anybody about anything. Hadn't he been the one to snap at Fern and tell her to leave him alone? Hadn't he been the one to insult her and give her a piece of his mind whenever he felt like it? Hadn't he been the one so oblivious to Fern's needs that he had no idea when or if she'd been eating?

Reuben was thoroughly ashamed of himself. He didn't even know where Fern worked or if she made enough money to support herself. How much money was she sending to her family? How many times had she walked because her bike broke down on her? He should have been taking better care of her. He needed to apologize immediately and convince her that he hadn't meant a word he'd said tonight. He'd been so angry, he could barely remember what he'd said, but it hadn't been nice and he'd seen nothing but devastation in Fern's eyes. Making things right with Fern suddenly took on an urgency Reuben had never felt before. "We need to go to the Schmuckers' house right now and make sure she's all right."

John never worried about Fern the way Reuben did, even when they'd been children. "It's Fern," John said. "She can take care of herself."

"Like that time she almost drowned?"

John shrugged. "Johnny took her home tonight. He seemed happy to do it, and they're not going anywhere near the water."

Reuben ground his teeth together. Of course Johnny Raber was happy. He had a crush on Fern, and

Fern was too nice to put a stop to it. "I don't care," he said. "I need to talk to her."

John's eyes flashed with surprise, and he studied Reuben's face as if he were trying to read something in high German. "Why?"

"I said some cruel things to her. I need to take them back."

"Can't it wait until tomorrow?"

Reuben kicked a hay bale and pieces of hay flew into the air. "*Nae*, it can't wait. It can't wait another minute."

"It sounds serious." Reuben couldn't tell if John was humoring him or just as concerned.

Humoring him. To John, Fern was a little sister who tagged along with the boys. To Reuben, Fern was so much more, but he couldn't even begin to explain it to John. He couldn't begin to explain it to himself.

"Are you going to come with me or sit here in the barn twiddling your thumbs?"

One side of John's mouth curled upward. "Okay, bossy pants. I'll come with you, but it's a waste of time. Fern is already in bed dreaming of nice boys like Johnny Raber."

"She is not. Fern isn't interested in Johnny Raber."

John nodded, his lips twitching with an aggravating tease. "Of course she isn't. Why else would she fall into his arms at the singing?"

John always knew how to cut Reuben's confidence down about four notches. "I can always leave you behind."

"You don't want to have to hitch up the horse again when I've got the Yoders' buggy right outside."

Reuben stuck his hat on his head and followed John out to the Yoders' open air buggy. The rain was coming harder now. "We'll be soaked before we even get down the hill," John said. "Let's just wait until morning. She won't be awake anyway."

"I'm going," Reuben said. "You can cower in the barn until I get back if you want."

John raised a very cynical eyebrow. "Cower? I'm not afraid. I'm smart enough to know I don't want to get wet. I'll catch a cold."

Reuben jumped up into the buggy seat and took up the reins. "See you later, smarty pants."

John groaned as if Reuben had stuck him with a pin. Resting his hand on the muddy wheel, he studied Reuben's face as if seeing him for the first time. A deliberate smile tugged at his lips, making Reuben slightly irritated at the delay. "Don't get all bent out of shape," John said. "I'm coming." He climbed up next to Reuben, snatched the reins from his hands, and rolled his eyes. "The things some people do for love."

Chapter Twenty-Three

Reuben awoke with a crick in his neck and a piece of hay sticking to his cheek. It was as dark in the barn as it had been at midnight, but he could feel the sky outside the window preparing for light. Amish farmers woke before the sunrise because of that feeling. It was as if everything in the world took a collective breath right before the start of the day.

John lay on a bed of hay bales a few feet away looking as if he'd had as bad a night as Reuben had. Hay stuck out from his hair in eight or nine places and a line was tattooed into his cheek from something hard and uncomfortable he had slept on. A ball of yarn lay at his feet as if waiting for him to wake up and play. Reuben curled one side of his mouth. He'd be happy to never see a skein of yarn ever again.

He'd been very irritated last night having to admit that John was right. They'd gone to the Schmuckers' house only to find it dark and closed tight like a prison. Reuben had wanted to knock and wake up the household, but John had talked him out of it. If Fern really was sick, Reuben would only make it worse by interrupting her sleep.

They'd come back to Huckleberry Hill, Reuben more downhearted than he'd ever been. He needed to talk to Fern. Nothing in his life would be right until he saw her.

They had unhitched the Yoders' horse, brought him into the barn, and fed him some good oats, then John had gone to the house for dry clothes, extra blankets, and Reuben's knitting. Reuben had decided that if he wanted to make amends to both Mammi and Dawdi, he'd have to finish his hopeless blanket. He and John had stayed up until three this morning knitting something that would pass for a baby blanket. He could never actually give it to anyone, but Mammi would be thrilled that he had been practicing his knitting, and Dawdi would be pleased that Reuben had tried to make things right.

Reuben had taught John how to knit—it was the blind leading the blind—and John had knitted half the blanket, further proving to Reuben that John was the best of friends. What other boy would stay up late to help a friend soften his *mammi*'s heart?

Reuben sat up and pressed his fingers to his forehead. Who knew that knitting could produce such a headache? He glanced over at Dawdi's workbench. A slightly lumpy, misshapen baby-pink blanket sat on top, folded as well as could be expected from two bleary-eyed Amish boys in the early hours of the morning. Mammi would love it. At least Reuben hoped so, because he was never going to pick up a pair of knitting needles again.

Reuben pulled out his pocket watch. Five o'clock. How long should he wait? Surely Fern would be up by five thirty. Or six. He'd wait no longer than six. First he'd milk the cow like lightning and shovel in some breakfast, then ride down the hill in Dawdi's buggy like a madman. *Nae*. He'd go horseback. That was faster. He'd rattle all the windows at the Schmuckers' house when he knocked on the door. He wouldn't even feel bad about waking them up. He'd waited long enough.

Reuben sat up and searched the floor for his boots. John stirred and yawned loudly enough to make the horses stir. "You should be grateful I'm such a *gute* friend. My back will never be the same."

"You owe me," Reuben said, lacing up his boots.

John nodded. "I suppose I do."

Reuben retrieved a galvanized bucket from the shelf and set to milking the cow. John fed the horses and turned them out to pasture, which was a small, fenced-in area behind the barn. Not enough room for the horses to run but enough to stretch their legs.

After milking, Reuben handed the full bucket to John, squared his shoulders, and picked up the blanket. Time to face Mammi and eat several pieces of humble pie.

Mammi stood at the stove stirring what looked like purple scrambled eggs in a frying pan. She looked over her shoulder, and her face brightened as if someone had turned on a whole sky full of stars. "Reuben! It's about time you came in. I was worried sick all night, but Felty said you were right as rain." She threw out her arms and marched toward him, leaving her steaming eggs still hissing in the pan. "I hate for my grandchildren to sleep in the barn. It's moist in there. I'm always afraid you'll catch cold." She looked at John and smiled. "And it's not just my grandchildren. I don't like anyone sleeping in the barn unless they can help it—Fern's brother especially. Oh, look! You milked the cow. Felty will be so happy."

"We did fine in the barn, Mammi. I fixed the roof in March, so there are no leaks," Reuben said, laying his bad excuse for a blanket on the table and taking Mammi's hands. "And it was only fitting that I sleep there after how I treated you last night." He squeezed both her hands in his. "I am very sorry about what I said, Mammi. I was angry, but not at you or your knitting."

Mammi nodded. "Sometimes when we are hurt, we lash out at the things and people we love the most. I never doubted your love for knitting."

He picked up the blanket and handed it to her, cringing when he saw a strand of yarn sticking out from the center of it. How did that get there? If he pulled on it, it was possible the whole thing would unravel. Lord willing, Mammi wouldn't be so unwise as to pull it and find out.

She acted as if she'd just gotten the news of seven new grandchildren. "*Ach, du lieva*, Reuben. Did you make this?"

"Last night. I couldn't sleep for thinking of my sins." And the thousand pieces of hay stabbing into his back.

Mammi gave him her warmest smile, as if there were no better person in the world than Reuben Helmuth. "Now, now, dear. Don't say another word. You are my grandson and a very *gute* boy. This blanket proves it. The children at the hospital will love it."

Reuben wanted to warn Mammi not to give it to the hospital, but he just couldn't, not with the way she was smoothing her hand over his rough and holey knitting. John's side was even worse. Surely someone at the hospital would see the wisdom of keeping this particular blanket as far away from the children as possible. Maybe they could remake it into a beanie.

Mammi set Reuben and John's blanket on the small table next to the sofa. "I'm so proud to think I have a grandson who knits. Today is a wonderful-*gute* day." The purple eggs, or whatever they were, bubbled on the stove and finally got Mammi's attention. She grinned. "*Ach.* I almost forgot breakfast." She bustled to the stove and picked up her spoon. "It's a new recipe I'm trying out. Blueberry Egg Hash. With cinnamon. Do you like cinnamon, John?"

The expression on John's face was much like the one Fern wore when confronted with Mammi's cooking. Reuben could never figure it out. Mammi might make some unconventional dishes, but they were always full of flavor and plenty of imagination.

"That sounds delicious, Mammi," Reuben said. As much as he wanted to get to the Schmuckers' house, he'd have to make time for breakfast. Mammi would be devastated if he skipped out on Blueberry Egg Hash. John looked as if he was thinking of running away as fast as he could. Reuben draped a hand over John's shoulder. "You'll love it, John. Mammi is the best cook in the world."

John swallowed hard and nodded. "I don't doubt it."

"Well, *gute maiya*," Dawdi said, coming into the room with his milking boots already on his feet. "How did you sleep last night?" He smiled at Reuben as if all was forgiven—which it was. He'd told Reuben so last night.

Reuben smiled back. "We stayed up sort of late to finish Mammi's blanket, but what sleep we got was adequate." Reuben liked "adequate." He didn't have to lie or tell Dawdi that he ached in about twenty different places.

Dawdi seemed satisfied. "A night in the barn is as *gute* a way I know to clear your head."

Mammi set the platter of purple eggs on the table along with a huge bottle of cinnamon. They said silent prayer and then Mammi divided the eggs evenly among the four of them. Reuben looked at John's plate with regret. John was not going to enjoy those eggs near as much as Reuben would have enjoyed eating John's portion. Reuben picked up the bottle of cinnamon and shook it vigorously over his plate.

John's eyes widened in surprise, but he kept whatever he was thinking to himself. He picked up his fork, scooped up a hearty bite of eggs, and shoved them into his mouth. He took a huge gulp of milk to wash down his eggs, no doubt hoping to finish them off in four bites and not have to linger over them any longer than he had to.

Reuben stifled a chuckle and took a bite. The cinnamon and sweetness of the blueberries melted together in his mouth. He sighed with pleasure. Mammi had done it again.

"Oh, dear, John," Mammi said. "You've finished your eggs already. I knew I should have made more. You are a growing boy. You need nutrition."

John forced the last of his eggs down his throat with a gulp. "*Nae*, Anna. I am so full I couldn't eat another bite even if Reuben held my mouth open. *Denki*. It was a delicious breakfast."

Considering John had cleaned his plate in less than three minutes, he probably hadn't the time to actually know whether it was delicious or not. "Do you want some of mine?" Reuben said, giving John a teasing smile.

John didn't seem to see the humor in it. He coughed. "*Nae, denki*, Reuben. I wouldn't want you to miss out."

Reuben finished off his eggs more slowly than John had, but he still ate quickly. He needed to see Fern. He didn't want to waste one more minute of time. He half groaned, half rejoiced when a knock came at the door. If it was Fern, he'd see her that much sooner. If it was someone else, he'd be irritated at the delay.

He was irritated. Dawdi answered the door, and Reuben gripped his fork so tightly, he thought it might warp in his fist. Sadie Yoder stood in the doorway, a tentative—almost humble—smile on her face, her pretty yellow hair mostly hidden beneath a black bonnet, a black shawl draped around her shoulders. "Is John King here?" she said in her most timid-sounding voice. Sadie knew how to be coy, friendly, indignant, or lovable at just the right time. She had a sense about such things, and Reuben couldn't help but admire how astute she was.

But today, he really needed to leave, and Sadie was the last person in the world he wanted to see. If he didn't clamp his mouth shut, for sure and certain he'd say something he'd regret. Sadie was the reason he was in the fix he was in. Reuben took a deep breath. That wasn't true and he knew it. His problems were no one's fault but his own.

John scooted his chair from the table so fast, you'd have thought his trousers were on fire. He really wanted an excuse to escape, even if it was in the shape of Sadie Yoder. "I'm here," he said.

Sadie took one step into the house and eyed Reuben doubtfully. "My *bruder* dropped me off at the bottom of the hill to fetch our buggy. We didn't know you were going to keep her all night."

"I'm sorry," John said. "It got to be too late and too wet to come back. I hope your *dat* doesn't mind."

Sadie took another step into the room as if pretending she wasn't trying to come in at all. "He isn't mad. He just wants to be sure we get our buggy back. He's gone to milk, and I've come to get the buggy."

John looked longingly at Reuben. Did he want Reuben to rescue him? From what exactly? When Reuben didn't respond—because he had no idea what John wanted—John nodded to Sadie. "Okay. I'll hitch it up."

"*Gute* morning, Sadie," Mammi said, buttering a piece of toast that looked a little greener than normal bread should look. "How are you after last night's debacle?"

Reuben wasn't sure what "debacle" meant, and from the look on Sadie's face, it was clear she didn't either. "*Ach . . .*" Sadie said, her eyes darting between Mammi and Dawdi. "*Ach*, I am right as rain. A wonderful-*gute* singing."

"It's appropriate we got lots of rain last night then," Mammi said, her eyes twinkling like she had a very *gute* secret to keep.

"*Jah*," was all Sadie had to say for herself.

"I'll hitch up your horse," John said, right before his long strides took him out the door.

Sadie bit her bottom lip and seemed to lose some of that calm assurance that had carried her into the house. "Reuben," she said. "Would you please come outside? I would consider it a very big favor if you and I had a talk."

The last time Sadie had invited Reuben to talk, it

had turned into a disaster. He didn't trust her, and if she meant to humiliate him, she'd be sorely disappointed. Maybe after today, he could be finished with her once and for all, because he'd never be humiliated by Sadie Yoder again. After last night, he didn't care what she thought or how many friends she had. He didn't even care that she was the bishop's daughter.

She didn't have beautiful auburn hair that curled at the nape of her neck or lively brown eyes that danced every time she smiled. Sadie had purposefully tried to humiliate him. He didn't have time for her anymore.

Reuben stepped onto Mammi and Dawdi's covered porch with Sadie leading the way. Dawdi shut the door behind them and closed the curtains to the window that looked out onto the porch. He must have thought they would need some privacy, though Reuben didn't care what Sadie had to say to him. He felt annoyed more than anything else. Sadie was an inconvenience he needed to deal with before he could see Fern.

Sadie took three giant steps that put her within inches of Reuben. He took three giant steps backward. She pursed her lips and took another step toward him. He stepped back, hoping he didn't run out of porch before Sadie gave up chasing him.

He shouldn't have been surprised when her eyes pooled with tears. "You don't have to run away, Reuben. I came to apologize."

He tried not to look distrustful. Maybe she'd had a change of heart overnight. Reuben had certainly come a long way in the last twelve hours.

She blinked back her tears. "I apologize for not having faith in you."

"What do you mean?"

"I should have known you were just trying to spare

Fern's feelings. I forgot what a *gute* heart you have, Reuben. Still, you should have had the courtesy to explain everything to me before I got carried away. You could have prevented a lot of embarrassment for both of us if you'd only explained things."

Reuben drew his brows together. He'd made things very clear that day at Esther's barn. "What didn't I explain?"

"Right before Johnny Raber took Fern home last night, she told me everything, though why you wanted to spare her feelings at the expense of mine I can't understand."

"What did Fern say?"

"What do you think? She told me the truth, which is more than I got from you that day in Esther's barn. Fern said you found out that she was in love with you, and you didn't want to hurt her feelings so you told me that you just wanted to be friends." A slight smile drifted onto her face. "I knew, I just knew, we were more to each other than friends. I didn't realize how protective you are of Fern, even though she is who she is. Fern says you set her straight last night. She understands how you feel about her. She understands her place, and you don't have to pretend to be her friend anymore."

Reuben's chest tightened until it was impossible to draw breath. Even after all the cruel words he'd said to her, Fern had tried to fix things with Sadie, to make it better when he hadn't been able to see any way out. She was still watching out for him, and he thought he might suffocate with guilt.

"I am sorry that I tried to embarrass you last night. I just . . . I felt so used and deceived and angry. I wanted you to hurt as bad as I was hurting." She squared her shoulders. "But I can see that was not the Christian way to handle it. I wish you would have told me from the start. I could have helped you with Fern. You spent too much time with her. It got her hopes up."

Reuben's ears started ringing and all he could see was Fern's grief-stricken face the moment before he had turned his back on her.

"It was the same with Esther. You were too nice, and she got her hopes up. Boys don't like Esther. She thinks she's in love with anyone who's nice to her."

The words seemed to explode from his mouth. "You're wrong, Sadie."

Sadie's long-winded speech sputtered to a stop, and she furrowed her brow. "Wrong about what?"

"Christian charity. Me. Esther. Fern. Fern has been nothing but kind and patient with me. I was telling the truth that day in the barn. I don't love you. I don't want to be your boyfriend. I don't even want to be your friend."

Sadie caught his words like a bad disease. "How dare you, Reuben Helmuth."

His heart seemed to explode until it pushed against his ribs and left him gasping for air. This feeling of utter and complete love was for Fern. It had always been Fern, and he had been too blind to see it.

John drove the Yoders' buggy to the front of the house. Reuben leaped down the porch steps and turned back to look at Sadie. "I don't like you, Sadie. I love Fern. I love her better than I love my *mammi*'s cooking, and I'm going to tell her. Right now."

He couldn't spare another thought for Sadie Yoder. Fern needed to know how he felt as soon as possible. He didn't want her to miss out on one more moment of his love.

"John," he said, running to meet the buggy as it pulled up to Mammi and Dawdi's sidewalk. "Take Sadie home. I'm going to get Fern." He burst into an uncontrollable smile. "I love her, John. And I want to marry her."

John tried to stifle a smile that would not be contained. "It wonders me why anyone would like my annoying little sister."

"You know perfectly well that she is the most beautiful, kind, *wunderbarr* girl in the world."

"Except for Linda Sue," John said.

Reuben shook his head. "Even better than Linda Sue, and I almost made the biggest mistake of my life. I could never love anyone the way I love Fern."

"*Ach, vell.* You might as well marry her. She'd never stop tagging along after you anyway."

Reuben glanced behind him. "Be careful of Sadie. She's wonderful mad. Don't go over any big bumps."

John chuckled. "I won't. And take care, Reuben. Fern won't believe you. She doesn't think all that much of herself. You'll have to convince her that someone as important as Reuben Helmuth could love a pig farmer's daughter."

John had meant it as a jest, but Reuben's joy drained from him like water from a leaky dam. He had been treating Fern as an afterthought. John was right. She might not believe him.

All the more reason to get over there immediately and convince her.

He loved Fern, and he'd make her certain of it—as certain as the sun rising in the morning of a brand-new day.

Chapter Twenty-Four

Barbara Schmucker lived up to her reputation. She answered the door scowling at Reuben as if he were a salesman and she had no time for such nonsense. She wore a ratty bathrobe, with uncovered head and bright pink slippers on her feet. "What do you want?" she said, revealing a mouth devoid of teeth.

"It wonders me if I could see Fern," he said.

"You've got no business coming over this early. Folks isn't even dressed yet."

Reuben would have to temper his eagerness. Barbara seemed like someone who despised the eager type. "I'm sorry. I need to see Fern. She wasn't feeling well last night. Is she still in bed?"

"How would I know? It's bad enough she's here. I can't be expected to look out for her comings and goings."

Fern had lived here for three months without complaint. It made Reuben even more ashamed. He'd never asked Fern about her living situation. She'd never volunteered any information. If Barbara Schmucker was as ornery as she seemed, Reuben would insist that

Fern move in with Mammi and Dawdi, and he'd sleep in the barn from now on. Fern had enough hardship in her life than to have to deal with Barbara Schmucker on a daily basis.

"Would you . . . do you think you could go check?" he said, even at the risk of making Barbara angrier than she already was. Fern's bike was leaning against the corner of the house. She had to be here, and he had to see her. He wouldn't leave without speaking to her, no matter how early it was.

"Go check for yourself," Barbara said. "You've got legs. The doctor took both my legs off when my babies was born."

Reuben stole a look at Barbara's feet. She definitely had legs. Was she unwell in the head? "Okay," he said, stepping into the house. "Which room is hers?"

Barbara took a step back and picked up a baseball bat that was propped against the wall. "Get out of here. I don't let robbers in the house."

Reuben's heart raced as he quickly stepped away from the bat and out of the house. Fern was definitely coming back to Huckleberry Hill with him. He wouldn't stand for her to stay one more minute in Barbara Schmucker's house.

Barbara slammed the door in his face, and Reuben stood motionless on the porch. What had just happened? Was Fern all right in there? How was he ever to find out? Maybe he should go back to Huckleberry Hill and fetch Mammi. She seemed to know Barbara Schmucker well enough. Reuben lingered on the porch. But how could he just leave Fern here with this horrible woman?

The door slowly opened, and Reuben stepped back just in case Barbara came after him with that bat. A small man with dark gray eyes, a weathered face, and a withered expression stood in the doorway.

Reuben kept his distance, in case of bats. "Hello. I'm Reuben Helmuth. I'm looking for Fern King."

The man grabbed onto his beard as if it were a handle. "Felty's boy?"

"He's my *dawdi.*"

He eyed Reuben carefully. "You have his eyes. And his height."

"I hope I didn't frighten Barbara . . . your wife?"

The man nodded as if the small movement made him tired.

"I meant no harm," Reuben said. "I came to get Fern." *And take her away forever.*

The man glanced back, as if getting permission from someone, then stepped out onto the porch and shut the door behind him. "Barbara is a *gute* woman, but she hasn't been the same since the last baby died."

Her own baby? Because Barbara and her husband couldn't have been much younger than sixty. "*Ach.* I'm sorry."

The man held out his hand for Reuben to shake. "I'm Wally. Any relative of Felty's is a friend of mine. Felty never looks at me or my wife cross-eyed."

"He's a *gute* man."

Wally started down the porch steps. Did he think to persuade Reuben to leave? Because he wasn't going anywhere without Fern. He'd neglected her enough already. "Fern's a sweet little thing," Wally said, strolling across his lawn, which was more weeds and wildflowers than grass. A rubber tire sat in the middle of the yard as did several pieces of rusty metal and some flattened grocery bags. Reuben couldn't do anything but follow. "I'm sorry I couldn't do more for her," Wally said, "but the way things are with Barbara make it hard. Fern said the barn was okay, but I never felt quite right about it. The most important thing is to keep Barbara happy."

Dread grew in Reuben's chest like a poisonous mushroom as all thoughts of happiness disappeared. What had Fern been up to? And why hadn't Reuben known about it?

Wally led him behind the house, where a substantial white barn loomed over a green pasture. They trudged up the gentle slope to the barn, where Reuben's disquiet grew louder. Wally opened a small door at the back of the barn and stuck his head into what looked like a tiny storage room. "Fern?" he said. He opened the door wider and motioned for Reuben to go in ahead of him. "She's not here. Must have gone out early this morning."

Reuben stepped into the room and felt dizzy. A rickety-looking cot stood in the corner of the old storage room with rotting wood shelves and a flaking cement floor.

"She cleaned it up real nice," Wally said. "The cobwebs were as thick as my finger when she moved in."

A half-eaten tub of peanut-butter-chocolate drops sat on one of the shelves, along with a watering can and four pots. A folded blanket was spread over the top of the cot with two more blankets neatly folded at the foot of it. She'd obviously used the one blanket as a mattress and the other two as her bedding. Had she slept here all this time? He barely had the heart to ask, for fear of the horrible answer. "What did she use for heat?"

Wally's weak smile faded to nothing. "It's warmer in here than outside."

Reuben sank to the cot and massaged the spot right above his left eyebrow. How could Wally have let Fern live like this? How had Fern kept it a secret? How had Reuben been so utterly blind?

Wally pointed to a small, enclosed space off the storage room with a hose sticking through an open window and a drain in the floor. "She rigged up a nice shower, and the outhouse is just over that little hill."

"What did she . . . how did she . . . did she eat with you?" Reuben lost the ability to speak. There were no words.

Wally seemed to shrink smaller and smaller with each word. "Barbara wouldn't allow it. Fern insists she's okay. She says she eats at her friends' houses. She seems content enough."

Content? Reuben wanted to upend the cot and smash every last one of those peanut-butter-chocolate drops. How could Wally think Fern was content?

Absentmindedly, Wally rubbed his hand along one of the shelves. "Nice and clean," he said, losing his smile when he met eyes with Reuben. "She came to us unexpected and said she was only staying long enough to help a friend. She has stayed many weeks longer than she said she would. What could I do? Barbara don't like folks in the house."

You should have given her a home and food and heat. That's what you should have done.

How could Reuben be angry with Wally Schmucker when he himself hadn't bothered to find out where Fern had been living?

He'd been too wrapped up in his own problems to

notice. She had come to Bonduel for him and only him. He'd wasted so much energy on trying to be liked that he'd forgotten how to be kind. Fern had been nothing but helpful and anxious for his well-being, and he'd gotten worked up over a thousand little nothings while Fern lived like a dog in Wally Schmucker's barn.

"It's a real nice little room," Wally said, but Reuben couldn't begin to agree. Wally was only trying to make himself feel good, and Reuben knew better. There was no justification for this. No reason for Fern to live in a barn for the sake of an ungrateful, arrogant boy like Reuben Helmuth.

And how had he repaid her?

He'd shown Fern—beautiful, gentle Fern—contempt he wouldn't have given an enemy, all because his pride had been wounded by insignificant, petty Sadie Yoder. The burden of his mistakes was too great to bear. A groan came from deep within his throat, and he rubbed the back of his neck.

"I'm sure she ain't gone far," Wally said. "Her bike's still here. I gave it to her to ride even though Barbara was against it. We weren't using it."

Short of wandering the town in search of the girl he loved, Reuben had no idea what to do. He had to find Fern, but she seemed to be further away than ever. "Maybe I'll wait here until she gets back."

"I don't think it's quite the right thing to have a boy wait in a girl's bedroom."

Reuben lifted his head and stared at Wally in disbelief. This wasn't a bedroom. It was a cold, empty, filthy storeroom where Fern had been sleeping for three months. What did Wally know about what was right and proper? Reuben worked hard to keep the nastiness out of his voice. "I just want to talk to her. That's all. And I'll be taking her to Huckleberry Hill to stay. She shouldn't be sleeping in your storeroom."

Wally pursed his lips. "Barbara didn't want her in the house."

"She'll be gone by nightfall."

"I'll come back for the blankets later. Barbara's been worried about them." Wally left the door open, and Reuben could hear his fading footsteps as he went back to the house.

With his emotions pulled so taut he could barely think, Reuben gazed around the storeroom, surprised at how barren it felt. Except for the peanut-butter-chocolate drops, there wasn't a sign of Fern anywhere. She wasn't rich by any means, but she did own more than one dress and an extra pair of shoes. She went without shoes so often that Reuben expected to see at least one pair.

As soon as she got back, he would move all her stuff, little or a lot, to Mammi and Dawdi's house. She wasn't staying here one more night.

How much longer would he have to wait for her? He was already so antsy he thought he might go crazy. Fern needed to know he loved her, and she needed to know it now.

He stood and peered at the rustic shelves. They were clean. Fern's doing, no doubt. He turned the water can upside down and examined the cracked ceramic flowerpots. He hesitated when he felt something inside one of the pots. With his heart beating in his throat, he pulled out a small, folded piece of paper. "John" was written on the outside. Reuben fingered the paper for half a second, wondering if he should read what was meant for Fern's *bruder*, but his curiosity got the better of him. If he took it to John, John would let him read it anyway, for sure and certain.

He unfolded the paper, filled with Fern's slanted handwriting.

Dear John, I know you mean to come home on Wednesday. I probably should have waited to ride the bus with you, but I found I couldn't stay in Bonduel for one more day. I'm sorry to be so silly about it, but you, of all people, know how stubborn and selfish I can be when I've made my mind up about something. I've tried to be a good friend to Reuben, but I am not the friend he needs or wants. He deserves better than a pig farmer's daughter who cleans toilets to earn money. I can see you rolling your eyes at me. Please stop. I will never be good enough for him, and I am giving up trying to scold him into forgiving you. I'm giving up on Reuben in general, so you can stop pestering me to come home. I will find someone in Sugarcreek to annoy—maybe you and Linda Sue. I'd be glad to join you on your honeymoon trip.

I'm teasing, of course, but I am afraid you are stuck with a tag-along sister for the rest of your life. My marriage prospects are dim. I will die an old maid with a pair of knitting needles in my hand. Reuben says knitting is only good for old ladies and spinsters. I will be both someday.

I will see you at home in a few days. If you're late, I will have eaten all your helpings of ham and bean soup.

Reuben blinked, and a tear splashed onto Fern's letter.

He wanted to reach into the page, grab her hand, and scold her for believing that she wasn't good enough. She was too good for Reuben, and everybody knew it but Fern.

He moaned and pressed his hand to his forehead. It was his doing. He'd been all smiles with Sadie and left Fern to walk home by herself. He'd cared more about what Matthew and Aaron thought than about Fern's feelings. What had he done but make her believe she was nothing?

And last night, he'd told her so to her face.

Reuben had no strength left for standing. The cot creaked angrily as he sat down on it.

The girl whom he had always counted on had given up on him.

There was no hope left.

He buried his face in his hands and sobbed like a little child.

Chapter Twenty-Five

Fern stepped off the bus and blinked in the bright sunlight. After changing buses three times, she still had to walk another three miles, but at least she was in Sugarcreek and closer to home with every step.

After hours of breathing in the stale, stifling air of a Greyhound bus plus two stinky city buses, Fern found the shade of a maple tree and took in the fresh spring scent of new leaves and lilacs. She told herself it was so, so *gute* to be home, even though she felt nothing but profound fatigue and breathtaking emptiness.

Stretching her shoulders back, she rotated her neck to work out the kinks she'd collected from her long ride. *Oy*, anyhow. She hated, *hated*, riding the bus. Would it have killed her to stay two extra days in Bonduel? At least then she would have had John for company on the return trip.

Jah. It probably would have killed her.

She should never have gone to Wisconsin in the first place. She'd been conceited to think someone like her could help Reuben. She couldn't even talk him into forgiving her *bruder*. She had convinced herself that Reuben had wanted her there, and she'd been foolish enough to be taken in by his smiles and his exceptional kindness. Too late she had realized that he was being nice to her, not because he particularly liked her, but because he had a *gute* heart. Sadie and Esther hadn't been the only ones taken in.

Fern couldn't blame Reuben. He was affectionate, charming, irresistible. Irresistibly handsome. He had no idea how many girls fell in love with him just because he gave them a smile or a kind word. Fern had wanted to believe. She had talked herself into hoping that Reuben took her to McDonald's and fixed her bike because he liked her, and she had no one to blame but herself for the pain that stabbed like a knife to her heart. Every moment spent with Reuben in Bonduel had only made her love him more and made the heartache that much more difficult to bear. She should never have gone. The pain would linger for a very long time.

She'd spent the first three hours of the bus ride crying her eyes out, despite the best efforts of the nice *Englisch* lady who sat next to her. The older woman had offered Fern her phone, her tissues, and her Flamin' Hot Crunchy Cheetos, which Fern ate even though they set her mouth on fire. She'd learned never to refuse food, especially when you didn't know where your next meal was coming from. Fern thanked *Gotte* that she had possessed the presence of mind to bring two bottles of Wally Schmucker's water with her. The Cheetos were bearable washed down with something cold.

Well. Lukewarm. She'd never had a fridge in the little storeroom she'd slept in. The water was only cold when the nights were.

Fern's feet felt as heavy as if she had a brick tied to each ankle. Three miles was an eternity when she hadn't slept since Sunday morning and hadn't eaten anything since the Cheetos hours ago.

She squared her shoulders and wrapped her arms around the canvas bag that held the few clothes and other personal items she'd taken from Bonduel. In less than an hour she'd be home. She could take a nap and eat herself silly. She planned on using the last of her paycheck to buy three Sausage McMuffins, two large fries, and an extra-large lemonade, and she wouldn't share her fries with anyone, not even her little niece Lily Rose, who loved French fries.

Okay. She would share with Lily Rose, but only because Fern had missed her so much.

Fern shook off her heaviness as best she could and put some spring into her step. She was going home. What could be better than seeing Mamm and Dat and hugging her many nieces and nephews and shoveling manure? It was time to move on with her life, without another thought for Reuben Helmuth.

Tears sprung to her eyes. *Ach, du lieva.* Resolving to put Reuben out of her mind was much easier than doing it. Maybe she'd buy four Sausage McMuffins.

She sniffed and wiped her nose with the nice *Englisch* lady's last tissue. Sausage McMuffins would only serve to remind Fern of the times Reuben had taken her to McDonald's and then watched to make sure she ate enough. She'd never forget the tenderness in his eyes when she'd fainted or the look of eager anticipation when he bought her a chocolate sundae pie at Burger King.

She'd never be able to eat fast food again.

Fern took a deep, shuddering breath, and willed

herself to stop thinking about Reuben. It was too hard to walk and cry at the same time. She couldn't breathe well with a stuffy nose, and she'd surely trip if she didn't keep a clear eye on the road. Besides, she was out of water. If she didn't want to get dehydrated, she'd have to stop the tears.

Trying to make herself feel numb, Fern took one determined step in front of the other. The houses thinned out the farther she got from the bus station, and the pastures and fields were abloom in their late spring splendor. She passed Pettys' house. Mr. Petty was an *Englischer* who bought a shoat from Dat every spring, then raised and butchered it every winter. The Barkers had painted their house last year, wanting light brown, but the color had turned out to be closer to pink. The Millers raised horses, and the Broomfields kept a few dozen chickens. Fern hopped the fence and trudged across the Masts' cornfield, being careful to step in the furrows and not trample the young cornstalks. Fern and her siblings had used Masts' field as a shortcut for years with the Masts' permission. Every time Fern cut across their field, she pulled a few weeds as payment for letting her tromp across their property.

She paused as the first whiff of the pig farm greeted her, stinging her nose and calling forth a flood of beautiful memories. She had never minded the smell of the farm, though the neighbors sometimes complained. Of course, Fern's being a pig farmer's daughter was one of the reasons Reuben was too *gute* for her, but she would be ungrateful if she didn't acknowledge that the familiar, acrid odor of manure meant there were hogs to fatten up and pens to clean. It also meant there was plenty of work to do and food on the table.

Fern would never take a full stomach for granted again.

Especially today.

Her empty stomach lurched as if she were still sitting on the bus. Reuben Helmuth stood in one of the hog lots holding a shovel and shooting the breeze with John. Was she having a nightmare? Hadn't she left them both back in Bonduel?

Didn't Reuben hate the very sight of her brother?

For sure and certain she was dreaming.

Dreaming or not, under no circumstances was Reuben to see her. Not only did she look a fright after the long bus ride, but she was in no condition to have any sort of a conversation with a boy who found a pig farmer's daughter repulsive. She'd burst into tears or wither under his upturned nose. She couldn't do it.

Just. Could. Not.

She wanted to kick herself for taking the shortcut. If she'd gone the long way around, she could have strolled up the road and slipped in the front door, out of sight of the hog lots behind the house. She stopped and crouched next to the Masts' short corn plants. They'd give her little protection, but at least she wouldn't be standing out in the open where Reuben was sure to see her. All he had to do was turn his head a few inches to the left.

Sweat trickled down her back. She could still turn around and go back the way she had come, but her legs shook from hunger and fatigue, and she didn't know if she'd make it to the house before collapsing in a heap by the side of the road. Although, if she did collapse in a heap, maybe the garbage truck would come by and pick her up and Reuben would never have to lay eyes on her again.

Nae. Some well-meaning neighbor would find her before the garbage truck did.

To her right stood a thick stand of trees. If she could make it to the shelter of the trees, she could skirt around the fence line and get close enough to the house to make a run for the back door.

Keeping low to the ground was more challenging than Fern had anticipated. Her knees protested with every step and her back was already sore from sitting on a bus for what seemed like days instead of hours. She caught her breath twice when it looked like Reuben might glance her way, but he seemed to be engrossed in a very serious, very important conversation with John and wasn't paying attention to much else.

Moving as quickly and quietly as she could, she slipped behind a clump of aspens, spied out from between two of them, and in profound relief, saw that Reuben wasn't looking in her direction. His gaze pointed toward the road that ran in front of Fern's house, looking for something. Or someone.

Her heart leaped into her throat. Was he looking for her?

Of course not. Reuben would be happy to have Fern King out of his life forever.

She tiptoed through the undergrowth, trying hard not to make a sound—her pulse pounding against her ears was loud enough. Once she got to the edge of the trees, she made sure Reuben and John weren't looking, then took a deep breath, leaped over the barbed-wire fence, and made a run for the house. An overhanging tree branch caught her bonnet and ripped it off her head as she ran. She didn't pause to rescue it. All that mattered was making it to the safety of the house before Reuben caught sight of her and started scowling.

She had always been a fast runner, but her legs felt like jelly and her feet were still dragging those bricks. She gasped as Reuben turned his head. A tree root reached out to grab her foot, and she made a spectacular dive headfirst into the grass. Thank the Lord, she caught herself with her hands and elbows. The pain traveled up her arms. *Ach, vell.* Better a skinned elbow than a skinned face.

"Fern!" Reuben called as he sprinted in her direction. "Are you all right?" Concern and something like hope joined together on his face, as if he was happy to see her but sorry she'd fallen. Or perhaps it was the other way around. Maybe he was happy she'd fallen and sorry she wasn't still on that bus.

"Fern, what happened?" John said, coming up behind Reuben and propping his hands on his hips. He chuckled. "You look like you've had a rough time of it."

Reuben knelt beside her and tried to help her up. She nudged his arm away, irritated that the mere brush of his hand against hers made her heart gallop around the meadow and down the lane. His concern deepened and there was no mistaking the hurt that flashed in his eyes. What was he up to?

She managed to sit up, but her legs refused to obey the simple command to stand. It frustrated her to no end that she had nearly made it to the house without being seen. She would have bawled like a baby if Reuben hadn't been kneeling there, a witness to her grand and painful humiliation.

"Fern, are you okay? Can I help you to the house? Do you need something to eat?"

Jah. She wanted a whole loaf of Mamm's honey-whole-wheat bread and a gallon of raspberry lemonade. She did *not* want to eat one more helping of humble pie. Couldn't Reuben leave her alone to let her wallow in her misery?

"I tripped," she said. Reuben was undoubtedly laughing at her even though he didn't make a sound. John made no attempt to be quiet about it. Her brother was the most insensitive, aggravating boy in the world. She regretted being related to him.

"Here," Reuben said, trying to take her hand without permission again. "Let me help you into the house. You need to eat. Your *mamm* made stew."

Stew sounded like about the best thing in the whole world right now. Too bad she couldn't make it to the house to eat.

"Can you stand up?" Reuben said. She wished he'd stop with the compassion. It was an act, and she couldn't bear the mockery anymore.

"You and John go back to what you were doing. I'll make it to the house on my own."

"I don't think you will." Reuben flashed a beautiful, tortured smile that normally would have turned her knees to mush and her heart to tapioca pudding. The little pieces of shattered glass that were her hopes and dreams crumbled to dust and blew away. Oh, how she loved him! Why hadn't she taken the long way around? Why hadn't he stayed in Bonduel?

He bent down, gathered her into his arms, and lifted her as if she weighed nothing at all. She should have resisted the tenderness of his touch. Any surrender of her precarious control would only hurt worse in the end. Instead, she melted into his embrace, wrapped her arms around his neck, and let herself savor the protection and warmth of his strong arms. It was only for a few seconds. She would play the fool in exchange for a few glorious moments of nearness to Reuben Helmuth. She'd never get so close again.

"How long has it been since you've eaten anything?"

"I had breakfast." A very early breakfast. Flamin' Hot Cheetos. They were delicious.

"You need to eat," he said, his tone laced with anxiety but without a hint of scolding. Was he back to playing the worried older brother?

No matter how hard she bit down on her tongue, she couldn't stop the tears from flowing. She buried her face in his neck so he wouldn't see, but he'd surely notice the wetness seeping into his shirt. Oh, *sis yuscht!*

"Shh, *heartzly.* Please don't cry," he said, soothing her as if she were a child.

John disappeared as Reuben carried her up the porch steps and into the kitchen.

Mamm stood at the kitchen sink washing the supper dishes. She turned when she heard the door open. "Fern!"

Reuben kicked a chair out from under the table and set Fern into it. Mamm rushed to Fern's side and cupped her hand around Fern's cheek. "*Ach,* my little bitty. We've been waiting for you since daybreak. I was so worried. Are you hurt?"

Fern threw her arms around Mamm, and the tears flowed like water from a faucet. "I'm okay, just happy to be home."

Mamm pulled away from Fern and gave her the once-over, clicking her tongue and frowning reproachfully. "But you look so skinny. Did Barbara not feed you? You should have come home sooner."

"*Jah*," said Fern. "I should have."

The lines burrowed deeper around Reuben's mouth. For sure and certain he was wishing Fern had never gone to Bonduel in the first place.

"You look exhausted," Mamm said, patting Fern's cheek.

Fern nodded. "I need a bowl of stew and a long nap."

Mamm's eyes darted between Fern and Reuben, and she seemed to force a smile. "But . . . now I must go upstairs. I think I left some water running." Before Fern could protest, Mamm backed out of the room and started up the stairs. "I'll be back. See that she gets something to eat, Reuben."

"I will," Reuben said, nodding as if he cared about her, as if her *mamm*'s request was his only desire. He tenderly took Fern's hands and turned them palms up. She shivered at his touch. "*Ach.* You're bleeding."

Hopefully he wouldn't see the elbows. "It's not even enough for a Band-Aid," she said, pulling from his grasp. She would not let Reuben lure her in, no matter how handsome he was or how concerned he seemed. She was the pig farmer's daughter. She must keep reminding herself or get hurt worse than she already was. Why had Mamm left her alone with him? She'd had enough of Reuben to last three lifetimes.

He went to the sink and wet one of Mamm's good towels, then brought it back to the table and dabbed at the blood oozing from the scrapes on her palms. She didn't dare lift her eyes to his face. "There," he said. "Almost as good as new." Except for the towel. Mamm would not be happy about the bloodstains. "Do you want a Band-Aid?"

"*Nae, denki.*"

He paused for a minute, probably wondering why he was tending to Fern King, the toilet cleaner, instead of flirting with the minister's daughter or painting Sadie Yoder's mailbox, but she wouldn't look at him, so she couldn't be sure what he was thinking. "I'll make you some tea."

Fern laced her fingers together and sat in silence as Reuben moved about the kitchen as if it were his own, filling the kettle, turning on the stove, retrieving the herbal tea from the shelf. When the water was on to boil, he poured leftover stew into a pot and set it next to the tea kettle. He turned and smiled at her. She'd never seen any expression so profoundly sad. She couldn't bear the beauty of it and looked away.

"I'll bet you're wondering how John and I got here before you did," he said.

"You must have hired a driver." She sounded mousy and frightened, as if one scowl from Reuben would break her like a twig. Maybe it would.

Or maybe she was more durable than that.

"When I found out you had gone, I raced to the bus stop with Dawdi's horse. Rhubarb used to be a champion, you know." He frowned and cleared his throat, probably remembering that Fern hadn't been invited to the buggy races and didn't know how fast Felty's horse could run. "Your bus had left by the time I got there. I rode back to Huckleberry Hill, packed my things, and called a driver. My *mammi* sends her best and asked me to give you a pot holder. It's in my suitcase."

Fern bit her lip. Dear Anna.

"We got here last night." Reuben stirred the stew, and the smell wafted from the steaming pot and made

Fern's mouth water. She'd eat every bite, even if it was Reuben who had warmed it up for her.

He steeped the tea and brought a cup to the table. "Chamomile. It will help you relax." He watched as she drank it, as if to make sure she didn't secretly pour it out while he wasn't looking. He didn't need to worry. Fern would have finished off a pot of Anna's turpentine-flavored *kaffee* just for the warmth of it. He dished up some stew, set it in front of her, and sat down at the head of the table next to Fern. There was only a sharp table corner separating them. He leaned toward her as if to supervise her eating.

And he did. With a mixture of painful emotions in his eyes, he watched her put every spoonful in her mouth. She didn't want to try to guess what Reuben was thinking. The answers held no happiness for her. She wished he weren't so close.

She finished every last bite, and the warmth of the stew gave her new energy. She still ached to take a nap, but she thought she might be able to walk upstairs to her bedroom without fainting.

"Feel better?" Reuben said.

Not really, but at least she felt full. She wouldn't feel better for a very long time.

"I have a present for you."

Ach. She hated that he was being so concerned. So nice. It only made her love him more when she wanted to hate him. Hating Reuben would have made things so much easier. It was why Reuben had insisted on hating John and Linda Sue. Hate was so much easier than love.

When she didn't reply or even seem interested, he got up from the table and disappeared down the hall. He came back with at least a dozen grocery sacks looped over his arms. "Before I left Bonduel, I went to Clara and Carolyn's and bought everything they had in the shop. Clara was ecstatic, but Carolyn was annoyed that they'd have nothing for other customers. But she was willing when I told her it was all for you." He placed the bags on the table and eagerly started emptying them. He pulled out everything from peanut-butter-chocolate drops to divinity, white-chocolate-macadamia-nut clusters, pecan turtles, peanut brittle to coconut haystacks.

Fern had never seen so much candy. She felt physically ill. Why couldn't Reuben have walked away instead of carrying her into the house? Why couldn't he have left the candy at Clara and Carolyn's shop instead of spending way too much money to bring it to Sugarcreek? If he wanted to be rid of her, why didn't he try to make her hate him?

He opened a tub of peanut-butter-chocolate drops and held it out to her. "Want one?"

She shook her head.

Reuben stumbled back to his chair, sitting down as if he was too weak to stand. "I hoped it might help." He searched her face as he reached over and laid his hand on top of hers. Her fingertips tingled. "I went to the Schmuckers' house to see you on Monday morning first thing," he said, so softly she had to strain to hear him. "I saw where you'd been sleeping."

She drew her hand from his as the ache in her heart threatened to escape. Clamping her mouth shut, she looked away from him, taking deep breaths until the need to cry subsided. How repulsive he must find her. Not only did she clean toilets, she slept in a barn and took a shower with a hose. It was ridiculous that it mattered to her, but to her sorrow, she knew that it mattered very much. Why, oh why, didn't he go away and leave her in her misery?

Something raw and painful flashed in his eyes. "I should have known about the barn."

She pressed her stinging palms to her forehead. "Then you would have avoided me from the very beginning."

He flinched as if she'd spit at him. "Avoid you? Fern, I would have taken you away from there and put you up at my *mammi*'s house. You would have had a warm place to sleep and as much raisin corn casserole as you could eat." The corner of his mouth twitched upward. "I would have taken you to Burger King every day."

"Why?" The word forced its way out of her mouth before she could pull it back. It came out more like a sob than a question. "Why do you care, Reuben? I am nothing to you, except a stumbling block."

"That's not true."

She stood up so fast, her chair clattered to the floor behind her. The room tilted a little to her left, but she took a deep breath and righted it once more. "You don't have to pretend anymore, Reuben. You don't have to try to make it up to me because you feel guilty that you're rich. I release you of any sense of responsibility you have toward me and my family. I forgive you for everything, and you don't have to feel obligated to come here ever again."

"I don't feel obligated."

"Guilty, disgusted, repulsed. Whatever it is you feel, you can just stop it. I won't let you torture me like this."

Reuben acted as if she had slapped him in the face. "Fern, please listen to me. I'm so sorry."

Even knowing how likely she was to faint before she even made it across the kitchen, Fern turned on her heels and stormed out the back door, slamming it behind her as she went. What did Reuben want from her? Hadn't he been telling her for months to leave him alone? Now, when she was finally ready to do what he wanted, he wouldn't go away.

Was he trying to get in good with John now that John was marrying the bishop's daughter? Did he want to make Fern sorry for ruining his chances in Bonduel? Did he want to gloat over the fact that he was still as rich and handsome as ever, and she was still a pig farmer's daughter? She'd lived in a barn for three months and cleaned toilets for a living. Reuben had plenty to feel smug about.

How much more of her pain did he want?

She heard the back door open as she stormed across the lawn. Of course he would follow her. He'd followed her all the way from Bonduel.

If she wanted to get rid of him, she'd have to go to the one place he wouldn't follow. She walked through the gate, into one of the hog lots, and ducked under one of the shelters Dat had constructed for the hogs. It was basically four posts holding up a piece of wood for shade and rain protection. The hogs were in the far corner of the pasture, so she had the whole thing to herself. She sat down in the straw and leaned against one of the posts so she wouldn't faint. Fainting was becoming a very bad habit.

She'd get a little peace here until Reuben got sick of waiting and went home. And then she'd avoid him like the plague for the rest of her life. Maybe she'd go back to Bonduel. Anna and Felty would probably take her in, or she could always live in the Schmuckers' barn. Anything was better than the torture of seeing Reuben in Sugarcreek.

"Fern, please can I talk to you?" Reuben didn't even hesitate to sit right next to her in the straw.

She wrapped her arms around her waist and turned her face from him. "Please, Reuben. Please just go." She sounded so weak. So defeated. One more thing for Reuben to gloat over.

Reuben braced his arms on his knees, bowed his head, and closed his eyes, as if he had spent all his strength coming from the house. "Fern, please forgive me," he whispered.

"I forgive you. Please go away."

He lifted his head and reached out his hand as if he were going to smooth one of her curls around his finger like he used to do. She raised her hand and leaned away from him. Her heart was broken. She wasn't going to let him grind the pieces into dust.

"Please, Fern," he said. "Please don't shrink from me. I can't bear it."

Ach! She hated that she loved him too much to ever refuse anything he asked for. She turned her face to him and held perfectly still as he tenderly smoothed the back of his hand down her cheek. She closed her eyes. His touch felt like heaven and perdition at the same time. "I made you feel so low, when in truth, you are everything to me. How can I make you understand?"

Even though she wanted to burst into tears, she didn't move. Didn't blink. "You're making fun of me."

"I'm not, Fern. I have never been more serious or more desperate in my life. I ignored you and excluded you and thought I would be better off with Sadie Yoder. I've been proud and stubborn and resentful, and I didn't see what was right in front of my face. I've made enough stupid mistakes to fill a warehouse. It's no wonder you don't believe a word I say."

She tried to breathe with an anvil pressing against her chest. "I told you already. I forgive you."

He took her hand in his, and she didn't have the strength to pull away. "I've asked your *dat* if I can work here and prove myself to you, no matter how long it takes."

Fern attempted a flippant smile. "Work on a pig farm? Why?"

"Don't you see? I'm so, so sorry. Sorry for everything I said. Sorry for how I acted and how ugly I've become." He ran his thumb back and forth across the back of her hand. She nearly lost her composure. "Fern, I love you. Please tell me it's not too late."

His declaration knocked the wind out of her. "You love me?"

He nodded, searching her face with those aggravatingly blue eyes.

"That's impossible, Reuben. That's impossible." She wanted to believe him. Ached to believe him. "I'm a nobody. You can't love a nobody." Her fragile control shattered, and she clapped her hand over her mouth. It did no good. The sobs rolled from her throat like waves on a stormy lake.

Reuben scooted closer and drew her firmly into his arms. He held on tight even though she made a weak attempt to push him away. He was so much stronger, and she was in desperate need of sleep. Any ounce of pride she still possessed evaporated with her happiness. "This is a cruel joke to play on a girl who has loved you for as long as I can remember."

His arms tightened around her. "You love me?"

"Go ahead and rub it in my face. I don't care anymore, just so long as you leave me alone."

He nudged her away and grasped her upper arms. The look in his eyes could have set her on fire. "My driver broke the speed limit all the way to Sugarcreek because I couldn't stand the thought of not being with you, of you not knowing how I felt. I said some terrible things to you, things born of anger, things I didn't mean. You lived in a barn and practically starved so that you could stay in Bonduel and reclaim me. *Me.* I didn't deserve any of it, but you did it anyway. You've got to believe me, Fern. I love you. I want to marry you."

How could it be true? Yet how could it not be true? Why would he tell such a lie?

"Why?"

"Because you are the most *wunderbarr* girl in the world. Tell me I haven't wasted my chances with you."

"I'm a pig farmer's daughter."

"I love that you are a pig farmer's daughter."

"I used to sleep in a barn and clean gas station toilets."

He reached up and curled an errant lock of her hair around his finger. Her whole body tingled. "I've slept in a barn too. And I am the best toilet cleaner in Sugarcreek."

She held her breath as her heart beat a wild cadence. Reuben was telling the truth. She could see it in the deep, icy blue of his eyes. She thought she might faint. A grin crept onto her lips as a breathless, joyful intoxication washed over her, filling her to overflowing. There wasn't room enough to contain her sudden happiness. "*I* am the best toilet cleaner in Sugarcreek."

"You're better than me at everything."

Before she could argue, he was kissing her—her forehead, her cheeks, the tip of her nose, and finally her lips, which had never been kissed before. He clung to her with the ferocity of newfound hope. His touch felt like a rainstorm after a long drought. A ribbon of warmth slid down her spine and radiated out through her fingers and toes. Who needed Sausage McMuffins or peanut-butter-chocolate drops? She could live off Reuben Helmuth's kisses forever.

A drop of water caressed her cheek, and she reluctantly pulled away from him. His eyes glistened with tears as he cupped her face in his hands. "Could you ever love someone as ill-tempered and proud as me?"

"I think you've lost your mind," she said, her voice shaking like a match in the wind.

"Could you love me anyway?"

"With all my heart."

He groaned and covered his face with his hands as great, shuddering sobs wracked his body.

"Hush. Hush," she said, stroking her hand up and down his arm. "All is well."

"I'll never forgive myself for hurting you."

"You'll have to," she said, with a mischievous grin on her lips. "You know how persnickety I am about forgiveness."

"I know how persnickety you are about everything. I wouldn't have you any other way."

"A peanut-butter-chocolate drop will make you feel better. I have a whole bag full in the kitchen if you'd like to come in. I'm willing to share."

He smiled his most dazzling smile. "I hear they're delicious."

"You haven't lived until you've tasted them."

"I haven't lived at all until today. I love you, Fern King."

He was sitting on a pile of straw on the ground in a hog lot with manure sticking to his boots. How could she not adore him? "And I love you, Reuben Helmuth. With all my heart."

He kissed her again, and she could have flown to Bonduel and back in an instant. It would have been a much more pleasant trip than the bus.

Chapter Twenty-Six

Anna sat back in her chair and sighed. She never got tired of seeing two young people aptly matched and happily married. Matchmaking was more fun than cooking, crocheting, and knitting put together. "Just look at the groom, Felty. Have you ever seen a wider smile?"

"Only on myself the day I married you, Annie."

"Now, Felty," Anna said. Felty was not only the handsomest man in Bonduel, he was also the world's biggest tease. "I don't think you got a look at yourself on our wedding day."

"But my lips ached for weeks from smiling so much."

The wedding had been lovely. The bishop had talked and talked and then the minister had talked and talked, but that was just the way things went at an Amish wedding. The elders must have taken satisfaction in torturing the to-be-marrieds, sermonizing for nearly three hours before letting the poor couple take vows. Of course, the bishop might feel cheated if he couldn't deliver a sermon at a wedding. Better to let the poor man have his time in the sun. Everyone wanted to feel useful.

Anna was glad she didn't have to give sermons. She was useful enough already, knitting pot holders for the needy of Bonduel and making matches for her grandchildren.

The bride's *fater* was handing out green pens with the bride's and groom's names on them, and Felty was just finishing his last bite of wedding cake. The wedding supper had been extravagant. They'd served two different kinds of chicken, celery *and* corn-bread stuffing, layered Jell-O, and four different kinds of vegetables. Little cakes had served as centerpieces that the guests cut right at the table. Both families had been waiting a long time for this wedding. They were definitely making the most of it.

Anna's heart nearly burst when she glanced over at Reuben and Fern, who were visiting with the happy couple. Well, Dorothy, Reuben, and Fern were visiting. Melvin, the bridegroom, had a smile anchored to his face, but he wasn't saying much. Dorothy never seemed to mind that Melvin seldom said a word.

Reuben and Fern and Fern's brother John had arrived last night in a van of wedding guests. Reuben and John had slept in their barn, and Fern had slept in the guest room. Felty said Reuben enjoyed sleeping in the barn, though Anna couldn't begin to guess why. She always preferred a comfy bed for her creaky joints.

Reuben and Fern strolled toward Anna and Felty and sat down in the empty seats opposite them at the table. Anna felt that special glow in the pit of her stomach that only came when she'd made a successful match. Fern and Reuben were definitely a match. Reuben couldn't take his eyes off Fern, as if every good thing lived in her eyes. Fern blushed and grinned and shone like a new penny.

Anna had known they were meant for each other the minute Fern came squeaking up Huckleberry Hill on Wally Schmucker's rusty bicycle. Fern was spunky enough to keep Reuben guessing, and Reuben was affectionate enough to keep Fern loving him.

"Dorothy and Melvin make a wonderful-nice couple, ain't not?" Reuben said, smiling at Fern as if she were the only girl in the world.

"They found New Hampshire yesterday," Felty said. "They couldn't be happier."

It would be a blessed marriage. They would never run out of license plates.

Reuben nodded at Fern, who glowed so bright, Anna thought she might need to put on her sunglasses. "Mammi and Dawdi, we have something to tell you."

Anna's heart beat faster, even though she knew exactly what they were going to tell her. It was still exciting news. She couldn't help herself. "You're going to be married."

Reuben laughed, and Fern's smile got wider and brighter. Anna would definitely need those sunglasses. And some sunscreen. "*Jah*, Mammi," Reuben said. "Come September."

Anna clapped her hands and then thought better of it and folded them quietly in her lap. She shouldn't draw attention if Reuben and Fern wanted to keep their engagement a secret.

"I am the happiest girl in the world," Fern said.

Smiling like a swimmer on a hot day, Felty reached across the table and clasped Reuben's wrist. "And you did it without license plates."

"Fern has kindly agreed to put up with me for the rest of her life," Reuben said.

Fern giggled. "He promised me chocolate for my trouble."

"He's getting the better end of the bargain," Felty said.

"Don't I know it," Reuben said. "I feel like I'm going to burst."

Anna had never seen him so happy.

Ah, the wonder of young love.

Fern's smile suddenly wilted. "*Ach*, Anna. Do you think you could find a match for Johnny Raber? He's been sitting at the far table all by himself for half an hour, and I feel like I'm partially responsible."

Reuben lost his smile too. "It's not your fault Johnny just happened to be there to catch you when you fainted. If anybody's to blame, it's me for being such a *dumkoff.*"

"I hurt his feelings when I left Bonduel so suddenly."

Reuben grunted. "You hurt my feelings too."

Anna raised her eyebrows and fastened a scold onto her lips. "Now, don't either of you worry. Johnny Raber is going to be just fine. I've already invited him to Huckleberry Hill to learn how to knit. He was so excited, I could have knocked him over with a ball of yarn."

"Mammi, you know how fond I am of knitting," Reuben said, "but how will that help mend his broken heart?"

Anna's sigh came from deep within her throat. These young people certainly had a hard time understanding the ways of love. "Well, dear, I'm inviting Lorene, Esther, and a couple of other girls to come up and knit at the same time. Esther is as cheerful as ever, and Lorene has such a delightful laugh. Johnny is sure to fall for one of them."

One side of Reuben's mouth curled slightly. "I don't know, Mammi. Johnny knows Fern. No other girl will ever be quite as appealing."

Fern's smile came back full force. "Reuben Helmuth, you are such a tease."

Mammi shrugged. "Johnny will have to settle. That's all there is to it."

Fern sucked in her breath and nudged Reuben with her elbow. "There's Sadie. We've got to go talk to her."

"Why?" Reuben said, frowning as if she'd asked him to take out the garbage. "She doesn't like me. I don't like her. Why stir the pot?"

Fern got to her feet and pulled Reuben with her. "We're going over there. She used to be in love with you, and you need to apologize for hurting her feelings. I know how it feels to have Reuben Helmuth break my heart, and I feel sorry for her."

He cringed. "Don't remind me."

Reuben might not have wanted to talk to Sadie, but he'd do anything for Fern. He didn't even put up a fight as Fern dragged him to Sadie's side. Sadie certainly was a pretty girl, but Anna didn't think she'd try to match Sadie with any of her grandchildren. She wasn't a diligent enough knitter. You could tell a lot about a person by their knitting.

Felty put down his fork and wiped cake crumbs out of his beard. "Reuben is a *gute* boy. I don't wonder that they'll be very happy."

"Of course they will, Felty dear. Reuben has a bit of a temper, but he also has your goodness. Fern will always find reason to rejoice. Just like I have."

Felty smiled, and his eyes got misty like fog on a spring morning. "Me too, Annie-banannie. Me too."

Anna patted Felty on the arm and looked at him sweetly, but one moment of tenderness was all she could spare. She reached into her pocket and pulled out a piece of notebook paper. "Now we've got bigger fish to fry, Felty. No resting on our laurels."

"I didn't even know we had laurels."

Anna unfolded her paper. "Reuben interrupted my original plans, and I can't regret it because we found him a *gute* match. But now it's time to focus on our granddaughter Elsie. She must come to Bonduel if she wants to get a husband. The boy I've chosen for her is not going to wait much longer."

"You want her to come and teach at the school."

"The school year is closer than ever and we've got to hurry before they hire someone else." Anna smoothed the paper in her hand. "I've written another letter, but I've given up on the big words. Short, simple, and to the point is what will persuade her to come. *Dear Elsie, Your future husband is waiting in Bonduel. Come and get him. Love, Mammi Helmuth.* What do you think?"

Felty raised an eyebrow as his lips twitched into a lopsided grin. "She'll come running."

For sure and certain.

Connect with U s

Visit us online at
KensingtonBooks.com
to read more from your favorite authors, see books
by series, view reading group guides, and more.

Join us on social media

for sneak peeks, chances to win books and prize packs,
and to share your thoughts with other readers.

facebook.com/kensingtonpublishing
twitter.com/kensingtonbooks

Tell us what you think!

To share your thoughts, submit a review,
or sign up for our eNewsletters, please visit:
KensingtonBooks.com/TellUs.